Kay Stephens was born and brought up in the West Riding of Yorkshire which forms the background to this novel. She spent the first seven years of her working life as a librarian, and since then has written several novels as well as short stories. She now lives in the South of England and is currently working on her next novel, also based in Yorkshire.

West Riding

Kay Stephens

HEADLINE

First published in 1988
by Century Hutchinson Ltd

First published in paperback in 1990
by HEADLINE BOOK PUBLISHING PLC

ISBN 0 7472 3330 6

Printed and bound in Great Britain by
Collins, Glasgow

HEADLINE BOOK PUBLISHING PLC
Headline House
79 Great Titchfield Street
London W1P 7FN

1

Rhona's brown eyes widened. She couldn't help staring. The woman was stunning, and so very elegant. Her black bobbed hair gleamed beneath the slanting brim of her hat, her coat was unmistakably mink. And yet she was crying as she ran down the lane – not weeping discreetly, but sobbing as a child would, abandoned.

Far more embarrassed than this stranger who was beyond caring, Rhona glanced away as the woman hurtled past, her high-heeled shoes slithering over the frozen snow.

Anywhere else, Rhona would have asked what was wrong, or if she could help. Here, the turrets of Farnley Carr jutting above the coarse grass and heather of the moor made distress readily explicable; questions were superfluous.

Panting now, her breath clouding the frosty air, she trudged upwards. She hadn't wanted to come, but who did only what they wanted? Pulsing through her head, Auntie Norah's voice prevented her giving up. 'It's my home, Rhona love, all I've got. I won't let them turn me out.'

She hadn't been daunted by the climb – a half hour's struggle from Auntie Norah's cottage, before that a similar distance from the town – she wouldn't let this strange woman's tears daunt her. She had come here to fight. If other people were dismissed, snivelling, by Wolf Richardson it was no more than she expected. Rhona Hebden, forearmed, would be that much more formidable. By heaven, she'd better be!

The house and its grounds were grim. Soot-blackened walls surrounded the garden she entered through a wrought-iron gate that clanged to behind her with a scattering of tiny icicles. Even the snow covering failed to soften the over-formal landscaping. And Farnley Carr itself with all its battlements seemed designed to keep out ordinary folk. Briefly, apprehension made her heart accelerate.

This is 1933, she reminded herself. Just because the place looked like something out of Dickens, she needn't let it scare her. No one, these days, intimidated a grown woman of twenty.

The tall, lean man who opened the heavy oak door was familiar. She had seen him at the wheel of the Richardsons' Daimler, swanking through Halfield's grey streets as if driving for minor royalty. She was unimpressed by glimpses of the butler collecting groceries for his London-born mistress. Evidently, Mrs Richardson didn't want to be seen shopping alongside working-class people; nor, for that matter, socializing with any of Halfield's citizens.

'Is Mr Richardson at home?' Rhona asked in response to the narrowing of blue eyes and an imperiously raised grey eyebrow. 'My name's Hebden – Miss Hebden, I've come about the reservoir.'

'Have you an appointment?'

'No, I haven't. I didn't stop to telephone. I came straight here. I couldn't mess about, this is too important.' And I never thought.

'If you would step inside, Miss. I'll inquire if Mr Richardson is available.'

The hall where she waited was by no means modest. From the expanse of chequered marble floor a majestic stone staircase ascended towards a large window which patterned cold steps with the fiery hues of its stained glass. Logs spat and roared in the great fireplace, flickered reflections over panelled walls, and made scant difference to the temperature.

Despite her closely fitted coat with its fur collar, Rhona was shivering. Outdoors, she'd been warmed by the effort of the uphill climb. Enforced inactivity was draining heat from her body, and more than a little confidence.

'Mr Richardson will see you,' the butler condescended, returning. His own disapproval undisguised, he reluc-

tantly extended a hand. 'If I may take your coat and your
– er . . .'

'My overshoes, oh yes.' Rhona bent to unfasten the
studs of the ugly rubber footwear. Deftly, she balanced
on first one slender leg then the other, extracting her black
court shoes from their protective covering. She felt better
now and smiled as she slid her arms from the tweed coat.

'This way, Miss.'

Following, her heels clattered on the marble. A year
ago, six months even, she'd have walked on her toes.
Now, she straightened her already poised back, breathed
more deeply, and strode forward.

'Miss Hebden, Sir . . .'

The tall, broad-shouldered man turned from the
mantelpiece only when the door had closed. He had been
staring into the blaze, heavy brown brows drawn together.
'Never trust a man with meeting eyebrows,' Rhona
recalled Auntie Norah warning her. But when he deigned
to confront her she saw that his brows merely appeared
to be joined, and the grey eyes beneath betrayed *his* ready
mistrust.

And whatever was wrong with his hand? Once she'd
noticed, she couldn't stop staring at the white handker-
chief in which it was wrapped. Blood was seeping through
its folds. Rhona forgot everything else. Fragments of
crystal lay on the tiled hearth, a goblet had been shattered.
And *not*, from his grave expression, in some fervent toast!

'You've cut yourself . . .'

'It's nothing.'

Rhona wasn't sure about that, but she could be equally
dismissive of the injury. She challenged his eyes levelly.
'I've come about Auntie Norah, someone has to speak up
and she won't for herself – can't, in fact. This weather,
she's completely housebound.'

'Your aunt . . . ?' Wolf Richardson demanded, his eyes
perturbed although his deep voice sounded cold and
indifferent.

'She's not my aunt really. I should have explained –
Miss Lowe of Branby Cottage, Vicar's Dale.' She noticed

7

his eyelid flicker as she mentioned the valley, but his rugged features were masked. He let her continue. 'She was my father's nanny. She's arthritic, and eighty-six – no, just a minute, she must be eighty-seven. Moving house would kill her.'

'Ah – Miss Lowe. But we wrote to her, surely. She will receive assistance, with the actual removal, and to cover all expenses.' The smile on his well-defined lips was bland, but still icy. 'We have suggested various cottages that might be purchased on her behalf. Each of which is considerably nearer to the town.'

'She doesn't want to live near the town, she's happy where she is – or was happy till you came, disrupting everything.'

Scarcely taking his glance from her, Wolf Richardson drew forward a chair.

'Sit down then,' he invited gracelessly. 'Before accusing me of disruption, Miss Hebden, acquaint yourself with the facts. My plans for Dale Reservoir have been generated by genuine need.'

'Yours?' she suggested in a quiet voice. 'To make money?'

'The need of the local people. The towns around here have potential . . .'

'A fact which you mean to exploit.'

'Why the hell do you all assume I'm motivated solely by greed?' His rather angular cheeks flushed with anger.

'Happen it's the way you live, with your flashy car and a house the size of this when there's only the two of you,' Rhona ventured, still quietly, trying not to be rude. But he seemed blind about himself!

'You haven't paused to consider that the area may benefit from acquiring somebody who possesses a degree of business acumen? You surely don't need reminding that the seven years since the General Strike haven't improved the lot of the West Riding?'

'I certainly don't need you to tell me. I've lived in Yorkshire all my life. I've one brother who's a carpet weaver, the other's a trainee loom tuner in Dawson's cotton mill. Neither of them can recall working a full week – it's four days, if they're lucky, three most often.'

Wolf Richardson was astounded – not because of learning that any recent expansion hadn't touched the textile trade, he'd done his homework on that – but by finding her brothers did manual work. He'd judged this young lady to be of a well-educated family. And had noticed her hands which were clean, pale and smooth, too dainty for working-class hands.

'And you – ?' he asked, before he could stop himself. 'Where do you work? You're not still at school?'

'Do I look that young?' asked Rhona fiercely. Unconsciously, she ran a hand over her auburn hair. The snow had made it curl even more tightly. But she'd long since ceased wasting time bemoaning the locks that yielded to no amount of brushing.

Wolf smiled. With her heart-shaped face, eyes the colour of sherry, and that tumble of red-brown hair, she'd all the appeal of a wickedly enchanting child. 'How old are you?'

'Old enough to teach,' answered Rhona pertly. 'How old are you?'

Wolf did not reply. He glowered. He hadn't needed her reminder that he seemed older than everyone, he'd heard that already this afternoon. *And* that all he considered was making money.

'So – you think yourself an intellectual, is that why you've decided to tackle me?'

The very notion was ludicrous, but she didn't feel like laughing. This man was so violent he'd crush a glass in his hand. But he'd not see he alarmed her either. 'Is it only intellectuals who'll approach your comprehension of what's right for Vicar's Dale? Has no one dared to question what you're doing? Maybe most folk round here are too worn down by the slump to fight much longer.'

'Then it's high time someone created work. I'll be employing men who haven't had a job in years. I'll improve the conditions of the entire locality, not destroy it. With an adequate, consistent water supply, manufac-

9

turers will look again at this part of the West Riding, will realize its potential . . .'

Rhona's eyes glinted. 'And farms will be submerged.'

'Two only. Both families are already preparing to move just a little farther up the valley, at no cost to themselves. To new homes, Miss Hebden, and greater acreage – which I have found for them.'

'So's you'll get your own way.'

'That's called forward planning, thinking ahead. From what I see around Halfield, there hasn't been enough of that.'

The fact that some people already had agreed to move out because of the reservoir was a shock. Rhona wished she'd known. Not that it would have prevented her trying to reason with him before it was too late. But she'd have had arguments ready, wouldn't have been made to feel so helpless. A part of her acknowledged that, meeting equally, she'd have loved the challenge.

'You're very smart, aren't you?' she said sharply, too upset to remember that she'd intended keeping calm, and speaking up for Auntie Norah with equanimity. 'You come from down South, and you can talk lovely. But you don't know anything about us. I've got a feeling you don't want to know. You don't really care. So long as nobody stops you doing what you want, you don't give a hang. *You'll* move folk, because they're getting in your way. But every one of them is an individual, just as much as you are. Even them that are getting too old to read your letters properly, and sit there fretting till someone comes along who can translate all those clever phrases. Don't you know that makes it even more scaring?' Her pause was only fractional, to gulp in breath. 'Haven't you the sense to see?'

Wolf Richardson admired spirit. He'd been watching her, noting the flush that fired her cheeks, and loving the glitter flecking those magnificent eyes with gold. In different circumstances he'd have enjoyed prolonging this into a rattling good argument. If he hadn't been drained already by such an almighty upheaval. The wounded hand was pulsing now, the cuts opening each time he moved. Defiantly, he used it to gesture her to be quiet. Several drops of blood spattered the blue carpet.

'If Miss Lowe has been perturbed, then I am sorry. Since she hasn't understood fully, I will see her myself, explain . . .'

'You haven't even the sense to look after your own hand!' Rhona exclaimed, smiling slightly. 'Want me to see if there's anything I can do?'

'No,' he said hastily. 'Thank you. Stimson will attend to it.'

'You mustn't go calling on Auntie Norah, though, you'd give her a seizure or something. She gets fussed enough having the minister visit, even the insurance chap. No, I'll tell her anything there is to tell.'

Afterwards, stumbling and slithering down the lane, Rhona felt far from satisfied. She'd said most of what she'd had to say, but not anything like as well as she'd intended. She'd let his jibe about her youth go home, that had put her off guard. Worst of all, though, Wolf Richardson perturbed her with his capacity for making folk do his way.

And she'd got too het up. She often did. Mum would testify to that, as would her half-brothers. And Dad? Jack Hebden, her stepfather . . . ? He'd grin, wouldn't he, and call her his plucky lass. Right from the day he'd first seen her when she was a cheeky toddler, he'd liked her spirit. And he'd encouraged her innate eagerness to learn and to question. She'd been lucky in Jack Hebden, luckier than she'd ever understood before, to have him for her stepfather. If it weren't for him, she might not even know how strong a spirit she possessed. She'd never have dreamed of going to Farnley Carr. From now on, though, she'd fight more subtly.

Between the gaunt mills and back-to-back houses of Halfield greyish yellow fog drifted, dank with moisture from the river and canal which once had drawn textile

11

manufacturers to the valley. Gas lamps were haloed eerily in its haze. Trams lumbered through its gloom.

'Your mother'll be wondering where you've got to, won't she, love?'

'Not really, Dad, I told her I was going to be late. I went to see Auntie Norah straight after school.'

'You've been a long time. Wasn't she so well?'

They'd met on the tram. Rhona had been glad to see Jack Hebden's smiling thin face when, with several work-mates, he got on at the gates of the engineering works. He wasn't much taller than her, and was wiry, but his blue eyes were very lively, and always had a special glint in them for her mother, and for Rhona herself.

Despite his relative lack of height, there could be no doubting Jack's energy, even after a hard day as a foreman at the works. Rhona had difficulty keeping up with him as the tram rattled away towards the People's Park, and they walked from the corner of Brunswick Road.

'Was Norah Lowe all right, anyway? She's always meant a lot to you, hasn't she, lass? And she must be getting on now.'

'Eighty-seven, I've just realized today. She doesn't hold with anyone sending even a card, you tend to forget how she's ageing. Actually, she'd be very well for her years, if folk like Mr Clever Richardson would let her be.' He'd made that sophisticated woman weep; it was no wonder he upset Auntie Norah.

'Her cottage is in Vicar's Dale, isn't it?' her stepfather said, suddenly serious. 'I know how I'd feel if they were trying to get us out of our little place.'

'Yes.' The grey stone terraced house that was home for the Hebdens was precious to Jack, the first of his family who wasn't living in rented accommodation. When there was short time at the engineering works, he'd a struggle to pay the mortgage. But Rhona knew he'd ensure that it was paid promptly, no matter what he had to sacrifice.

'I read in the paper that Richardson's offered them somewhere to live. Doesn't Norah like the new cottage?'

'Right at first, she didn't want to go and look. Since this snow's set in she hasn't been going out.'

'I don't suppose being isolated on her own has helped her to feel any better about it.'

'She was in a right tizzy when I got there. I could murder him for what he's doing! Who does he think he is – Lord Muck?'

Briefly she paused, staring across the dark road, wondering why the man she pictured so clearly against the rolling fog didn't quite tally with her verbal image of the dictator.

'Just because he has a tidy bit of brass and can set her up in a new place, pay all expenses, compensate her for giving up her home.'

'Though nothing would compensate Norah Lowe,' Jack Hebden observed.

'Quite. She's happy in Branby Cottage. More important, she's used to it. She's been there since Exton Hall was sold. One day, he'll know what it's like to be old, to get a bit confused. Though I don't expect it makes much difference to folk like him.'

All at once, though, she could see that makeshift bandage on a bleeding hand, the way he'd winced. Well, he'd only his own temper to blame – hadn't he?

'Anyway, Rhona love, the old lady has you to help sort things.'

'Maybe. Trouble is I don't go there often enough. She'd been getting herself into a state for days, this time. It's all so daft – he ought to know she'd not fathom all that rigmarole.' As they turned into Gracechurch Street she grinned at her stepfather. 'He said as how they were willing to move all her "furnishings and accoutrements" for her. Poor Auntie Norah was worrying because she didn't believe she had any accoutrements. And if she hadn't, would this posh Mr Richardson think she hadn't been brought up right?'

Passing beneath the gas lamp, three doors from number 46, Jack Hebden glanced affectionately into Rhona's eyes. She possessed an understanding beyond her years. 'It's sad, isn't it, love – how . . . reduced people become by age.'

'I tried to reassure her, explaining. *And* I reminded her that she brought my father up, and helped with *his* father before that. The Extons wouldn't have kept her on that long if she wasn't very special.'

'You're right there. They always had a name round here for being careful and – well, sensible.'

'They were Yorkshire, weren't they?'

'Aye – there is that.'

They exchanged a knowing smile as Jack opened the door. Crossing the step which had been cleared of snow and was freshly yellow-stoned, Rhona sensed somebody just behind her. Her half-brother, Dan, followed them into the cosy living room.

'That cistern's frozen up again,' he grumbled, hurrying past the two of them as they removed their coats and hung them on the back of the door. Shivering, he contracted his burly shoulders.

'Well, you know what to do,' Jack told his son cheerfully. 'I suppose the candle's burnt down again.'

'Aye. It just flickered its last when I went down there. It's bad enough sitting out there in the cold, without it being dark as well. And no flush.'

'You do go on, don't you, lad? You could have done something about it while you've stood moaning there.'

'All right. I just wish we had an indoor one. Nobody else . . .'

'Has as much lip for their father!' Rhona exclaimed.

Her half-brother grinned. 'Whose side are you on? I'll just tell our Mum that it needs a new . . .'

'You'll do nowt of sort!' his father corrected him, trying to appear stern. 'You know where them candles are, and the matches. See to it.'

'Aw, Dad . . . I've only just come in from work.'

'And your mother's been working all day, same as the rest of us. And will be working tonight when we're sitting in front of the fire.'

Eve Hebden didn't emerge from the kitchen until her

14

younger son had done as his father asked. When she married Jack Hebden she'd made up her mind that he would wield the authority, and always had kept to that. At first, accustomed to her rather different role as Paul Exton's wife, she had experienced some difficulty in curtailing her instinct to organize. When Stanley had been born a year later, followed in fifteen months by Daniel, she'd found plenty to occupy her coping with them and with Rhona. And without the housekeeper she'd been used to at Exton Hall, she'd made cooking her speciality.

'I've done a nice bit of hake for tea,' she told them, and kissed Jack and Rhona in turn. Rhona smiled to herself. The 'bit' of hake would be enough for seven or eight, with great mounds of mashed potato and some other vegetable.

'You've been baking as well, haven't you?' she remarked, loving the aroma of the cakes cooling on their wire tray.

Her mother's face, pink and glowing from the warm kitchen, lit up. Eve Hebden needed only a word of appreciation from any of her family. 'Just a feather cake, love, and a few buns.'

'Feather cake! My old ma's recipe,' Jack exclaimed, smiling as well. He couldn't wish for a better wife. His mother had been anxious when he'd married Paul Exton's widow, thinking Eve might have grand ideas and could have lacked practicality, But his Eve lacked nothing, and nor did their family. She was a beauty, as well – tall, willowy, graceful as one of the translucent figures that were all the rage, these days. And a good homemaker, he thought appreciatively, glancing round the walls distempered in peach colour with a decorative paper frieze.

'Do you need a hand, Mum?' Rhona inquired, following her into the kitchen.

'I don't think so, thanks, love. You go and sit by the fire and get warm. We're waiting for our Stan.'

'I didn't know he was down at the mill today.'

'He wasn't. Said he was going to the billiard hall this afternoon. He spent most of the morning hanging round the street with the Taylor lads. Smoking . . . Did you hear that, Jack?' she called to the other room. 'Our Stan's smoking again.'

'Then tell him . . .' He paused. From the kitchen, they heard his sigh. 'I'll have another word with him.' He began winding the gramophone.

'I don't know why he has to smoke,' Mrs Hebden continued to Rhona. 'He's the only one of you who's wanted to give it a try.'

'I could never afford it. And there's time yet, where our Daniel's concerned . . .'

'He'd better not start,' Jack Hebden observed, just as Dan came in again. Ernest Lough's recording 'Oh, for the Wings of a Dove!' began.

'What had I better not start?' Dan asked, standing in the doorway between kitchen and living room, on the way to washing his hands at the sink. Nearly six feet tall, he towered over Rhona by five inches.

'Smoking.'

Dan grinned wickedly, glancing first to his mother then to Jack. 'How do you know I haven't? Happen I was having a quick fag now, down the steps.' His brown eyes glittered, and his dark hair was awry.

'Well, if you were we'll all know next visit, won't we? Don't think the cold'll kill that filthy tobacco smoke.'

'And I'm not too old to receive a clout, eh, Dad?' Dan enjoyed taking advantage of his father's habit of remaining in his fireside chair until tea was on the table.

'I wasn't smoking, anyway, you know,' Dan said. 'It's a daft game – I've got summat better to do with my brass.'

'Something,' Eve corrected him gently, and smiled, her eyes tender. 'How much have you got saved now, love?' Daniel was hoping to buy a motorcycle.

'Ten pounds – no, guineas. I'll have to borrow off our Rhona, won't I, in the end?'

They all laughed again. It was a family joke, and Rhona loved them for their refusal to be resentful. Paul Exton, when he went away to war, had made a will. He had left a substantial amount to his wife, Eve, but also had settled on Rhona a sum which she would inherit at twenty-one.

'Only another year, eh, our Rhona?' Dan persisted, giving her a wink and nudging her ribs.

'I'll consider you for a loan,' she assured him gravely. 'At the rate of interest current at that particular time.'

'Hellfire!'

'Daniel!' came the roar from the other room. A mild-mannered man himself, Jack Hebden deplored swearing. 'What have I told you? I'd prefer it if you didn't use that sort of talk outside, with your pals. In this house . . .'

'But Rhona's the one who made me swear, Dad . . .'

'You will watch your language.' Jack continued doggedly. 'And if you've so little control over your words that somebody can "make" you swear, I'll have to look more closely at your education. It's not too late yet to send you to night school.'

In the kitchen Dan raised his eyes heavenwards, silently mouthing the echo of his father's words. Trying not to smile, Eve suddenly became very busy, lifting saucepan lids and inspecting the food. Her youngest was a bit of a lad, all right! Give him half a chance and he'd make you laugh as much as some of the comics on the music hall.

Dan was good, though, sound. And he tried to be patient about that motorcycle. Sometimes she wished she still had the bulk of the money Paul had left her. But that had gone years ago, when her own mother was so ill. They'd been told a private nursing home would be best, and into a nursing home her mother had gone. It hadn't helped. Her sugar diabetes had got worse and worse, and then gangrene had set in and she'd had to have her leg taken off.

'Mum – what is it?' Rhona sounded anxious.

Eve smiled. 'I was just thinking – about my mother, as a matter of fact. It isn't often I do now, it all seems a long time ago. Happen it was for the best,' she added, half to herself, thinking of the money spent before her mother's death at fifty-one.

They managed very well on Jack's pay packet, especially now the lads were earning a bit besides. Dan would get what he wanted – in time. His father said he wouldn't be allowed to ride till he was twenty-one. To a sixteen-year-old that must look like for ever. But, knowing Jack, he would consent long before then.

For Dan's sake, she was glad; though she knew no mother had much peace of mind when her son was out on one of them things. 'Those' she corrected herself inwardly, and was surprised. She'd changed, hadn't she, since she was Mrs Exton of Exton Hall? Mind you, some of it was for the better.

She'd loved Paul Exton, though, just as she loved Jack. The two men were very different, in more than background, but both fine husbands. Paul had been assertive, as befitted a mill owner. But he'd not had Jack's tolerance, and maybe his impulsiveness was confined to business. His daughter seemed to be inheriting that trait in every aspect of life. Not that their Rhona caused them any anxiety. They'd enough to worry about with Stan.

There'd been a right to-do the other week. One of Jack's workmates let on that Stanley was attending meetings organized by that Oswald Mosley. Jack had told Stan straight: he wasn't having any Fascist living here. But they were both worried. Stanley seemed to be taking it all to heart so – as far as he was concerned, Oswald Mosley was the only one who cared about the working class. Eve didn't know so much about that. She just hoped Stan kept out of trouble. There'd been a lot of violence since Mosley founded the British Union of Fascists last year.

'What did you do about Auntie Norah, love?' Eve asked Rhona, remembering. 'Did you help her write a letter?'

'I did more than that. I went up to Farnley Carr.'

'You never let on, walking home.' Drawn by her news, her stepfather even deserted the Gracie Fields record that was starting, and came to stand in the kitchen doorway.

Rhona faced him. 'Happen I wasn't over pleased with the way it went. I'd had it all worked out. What I wanted to say, and how. But it didn't quite come out that way. Maybe *I* need to go to night school . . .'

Jack shook his head, blue eyes warming, aglow. 'Nay, lass. I'll bet you're soft-pedalling what you've done, as usual. And I'll tell you something – no matter what the outcome, your father would have been proud of what you've done today. Right proud.'

Rhona gave a tiny shrug, but her gaze met his and her cheeks coloured.

Eve stopped stirring the sauce and looked towards her husband. Her glance locked on his and she breathed deeply, loving him perhaps more than ever in the past. How good Jack was, to her and for her daughter, as well as the lads he'd given her. 'Stan's late,' she said. 'We'd better begin without him.'

Rhona was on her way out that evening when she met Stanley on the corner of Gracechurch Street and Brunswick Road. For all his six feet two inches, he looked like a small, shamefaced boy.

'Has our mum sent you to fetch me?' A frown wrinkled his high forehead and narrowed his brown eyes. 'Clean forgot the time, we were having a game of snooker and you know how it is . . .'

'Better than hanging round street corners?' There was no sense in going on at him. If he didn't want to admit where he'd been, nothing would shift him. 'Mum didn't send me, but she isn't very pleased. She likes us all to sit down to tea together.'

'Can't see why. They've got no time for me, these days.'

'Where've you got that idea from? Nay, Stan – be fair.'

'Well, they go on at me enough. First one, then the other. "You oughtn't to smoke, Stanley." "Why can't you be more careful with your money, like our Dan?" It's my brass, isn't it? What little there is.'

'I don't think they really mind how you spend it, lad, so long as it isn't on cigarettes.'

'That's still my affair. I manage to pay my way . . .' His voice trailed off as his sister raised one auburn eyebrow. 'Most times,' he added under his breath.

Rhona smiled. 'How are you placed for tomorrow?' she inquired. 'I've got a shilling or two to spare.'

'Thanks, Rhona, you're a good lass. But I shan't be needing it. I'm working tomorrow. The weaving shed's closed officially, none of the looms are running. But there's a big breakdown, all us tuners'll be in. It'll be nice and quiet and all, without that clacking from the looms.'

'To say nothing of the weavers!'

'That just shows you know nowt about it! The weavers lip-read, didn't you know that, even?'

'I had heard,' she said dryly. 'I just wasn't thinking. Does the noise get you down?' She hadn't considered, until now, that Stan mightn't find the work entirely congenial. A job was a job, these days, and he'd seemed happy enough when he got the chance to start in the mill.

Stanley grinned. 'It's all right, I suppose. We can't all be school teachers!' He said it as if school really resembled Angela Brazil stories.

'Sauce! You're the second one today to bait me about my job – and *you* know that teaching ten-year-olds to knit and sew isn't much cop!'

'At least you don't get your hands mucky.'

'And I better hadn't either! It's bad enough getting the kids to keep their sewing clean.'

Rhona shivered and drew up her scarf round her ears. The tweed coat was thick and its fur collar warm, but tonight it was so cold nothing would prevent the chill penetrating. 'Look at me – standing here talking to you, I must be wrong in my head!'

She had a soft spot for Stan, though. And he did seem to not quite fit in at home these days. She could understand them worrying in case he got mixed up in politics that he couldn't handle. But she admired him for keeping abreast of what was going on.

'Are you off somewhere nice?' Stanley inquired, wondering where his half-sister was going on her own. 'Meeting Betty Marshall?'

'Not tonight.' Betty was courting now, she rarely saw her. And Rhona didn't want to say any more. She wasn't at all certain she was doing the right thing. She'd wasted her time calling on Wolf Richardson. If her evening visit proved even more fruitless, she wasn't going to answer questions from her interested family.

2

Hardly darkened at all by soot, the house was York stone, gleaming a sandy gold in the light from the gas lamps. Less than a couple of miles from Gracechurch Street, the area was clear of fog, and very different from the rows of terraced houses which, for Rhona, now were home. And yet her own home, once, had been only a hundred yards along Apsley Road from Lavender Court where the Ayntree family lived.

The Ayntrees' elderly housekeeper, neat in a dark blue dress, smiled instantly when she opened the burnished mahogany door. 'Miss Rhona – it is, isn't it? Oh, come in, lass, do. And let's have a look at you . . .' Jane Bishop, who'd been housekeeper to the Ayntrees since the Extons were neighbours, was gazing at her and nodding her iron-grey head.

'Eeh – you are like your dad!'

Rhona smiled. 'I must be! You recognized me quickly enough, Mrs Bishop.'

'I should think so, as well! You're an Exton, all right, even if you did take your stepfather's name. And how's your mother, bless her?'

'She's very well, thank you, Mrs Bishop. And will be pleased to have news of you. But how are you? You don't change much. And how is everyone?'

'I'm not so bad, you know, for an old 'un. But I'm afraid Mrs Ayntree's not very well at present, her bronchitis always plays up in winter time. The master's all right, though. Working too hard, as usual, with the mill and all that travelling back and forth to London. But he always wanted to go into politics, didn't he, he doesn't grumble about the hard work. Is it the mistress you've come to see? I don't know what to say, I'm sure. We had

21

the doctor in again only this afternoon, he's prescribed absolute rest . . .'

'Actually, it's Mr Ayntree I want to see. I did telephone him, he said it would be all right.' She knew now about appointments.

'Then I'll just tell him you're here. You give me your coat and your overshoes, and go through to the sitting room.'

Rhona scarcely had time to sit in one of the comfortable grey moquette armchairs before Rupert Ayntree MP came striding into the room.

'Rhona – little Rhona Exton!' He extended both hands to take hers.

'Well . . . Hebden, actually,' she corrected him gently, and smiled.

'Ah – yes. Of course. But there's no concealing your genealogy, is there? You're the image of Paul. But you must have been told that so often that it bores you.'

Still smiling, Rhona shook her head. 'Not really. Sometimes Mum would mention the likeness, but not too often. As with the surname, she didn't want to keep reminding Dad that she'd known a rather different life with my father.'

'And how is she?' he asked, releasing her hands.

'Very well, thank you. And happy.'

'I'm glad, my dear, very glad. I'm only sorry we seem to have lost touch over the years. How long is it this time since I saw you?'

'Must be eight or nine years – I'd just started at the grammar school. But you're a busy man, and have a lot of anxiety. I'm sorry your wife isn't any better.'

Rupert Ayntree sighed, his green eyes clouding. 'Yes, I'm afraid this winter is taking a heavy toll. She's hardly left her room since November.'

Wondering if she'd been wrong to come here with further problems, Rhona glanced around the room. The three-piece suite was new, but she recalled the polished walnut sideboard and matching side table. Their familiarity reassured her.

'Well – tell me why you're here, Rhona. You did say it was important. It sounded terribly businesslike . . .' He was smiling again now, the sort of smile she imagined him using with his constituents. It suited his rather florid face and portly build far better than the anxiety generated by his wife's condition.

'It's about Wolf Richardson planning to flood Vicar's Dale. Can't you do something to stop him?'

'Stop? Oh, my dear, there's nothing anyone can do now. The plans have been approved. I'm afraid, whether you like it or not, the scheme will go ahead,' he said, appalling her because everything was settled.

'But what about the people who're going to lose their homes? Surely you care about them, Mr Ayntree?'

'Naturally, we are concerned for their wellbeing. But I have had the personal assurance of Mr Richardson himself that they are being re-housed. Indeed, those who farm the valley are being offered greater acreage, along with superior housing . . .'

'I'm not worried about the farmers,' she told him, 'they can speak for themselves. But it's some of the people who live in cottages in the dale – like Norah Lowe, who was my father's nanny.'

'Why, I'd completely forgotten where she'd settled after the house was sold.'

'And she *has* settled there, that's the trouble. Having to move will be the finish of her.'

'Oh, surely not. I understood most of the cottagers were being offered accommodation that is far more convenient, much nearer town.'

'Auntie Norah is happy where she is.'

Again Rupert Ayntree sighed. 'I understand. She must be getting on in years now. Nevertheless, I fear that this particular change is one that has to be made.'

'But why? Who wants a new reservoir – except people like Wolf Richardson who're going to make a fortune out of its construction? We've managed all these years without Dale Reservoir, I can't see . . .'

'Managed? I think, my dear, you've identified the

23

reason for the scheme. After all, managing isn't quite sufficient, is it? The whole area will benefit from an improved water supply. The idea is that it will attract new businesses to Halfield. There are signs of increasing industrial development, even if they aren't yet very apparent to the layman.'

'That's what he said; you've been listening to him, haven't you?'

'To Wolf Richardson? I'd be a poor representative of my constituents' interests, wouldn't I, if I didn't find out all I could about such a major project?'

'And you side with him.' Disappointed, Rhona bit her lip.

'I also have a duty to my people,' he reminded her gently. 'Do you wish me to look into Norah Lowe's case?'

'It's difficult to know what to do for the best,' she admitted. 'She might get into a state, even with you. She can't do with anything out of the ordinary, you see, not now – she's eighty-seven. I was saying to Mr Richardson . . .'

'You've seen him then?'

Briefly, Rhona met his surprised glance, then lowered her gaze. 'This afternoon, not that it did any good. He seemed to be in a foul mood when I arrived, it certainly didn't improve while I was there. And he wanted to go and see Auntie Norah himself. I told him that was no good, he'd have had her in a right tizzy.'

'And you're afraid I'd be as bad? Wouldn't she remember me?'

'She might – then again, she might not. You know what old folk are like. Sometimes they can describe things that happened fifty or sixty years ago, and can't remember if they've eaten any dinner today.'

'Has Norah Lowe any relations?'

'Not any longer. There was a brother who used to live in Todmorden, but he passed away a few years ago. There's only us now.'

'And you visit regularly. Your father would be pleased.'

'I like to think that as well. I was too young when he

24

died to have many real recollections of him, but I do sense sometimes what he'd approve of – *and* what he wouldn't!' She grinned, brightening. 'I've been spoiled, you know, having Jack Hebden for a stepfather. He's too easygoing, specially with me.'

'And with his own two . . . ? Boys, aren't they?'

'Almost young men now. Stan's training to be a loom tuner at Dawson's mill, and Dan's weaving – carpets.'

'Good West Riding trades both of them. And what are you doing, Rhona?'

'Teaching sewing and knitting, but that's only the beginning.' She wanted to teach other subjects as well, when she could afford to take time off for the necessary training.

They were interrupted by the door opening. A young man and woman came into the room. They were about her own age, Rhona knew, but she felt they were older, felt shy with them. Twins, they were so like each other they appeared to exclude everyone else. Their pale hair was straight but glowed round their lovely features, both pairs of eyes glittered green like their father's.

'Phyllis, Clive!' he exclaimed. 'Don't you know who this is?'

The twins shook their heads, unsmiling, as though they had no wish to know her. Together, they glanced pointedly at the new electric clock.

'Rhona Hebden – used to be Rhona Exton,' Mr Ayntree explained, while Rhona wondered if she really had been friendly with these two all those years ago. 'Her parents lived just along the road when you were small.'

'Hallo,' they chorused, well drilled in good manners, but when Rhona responded warmly and smiled, they remained implacably gloomy.

'You're not busy, are you?' Phyllis asked her father, irritating Rhona with her assumption that her business here might be dismissed. 'My dress hasn't arrived. It was promised for yesterday, you know, but it's still not here. If it doesn't arrive in time for the ball tomorrow I shan't go.' Just like somebody out of Jane Austen! thought Rhona.

'You are stupid,' her brother reproved. 'I keep telling you it doesn't matter what you wear.'

'Of course it matters. Tell him, Father. You know how special this dress is.'

'Have you telephoned the shop?' Mr Ayntree asked, trying not to smile at his daughter's devastated expression.

'They say the delivery van broke down today, but they've promised the dress for tomorrow morning.'

'Let it rest, Phyl,' her brother said, sighing. 'You do create! Nobody'll look at you, anyway.' I've heard that before! Rhona reflected.

'That's just like brothers, isn't it?' she said sympathetically. 'They can be very scathing at times.'

'My dear, I don't know how I survive!' Phyllis observed, thawing a little now that Rhona seemed to take her part. 'And I know precisely how it'll be at the ball, as well. Daddy and Clive will gravitate towards the other men for drinks, and that will be the last I'll see of them until time to leave.' She looked at Rhona. 'I suppose you won't be there, will you? I've never seen you at the Mayor's Ball.'

Rhona smiled, shaking her head. 'I'm afraid it isn't an occasion I usually attend.' She was astonished that Phyllis seemed to want her there.

'Then you should,' Rupert Ayntree insisted.

Rhona gave him a surprised look.

'If you're genuinely concerned for the welfare of local people, you need to get to know those who can assist. All the councillors will be present, and the Mayor, of course.'

'Well, much as it might be useful,' Rhona continued, 'I've done nothing about a ticket. For this year, at least, it's too late.'

'Not at all,' Clive Ayntree said quickly. 'You have an extra ticket, don't you, Father?'

'For your mother, yes, but there's no chance of her being anywhere near fit to attend.' He turned to Rhona. 'Won't you make use of it, my dear? And make the three of us very happy to have your company.' Phyllis was nodding, encouraging her.

Rhona thanked him warmly, but didn't quite know how to reply. It was scarcely the kind of event she was accustomed to. Church soirées and tennis-club dances were the extent of her social evenings.

'You might as well come,' Clive told her practically. 'The ticket will be wasted, otherwise. And Phyl will be glad of another female, if only to moan to!'

Sitting beside Phyllis on the following evening, Rhona realized how well Clive knew his sister.

'It is a bore, I knew it would be!' Phyllis exclaimed as she set down her glass. 'Even the cocktails taste weary!'

Rhona smiled. 'Well, I'm enjoying it all. I'm glad I came. The dresses are so lovely – yours is an absolute dream!'

Phyllis glowed, a smile softened the carefully painted line of her lips, and she affectionately smoothed the gleaming gold tissue. 'It is rather special, isn't it? They had to take it in, you know. My waist is fully two inches smaller than average.'

'I love the way the material shines,' Rhona continued. The dress was fitted to Phyllis's boyishly slender figure, had a daringly low back, and a skirt that fanned out to ripple round her ankles.

In her own primrose yellow which she'd first worn as bridesmaid at Cousin Helen's wedding, Rhona felt far younger than Phyllis and decidedly ordinary. And yet tonight she didn't care, she was so interested in everything that she felt extremely happy. Mr Ayntree had introduced her to the Mayor, Alderman Pearson, and a group of local councillors, and although this wasn't the occasion to raise the matter of the reservoir, there was nothing to prevent her contacting them later. She might have been told that it was too late now to halt construction of the reservoir, but Rhona refused to accept that nothing could be done.

'I hope you didn't come here expecting to dance,' Phyllis said wryly, glancing across to the men assembling around the bar. 'I don't believe half of them understand what all this is supposed to be about!'

Rhona smiled. She was discovering that Phyllis rather enjoyed complaining. And that it wasn't intended that seriously. And besides, Phyllis had already danced three times – two of them with the most attractive fellow present, a tall, dark-haired young man with friendly grey eyes. Sir Reginald Newbold's eldest son, he'd seemed very pleased to meet Rhona, and interested in the school where she taught.

'Miss Hebden,' a masculine voice exclaimed just behind their table. 'May I have the pleasure of this dance?'

Rather amused by his formality, Rhona turned to look at him, and was shaken. He was the last person she wished to partner. But she'd never had reason to refuse anybody at church soirées, or other dances, would she be justified in refusing Wolf Richardson?

Thanking him, she stood up. Embarrassed, she realized she was staring at his hands – all trace of blood had vanished.

'How young and fresh you look, Miss Hebden, your gown is well chosen to complement your glorious hair, and to show a very straight back,' Wolf murmured as he drew her into his arms to begin a waltz.

Despite all her misgivings, Rhona smiled. 'Thank you. Actually, I altered the back only last night, when I knew I was coming here.'

'*You* altered it? What talent! Teaching school, *and* being a skilled needlewoman . . .'

'Actually, sewing is one of the subjects I teach,' Rhona began, and checked, furious with herself. Not only had she told him about altering the dress, something she had meant to keep from everyone, now she was blabbing about her work. She'd thrown away any possible advantage by confiding so much. If Wolf Richardson was so disconcerting, she would harden herself against letting out further revelations.

'I do so agree that dancing should not be spoiled by too

much idle chit-chat,' he said quietly, apparently misreading her sudden silence.

Rhona sighed heavily. And said nothing. There was one way only of dealing with a wayward tongue that couldn't be trusted.

He appeared to misinterpret the sigh. 'It is wonderful, isn't it, to concentrate on dancing – and one's partner.'

Rhona was trying to think of a cutting response that would shatter his illusions. 'You know what they say – they can't get you for thinking!' she exclaimed, wishing she'd come up with something original.

His laugh startled her, and she felt his arm tighten, drawing her closer. 'Agreed. And you've decided to guard your lips, before you let me know too much. Because you enjoyed my astonishment when I learned what your job is. Inwardly, you're kicking yourself for letting my flattery encourage your innate honesty.'

'Quite the psychologist, aren't you?' In fact, she was suppressing her amusement. He wasn't daft! 'If you're so astute you'll know also that I only danced with you because I was embarrassed about refusing.'

Wolf laughed again. 'Splendid! I was hoping I'd see that spirit of yours tonight. Without a bit of spice, you're altogether too sugary for the Rhona Hebden that I respect.'

There was no answer to that one! And she shouldn't feel this surge of elation because this man was saying such things. She ought to be totally alarmed – deep within her a rhythmic pulse was stirring, insistent as the waltz tempo, so powerful that she only now became aware that the band had finished playing. Without looking at Wolf, she knew his steady grey eyes were gazing at her, that he generated this undeniable magnetism. She ought to move away, but her head felt light as drifting smoke while her legs were leaden; *not* leaning towards him required all her willpower.

The band was playing again. Delight warming his rather harsh features, Wolf led her into an elegant foxtrot. If he had been less skilled, Rhona might have steeled herself against enjoying the dance. Fitting her steps to his, she was moving more gracefully than ever in her life. Just for these few minutes, she felt . . . beautiful. When the final bars faded, she smiled. 'That was good,' she said appreciatively.

He smiled back at her. 'Don't say I'm making you reverse your opinion!'

She stilled the quiver deep inside her. 'Only in less serious areas. You can dance. I'm not saying more than that.'

They had reached the edge of the dance floor when someone requested a tango. Wolf had locked his fingers over hers, she felt his grasp tighten. But she wasn't some Edwardian miss, swooning over her partner!

'You're out of luck – I can't do this . . .' Rhona began. And she couldn't, mustn't, be feeling so *right* while she was with him.

'With me, you can,' he asserted firmly and took her with him back on to the floor.

She sighed, her sherry-brown eyes rueful. Wolf, undeterred, started his suave interpretation of the dance. Rhona was exhilarated. She'd never believed she'd experience something so exotic. She closed her eyes. They might have been skimming through the balmy south of France, with palm trees stirring in a soft breeze wafting in off the Mediterranean. She was transported from wintry Halfield, smiled up at him, and danced more exuberantly.

'After this,' he told her quietly, 'you won't remember anything but my clever dancing!'

'That's what you think.'

'I don't, actually,' he admitted regretfully, sweeping her around him in a stylish spin. 'But I have to demonstrate there's more than one side to me.'

'I haven't said there wasn't.' There was this crazy attraction also!

'I know. I'll acknowledge that, above all, you are scrupulously fair.'

Rhona resisted the impulse to give him another searching glance. If Wolf Richardson was trying to perturb her he couldn't have generated more agitation deep inside her. But she would show him that she wasn't succumbing to his technique. The moment this dance finished she would thank him coolly, but politely, and return to her seat.

Even before the lively beat ceased, Wolf steadied her briefly, one hand lightly on her waist. 'That's enough for me,' he announced hastily. 'You'll have to forgive me for excusing myself.' He escorted her back smartly to her table.

Rhona concealed a wry smile as she watched him walking away from her. He might have known how much she wanted to dismiss him – *and* have known precisely how to forestall her!

Bubbling with excitement, Phyllis disengaged herself from her partner a few tables away and hurried to flop on to the seat beside Rhona's. 'Gracious, you've a nerve,' she exclaimed merrily, 'setting your cap at the only millionaire present!'

'He's a married man, don't be silly,' said Rhona quite sharply.

'Not any longer, not from what I hear.' Phyllis's green eyes were glittering as she studied Rhona's puzzled expression. 'You don't know, do you! Sorry, old love, I was doing you an injustice. Wolf Richardson's wife has deserted him.'

'Are you sure?'

Phyllis flicked back her pale hair. 'She's not with him tonight, is she?'

'I don't know. I've never met the lady.'

'But you'd met him before, hadn't you?'

'Only yesterday. Because I went to complain.'

'Complain? To him? Nobody does that. You wouldn't dare.'

'Someone had to put him right on what he's doing, to speak out about the folk being turned out of their homes for his wretched reservoir.'

'So that was it. And was that the reason you called to see Daddy?'

'Yes.'

31

'Good for you! I wouldn't have thought you'd had it in you. You're a plucky girl, aren't you, Rhona Exton!'

'Hebden.' she corrected automatically, then smiled. 'My stepfather adopted me, and gave me his name.'

'Anyway; to go back to Wolf Richardson,' Phyllis went on, with a mischievous grin.

'Must we?' She wasn't interested in scandal; would keep well away!

'Since he's become such a friend of yours, you ought to know. His wife walked out on him, went back to London. For good. Everyone says they'd had a terrible row.'

'I wonder how "everyone" knows,' Rhona said quietly. Wolf Richardson was hardly the man to broadcast his personal life.

'They have servants, haven't they? By all accounts, unless they were stone deaf, they could scarcely miss what was happening.'

Rhona said nothing. Wolf would have given as good as he got. And yet . . . in a way, she sympathized. From what she'd seen, he seemed determined to stand by his own beliefs, and his decisions. If they were opposed, he still wouldn't sacrifice what he considered right, even to his personal happiness. What're you doing, defending him, she wondered, why care?

'You're looking very solemn, young lady, aren't you enjoying the ball?' Jolted back to where she was, Rhona managed a smile. Rupert Ayntree, with Clive close behind, had returned.

'I'm thoroughly enjoying the evening, thank you very much.'

'Then I'm going to claim at least one dance, before all these young fellows take you over completely!' Mr Ayntree insisted.

'Was Wolf Richardson responsible for your frown?' he asked as soon as they reached the dance floor. 'If he's been irritating you . . .'

'He hasn't,' Rhona assured him. 'He's proving far less irritating than I expected.' And, she thought, look how dangerous that is! She'd just been shaken by learning that Wolf's wife had deserted him. Now, Mr Ayntree had as good as told her that he'd been keeping an eye on them as they danced together. Already, people were gossiping about the Richardsons, *she* wasn't going to get involved. He needn't think she'd heal his vanity!

'He has the reputation of something of a boor – and a bore – on social occasions.'

What was there to say? She'd found him more of a charmer than a boor. So much of a charmer that she couldn't take him too seriously. Anyway, Rupert Ayntree was her partner now. And he soon had her smiling, he was compensating for any inadequacies in his dancing by giving a succession of rapid assessments of many of the local dignitaries.

'Forgive my naughty humour,' he murmured, taking her back to the others. 'Without it, I'd become as stuffy as Members of Parliament are supposed to be!' He made her feel very mature, accustomed to such occasions.

Warming to him, Rhona would have been happy to dance again with this friend of her father. But then Clive partnered her for several numbers and took her through to supper.

The Ayntree family were popular, their table was approached by many of their friends who included Rhona in their conversation and laughter. But she couldn't avoid noticing Wolf Richardson eating alone at the far end of the room. Had the reservoir scheme made him so unpopular?

After supper he came again to ask her to dance. She'd intended keeping out of his way, but doing so seemed churlish now. And how would she tell him?

'Without you, my evening would have been very dull,' he told her.

'You've a smooth tongue, Mr Richardson. Is that how you get your own way?'

'I wish I did!'

'Is it the money that talks, then?' Rhona suggested. She felt safer with some conflict between them. She wasn't falling for his compliments.

'The wealth which you seem to resent was hard earned, you know. I followed my father into civil engineering, and we've neither of us been afraid of tackling ambitious projects. Ours was one of the companies involved in constructing the Mersey Tunnel. Just before his death, he was working on harbours, I'm specializing . . .'

'. . . in reservoirs?' she prompted wryly.

He sighed. 'Ah. This local scheme will do good, you know, attracting business. But I was hoping we might get through the evening without reverting to a matter on which clearly we never will agree.'

He'd been justified in reproving her. Rhona was about to admit as much when someone tugged at her arm. Phyllis was standing there, her green eyes staring with anxiety, her lovely face pale.

'Oh Rhona – I am sorry, we'll have to leave at once. It's Mother . . . Mrs Bishop telephoned. Mother's much worse and the doctor's sending her to hospital. Can you come now, quickly?'

'Oh, Phyllis, I am sorry.'

Rhona hastened after her towards the entrance. She was so disturbed she hardly noticed that Wolf went with her, his hand still grasping hers. Rupert Ayntree and his son were hurrying towards the outer door, already thrusting on their heavy winter coats.

'Look,' Rhona began as she joined them, 'you don't have to worry about me, you want to get home as fast as you can.'

'But, my dear, we must see you safely home,' Phyllis's father protested.

'No – really. I'll be all right, thank you. I can easily get a taxi. You go along. I hope Mrs Ayntree soon recovers. And thank you for a wonderful evening. I'm ever so sorry it's been spoiled for you like this.'

It was only after they'd gone that she really noticed that her hand was still grasped in Wolf Richardson's. He was gazing at her, his grey eyes serious.

'I hope that when the ball ends, Miss Hebden, you'll let me drive you home.'

'Thank you, but I wouldn't dream of putting you to so much trouble.'

Raising an eyebrow, Wolf smiled. 'Well, leave the matter in abeyance, while we finish our dance.'

Rhona couldn't pretend that she didn't enjoy dancing with him. Neither Rupert Ayntree nor Clive had a fraction of Wolf's style. But she decided, all the same, that he needn't think he could have all the remaining dances with her.

Once again, however, he took decision-making out of her hands. As soon as the dance ended he took her back to her table. 'I won't be selfish. I'll leave you free to accept other partners.'

It seemed, though, that those who were seeking someone to dance with had done so by now; the only men still unattached were gathered around the bar.

Feeling conspicuous on her own, she hurried towards the ladies' cloakroom. Glancing in the mirror, she noticed the flare in her cheeks and the vivacity of her eyes. She'd never seen them so bright – gold-flecked, glowing with stimulation. Why, great heavens, she looked quite – pretty!

She ran cold water over her wrists, slowly dabbed them dry, then held them to either side of her face. The state she was in must be with dancing so much, she told herself – and knew that it wasn't. No one, ever, had brought the blood surging through her veins like this, exciting and exhilarating her, until she felt like a different person.

A stranger, that's what she'd become. And she felt a whole lot safer with the Rhona Hebden she knew. You're scared, she silently reproached herself, you keep going on about safety. What are you doing hiding away in here? Just get out there, order yourself a taxi, and tell the man you're leaving. She raised her pointed chin, and hurried through the door.

But Wolf was waiting for her. Crossing the ballroom, she walked straight into his path. He detained her with a smile, and he had a plan worked out.

'My car will be outside the main entrance whenever

you're ready to leave. Just take your time if you wish to go home now, don't give anyone scope for talking.'

'Because you're a married man and are here alone?'

'Because I'm no longer truly married. Most people know my wife has walked out. And most will relish dragging my name in the mud. I'll not have them do that with yours.'

He was very serious. How could she throw his thoughtfulness in his face?

The Daimler was parked at the kerb, Rhona noticed some time later when she walked down the steps of the Victoria Hall into a flurry of snow. Wolf Richardson stepped out on to the pavement.

'You're not thinking of looking for a taxi, Miss Hebden? I'm going your way, I'll give you a lift.' Snowflakes melted into his brown hair.

'That's a nice surprise, thank you very much,' she said as he opened the passenger door. She felt rather special as he waited until she'd settled into her seat. This *isn't* going to my head, though, she reminded herself.

Getting into the driving seat, Wolf smiled sideways at her. 'I trust that will allay a few suspicions, at least.'

Rhona drew in a deep breath. Could he tell how afraid she was of becoming mixed up with him? 'I hope so, for your sake. I'd hate your wife to think I chased you the minute her back turned.'

He snorted. 'The attempt at discretion was entirely on your behalf.'

'Thanks,' she said hastily. She was agitated, without fully understanding the reason – except that this little scene they'd acted out had seemed quite conspiratorial. In a way, she'd enjoyed it. And she hadn't for one moment intended liking anything about him.

The inside of the car was so luxurious, she was enchanted. Its driver, though, had withdrawn, was frowning. Suddenly, Rhona felt awkward, didn't know what to do or say. How could she have felt as if she and this man might have something in common, how could she have loved dancing with him?

The Daimler glided so smoothly over the setts that they seemed to be riding through a dream. The gas lamps appeared to be flashing past very rapidly, and yet a lone constable on his beat gave them merely a glance. They couldn't be travelling excessively fast.

'Which house is it?' Wolf inquired coolly, turning into Gracechurch Street. Rhona started, afraid there'd be insufficient room for the Daimler between one flagged pavement and the other.

'Number forty-six, nearly at the far end.'

Wordlessly he nodded, concentrating on negotiating the unmade road which was worsened by icy patches.

'Thank you very much,' Rhona said as he slowed to a halt outside her home. Half of her wanted to dart indoors before anyone saw how she'd returned; the other half wanted the entire street to notice. Wildly, she pictured inviting him in.

'My pleasure.' He faced her then, as he switched off the engine. 'My wife won't be coming back,' he announced wearily. 'I heard today from her solicitor. She's wasted no time before seeking legal separation.'

His bleakness engulfed her making her shudder. 'I'm sorry.'

'So am I. I – hadn't realized we got along that badly. It seems she finds me absolutely intolerable. Maybe you would understand her reasons – she blames my determination to proceed with constructing the reservoir.'

'That's hardly grounds for divorce!'

'She claims I'm obsessive to the point of insanity. Perhaps you'd understand that better?'

Rhona was compelled to smile. 'Not really, certainly not tonight.'

'But yesterday – when you came to Farnley Carr?' When she didn't reply he persisted: 'I can't imagine what kind of impression I made then. It was only minutes earlier that Beatrice had stormed out.'

And I saw her, Rhona realized with a jolt, recalling how the woman had been weeping, quite uncontrollably. She also remembered the shattered goblet and the blood on his hand. He must have been extremely angry.

'How's the hand?' she asked, without meaning to mention it.

Again, his lips curled wryly. 'Better, thank you. Given time, everything heals.'

'Well – thanks again, for bringing me home.'

Her hand was on the door when he checked it with his own. 'One moment, please. Miss Hebden – Rhona, I'm the one indebted to you. I only went tonight out of sheer pig-headedness, determined to show everyone that I wasn't destroyed by the shattering of my marriage. If I'm to achieve anything at all here I've got to hold my head high. Already, there are enough people who despise me. Rightly or wrongly, I'm going to show them that Wolf Richardson isn't easily cowed. Without you, my dear Miss Hebden, I'd have shown them I'm just as susceptible as the next man to being kicked when I'm already down.'

'Kicked?'

'Didn't you see me alone at supper? How many times did I dance with anyone other than yourself? I'm a stranger here, remember. And proving myself is damned difficult. If I succeed they'll say I'm too clever by half, and question my methods. And if I fail – it'll provide good excuse for avoiding me.'

Despite all her misgivings about the man, Rhona couldn't control her upsurge of sympathy, and admiration. Unfortunately, she mustn't show either.

'I'd be glad of your friendship, Rhona. You should realize that by now.'

She thought of Auntie Norah. 'And you should realize you're taking a mean advantage of having driven me home. And of giving me such a good time this evening. You've made me want to agree to anything you suggest. Yet you know I can't. We can never be friends. Unless you abandon that diabolical scheme for a reservoir.'

3

The lights of Halfield were going out. He watched as, one by one, each gas lamp flickered and was extinguished. This far out, high on the moor, he'd expected any light from so far away to be diffused, a blur. He'd never noticed before how much he could see of the town from the front windows of Farnley Carr. Maybe he hadn't cared.

Sighing, Wolf stretched in his high-backed brocaded chair, closed his eyes to rest them. It had been a long night – in some ways. And yet he still seemed to hear her voice, echoing in his head.

'We can never be friends. Unless you abandon that diabolical scheme for a reservoir.' It might be less than an hour since he'd left her in that dismal street of back-to-back houses. If he hadn't sat through the night at the window of the master bedroom, if he hadn't remained here through the first faint glimmer of a winter's dawn, he might believe it still was only a matter of minutes since they'd said goodnight.

Her face was vivid before the eye of his mind, her brown eyes aglow, her glorious red-brown hair gleaming with vitality. And her spirited voice which didn't *always* condemn him was a teasing and tantalizing presence that seemed to fill this room.

What was there about her? Was it her youth? Certainly that had made him feel jaded by comparison – until she effortlessly infected him with her enjoyment of the ball. Was it her ingenuous nature which, right from the start, had delighted him by dismissing obstacles and minimizing the workings of bureaucracy? If she did but know it, she'd come close to convincing *him* that her intervention might yet prevent the reservoir going ahead! Impossible though it seemed, she'd made him question the validity of the planning permission already received.

More alarmingly, throughout this night, she'd made him question his desire to see the project completed. Was he insane? What other explanation could there be for this reversal of his intention? Or near-reversal. He was over it now. No one would ever know that he'd approached the brink of tearing up his plans.

None of it made sense. He'd let the reservoir scheme become the final contention between Beatrice and himself. She was an intelligent woman, would have understood his reasons for going ahead, she'd given him time to enlarge on what he saw as a very necessary construction. And she'd left for London only when he'd refused to explain.

Never explain, and never make excuses – that was the code he lived by. A code inherited from his father, and his father before him. Men who'd won respect throughout civil engineering. His father had died suddenly, his heart worn out at fifty, the doctors had said. Wolf had continued ever since, designing and contracting at home and abroad, without let-up. And he surely was not going to be weakened by this girl who could not accept that he made his own decisions . . . and stood by them.

Who was Rhona Hebden, after all, to suppose that she might stop him?

At last! The classroom was empty now and, thank goodness, silent. What an appalling day! The only good thing had been learning that Mrs Ayntree was improving when she telephoned Lavender Court. Phyllis had been so relieved about her mother that she'd remembered to ask if Rhona had managed to get a taxi home.

'No problem at all,' she'd answered quickly. 'I didn't wait till the end. With school today I didn't want to be too late.'

Afterwards, she'd felt guilty about leading her friend to believe she'd gone home by taxi. But Phyllis always had loved to tease, the years hadn't changed her.

And the less said – *and* thought – about Wolf Richardson the better! She'd been enough of an idiot dancing with him so frequently, there was no need to let his attention go to her head. If Wolf had had a motive, other than passing a dull evening, it could only have been to ensure that she came over to his side regarding that reservoir.

She had no intention whatsoever of making a habit of seeing him. Whatever he might say, he was still a married man. And people had noticed them dancing together. What good would all her extra training be if she was refused a good teaching position because of gossip that she was involved with a man who wasn't free?

She'd had her bit of fun last night, now she'd be careful. Keeping out of Wolf's way wouldn't be difficult. And she was learning not to act so impulsively.

Perhaps it was as well, she added silently to herself. Despite the late hour, she hadn't slept so well as usual, troubled by a stimulation that left her feeling utterly perturbed and embarrassed.

She'd had boyfriends, of course. Boys to hold hands with in the pictures, or to dance with at the tennis-club socials, to kiss when they'd been going out together for a while. And she thought she knew quite a bit about being attracted to someone.

Last night, though, hadn't been the same. Trust her to let herself go, and let Wolf Richardson of all people so close that when he danced, and danced, and danced again with her he created an unforgivable longing. And the need to merge her steps with his had generated an ache for a much more alarming merger.

Sex wasn't discussed at home, it never had been, but her Cousin Helen had been less reticent shortly after her honeymoon. For Helen, being married had proved an enormous excitement.

'Don't believe them when they tell you it's just something that a woman has to endure, Rhona,' she exclaimed. 'There's nothing like giving yourself entirely to the right man – and nothing, but nothing, produces such a glorious feeling of satisfaction afterwards!'

Rhona had been used to her cousin's superlatives. Helen was a girl who'd always lived every moment, and had ensured that everyone knew about it. Last night, though, alone in her chill little room she had begun to wonder if there could be some truth in Helen's claim. *With the right man*, though, of course. And no matter what feelings he generated Wolf Richardson never would . . .

Rhona started, and her heart began thundering in her chest. The knock on the classroom door had been timorous, but to her it had sounded loud enough to alert the entire neighbourhood! She could feel her face reddening. Thank goodness no one could guess what she'd been thinking!

Through the brown-painted glass panel she saw the outline of a girl. The bulk of the silhouette immediately identified the pupil, and Rhona quelled a sigh. Poor Amy had caused trouble enough today by crying her way through the lesson. Having her hanging back after the others had left was more than Rhona could face.

'Amy – what is it?'

'Can my mum talk to you, Miss Hebden, *please*? It's about me getting upset . . .'

Mrs Lightowler stood hesitantly near the door of the next classroom. She might have been about to bolt for cover there. Rhona was compelled to suppress a laugh at the incongruity of a tiny woman like Mrs Lightowler producing a hefty ten-year-old like Amy. To see them now, with Amy hustling her mother through the door, you'd believe their roles were reversed.

'Do sit down, Mrs Lightowler,' Rhona invited.

'Go on, Mum,' Amy prompted. 'Tell her what you said to me.'

'I could see our Amy had been crying as soon as she came in,' Mrs Lightowler began. 'It was because of your lesson, wasn't it? And it seems such a pity. Our Amy's a good little knitter, you know. She tries right hard at home. And she never drops any stitches now. It's not her fault that she's so big. Takes after her dad, she does, and her brothers.'

'I see.'

Before Rhona could say any more Amy was speaking

42

again. 'Haven't you got any nice patterns that would fit me, Miss?'

Rhona swallowed. So that was it. The other advanced knitters in the class had been selecting patterns to make simple cardigans. And Amy . . . ? Guiltily, she remembered suggesting that Amy might knit a scarf instead.

'She's made a scarf already, you know,' Mrs Lightowler reminded her. 'She only wants to be more like the others.'

'I know they laugh behind my back,' said Amy, standing for once to her full height. 'I don't really mind the names they call me. But I can't help being bigger than them, and I like doing knitting.'

The school stock of patterns didn't include anything anywhere near Amy's size, and Rhona felt that adult cardigans would look all wrong on a ten-year-old child. She would have to suggest altering a pattern to accommodate Amy's girth. If she'd been feeling less perturbed by her own emotions in class, she'd have made the suggestion earlier.

'I'll see what I can do,' she promised. 'I might be able to adapt a pattern to fit her. Just let me take a few measurements.'

Watching mother and daughter crossing the school yard, Rhona felt affectionate amusement bubbling up into her throat. Elated now, Amy was bounding along beside her diminutive mother, pausing now and then to give her arm an eager tug, encouraging her home for tea. The girl might have been a massive St Bernard pup, mothered by a neat little toy poodle! Still, St Bernards were lovable dogs, and certainly useful.

Working that evening in her room, Rhona found herself enjoying calculating the number of stitches that would produce a garment large enough for Amy. And even working out how much additional wool would be required wasn't so fearsome as she'd imagined. By the time she went to bed she had copied out the instructions in a form which the girl would be able to understand. She felt more satisfied than she had for several months; and glad to have her mind occupied . . . ?

Few parents came near the school, having Mrs Lightowler show such willingness to cooperate like this had given Rhona a nice surprise. Between them, they would ensure that Amy completed an acceptable garment and, who knows, that could give the girl a brighter picture of herself. That couldn't hurt, could it? Who knew what good it might do by stimulating the girl's pride in herself?

Rhona stared disbelievingly at the invitation, then read it a second time and a third.

Mr & Mrs Rupert Ayntree MP request the pleasure of the company of Miss Rhona Hebden at a reception to celebrate the engagement of their daughter Phyllis Leonie to Mr Adrian Newbold, elder son of Sir Reginald Newbold JP . . .

The details were a blur, she was so close to tears. In the accompanying note, Phyllis explained that she had known Adrian Newbold for years, his father and her parents were friends. And Rhona had learned only this week that Sir Reginald Newbold's company was the major contractor involved in constructing Dale Reservoir!

Seething, Rhona wrote back thanking them tersely, and declining the invitation. And she offered neither reason nor excuse. Mr Ayntree surely would understand that she now recognized his refusal to oppose the reservoir scheme as rather more than a decision based on what would most benefit the community.

It was only a month now since the Mayor's Ball; surely Phyllis must have had some idea then that she would agree to marry Adrian Newbold? The entire Ayntree family must have known. She didn't blame any of them for leaning towards the interests of their friends, but she'd have thought more of them if Phyllis or her father had explained why they couldn't oppose the project.

Feeling that the Mayor's Ball had been a regrettable occasion in more than one way, Rhona pushed it to the back of her mind. She was busy enough, anyway, if only with Amy Lightowler.

Since she'd produced that cardigan design for her the girl had surged ahead, filled with enthusiasm. She'd already nearly completed the garment and was pestering Rhona for the adaptation of another pattern.

Because Amy had shown such interest, and suspecting that the girl was somewhat overshadowed by her father and brothers, Rhona asked her to spend one evening each week at Gracechurch Street. Working together on altering a knitting pattern proved laborious, but Rhona felt she was compensated by Amy's very evident pleasure.

'I've got something to look forward to now, Miss Hebden,' she confided, her round face aglow.

Fitting in visits to Auntie Norah, and her church-going and teaching Sunday School, then tennis-club committee meetings in preparation for the new season ahead kept Rhona's mind off the Ayntree family. When she bumped into Phyllis in the town centre one Saturday morning, she greeted her instinctively as the friend that she so quickly had become. And then she remembered the engagement invitation.

Immediately embarrassed, Rhona tried to think up a polite excuse for hurrying away before the topic was raised. She was too late, however.

'It's my party tonight, Rhona, I do wish you were coming.' Phyllis sounded sincere, and Rhona felt sorry that she'd been obliged to refuse. 'Are you going somewhere else?' Phyllis persisted. 'You didn't say . . .'

Rhona sighed. 'And you didn't say, at first, how well you knew the Newbold family, did you? You let me go on about the reservoir scheme, and Wolf Richardson, and not for one minute did you let on that you were involved with the family who were going to build the wretched thing.'

'Oh, that!' Phyllis said dismissively. 'As if it mattered!' She glanced down to adjust the fox fur draping the shoulders of her fine woollen coat the shade of her ash-blonde hair.

'It matters to me to know where I stand with my friends.'

'You make it sound as though Father has a financial interest in the scheme. I don't think he has, you know.

And although Adrian works for his father, all they consider is the company and making it successful, they have to take what work they can get. Not everybody's building something on the scale of the reservoir, these days.'

Rhona said nothing, could have hit her for sounding so *reasonable*.

Phyllis shrugged. 'Oh, well – please yourself. But I think you're jolly mean staying away because we don't all agree with you.'

'That isn't the point. I'd have preferred you all to be honest.'

'We were. We've done nothing underhand, nothing to be ashamed of. And you're a fine one to talk! Who spent the whole evening with the one man who's going to make a whacking profit out of the reservoir?'

'I didn't, not the whole evening.'

'And he saw you home afterwards, didn't he?'

Rhona darted her a sharp look, but didn't speak. Somebody had been talking. She'd told Wolf Richardson that she didn't care about gossips. But she did care enough to want her own name kept out of any possible scandal.

'There aren't that many big black Daimlers in Halfield yet, are there?' Phyllis remarked with a knowing grin. 'He'll be there tonight – why don't you forget our differences and come along?'

'I've said no, thank you – and I mean it. I'm sorry, Phyllis, I didn't want us to fall out. And, for your information, the fact that that man's going to be there is the last thing that'd make me go.'

It was a crisp February day with the sun shining from a sky blue as many a one in June. But as she and Phyllis stalked away from each other Rhona was miserable, it might as well have been pouring down.

She would have enjoyed herself at that party. She'd thrown away her friendship with the Ayntrees, and was sickened.

Oh, well, she thought resignedly, I've done it now. No more outings with the Ayntree family. And none with

Wolf Richardson, something deep in her subconscious added, and increased her gloom. She'd better walk home instead of waiting for the tram. The exercise would work the bad humour out of her system.

Even though it was Saturday morning one or two mills were as noisy as any day during the week. Black and forbidding with its high stone walls, the last one before she turned into Brunswick Road was Bridge House Mill, once owned by Paul Exton.

Most times when she passed, Rhona didn't even think about her connection with the place; today, she experienced a sudden longing to talk to Bill Brightstone, its manager.

He was in the office whose dull brown paint and old wooden desk strewn with papers seemed not to have altered since her last visit. When she approached, Mr Brightstone looked up, and a wide smile transformed his round, ruddy face. 'Rhona – little Rhona Hebden! Come in, lass – let's have a look at you. You don't come here often enough, you know.'

'I know, Mr Brightstone. There never seems sufficient time for all I want to fit in.' She added silently to herself that he was right – she didn't indulge herself often enough in the welcome she received here.

'Well, so long as you haven't forgotten us. You're always welcome here, you know.'

'I was just realizing that.' Rhona smiled. 'I think I need one place that never changes.'

'Never? You'd be surprised! Since you were here we've made quite a few alterations. For one thing, our Timothy's working with me now.'

'Tim? Really?' Rhona's eyebrows soared while she settled on to the chair Bill Brightstone offered. 'I never thought he would come into the mill when he'd been away to Cambridge.'

'Nor did I, lass. But it was his suggestion. Fact is my ticker's been playing up this past twelve months, and the doctor's told me to ease up. I think young Timothy understood how I couldn't bear to have anyone else

47

managing this place. Any road, he said he'd like to learn all there is to know about the job.'

'And I'm sure there's no one better qualified than you to teach him. I'm right sorry about your heart, though, how bad . . . ?'

'To teach me what . . . ?' a voice inquired from the doorway, and Timothy Brightstone strode in. 'Don't let him fool you, Rhona, I'm learning everything the hard way.'

She smiled wryly. 'Happen that's the only way it'll stick in your mind!' she said jauntily. But she was having difficulty with her hastening pulse. Tim had grown up at Cambridge, and grown into an attractive young man. She rose and crossed the few paces to greet him.

'Happen so!' Tim pulled her close, a friendly arm across her shoulders. He was a lot taller than her now, and seemed to have slimmed down. He'd never be plump like his father. His hair gleamed as fair as the Ayntree twins', and was wavy, giving him rather a devil-may-care look. 'What do you think about me being in the mill, then?'

'It's a good idea. If you do no worse than your dad, you'll be all right.'

'I'll do better.' Timothy, his blue eyes glittering so that they reminded her of Jack Hebden's, gave her shoulders a squeeze.

Rhona grinned up at him. 'They didn't teach you modesty at Cambridge, I see.'

'Not a great deal, no,' he responded, in similar light tone. But his expression grew serious, making her want to get to know him all over again, and to know him better.

'They did teach us self-reliance, which has something to recommend it,' Tim continued, while Rhona stood there, aware that she was being impressed, and somehow unable to say anything to break the magnetism willing her attention. 'And how to appreciate an attractive girl. You've blossomed, Rhona Hebden, do you know that?'

His too-obvious flattery severed the attraction. 'Thank you, kind sir!' she mocked. 'It's a wonder you didn't say how I've grown. And what makes you an expert on the fair sex? You're not that much older than me, don't forget. And I've known you all my life. Don't pretend with me that you've come home, after a couple of years, the sophisticated man-about-town. You'll always be young Tim whose dad used to take us both on picnics down by the beck.'

'But I am a man-about-town, and that's why I can speak with the authority of a connoisseur. Let me take you out, Rhona – I'll show you, I'll give you a good time.'

Rhona felt Timothy's father's disapproval; when she turned, sure enough he was frowning. 'Nay, Tim – you know that's not right. At least, tidy up the loose ends first. Don't go asking one lass out while you're courting another.'

'Hazel Wright and I aren't courting,' Tim protested. 'We're both free to do as we like.'

'Are you? I doubt if Hazel thinks that. Be fair, lad. She didn't go out with any other young fellows while you were away.'

'That was her hard cheese. Anyway, Rhona here's an old friend – that doesn't count.'

Rhona laughed. 'Gratified though I might be by your interest, Tim, I rather think I'll curb my eagerness till you've sorted out your love-life . . .'

Tim grinned at her. The hand on her shoulder had slid up beneath the fur of her collar. Even through the thick tweed of her coat she could feel his fingers caressing the curve of her neck. She'd have to keep a sharp eye on Mr Tim Brightstone if she kept coming across him now he was back in Halfield.

'Take no notice of what he says!' he exclaimed, with a careless nod in his father's direction. He leaned over and kissed her, on the cheek but with a force that couldn't be ignored. 'Think on now, that's just to whet your appetite.'

He stopped flirting after that and the three of them settled round the desk to talk about the mill, and about times long past.

Rhona relaxed, soothed by Bill Brightstone's familiar voice, and by the half-forgotten smell of processed wool from the spinning frames beyond the office windows. From time to time Timothy or his father would glance towards the operatives as they passed between the heavy machines but for long enough nothing interrupted the steady production of yarn. She took the smooth running of the frames as proof of the efficiency of Bill Brightstone and now of Timothy.

Eventually, the hooter sounded at twelve o'clock. Gradually the spinning ceased. Rhona sighed appreciatively, revelling in the sudden quiet.

'Grand, isn't it,' Tim remarked, 'when it's stopped?'

'Nay, lad, you don't know what you're talking about,' his father reproved. 'Aren't there enough mills in the West Riding on short time for you to know that we're fortunate to have work for a full week?'

'Well, you know what I mean . . .' Tim began uncomfortably. 'We can talk properly now, without all that racket.'

'If we do all that you speak of here,' Bill went on, still frowning, 'you'll know what noise is! You've heard nothing yet. That lot's silent compared with some of the machinery we'd have to have. But I'm sure Rhona doesn't want to hear all the boring details of your schemes.'

Even though father and son hadn't shared with her their future plans for Bridge House Mill, Rhona came away from there that morning feeling that she'd been warmed by somewhere where she belonged. Bill was a good bloke and always would be, and Tim, despite his chat, seemed set to emerge with many of his father's attributes.

She had promised to go back to the mill before too much time elapsed, and meant to keep that promise. They were her sort of folk, living the kind of lives she understood, and they readily accepted her. Tim's words needed to be taken with a fair sprinkling of salt, never mind a pinch, but she was level-headed enough for that not to matter.

She wouldn't be surprised if he married Hazel Wright, she was a bonny girl who'd been in the same infants' class as Rhona, but then had moved to the other side of town.

They'd met on occasions since, because Hazel was in a tennis club as well. She was a dazzling girl in white, her hair being as black as coal, and her eyes nearly as dark. He's daft if he doesn't stick with her, Rhona thought as she walked along Gracechurch Street. And Hazel would be wrong in her head if she didn't continue to wait for Timothy.

Nearing the house, Rhona slowed almost to a stop, pensive now, realizing as she thought of Tim marrying Hazel that she rather envied them. Don't be so soft, she rebuked herself. He's an attractive fellow, that's all. He's got nice eyes and wavy hair, that's what's done it. That, and standing closer than he ought, giving her the glad eye while his hand through her coat proved what an expert touch he had. She'd go back to the mill, all right, he wouldn't stop her doing that. But she'd not succumb to his sort of nonsense.

She wouldn't have time for courting for many a long month, would she? At last, she was approaching twenty-one and was gathering information about courses that would provide qualifications for teaching more subjects. As soon as she learned how much money would be coming her way, she was going to have a long talk with her headmistress.

She would need to be absent for a couple of years or so, studying. It wasn't reasonable to suppose that her old school would automatically offer her a position after that. Rhona didn't really care. Suitably qualified, she would feel she had more authority when seeking a new place. Teaching somewhere different would be exciting, more of a challenge.

Let's just hope there'll be enough to keep me until I'm fully trained, she thought, going into the house. She'd set her heart on this, nothing less than a major crisis was going to stop her.

Taking off her coat and hanging it behind the door, Rhona shuddered. All at once, she sensed that something might occur to alter all her plans. Alarm quivered right through her, numbing her limbs so that when she tried to walk away from the door she could not do so.

Now less of that! she silently chided herself. That's defeatist thinking. She was Paul Exton's daughter, wasn't she. He'd not have given way because of an inexplicable feeling that something would go wrong.

Rhona glanced across the comfy living room, then through into the kitchen. Mum, Dad, Stanley, Dan . . . they were all there, chatting away as usual, busy. Why on earth had she thought something dreadful might happen? I need more confidence, she decided, somehow I'll get it! One day, she promised herself, I'll be sure where my life is going – surer even than brilliant people, like Wolf Richardson.

4

Relief flowing through her, Rhona smiled across the desk at Marcus Feldman, the white-haired solicitor, who'd finished reading the first extract from her father's will.

'It does sound a lot,' she exclaimed. 'I don't mind telling you I've been ever so worried, these past few months. I'm going to training college, you see, that's why I've got to have something behind me. I didn't realize how much my father had left me. It'll be more than ample to live on.'

'There's more besides,' Mr Feldman continued, smiling back at her and making her feel easier than she had since entering the old-fashioned office.

'More . . . ? But I don't understand. You said this was the approximate total to be realized from his investments.'

He nodded his snowy head, fingered the matching beard, and leaned back in his massive leather chair. 'There are shares also, Miss Hebden. Shares in Bridge House Mill.'

'*What*?' Disbelief made the word emerge with a funny little laugh. 'Nay, I was only a little lass when he went away to war, he'd not have left me shares.'

'See for yourself . . .' Faintly amused, Marcus Feldman slid the document across his polished walnut desk.

'I'll take your word for it.' She could read everything later. She needed no proof of her father's action, but she was far from happy about what he'd done. *Shares*. Shares sounded like responsibility. 'Can – will it be all right if I sell them?'

'Legally, there's nothing to prevent that course. I feel sure, though, that your father's intention was that you would involve yourself, to some degree, in the mill.'

'Yes, but – he wasn't to know I was going to be a teacher. If I'd been a lad, giving me shares would have been different. But he'd never have wanted me *not* to teach . . .' Rhona felt quite sick, trapped.

'Don't act in haste, Miss Hebden, please. Take time to consider what you really wish, then come and see me again. If you feel you still must continue with your chosen career and need advice for disposing of the stock, I can put you in touch with the best professional advisers.'

'Thank you, Mr Feldman, thank you very much,' Rhona said hastily. She rose, then glanced apologetically towards him. 'I'm sorry – was there anything else you wanted to mention just now?'

There was not, and Rhona couldn't have been more thankful. Clutching a copy of the will, she fled from the offices. Out in the street, she had to stand still, gasping rather dizzily, badly shaken.

All the way back in the rattling tram, she kept telling herself that there was no reason to feel so appalled, that she could simply be glad that she'd inherited the money she needed, and that was it. Nothing, though, could dull the apprehension gnawing into her, inducing a pain beneath her ribs and catching at her breath.

She sprang off the tram at Bridge House Mill and pushed back the big heavy door so that it clattered against the wall, she was so anxious to see Bill Brightstone.

His office was empty. From between the clacking spinning mules, Bill saw her despairing look and strode towards the office.

'Hallo, Bill. I was just wondering if I should come looking for you, but I thought you mightn't like folk wandering through the shed.'

'I don't normally. You're different, though.' Although smiling, Bill was very out of breath, his cheeks flushed, but his lips blue-tinged.

'Are you all right?' Rhona inquired quickly.

'Aye – aye, thanks, lass. I'll just have a bit of a sit down.' He settled his bulk behind his desk, which was piled higher than ever with papers, samples of wool and bits of machinery.

'What's to do, lass? I can see summat's bothering you.'

'I've just come from the solicitor's.'

'Oh?' Bill scrutinized her expression. 'What's up then?'

'It's what my father's done, Bill. He's left me a lot of shares in the mill.'

'Aye – and . . . ?'

'You knew!'

'Naturally. When Mr Paul went off to fight he left me in charge, didn't he? He told me what he was doing, that them shares would be tied up, like, till you came of age. *If* anything happened to him, of course . . .'

'But you never said, never breathed a word! All these years.'

'Look, love, you only turned up here a few weeks back, I hadn't seen head nor tail of you since you were a bit of a lass, had I? I didn't have chance to say owt. T'weren't my place to. That were your dad's business. So long as I knew that sooner or later we'd have another Exton around, that were all I cared.'

'And who else knew – my mother?'

'I've no idea, have I? Haven't you asked her?' Bill fidgeted uncomfortably with a gadget from one of the combing machines which was leaving a greasy trail across a heap of invoices.

'I haven't been back home yet. I came straight here. I wanted to hear what you had to say, Bill. I'm going to training college, you know. I've only been waiting till I could afford. Now . . . Bill, you'll take these shares off my hands, won't you? I'll see it's worth your while, at a price you can manage.'

'Nay, Rhona lass, don't talk of getting rid. Come in with us properly, take your share of running the place.'

'*Me*?' She was incredulous, she'd never contemplated any such possibility. Hadn't she just said – she was going to study again, so she could teach, *teach* – more subjects, and more thoroughly, *teach* . . .

'Yes, you. I've had a bit of a setback since you were here before, we need somebody else to help keep an eye on things.'

'Setback? Bill . . . ?'

55

'I thought it were summat and nowt. But the doctor will have it that I had a slight heart attack. He's filling me up with all sorts of medicine – I'll be as right as a bobbin before long. Only . . .' Bill sighed, looked down at his desk, and then straight into Rhona's eyes. 'Well, it has taken it out of me. Our Timothy's having to shoulder more and more responsibility, and that wasn't what I wanted, at all. Not yet awhile, any road. He might have finished at Cambridge, but he's still studying. And he's got to continue. He's had chances that I never dreamed possible, I'll not see him chuck them away.'

As if to add weight to his father's words, Timothy came hurrying in.

'Is – is it spinning you're studying, Tim – is that it?' Rhona asked when they'd greeted each other. She felt utterly bewildered; getting him to talk for a while might give her an opportunity to think.

'In a way. Or exploring what's new these days, and how we might best utilize space here. Dad's often talked in the past about extending the mill.'

Bill nodded. 'We have the room. When the old carpet mill next door burned out, our board of directors put in a bid. We got it for next to nothing.'

'I want us to go over to weaving as well as spinning,' Timothy continued. 'But whatever we decide on has to pay for itself. That's why I've got to have time to look into it properly. There's a lot of new technology on its way. New, automatic looms. And that's what we'd have, or leave it alone altogether.'

'Development – that'd be Timothy's special responsibility. That, and helping with the day-to-day running of the place.'

'Well, he'd do that, I'm sure,' Rhona said quickly. 'You'll manage without anybody else. And whatever do you think I could help with?'

'Keeping the books, for one thing.'

'Don't you have a clerk who does that already?'

'Miss Perkins used to, but she's retired.'

'But somebody must be doing the books now.'

'I am – leastways, I was till I had that bad do with my heart. I've tried to catch up since, but there's always something more urgent needing my attention.'

Sighing, Rhona shook her head. 'I'm sorry, Bill. I haven't a head for that sort of thing at all. I was always hopeless at sums.'

'You'd a cheek to ask her, Dad,' Tim reproached his father. 'You can't expect Rhona to give up teaching for that.'

'You'll have to do it yourself, then,' Bill responded sharply. 'Happen that's something you can manage.'

Bill was glaring from Timothy to some green woollen fibres that had been dropped on to the desk among the paperwork.

'It's not my fault that I've got no eye for it,' Timothy said quietly, trying to rein in the annoyance created by his father's mentioning this in front of Rhona. 'I've said I'm sorry, and I mean it. I simply could not see any difference between them.'

'There's nothing to seeing it. It must be summat lacking in you, lad!' Bill turned to Rhona as he picked up two lengths of partly processed wool. 'You can tell them two slivers are different, can't you?'

'You mean that this one's much yellower than the other?'

'There – you see?' Bill said to his son. But then he forgot his irritation and looked at Rhona again. 'You know what, don't you, lass – that's how you could help.'

'I'm going away, Bill, to college.'

'Listen, *please*,' he implored, but *he* hadn't listened to her. 'It's not imperative that we have someone here all the time to keep an eye on colour control. You could still carry on with your teaching. But, if you'd a mind, you could come here after school once or twice a week. And maybe on Saturday mornings.'

'I'm taking a training course,' Rhona reminded him firmly. 'I shan't even be in Halfield.' Her father would have loved her to work at Bridge House Mill, she thought,

57

in whatever capacity. 'I'm sorry. It's only today that I've known for sure that I could afford any more training.'

'You haven't made concrete arrangements to go, then,' said Bill very quickly.

'Nothing's finalized,' she admitted cautiously. 'But I know exactly what I want to do.' Exhausted by the tension generated within the office, she hastily made an excuse and got herself out of the place.

Out in the fresh air she stood still, hauling in deep, calming breaths, her face upturned as she revelled in the lightly falling rain. She'd been scared stiff that she'd never get away! Back there she'd felt trapped. As if all her plans were doomed. She wouldn't throw them away, not for anybody. Why on earth should she?

'How did you get on, love?' Eve Hebden asked as her daughter came in.

'You knew, didn't you?' Rhona exclaimed. 'You were well aware that my father had left me all those shares.'

Eve sighed. 'Yes, I knew all right. Hundreds of times I reckoned that maybe I ought to warn you what you were in for . . .'

'But you didn't.' Grimly, Rhona smiled. 'Scared?'

Eve nodded. 'Daft, isn't it? You were that set on going on studying, I didn't want to place any obstruction in your way. I'm only glad Paul couldn't know what he was doing to his only child.'

Rhona laughed. 'Aye, happen it was as well! But nobody needs to get all upset about it. Nothing's going to make any difference. I haven't quite decided what I shall do about the shares, I've got to get used to the idea first; but I'm going to carry on just as if they didn't exist.'

Eve nodded, but as she returned to the gas stove another sigh gathered deep inside her chest. Rhona might *say* things remained the same, but who could ensure that?

People had told Rhona that once she was twenty-one time would fly so quickly she'd wish she could slow it down. She had laughed but suddenly they were in 1934 and spring was coming, and it didn't seem more than a few days since last spring.

When she last visited Auntie Norah she'd been astonished that the old lady was already preparing to move into her new home.

'I shan't like it, you know,' Norah Lowe confided, 'but I'll make myself live with it. You did your best to fight yon young man, now I'll do my best to show him he can't get Yorkshire folk down.'

Sitting in her worn old rocking chair, beside the black-leaded range dominating the little room, she'd folded her arms and smiled across at Rhona, who fidgeted slightly on the prickly horsehair sofa. 'It's cost him a packet, you know, just to buy the place. That cottage were close on three hundred pounds! I daresay he'll get that back when anything happens to me, but there's two lots of solicitors' fees and all. One of them is charging six guineas, whatever do you think to that? They don't know where to stop, these days.'

'I didn't realize you'd be going quite so soon.'

Rhona had felt weighed down with guilt. She should have kept a check on the old lady's plans. But she'd been too perturbed about her own future to spend long thinking about anything else.

Time and time again, she'd pictured Bill Brightstone as he'd looked that day, and had felt torn. Ought she to help out there? But that would mean there'd be no college, no getting away from only teaching sewing and knitting, no higher qualifications.

'What day did you say you were moving in? Do you want me to give you a hand?'

'No thanks, lass. That'd mean you taking time off your work. He said he'd see to everything. He'd jolly well better keep his promise.'

It was the day after Auntie Norah was being transferred to the new cottage, a Saturday. Determined to do everything she could now, Rhona was up early, but Jack Hebden was downstairs before her.

'Don't let on to your mother, there's no need, but I've

got a bit of something I want you to take with you.' Like a conspirator, he drew Rhona with him across to the sideboard. 'I put it in my drawer, so's – well, you know . . .' Half embarrassed by his own wish to contribute something to Norah Lowe's new home, he shrugged. 'It's not much, I'm afraid.'

Carefully he brought out from beneath a pile of neatly laundered handkerchiefs a Saxby Melton Mowbray pie and a quarter of ABC Empire tea.

'They're both nice and fresh, I only bought them last night.'

'You're very thoughtful, Dad. Auntie Norah will be pleased.'

Jack shut the drawer hastily as he heard his wife coming down the stairs. 'Better slip them into your basket, love,' he whispered, then went into the kitchen to shave.

Making sure that her husband was fully occupied sharpening his razor, Eve took Rhona aside. 'I've baked an egg custard for Auntie Norah,' she confided. 'It's down the cellar, so it'd keep all right. You don't have to mention it to Dad, I know money's tight but it'd be a poor do if we couldn't think of an old lady like that. She'll have been too busy to think of baking.'

Auntie Norah wouldn't go short of much this weekend with Rhona's half a dozen eggs, and biscuits, and these contributions from Jack and Eve.

The new cottage was only half a mile the far side of the town. As she walked there, Rhona thought, I'll have to try and cheer Auntie up. Maybe the things she was carrying would help. But nothing could alter the fact that Auntie had had to leave her old home. I just hope she doesn't start crying, or I'll be at it, as well. Poor old thing. Uprooted. Dumped in a strange house where only her few belongings would be the same.

From outside the cottage looked well enough – solidly built of good Yorkshire stone to withstand the keen winds that swept down off the moors. There was a square of garden in front, and it looked as if somebody had trimmed the privet hedge and tidied up the roses. Once they started growing in summer Auntie Norah might feel like sitting out.

There were some new slates on the roof. Wolf Richardson had ensured the place was weatherproof. And the door and window frames were freshly painted.

If only the old love could grow to like the place, Rhona thought as she opened the little iron gate. It's a decent enough home and would do nicely for the rest of her days.

Norah wasn't long answering the door when Rhona clattered the brass knocker.

'Eh, lass, come in . . . I'm that glad to see you!'

'Hallo, Auntie Norah. How are you – worn out with all the upheaval?'

'Bless you, I'm as right as a bobbin. It was all done for me, like Mr Richardson promised. He'd arranged for them to come and pack everything up for me, and to unpack it all when we got here. But take your coat off, love, and come and sit down.'

Rhona was shown where to hang her coat on a smart new hook, one of three on the back of the door. 'The old hooks were going rusty so they fitted me up with those. And they've put up new deal shelves in the kitchen. *Low* shelves – special for me, because I couldn't reach t'others.'

'I'm glad they're looking after you so well,' Rhona said, glancing round the cosy living room.

Auntie Norah's good stout table with its red chenille cover looked as right here as it had in her old home, and the walnut sideboard fitted nicely against the long wall at right angles to the fireplace. Above it had been hung her copy of Landseer's *Monarch of the Glen* as if that might guard her new home as it had the old. The dark horsehair sofa stood against the wall that faced the fire.

'They wanted to put in a fancy tiled fireplace instead of the old range, but I wouldn't let them. I like a nice range and a coal oven. They couldn't understand why I didn't want to be rid of all the black-leading. I told Mr Richardson, though, I've done black-leading all my life, and polished brasses, I'd be lost without summat to do.'

'I've brought you a few things, Auntie Norah,' Rhona told her, indicating the basket.

'You're a good lass, and no mistake,' Norah exclaimed, her dark eyes suddenly glistening.

'Oh, it's not just me. The eggs and biscuits were my idea but the other things are from Mum and Dad. He got the pie himself, and the tea.'

'Well, I don't know! And them on short time, and all. I've just been reading about it in the *Courier*.'

'Yes. Engineering's been doing better than textiles up to now. It was bound to come, I suppose. But we manage, and ought to – there's enough of us earning.'

'And only you working full time,' Norah observed solemnly.

Rhona smiled. 'I didn't come here to bring you our troubles, you know. How are your legs today, Auntie?'

'Mustn't grumble, love. They made me rest yesterday, you know. Had me sat like a queen in the middle of each room in turn, telling them where I wanted everything put.' She chuckled mischievously. 'Gave me quite a taste for giving orders. If I had my time again, I'd quite fancy being well to do!'

Her misshapen hands slow, she began unpacking the basket, setting each item in turn carefully on the chenille cloth. 'You've been right thoughtful, lass. If I'd brought you up myself, you couldn't have been much better, and that goes for all three of you. People are kind, you know. When I got here, I got such a surprise. You just come and see my kitchen – I'll show you . . .'

Auntie Norah took her stick from beside the fireplace and led the way to the kitchen. In the doorway she paused and tapped with her stick.

'There was a step here, you know. What do you think Mr Richardson had done? He only gave orders for a wood floor in here, to make it all level. And it's warmer, of course, as well.'

'Very good,' said Rhona, and wondered if there was no end to Mr Richardson's consideration. So long as he was getting his own way.

'Here – look at this . . .' Norah flung wide the door of a tiny pantry. 'I didn't bring one half of that with me. He'd had that man-servant of his buy it in for me. You could have knocked me down with a cobweb when I had a look! And that's another thing – the whole place is spotless, been cleaned right through. I shan't need to clean down this spring, and that's for certain.'

'I'm very pleased. I didn't think it'd be anything like this.'

Norah hobbled across to the stone sink and filled a kettle. 'You'll have a cup of tea now you're here, won't you? I'll put this on the gas, it'll boil directly.' She crossed to the small gas stove. 'They insisted that I have this, though I could have managed with the coal. I'm used to boiling up on a hob. But they insisted that it'd be more convenient to have the gas, specially on a hot day when I don't want to light a fire.'

Norah motioned Rhona to sit with her at the scrubbed deal table. 'We'll have a bit of a sit down while we wait for the kettle.' Suddenly, she laughed away to herself and glanced across, her dark eyes glinting. 'Bet you can't guess how I got here yesterday!'

'You'd better tell me. You seem full of surprises.'

'And this is the best of the lot. He sent that man of his over for me, didn't he, in that big posh car. I felt like Lady Muck, I can tell you! It were a pity we didn't have to go through the town, I'd have liked to have seen a few folks' faces.'

Rhona smiled back. 'Well, I'm glad it didn't prove to be the ordeal that we feared. So long as you manage to settle in soon . . .'

'Settle? Ay lass – I've settled already. I like my little home.' She chuckled again. 'I kicked up a bit of a fuss, didn't I, at first? About having to move. Happen it were that as did it.' She glanced wickedly over her shoulder at Rhona as she slowly stood up and went towards the stove. 'If only to make sure of a ride in a car like that!'

Rhona smiled to herself, trying to picture the Daimler travelling along the narrow lane to the cottage, with Auntie

Norah sitting in state. Her legs would hardly be long enough for her toes to touch the carpeted floor, and her head would barely be visible through its windows. And then while she was imagining Wolf's car Rhona seemed to hear it. She even fancied she heard a car door slam. Someone rattled the door knocker.

'Will you see who that is, Rhona love, you'll be quicker than me.'

As she crossed the living room Rhona glanced through the window and saw the car parked in the lane. It was the Richardson limousine! She expected to find Stimson when she opened the door; she found Wolf Richardson, and had to swallow to contain her rising agitation.

'Good morning, Rhona. Miss Lowe isn't indisposed, is she?' He seemed to be composing his expression, she might have caught him smiling to himself.

'No, she's all right. It was just that I'm quicker at answering doors.'

'Eeh – well, I never!' From the kitchen doorway Norah Lowe was gazing through to Wolf, her expression a mixture of astonishment and delight. 'Come in, come in. I didn't expect to see you again for a while. But I'm right glad you are here!'

As he passed her Rhona noticed Wolf's well-cut sports jacket and expensive-looking flannels. He was wearing a flashy pullover, like one she'd seen in a magazine somewhere, in alternating squares of yellow and brown. As if that weren't innovative enough, his shoes were brown and white, the latest fashion. Showy, she thought.

He certainly was dressing to impress somebody. Had he patched things up with his wife? Or had she missed something and he was courting somebody local?

'I thought I might find you here,' Wolf said, turning to her with a smile. 'Like me, you'll be checking that Miss Lowe has no complaints.'

'I can't think of one,' Norah assured him. 'And I'm glad I've got this opportunity to thank you for all you've done. I'm ever so grateful, Mr Richardson.'

'And I'm grateful, too, Miss Lowe – for the way you've

cooperated. You know as well as I do that this situation could have been very difficult. Your understanding has ensured that the whole matter has been concluded most smoothly.'

'Aye, well – it's been smoother than ever I dared hope, and all. And I was just saying to Rhona, here, that I'm going to be right comfortable.'

'Good. I'm very pleased.'

'You'll have a cup of tea with us, won't you?'

'That's very kind. Tea would be most welcome.'

'Get another cup, will you, Rhona love. And bring that pot in here now, we can't go sitting in the kitchen . . .'

Wolf smiled. 'Now no formality please, Miss Lowe.'

Norah laughed. 'You're a right one, aren't you? No formality indeed, and here you are calling me Miss Lowe at every verse end! I'm Norah to everybody . . .'

For once, Wolf appeared somewhat disconcerted. He could hardly say that she was old – too old to treat so disrespectfully, but . . .

She looked at him and grinned. 'You feel it's disrespectful, that it? Then call me Auntie Norah, like Rhona does. I've no kin of my own any longer, I don't mind adopting a sort of nephew.'

'Thank you, Auntie Norah,' Wolf agreed readily. He had warmed to the old lady since getting to know her, and he couldn't remember anyone, ever, wishing to claim any relationship with him, unless that might further their own ends. Norah Lowe was a dear, and he welcomed anything that might help Rhona to drop this wariness.

She was coming through from the kitchen now, carefully avoiding his gaze. At least that didn't prevent him absorbing every detail. Her dress, a soft green wool, moulded her breasts and waist. There was an attractive flush to her cheeks which hadn't been there in that split second between her opening the cottage door and seeing him.

Her hair was longer than when he'd seen her last, and the red-brown curls framing her face gleamed from a thorough brushing. Long, auburn lashes swept her cheek as she gazed down.

'Will you pour, Rhona, your hand's steadier than mine.'

'If you like, Auntie.' *Steadier*? She could have been cross with the old lady. Except that she didn't know what effect Wolf Richardson had upon her; no one knew. Thank heaven!

'Milk and sugar?' she inquired, darting Wolf a hasty glance.

'Please,' he said easily. She was reacting well, he thought, betraying in half-concealed awkwardness her awareness of him. It hadn't mattered that they hadn't met for far too long, maybe it never would matter. If only he could be patient, and wait. But he wasn't a patient man, never found waiting easy. And he was acutely conscious that, even when he ultimately was free, this massive need of her might remain repressed. Through her choice. 'Thank you,' he said warmly as she passed across his cup.

'You're welcome.'

. . . To tea, he thought wryly. Accompanied. Wouldn't she trust him even to drive her home? For those few minutes, to be alone together. I'm ten years your senior, my dear, have learned some discipline.

I'll have to get a car of my own, Rhona was thinking as they finished their tea. Ever since she'd come into all that money she'd been promising herself a little Morris or an Austin Seven. Round about a hundred pounds was all it would cost. Not a lot, if you said it fast! Although it still seemed quite a bit to her. Not that it was, really – with the amount she'd inherited. And it would avoid situations like this. Every meeting with Wolf ended with him offering to run her home.

'You're going to decline, aren't you?' he observed, smiling wryly across Auntie Norah's table. 'I only offered you a lift, I don't propose making off with you. And I don't traffic in white slaves!'

Her cheeks were flaring again, but only because she'd not been aware of how long she'd been considering, instead of giving him an answer. Now he was making a joke of it all and she'd look dafter than ever if she refused.

'Thank you, you're very kind.' She smiled, as much at herself as at anything. But hadn't meeting him decided her to curb her impulsiveness?

'I should think so as well, young lady,' Auntie Norah remarked. 'You'll not find a nicer, more straightforward young man, not anywhere in the Northern Union!'

'Ah, but Rhona takes great care over preserving her prejudices!' Wolf said, his grey eyes glittering with suppressed amusement. 'And she isn't readily impressed by me or my possessions.'

'Did you say you didn't want to be too long before you left?' Rhona asked him tersely. She'd intended spending the whole morning with Auntie Norah, but she'd certainly had more than she could take. Even though the atmosphere in the cottage was congenial enough, so congenial that if she'd been less physically aware of him she might have supposed Wolf to be a friend of many years' standing.

'I've troubled Auntie Norah with enough of my problems for the one day,' he said, rising.

And that surely was true, Rhona thought. Their conversation today had shown that Auntie was well acquainted with the fact that divorce proceedings had begun.

'I've been surprised,' Wolf had told them. 'Beatrice is a beautiful woman, and during our seven years of marriage I'd naturally grown accustomed to living with her. I miss her of course, but, strangely, I can't honestly say now that I regret her departure too deeply. There was a certain – *pretence* about our marriage. In London, both a part of the fashionable set, there seemed to be fewer inadequacies between us. Here in Yorkshire, I'm beginning to understand there might be other young women who'd provide a more meaningful relationship.'

'No doubt as soon as you're free you'll enjoy playing the field here while you complete the search,' Rhona had remarked, not liking the picture of Wolf as the classic predatory male.

'Happen you'll get the girl you deserve another time,' Auntie Norah had said.

Rhona had given her a look. But happen he would, and all. Some brittle girl who'd appreciate his flashy car and his flashy clothes, and the way he used his brass to make even more. Regardless of who he put out of a home.

'This is a lovely little home you've given me. I'll be happy here the rest of my days.'

So much for that! Rhona thought. Maybe she wasn't meant to dislike Wolf, after all. She didn't know how she felt about that notion – except rather shaken. She was glad the old lady liked this cottage, very, very glad, but she felt a fool having made a fuss on Auntie Norah's behalf, only to find that she need have done nothing.

Her back was to Wolf as he helped her on with her coat, she couldn't see his expression. And he couldn't see hers! she thought thankfully. She wasn't in any state to exercise tight control over her features. Instead of moving away, Wolf had rested a hand on each shoulder; their pressure was so intense that several moments later – after they'd said goodbye to Auntie Norah – Rhona suspected his palm prints were scorching through her coat.

She felt uncomfortable in the car – regretful about some of the things she'd said to him that first day at Farnley Carr. And physically uncomfortable because of sitting so close while attraction danced like some newfangled firework between them. No one, ever, had made concentration so difficult for her.

'You've been very good to Auntie Norah,' she said quietly. 'Happen I shouldn't have gone on at you so much about kicking her out of the old cottage.'

His smile pleased her, and there was no trace of 'I told you so' in his voice either. 'So long as she's happy. And I've never been sorry that you tackled me that day.'

'You like to see young women making fools of themselves, do you?'

'Nothing of the kind. Rhona . . .' He parked the car at the side of the moorland road and turned towards her, his grey eyes serious. 'I wouldn't have met you otherwise, would I? And you've a gift for being more concerned for someone else than for yourself.'

Rhona didn't reply. Why was she thinking about Bill Brightstone again, and helping at the mill? Nobody'd expect her to give up her ambitions.

Wolf continued, his tone still warm: 'I was glad, though, that you didn't persist in opposing the scheme. Why didn't you?'

'There wasn't much point, was there? Not with everyone telling me that you'd obtained all the permission you required for going ahead.' But she'd never acknowledged, even to herself, the real reason why she'd dropped the matter. Her caring too much for him, and that *his* ambitions succeed.

'Was that all there was to it?' Wolf asked, looking at her keenly. She was startled. Could he know there'd been more to her decision?

His beautiful translucent eyes seemed to search through to her soul. Gazing back, Rhona could conceal nothing. 'You'd gone into it far more deeply than I had. It's rather daunting to be confronted by someone who's so certain about what they're doing. I suppose I stopped wanting to oppose you. Helping Auntie Norah to cope with the situation made more sense. Only you beat me to it there, didn't you?'

Wolf's kiss interrupted her. Totally unexpected, it caught Rhona off guard, otherwise she'd never have let him near enough. His lips were pressing firmly on to hers, she felt her own mouth yielding. She could smell the soap he'd used that morning, a ferny aroma, acutely masculine. All the attraction she'd been fighting came soaring through her from some source that she'd barely suspected might exist.

His breath mingled with her own and both seemed to speed like her accelerating heart. Longing overtook any thought of caution, driving her with insistence that pulsed through her being until she couldn't prevent her tongue testing the mouth that generated this alarming hunger.

With this first hint of her response, Wolf's lips parted.

Rhona tasted the tea he'd drunk, heard his gasp, and felt the sharpness of his teeth. And then his tongue was probing, escalating her excitement, promising delight that he would create within her.

Her own urgency was scaring, she'd never believed desire could be like this, nor any man so unresistible. Everything she'd ever learned should have been warning her to cease, but her need of Wolf seared right through all that she had believed, everything she had been. Every nerve was thrilling to his wordless pledge of fulfilment. And she was ripped apart by emotions – frightened by the prospect of his touch, which surely would follow, yearning to experience the joy of his caress.

At last Wolf himself ended the kiss. Rhona had to will herself not to draw him back to her again.

'Whatever made you start that!' she exclaimed, trying to sound as stern as she ought to be feeling.

He laughed sharply and started the car engine. 'I could leave you in no doubt if I thought you needed, or wanted, the answer.'

'I daresay,' she said grimly. 'Just don't consider your experience an advantage.'

'Believe me I'm acutely aware it's anything but that.'

Neither of them spoke again until he'd turned the car into Gracechurch Street. Rhona still felt she was shaking, and *shaken* – still needing him.

'Just understand this,' said Wolf quietly as he slowed the car outside number 46, 'that wasn't merely desire. You're a lovely girl, Rhona.'

He drove off the minute she'd got out of the car, leaving her feeling as if her legs dangled from her elastic suspenders.

And that's enough of that, Rhona decided that night when she again had difficulty falling asleep: for a change, because of worrying about something different from Bridge House Mill. Wolf Richardson was an exciting man, all right; he made her gloriously alive! But there wasn't going to be any funny business between them. She hadn't been brought up to carry on with a married man. And even if he was going in for a divorce, whatever would her family think; supposing she got herself roped in as the *other woman*! She shouldn't be looking for excitement, but somebody who'd be reliable, her sort of chap – ordinary.

And anyway, she'd enough on for the present, time was far too scarce. Although work had never frightened Rhona Hebden, she'd got out of the habit of studying. She'd have to do some serious reading in preparation for college, she'd been trying to concentrate ever since she'd found she could afford the further training.

At least avoiding Wolf wouldn't be difficult once she was away from Halfield, she thought, and then: 'I always seem to be avoiding something.' *Like the mill, and Bill Brightstone?* She hadn't been near since that alarming day when he'd suggested her working there part time.

I'll never make anything of my life if I don't go to college, she thought. There was an ache in her chest, just thinking how much she longed to better herself, to teach more subjects – happen, some day, to head her own school. She just wished leading her own life didn't mean disappointing other folk.

5

It wasn't until weeks afterwards that Rhona admitted she had made her decision. The only person who wasn't delighted was herself. It could have been worse, though. As soon as she started her regular visits to the mill she discovered it wasn't as uninteresting as she had feared.

Secretly she even looked forward to going there. Maybe some understanding of spinning had been born in her. And her enthusiasm for knitting had given her a knowledge of yarns, even if they were of a different weight from those produced at Bridge House.

Stanley and Daniel teased her, at first, trying to make out that now she'd inherited a bit of money all she could think of was earning more. Her cheeks flaring, she soon put them right on that score.

'You're talking out of the backs of your necks, the pair of you! I wanted to become better qualified for teaching, but I couldn't see Bill Brightstone stuck for a bit of help. He's kept that place going since my father died – most of them on the board of directors are too old to take much notice so long as the place is making a profit. I'm not just going to take my share, then take him for granted!'

Eve didn't say very much at all about her daughter's involvement at the mill, until Jack expressed his opinion.

It was the first Saturday that Rhona had been working. 'You look tired, Rhona love,' he remarked as she came to sit by the fire.

'Just a bit. Happen you'll say the trouble is I'm not used to real work!'

'Nay, lass, that's the last thing I'd say. I've said before that your dad would be proud of you. I only hope today that wherever he is he can see what you're doing. Many a young chap would have baulked at taking on more than one job, like what you're doing. You're a grand lass,

Rhona. You know how highly I think of your mother, but even she wouldn't tackle some of the things you turn your hand to.'

It was a long speech for Jack Hebden. Rhona felt too choked to say anything straight away. Eventually, she gave a tiny shrug. 'Ay, it's nothing that special,' she began.

Her mother interrupted from the kitchen doorway. 'And I suppose that's what you'll say about all this knitting advice you give as well, is it, love?'

'I'd be right, and all – anybody with a bit of common sense could have done everything that I've done, and more.'

'Then it's funny they didn't try, isn't it?' Eve observed, exchanging a smile with her husband. 'Funny it's *you* that half of Halfield turns to for patterns that'll fit, and to sort them out when they can't fathom what the experts mean by increasing here, and decreasing there . . .'

Rhona was compelled to smile. Jack Hebden was prodding fiercely at the fire until shifting coals produced showers of sparks and a brilliant flare of flame. And then he turned to face Rhona, his cheeks flushed from the heat and his blue eyes all a-glitter.

'I'll tell you something, our Rhona,' he said, stabbing the air with the poker to emphasize his words. 'I've always treated you like my own daughter, and there's times like today when, by golly, I wish that you were! If them two lads turn out with anything like your mettle, I'll be well satisfied.'

'Dad's right, you know,' Eve added gently, her eyes misting. 'You don't seem able to say no when somebody presents you with a job that needs tackling. You have a lot of Exton in you, you know. You'll go a long way if you've a mind to.'

It had been nice to have the two of them speak so frankly. A kind of glow had settled around her heart, a glow that lasted for many a day. But then, gradually, Rhona came to realize that even what she was doing now would not be enough.

Helping old Bill and keeping on her job at school wasn't

nearly what she'd intended. Many a time she thought regretfully of how she might have been attending college now, but she did still teach. And brooding led nowhere.

Her days in the schoolroom grew more precious, too – there was about her classes a strange air of impermanence. She guided pupils in casting on their knitting, on cutting out simple garments, and caught herself suspecting she might not be there to see their completion.

I'm not suffering some mortal illness, she reminded herself constantly, there's nothing to prevent my continuing to teach. Perhaps she was growing morbid, preoccupied with this feeling that further changes would be forced upon her. Perhaps the responsibilities had been accepted more unwillingly than she had understood and she was experiencing a deep, subconscious resentment that generated its own insecurity.

I'll try to relax more, she promised herself, but smiled at her own refusal to accept reality. Relaxation was being crowded out.

The day that Rhona stopped teaching was the day that the Prince of Wales attended the ceremony marking completion of the initial stage of Dale Reservoir.

The fact that an important episode in her own life was closing on the very day that Wolf Richardson reached a milestone in his caused her a wry smile. She tidied her desk for the last time, then she briskly picked up her handbag, gloves and the daring sunglasses that had modern white frames. She was too busy to devote more than a moment's attention to the local event that was receiving so much publicity. Just as she had been too busy during the past year or so to toss more than a passing thought in Wolf's direction.

Her own life was full, so full sometimes that she wondered if it ever would slow down so she could start enjoying herself. Not that she was unhappy; but from time to time she had noticed that most of her contemporaries appeared to have far more capacity for light-hearted amusement.

When she had adapted that first knitting pattern for young Amy Lightowler, Rhona hadn't considered that she might be beginning something that would escalate. With Amy proving so quickly to be a talented knitter who produced a cardigan that would have done an adult credit, news of Rhona's skill rapidly spread.

Her own headmistress, recognizing at last that Rhona's methods of encouraging the class to knit and sew were producing extraordinary results, soon ensured that the rest of the town got to know of her – publicity which Rhona would have preferred to avoid.

And then the wife of their local vicar had begged Rhona to hold classes one evening each week in the Sunday School. Grown women as well as schoolgirls came along – everyone in Halfield who experienced difficulty with any aspect of knitting automatically sought her advice.

This, her other interests, teaching, and her few hours each week at the mill seemed quite sufficient to fill her time. But then she was thrust into a responsibility that threatened to change her whole life.

I only hope it's going to be in the right direction, Rhona thought now, recalling her mother's words about going a long way. Denying herself a last look around the class-room, she headed down the corridor. The rest of the staff were in a meeting, she'd said her goodbyes.

Crossing the school yard she saw Amy Lightowler waiting just beyond the rusty iron gates. She'd long since moved up to the big school, but most afternoons in summer she waited for Rhona coming out, and chatted as they headed home. She was sad, though, now. Her heavy body somehow expressed in its increased lumpishness her sincere regrets.

'Hallo, love.' Rhona smiled. 'Nice of you to wait. Put your shoulders back, though. Remember what I told you.'

With a grin, Amy complied. And she did look better. She had grown taller in the past two or three years, and because of her interest in the clothes she made was careful to restrict her intake of stodgy foods. She might never be a neatly proportioned girl, but she now had the makings of a handsome one.

'Aren't you even a little bit sorry you're not going to come back?' Amy asked.

'I'll miss the school, of course. If I've time to think about it while I'm at the mill. But I'm not going to say I'll miss you, am I, because I'll still be seeing you a lot.'

Amy was an enthusiastic member of Rhona's knitting course, and had advanced so greatly that she now helped some of the newcomers with their work.

'It won't be the same, though, will it?'

'And nor will we, *will we*?' Rhona countered sagely, and then took pity on the girl. She was only thirteen and couldn't be expected to be philosophical about changes. 'I try to look at it this way, Amy – every new interest we take up, whether it's our work, or just a pastime, is simply another stage in life . . .'

'That's all right. But *you* decided to alter everything, didn't you?'

'Ah.' Did she decide, though? Perhaps – but only because refusing was impossible.

'What does that mean?' Amy gave her a look as they began walking down Brunswick Road.

Rhona smiled and took the girl's arm. 'You've noticed that we don't like changes that we haven't decided on ourselves. It's strange, though, how often we accept them better than ever we expected.'

Vividly, she was picturing Auntie Norah in her new home on the day that Wolf Richardson called to see her. She'd never forget the old lady's very evident satisfaction with the new cottage, and her satisfaction with *him*.

Thinking about Wolf, it was a shock to see his car approaching. She felt peculiar, as if she herself had conjured him out of space by the simple expedient of visualizing him. And this, or something similar, had happened that last time she'd seen him, hadn't it?

'It is a long time since we met!' he exclaimed, winding down the car window after directing Stimson to stop.

Wolf was immaculate in a morning suit, and smiling so

76

brilliantly that Rhona marvelled at how handsome he could look when he cheered up. But then, he would be smiling, she supposed, when his project had only today received the accolade of a royal ceremony.

'No doubt you're well pleased with everything,' she said, smiling back at him. 'Congratulations on all you've achieved this far.'

Wolf was delighted by her generosity. The warming of his grey eyes revealed how much pleasure it gave him. 'Why not let me tell you all about it? I can give you a lift, your young friend as well . . .'

'Why not?' Rhona agreed, surprised by how much she wanted to hear him describe the occasion.

Amy, however, was less enthusiastic and hung back, reluctant to share Rhona with anyone, much less with a man who dressed so formally, and rode in an enormous car behind a uniformed chauffeur.

'I'll see you at the class next week,' the girl said hurriedly. 'I've got to call and get a loaf of bread for my mum.'

Rhona hesitated, staring anxiously after her young friend.

'Daren't you get into the car, Rhona?' Wolf asked, his familiar wry smile reminding her that nobody else treated her with such a strange mixture of seriousness and teasing.

The car door held wide, he was on the pavement beside her now, standing so close that she felt overwhelmed by his presence.

'You've lost your chaperon, I know,' he continued, still amused. 'But you're sufficiently mature to take care of yourself. And a businesswoman as well, now!'

Rhona gave him a look, then shrugged and got into the Daimler.

'Right, Stimson,' was all Wolf said when they were seated.

Rhona was wondering who had told him about her position at Bridge House Mill, and how much he knew, when they drove past Amy. She saw the corner of Wolf's mouth twitching and he seemed about to say something.

He half turned towards Rhona and she read in his eyes the comment he hadn't made about the girl's size.

They smiled at each other in silent acknowledgement of his suppressed opinion. Rhona felt intensely thankful that nothing further was required of her. Now Wolf was sitting so close, consideration of anything or anyone else seemed unlikely. Out in the street she'd been fully aware of him; here in the car she was quivering – if not outwardly, mysteriously, deep inside her.

'So – did everything go smoothly today?' she asked, making an effort to appear at ease. Whatever else, she mustn't let him guess that he still affected her, and mustn't permit her own emotions any hint of expression.

'Better even than I hoped, thank you. The Prince spoke very highly of the whole scheme, and was kindness itself during the luncheon. I reckon that after today there'll be more people prepared to accept the necessity for the reservoir.'

'Is that aimed at me?' she asked, glancing sideways at him.

Wolf laughed. 'I don't expect you'll come round. But I think we're both too busy to lose much sleep over matters on which we agree to differ.'

Rhona remembered his earlier reference to her new work. 'You seem to have heard that I'm changing my job. Or, rather, starting full time at the mill.'

'Yes, Bill Brightstone was only too happy to fill in the details.'

'Oh?' She was so astonished that it took her mind away from the turbulence sitting near Wolf was generating. Both Bill and Timothy were as opposed as she herself had been to the reservoir.

Wolf laughed again. 'You haven't learned, have you? I don't automatically cut people because they don't applaud all I'm doing. Bill Brightstone is a fellow governor of Littlewood School.'

Rhona smiled inwardly, aware that Wolf was waiting for her to comment on *his* being a member of the governing body. Littlewood was a fine private school, whose astronomical fees ensured it remained exclusive.

'So,' he continued, 'if you find life at Bridge House Mill falling short of what you expect, I'll put in a good word and secure you a post at Littlewood.'

'Thank you, but that won't be necessary,' said Rhona, unable to joke about the decision she had made. 'I'm not looking for fun at the mill, I'm going there to do a job.'

'And if you hate every minute you'll stick it out. Because of your father, and who he was . . .'

And who told you that? she thought. Bill? But she didn't say anything. She didn't want to quarrel with Wolf, nor now to argue. She was just discovering how much she had missed him. And that was daft – how can you miss somebody you hardly know? Especially when you've contrived to keep out of their way, have been so disturbed that you've avoided anyone in their particular circle.

'I wanted to know more about you, Rhona. Is that so very wrong?'

Careful, she thought, don't look at him, or he'll know he's surprised you again – *pleasantly* surprised.

'You must be thankful construction's going so well,' she said evenly.

'Indeed. But we still must surge ahead. I don't like the European situation, I want the reservoir finished before any confrontation.'

'Confrontation?'

'There are too many indications of trouble. I've been disturbed about Germany ever since the burning of the Reichstag.'

'That's a day or two since.'

'Just about the time I began the reservoir. But there's nothing to say something simmering so long won't boil over. There's a great deal hanging on who retains control over there.'

'But, today, you won't let that get you down. I thought you'd have been tied up till nightfall.'

'I'm on my way to Farnley Carr to change. There's a big affair tonight in the town hall.'

'In your honour? You must feel very proud of yourself. Will His Royal Highness be there?'

Wolf shook his head. 'He had to leave immediately after luncheon.' He paused, and Rhona grew aware that *he* now was tense. 'You could radically improve the evening, you know, by accompanying me.'

'*Me*? That's a laugh! Wasn't I out of place enough at the Mayor's Ball?'

'Not as much so as I myself.'

'This is your night, anyway, it'll all be different.'

'It could be . . .'

'Are you crazy? You're marr . . .' Wolf stopped her lips with his fingers. Their touch felt like a kiss, and reminded her too much of his kisses.

'I'm not, Rhona. The divorce is going through. Having it made absolute will take time, agreed. But to all intents I am free now to . . .'

She jerked back her head and his fingers fell away. 'That doesn't make any difference, not to me. I don't hold with divorce.'

'But you're not Catholic.'

It wasn't a question. He *had* been finding out about her.

'No, I'm not. You can just say I'm – old-fashioned. I suppose, these days, it seems acceptable to marry, then to free yourself because everything doesn't suit. I imagine it all depends on what sort of folk you mix with.'

'If you knew me better you'd be aware that I rarely mix with anyone.'

'You know what I mean. You give the impression of having quite a comprehensive circle.'

'Because I got the Prince of Wales to attend today?'

'If you like. I . . .' Rhona hadn't really considered who was responsible for inviting His Royal Highness. She hadn't cared. She wasn't certain now how they came to be developing an argument.

'He's all right,' she conceded. 'But he does seem to have friends with very modern ideas.'

'Perhaps that's the only way he can alleviate the pressures.'

'Happen so.'

'I'm only suggesting that you accompany me to a reception, Rhona. I'm not thinking of compromising you!' He was using the same kind of arguments he'd used before. And that had ended with him kissing her. But the mockery in his steely eyes made her laugh. Or was that sheer relief because there was no need to continue making excuses for refusing?

'I've nothing suitable to wear,' she began, half-heartedly.

Wolf whispered an order to Stimson and they stopped, about to turn into Gracechurch Street. Stimson reversed and drove towards the High Street where he stopped again, outside the Jonquil Gown Shop.

'If there's somewhere you prefer for selecting something special, you've only to say. Stimson and I are at your disposal. But I must point out that the shops will be closing before very long.'

'What makes you so sure I've really made my mind up about going with you? And how do you know I can afford Jonquil's prices?'

'If I didn't know I'd get my head in my hands, I'd offer my cheque book. As it is, I'm reassured by the knowledge that you're Paul Exton's daughter.'

'Heavens, you have been checking!' Despite herself, Rhona grinned.

Wolf opened the car door for her. 'Go on – treat yourself. Think of it as an investment, if that'll ease your careful Yorkshire soul.'

Already too excited to be intimidated, Rhona smiled when an elegant woman wearing dove grey, which almost matched her hair, approached inquiring what she wished.

'I'd like to see some evening dresses, please.'

'Certainly, madam, any particular colour?'

'I have to be rather careful, with hair the shade of mine . . .'

'I'll show you what we have.'

The first was beautifully cut, but in yellow, and Rhona hadn't forgotten how ordinary she'd felt in that other yellow dress.

'No, I don't think that's the shade, thank you.'

She saw it then, displayed on one of the models, and bringing even the dummy to glowing, vibrant life. Of gleaming silk, like burnished copper, simply but exquisitely styled, the gown dared her to try it on.

The saleslady was watching Rhona's eyes. 'It is just your colour, madam. If you'd like to try it . . .'

Rhona was ushered across the thick carpet to one of the cubicles while a girl was called to remove the dress from display.

The touch of the material was luxurious, cool and smooth. When Rhona glanced in the mirror she swallowed back a gasp of sheer astonishment. No garment anywhere could have fitted more perfectly. The rich silk emphasized every curve from shoulder to thigh, then gradually flared out, swishing into a cascade about her ankles. But the coppery shade was what Rhona could not resist. She'd never worn anything that so effectively brought out the lustrous glints of her hair. For once in her life, she looked as she would have chosen – poised, radiant, even beautiful. She'd never be more thankful she could afford the price.

In the car, Wolf teased, but Rhona refused him even a glimpse, aware already that he would be as stunned as she herself by her appearance.

Eve met her at the door, the eyes so like her daughter's anxious. 'Are you all right, love? Didn't expect to see you brought home by car.' She saw Rhona's smile. She hadn't expected either that she'd be so cheerful after leaving the school where she'd loved teaching.

'I'm fine, Mum, don't worry. It's just that I'm in a bit of a rush. I've been invited out. There's a do on at the town hall.'

'For Wolf Richardson? That was his car, wasn't it? You've changed your tune, haven't you, lady?'

Fleetingly Rhona grinned. 'I like to think I'm flexible!

82

I do know what I'm doing, Mum. And so does he. No involvement, no nothing. We're just having a night out. He's expected to be there, and he wants to take me with him. Curiously, that's what I want as well.'

'You've got it all worked out, haven't you?'

'Happen I have. And you *can* stop worrying, you know. I've told Wolf. It is just a night out. *One*. And I don't hold with divorce.

Eve Hebden was compelled to laugh. 'Well, you're nothing if not outspoken! I wonder who you get that from? I suppose I'd better heat up the copper for your bath.

The town hall looked grand, very grand. Tonight, with this year's Mayor, Alderman Sutcliffe, in his robes and gold chain, and all the councillors and everybody done up in their evening clothes, it couldn't have been more impressive. And I'm just the one to be impressed, she thought wryly, entering on Wolf Richardson's arm. If she had any control over it, though, she'd not let being impressed show too obviously.

Wolf made things easy. He certainly knew all the town council very well. He introduced Rhona with undisguised satisfaction, she might have been somebody important. And something in his steady gaze challenged each of them in turn to question the nature of his relationship with her. And if some of the glances Rhona received were speculative, she quickly discovered that she didn't mind. She loved a bit of fun, and revelled in the secret amusement generated by others' curiosity. Tonight, she meant to enjoy every minute.

The meal was sumptuous, an absolute banquet! At the back of her mind a small wordless protest deplored the presentation of so much food when everybody attending was already well fed. But, again, she was determined no criticism, even unvoiced, would spoil the occasion.

Wolf sensed and appreciated her determination to give herself whole-heartedly to being there. Suddenly, he felt choked by her ingenuousness. He'd known no other young lady still so innocent at twenty-three. And, God, was she lovely! He scarcely found time to eat, he was so entranced with her.

Jonquil's had done her proud, and no mistake. He doubted that she'd ever shopped anywhere like that before, but this dress – this *gown* was a real stunner! Rhona was a clever girl; she'd chosen gleaming silk in a coppery shade that toned magnificently with her hair, and brought out the subtle shading of her eyes. The silk clung to every curve of her slender body, stirring within him an ache that he was struggling to suppress. Around her legs the material was expertly cut to swirl out wide, revealing glimpses of her neat ankles.

Wolf swallowed, trying to concentrate on the meal. He felt his eyes clouding with a passion that he'd feared never to feel again. Inwardly, he smiled at his own susceptibility. Much as he wished this evening to last, he couldn't resist wishing away the protracted eating and the speeches that would follow. Afterwards, there would be dancing. He'd waited over two wearisome years to hold this partner to him again.

Rhona was laughing softly now, bubbling with excitement, her evident joy simply because of being there making him feel abnormally humble. *He'd* made her happy, if only for these regrettably short hours, and she was displaying no pretence of being blasé about any of it.

'I can't believe this is me,' she confided, 'not little Rhona Hebden from Gracechurch Street.'

Her breath caressed his cheek, making him long to draw her close against his side. He caught the aroma of tangy grapefruit which had preceded the fish now being served. He experienced an unbearable urge to savour her moist lips, to taste from her the sharpness of the fruit. Thank heaven he'd found courage to invite her. How he avoided kissing her, here at the table, he did not know.

When it came time for speeches Wolf's obsession with her loveliness increased. In order to see along their top table Rhona angled her chair slightly. Her bare arm was resting against his sleeve. As she'd moved, her leg had touched the braid of his evening trousers and there she let it remain. The folds of silk felt cool no longer through the black cloth separating them from his leg, but burned instead, an exquisite assertion of her nearness. He dreaded his turn to speak, and the requisite withdrawal from her.

His speech, though, brought its reward in acute consciousness of Rhona's close attention. If she still resented the reservoir scheme she was generous still in concealing her disapproval. He would defy any man alive to remain impervious to those brown eyes that never wavered from his face, and made him oblivious to three hundred other guests.

'You know how it's done, don't you?' she whispered as he sat down afterwards. 'Somebody taught you how to express yourself.'

Express, Wolf thought, there's a laugh! When the one feeling he ached to express had to be contained while it thundered through his veins.

It seemed only minutes later that they were in the car. Rhona hardly stopped talking, all the way over the dark setts of the roads out to Gracechurch Street. She was like a little girl who had been to her first party. Wolf continued to marvel that he'd given her so much pleasure. The only trouble was that she wasn't a little girl, and he was far from being a child either. He was in every way a man – a man too long alone, and, Lord, how he needed this woman!

The wine, together with excitement, had dulled all Rhona's misgivings about previous meetings. When Wolf stopped the car, she kissed him. If she hadn't, he might have remained resolute about not touching her. He drew her to him swiftly, finding her mouth, as he had longed during the hours of dancing to find it.

There was no containing his kisses now, no means of checking the surge of emotion that made him go on and on, pressing and probing at her lips until, with a tiny moan, Rhona welcomed his searching tongue. She tasted of good wine and promised to appease all healthy appetites.

But Wolf reminded himself of *his* promise of discipline. This time, he'd risk nothing that might alarm Rhona. He'd been well aware on that previous occasion that he'd perturbed her. Tonight, he'd govern the seemingly ungovernable.

God, how desirable she was, though! He longed to press her to him, and prove the strength of his need of her. Again, he slid his tongue between her lips, and felt that need increasing. She seemed to quiver in his arms, coming alive. He ached to trace the line of her breast, to caress every curve through the silk of that sensuous gown. And yet he knew what would follow, and that it would be the end. He'd waited too long to sacrifice everything for a few minutes' fevered fumbling in a car. One day, God willing, he'd love this woman, but only when the time, place, and their coming together were right.

'You weren't supposed to do that,' Rhona said dryly when, breathlessly, he withdrew his mouth from hers. But she didn't reprove him for his passion, and didn't move away.

Her head was comfortable against his shoulder, as she now felt comfortable with him. Her pulse was slowing fractionally and, recognizing how hard curtailing their kisses had been for him, she tried to ease the tension.

'It was a lovely evening, Wolf, one to remember. Always,' she murmured, heard the huskiness in her own voice and swallowed. What was she doing, risking falling for a man who was divorced? Or not even divorced, really. She'd told herself there was nothing in it, and had believed that. She had to go on believing it.

He took her hand in his, smiled at her, and her heart felt as if it would leap right out of her chest, or burst. But his fingers were warm over hers, she couldn't withdraw from their grasp. Briefly, she closed her eyes, longing to hold on to the moment, to that night. Because tomorrow and the succession of tomorrows wouldn't be the same, they never could be. Wolf and she were worlds apart, in their thinking, in their life-style.

And she wasn't getting involved with a man who'd been

married. A man who'd lived for seven years with that striking beauty whom she'd seen only the once and hadn't forgotten. Just as she never would forget her. No, being the second woman in any man's life wasn't for her. Folk might think she had plenty of self-confidence, but she wasn't a bad little actress on the quiet, she didn't believe in giving away how she was feeling. She was ordinary, though – too ordinary to contemplate soaring through the upheaval that would come from heeding this intense attraction.

'I'm glad Phyllis and her husband were there,' she said, quite briskly. 'I'd let our falling-out run on too long. I like Adrian Newbold, and he seems very good for Phyllis. She often used to sound so discontented.'

'I suppose it was just that she hadn't found what she needed to make life complete. We're all better for having one person who always has our interests at heart.'

Wolf was looking at her, and Rhona couldn't face the intensity of his lustrous grey eyes, a quick glance was all that she could take. Even that sent her heart hammering again. Whatever he might or might not say, Wolf was telling her tonight how much she mattered to him, that he needed to matter to her. If only, for this once in her life, she could stop thinking ahead, stop being so *sensible* . . .

'Maybe,' she heard her own voice saying carefully. 'I can't worry about that just now. I'm too busy with all I'm taking on at the mill.'

'There's always time for something we set our hearts on.'

Don't, something inside her pleaded silently, don't, Wolf! I'm not strong enough to resist. 'Happen so. Anyway, I'm all right as I am.'

Wolf swallowed down a sigh, and contained the impulse to kiss her again and again, and hold her close until she couldn't ignore the yearning that could supersede all other needs and override her composure. If she was all right, which he doubted, he most certainly was not. When first married to Beatrice he'd thought they had a healthy relationship, but Beatrice had been a cool lover. He sensed that Rhona would match his own passion, and give unrestrainedly.

And desire isn't everything, he reminded himself again, it's not worth losing Rhona for. If you *can* lose what you've never had, he thought ruefully, then wondered. So frequently tonight, and other times in the past, he'd felt this overwhelming affinity, that they belonged . . . *Might* belong, one day. If he did nothing. But doing nothing was the last thing he was any good at . . .

'It's late,' he said abruptly, and touched her cheek with his lips, but he permitted himself to squeeze her hand before he let it go. He leaned across to open the car door. 'Sleep well, Rhona. Thank you again for being with me.'

Starting full time at Bridge House Mill was coming down to earth, and no mistake! By the following Monday, though, Rhona had done a lot of thinking. And seeing Wolf Richardson was something that she had decided she must do without, or risk being carried away into an affair.

She wasn't so dissatisfied with being single that she'd settle with any man who'd belonged to somebody else. That'd mean facing disapproval from her family, and church. She didn't even *know* anybody who'd been divorced. She'd simply been swept off her feet – Wolf's kisses were much more romantic than anything she'd seen at the pictures, he was as good a dancer as Fred Astaire, and far nicer looking! But then he was experienced with women, knew how to make her want him.

Tim's friendliness helped. She'd been flattered that Wolf found her attractive. And Tim was equally aware of her as a woman, a timely reminder that attraction wasn't particularly unusual. It happened often enough, even between the most unsuitable people. One day, she'd be drawn to somebody again – to a man who was right for her. And meantime she hadn't been joking when she said how busy she was going to be.

At the end of her first full week at the mill, Rhona was so exhausted she wondered how she'd walk home. But she also felt well-pleased. The work was hard, she'd begun immersing herself in the day-to-day routine of a spinning mill. She went from one department to the next, watching the skilled operatives of the combing, drawing, and twisting machines, and asking questions.

Adding a weaving shed alongside the spinning hadn't come to anything yet, and Rhona was thankful. At least, she was having the opportunity of grasping the essential stages of one process before absorbing the intricacies of another. Work was going ahead, though, on the adjacent site, combining the noise of reconstruction with the rattle of spinning frames.

'I seem to have trudged nine times round this place today!' she exclaimed to Tim and his father. She'd been seeing how Herbert Shackleton, one of the maintenance men, repaired machines that had broken down.

'Herbert's been having a go at one of those round combing machines . . .'

'The Noble,' Tim prompted, smiling. 'We do have quite a bit of bother with that one. But you shouldn't go dirtying your hands with that side of things.'

'I've got to learn. I can't go fussing about my appearance,' she reminded Tim. 'And you two'll often see me when I'm looking anything but my best.'

'You look champion to me, any road,' Tim persisted. 'I haven't forgotten my intention of taking you out, either.'

Rhona sighed. She'd no time now for complications. And having Tim find her attractive was reassuring only so long as he *wouldn't* do anything about it. 'Don't start that again, Tim. You're courting Hazel. You shouldn't be flirting with me just because we're thrown together.'

'That's just where you're wrong,' Tim assured her, ignoring his father's startled look. 'I'm trying to finish with Hazel, only she won't have it.'

'I hope you're not thinking of using me to make that plain to her! I'm surprised at you, Tim Brightstone, a grand lass like that, and you're not satisfied.'

'That's what I keep telling him,' Bill interjected heatedly. 'Both me and his mother want to see them saving for their own little place. What more could anybody want?'

But Timothy was gazing hard at Rhona, his blue eyes intense before they veiled. Across the few paces separating them, she heard his deepened breathing. She hadn't bargained for this. There was nothing special about her, why were two men in the space of a week making it so obvious that they wanted her? She hadn't quite known how to cope with Wolf, but she did know how to stop Tim being so daft.

'Try and be sensible, please. You and I aren't going to be able to work together for long if you don't shut up about taking me out.'

For the next few weeks learning all she could about the mill took all her attention. And Tim made no more overtures.

The shock came one Saturday morning when Rhona left the house and met Hazel Wright, almost on the step.

The dark-haired girl's greeting was perfunctory, and she fell into step beside Rhona, her dark eyes glittering dangerously. 'You'll have to put up with me waiting for you like this, it was the only way I could be certain of seeing you. And I've got to protect my interests.'

Rhona's heart plummeted. She knew what was coming, and who was to blame. She could have thrashed Tim Brightstone.

'I can imagine Tim must think he's doing well for himself, getting hitched to one of the mill's directors . . .' Hazel was continuing.

'Just a minute,' Rhona interrupted, she wasn't having this! 'Whatever has he been telling you?'

'That him and me are finishing, don't pretend you don't know. Because he's fallen for you. I think you've the cheek of Old Nick, Rhona Hebden! You knew Tim and me had an understanding.'

'I'm not trying to take Tim away from you,' Rhona corrected her, distressed. 'There's nothing between us, and there wouldn't be.'

'So *you* say. Well, you would, wouldn't you, *to me.*

90

That's not the way Tim tells it. All I can say is you'd better lay off, because I'm going to have him, and there's an end of it . . .' Hazel gulped, near to tears.

Rhona wasn't far from crying as well, with fury. She'd been badly let down by Tim. Whatever he'd said to Hazel had been groundless. She'd never encouraged him, in any way, never for one moment.

What on earth can I say to her? she thought, sick with despair.

'Just think on – I'll find a way,' Hazel said, turned abruptly, and darted off down the passageway between the backs of two rows of houses.

Tim was approaching the mill from the opposite direction. Rhona didn't think he'd noticed Hazel but he couldn't have been quicker in through the door if he had seen her.

Rhona had to wait nearly all morning for the chance to tackle him out of his father's hearing. They were down at the far end of the mill examining a faulty yarn. Waiting had made her even more annoyed.

'I want a word with you, Timothy. I told you not to make me the excuse for breaking with Hazel.' She outlined Hazel's accusation. 'I don't want second-hand goods, you know, I never have wanted them.'

'No?' Tim retorted sharply. 'I thought you'd set your cap at Wolf Richardson . . .'

'You thought *what*?' Rhona snapped, hoping to goodness the clattering machines were drowning her voice to anyone further than three feet away. 'I went out with him *once*. And there was nothing in it. I wasn't brought up to go for a divorced man, he knows that as well as I do. Even if he was considering me in that light, which I very much doubt. We're from totally different environments, Wolf and I, not a bit alike, nor well suited.'

'Then there is hope for me.'

Rhona gave him a searching look, then ran a hand agitatedly through her hair. This was terrible: Tim looked and sounded so serious.

'You needn't go thinking that,' she said hastily, but his

91

earnest expression prevented her being quite so firm as she'd intended. 'You're a friend, Tim, and I hope you always will be. But you're going the fastest way you can towards destroying that.'

'What are you waiting for then, a perfect man, or something?'

'Maybe I am.'

'There's no such person exists, love. You'll be waiting the rest of your life if . . .'

'Let me worry about that. And just remember what I said before, about us not going out together.'

'And if I can't dismiss it, if I have to go on and on at you, because I'm so positive that we're right for each other? Because I feel it in my bones. Because the only way we'll find out is for you to give me a chance and see me away from this place . . .'

'You mustn't pester me, you should have seen that by now. It won't do any good. And certainly not like this. Hazel's a nice girl, Tim, I'd never dream of going out with you behind her back.'

Suddenly, he smiled. 'All right,' he agreed, surprisingly acquiescent.

Thank goodness for that, Rhona thought. She'd been afraid he really wouldn't listen to reason.

6

Six months had passed since Rhona had begun working full time at Bridge House Mill. And although she often was so occupied that she scarcely had time to think, those six months had been far happier and more fulfilling than ever she'd expected. She enjoyed working with Tim and his father, and believing she was easing the burden for Bill Brightstone helped to compensate for giving up all her teaching ambitions.

Bill's wife, Ellen, had invited her for tea one Sunday and while Tim and his dad went for a walk, the two women had talked. Ellen Brightstone, a likeable little body whose greying hair and wiry frame made her appear deceptively fragile, had gone on and on about how much better Bill was, these days. From something Ellen said, Rhona had gathered that Tim and Hazel were still seeing each other, which increased the relief she'd felt when Tim ceased asking *her* to go out with him. Gradually, over the weeks, the old easy friendship between Tim and herself had been restored.

She had no other relationships, but that was the way she had decided it must be. Until something came up. Wolf had telephoned her once, at the mill, inviting her to a concert in Leeds. She'd thanked him, and turned him down, making the excuse that she was going somewhere else that evening. But it had been an excuse. She hoped Wolf hadn't realized, and that refusing hadn't hurt him as much as herself.

That was a long time ago now, though, last August. They were into 1936, February. The winter ought to be nearly over, she hoped it was. It had been a bad winter for the Hebdens. Happen it was a good thing she wasn't away at college. One by one, they'd gone down with the flu, and were taking a long time to pick up again. Her mother and Stan both had coughs still and even Jack Hebden didn't seem to have his normal energy. Fortunately, she could afford now to lash out a bit and spend, when one or other of them needed a bunch of grapes or a jar of calf's foot jelly to perk them up. And there was no need to hesitate when the doctor ought to be called.

It was funny the way things turned out. The prospect of her inheritance had been a family joke, now they teased her about not spending. They called her tight-fisted, but they knew as well as Rhona herself that she didn't have time for throwing money around. She'd bought herself a smart little Oxford-blue Morris Eight, but the car didn't get used very often.

The mill was worth it, though, she hardly thought about anything else. She hadn't enough false modesty to pretend she didn't recognize how swiftly she'd picked up knowledge, about management as well as about the yarns they produced. Last week she'd discovered she'd earned the respect of the board of directors as much as the employees.

She'd got over being daunted by the darkly panelled room with its long mahogany table, and the forceful manner of some of her fellow directors. Although dubious about her own temerity, she'd spoken up about an idea that had come from her knitting classes.

'Before we launch out into this weaving scheme of Tim's,' she'd begun, 'I wonder if we couldn't do something about spinning a different kind of wool, for knitting.' They'd all stared at her then, even Bill who'd been told of her idea. 'There's a lot of complaints about the yarn they can buy in the shops. Some of the colours aren't so good, lots of the wool either splits on the needle point, or breaks altogether . . .'

'And . . . ?' the chairman of the board prompted, his eyes narrowing as he studied this good-looking lass who seemed capable of putting forward her own notions.

'We can do better – produce a wider selection of top-quality yarn. We've experience of spinning and dyeing, and could install the necessary machinery in the new section of the mill. I know what knitters want.'

Initially the board had been divided; two of them had worked in weaving themselves and favoured Tim's scheme. But Bill liked Rhona's idea from the start and soon they were all agreed that there'd be less of a risk in diversifying within spinning.

Rhona was enjoying herself now, researching other suppliers' knitting yarns, testing them for quality, durability and how well they stood up to frequent washing. Tim was busy, too, looking into the number and type of machines that best would fulfil their production targets.

'We've got to do this on a grand scale, or not at all,' he'd asserted.

That had scared Rhona a bit, delighted though she was that her idea had been approved. She was apprehensive about sinking a lot of capital into a scheme that she'd originated. She'd tried to convince the board that they ought to begin more cautiously by keeping their outlay to a minimum.

'You're scared, lass,' Bill had said afterwards, smiling sympathetically. 'That won't do, you know. In business, you've got to be venturesome. Your dad would have told you that.'

'Happen so. But my dad knew spinning inside out. I don't, not yet.'

'Don't talk rubbish. You've picked it up a treat, there's a lot of your old man in you! And you don't want to quell your imaginative ideas, neither. We need folk like you. There's some like me'll always make decent, hard-working managers – then there's some that have that bit extra – the gift for foreseeing how things *might* be . . .'

'Go on, you old flatterer,' she'd laughed. But Bill's words gave her courage.

'We're none of us daft,' he'd reminded her. 'None of us on the board would let you toss our brass away. Yon's a good idea, we're trying it out. And you know, lass, if you don't risk failing now and again, you might as well keep out of business altogether.'

This isn't going to fail, though, Rhona thought. And that particular evening she went home happier than ever.

She'd put up with any amount of hard work so long as it came to something.

The minute she opened the door of number 46 Grace-church Street she knew something was wrong. Jack Hebden was talking in a grave voice to a white-faced Eve who, when she saw Rhona, sighed.

'What is it?' Rhona asked, her heart jumping already as she glanced anxiously around. 'Not one of the lads – has something happened?'

'Not to them – no,' her stepfather said carefully. 'There's a lass gone missing. You – you haven't heard anything then?'

She shook her head. 'I wouldn't, would I? You know what it's like at the mill.'

'I only thought . . .' Looking awkward and embarrassed, Jack ran a hand through his dark thatch of hair, shrugged helplessly, cleared his throat, and couldn't continue.

Her mother went on for him: 'We only thought Tim might have been sent for. This girl who's disappeared is Hazel Wright, you see . . .'

'*Hazel?* Are you sure? Tim would have said, surely. He'd have been upset.' All the time she was speaking she was seeing Hazel's face, as she'd seen it that morning last year, when she'd been nearly out of her mind because of fear of losing Tim.

'If he'd known. Maybe he doesn't yet.' Eve swallowed. 'I can't help thinking how you used to be in the Infants' together. It might have been y . . .'

'But how did you hear? Happen there's been some mistake.' Why did she feel so . . . *guilty?* As if it was her fault Hazel had been so upset. But that was months ago, anyway.

'I wish I thought there was a mistake,' Jack said fervently. 'It was Stanley dashed in with the news, not half an hour ago. Hazel's brother is a regular at the billiard hall, he's getting a search party together from among the lads that play there. Stan came to collect our Daniel, they want as many people as they can get.'

'But I don't understand – Hazel isn't a child. She can't have wandered off and got herself lost. Happen she's just decided to go and visit somebody, without saying. How – how long has she been missing?'

'Since this morning just before dinner.' Her mother was pulling at a corner of the teatowel, shredding it.

'Well, that's no time at all, is it? How can they be certain that she's missing?'

'There was a row, so her brother says, love,' Jack explained sadly. 'She was in trouble.'

'In the family way,' Eve enlarged. 'I think her mum and dad only got to hear of it yesterday. Naturally, they were upset. I suppose they gave her a bad time – what respectable couple wouldn't if they found out their only daughter was . . . ? Anyway, Hazel and her mother were still at it hammer and tongs this morning. Then while Mrs Wright was out shopping Hazel disappeared.'

Rhona was frowning. 'It's worrying, of course. But I don't see why everybody's going into quite such a panic. In that condition, feeling nobody was on her side, her first instinct would be to get away. She must have lots of friends, she's always been popular. Hasn't anybody checked . . . ?'

'She left a note, love,' Jack announced solemnly.

'Not – I don't believe this, not a suicide note!'

'Evidently she said they wouldn't find her alive.'

'Oh, Lord! The silly girl . . . ! Tim would have married her, she needn't have . . .'

Rhona saw her mother and stepfather exchange a glance. The less she said the better. If Tim had refused to do right by Hazel it wasn't ~~really their~~ business. Too many folk would get to know all about it, anyway, without them working over the details.

'Where are they searching? Did the – the note give them a lead?'

'No,' Jack told her. 'But one of their neighbours saw her heading towards the new reservoir. Seemingly, he passed her in his van. Called out to her, but she didn't take no notice. It wasn't till he got home and heard what had happened that he began to put two and two together.'

'I'd better get after the lads. If they need lots of people to look, one more'll be a bit of help.'

'You can't swim, love, can you? That's why I'm still here. There's nowt else to be done now.'

'Swim? It's *February*, Dad.'

'It's the reservoir itself they're searching now.'

'Oh, God!'

'The police seem convinced she's in there,' her mother told her quietly. 'They've scoured everywhere in the vicinity of the reservoir. I think, from what Stan said, they found some clues.'

'How dreadful! How absolutely dreadful!' Rhona felt sickened. She couldn't get out of her mind that morning when Hazel had confronted her outside this very door, had accused her of trying to take Tim away. Because she'd heard nothing further, she'd believed that things were all right again between Hazel and Tim. Had wanted to believe that. Because Tim had wanted to break with Hazel, hadn't he, on account of *her*. He'd been saying that a long time ago.

'We'd better be having our tea,' Eve said wearily, glancing though the kitchen towards the stove.

'Can't we wait till the others come in?' Rhona suggested. She might feel more able to eat something by then, though she doubted it. They might have found Hazel alive. She doubted that as well.

Dan stumbled in with the news. It was half-past ten that night, and he'd left Stanley trying to talk to Hazel's brother. Police divers had found the girl. Where the water was too deep to be reached by any of the volunteers.

Dan had been weeping. Tough young Dan who'd been so carefree, who'd not had a serious thought in his head beyond earning enough to deck out his new motorcycle with all the latest gadgets. Dan, who loved roaring off down the street, shattering all the neighbours.

'That water didn't half sting your eyes,' he said hastily.

He'd noticed Rhona looking at him. 'Must be something they put in it. Or the cold – yes, it'd be the cold.'

When he reappeared after changing into his striped pyjamas he was whey-faced still, shivering – or shuddering. It was hot in the tiny living room. Jack had built up the fire until it was blazing halfway up the chimney ready for his lads coming home.

Rhona longed to put her arms round their Dan. Tall though he was, and broad-shouldered, in his pyjamas with his brown eyes perturbed, he looked as vulnerable as he had when he was little and had wet the bed.

'Two lives wasted,' he exclaimed angrily. 'And all their Derek could keep saying was that she was a bonny lass.'

She was, Rhona thought, but couldn't manage to utter one word.

'What I don't understand is why it was so awful for her to have a kid,' Dan went on earnestly. 'We all know how they're made – there can't be so many folk as haven't wanted to – well, you know . . . without waiting to be wed.'

Both Eve and Jack looked as though they felt like saying something, but neither of them spoke. Inwardly, Rhona sighed with relief. Along with her distress regarding Hazel she couldn't help recalling certain occasions. And the longing that had surged alarmingly, of its own volition, in response to a few kisses. Was it really that easy to fall for a youngster?

'Will you try and have something to eat, love?' Eve asked her youngest son. Her heart was aching for the mother who'd lost her daughter – grandchild, as well. And for this boy of hers who seemed to have grown into a man in one evening. Even if he didn't look it.

Dan shook his head. 'Sorry, Mum. It'd choke me.'

Food would have choked any of them.

Next morning Tim was at the mill as usual. Rhona hadn't expected that, and one glance towards his grey face made her wish he'd stopped at home.

As soon as she walked into the old-fashioned office she sensed that Tim and his father weren't speaking. Bill

Brightstone was pale as well, and appeared to have aged by fifteen years. His lips were clamped together, blue-tinged, his eyes shadowed.

Rhona had decided already that she would tell Tim she was sorry, but that would be all. If she said any more she'd really let rip. Stanley had come home just after midnight with the story that Derek Wright had tackled Tim only two days ago on his sister's behalf. Nothing the girl herself had said could make Tim agree to marry her, and Derek hoped to put the matter right before their parents had to know.

Rhona said what she'd planned while she and Tim were well away from the office, concealed by spinning frames from his father's troubled gaze.

'I should think you're sorry, and all,' Tim said roughly, astounding her. And frightening her as well, he sounded so furious. 'If it hadn't been for you none of this would have happened.'

'Me? You're actually blaming *me!* How on earth can you?'

'If you hadn't come on the scene again, making me want you, I'd have been married to Hazel long before this.'

'I won't have that, Tim Brightstone! I told you ages since there wasn't going to be anything between us. And you were messing about with Hazel. She was in the family way, wasn't she?'

Tim had the grace to look down at his hands. Rhona saw they were shaking slightly, gripping some broken part off the Noble combing machine.

'And you wouldn't stand by your responsibilities. You're a rotten coward, refusing to do the decent thing. I don't know what they taught you at Cambridge, but it certainly wasn't the difference between right and wrong. And it had nothing to do with growing up.'

Rhona turned and hurried away from him then, right to the far end near Bill's office. If she hadn't she'd have landed out at Tim, walloped him for trying to make her responsible for this mess. She felt like walking straight out of the mill and never coming back. She couldn't even think how anything could be all right here ever again.

This was her job, though, wasn't it? And turning her back on it because Tim was a fool wasn't going to help his father, was it? Bill had enough with his weak heart, without any of this lot to worry him.

After she'd calmed down a bit Rhona went into Bill's office and sat at the other side of the desk, trying to appear normal while they worked on costings for the new knitting yarns. And throughout that day she remained near him; if he went out to attend to some problem in the spinning or dyeing, she went with him. And she kept out of Tim's way. It was only by doing that that she kept her hands off him.

It was a quarter to five when Bill said he was going home.

'See everything's locked up all right, will you, Rhona love? Our Tim's about the place somewhere, I expect, I don't rightly know where – and I don't want to. I can't be sure he'll see to anything, frame of mind he's in, so if you'll . . .'

'Of course I will. Leave it all to me, you get home to your wife. And try to leave Tim to worry about – th – this bad business. He was old enough to bring it on himself, he'll happen find the maturity from somewhere to cope with the trouble he's caused.'

Bill met her glance, and she read the pain in his eyes.

'It was nothing you could have helped, Bill.'

'I brought him up, didn't I?'

'Well . . .' There was nothing she could say.

Tim came into the office as soon as his dad had gone. Rhona had been steeling herself for this. It was no good pretending there was any way they could continue avoiding one another.

'Rhona, I'm a swine,' he began, before she could stop him. 'I'm out of my mind with what's happened. I shouldn't have tried to lay it all at your door.'

'That's right, you shouldn't. Now shut up about it. Or

101

you'll hear everything that I think, and I don't believe this is the time. Nor the place.'

'But some of it was true, love. You wouldn't see it, you've never wanted to. I did fall for you that first day I walked in here and saw you talking to the old man. You came to me, don't you remember – we met just under that horrible old-fashioned lamp.' Her hair had gleamed with red lights and her eyes had looked glorious when she smiled at him. 'I wanted you then, Rhona, and I haven't stopped wanting you since.'

Anger was making her cheeks blaze, sending a rush of heat right through her body; she could have seized him by the shoulders and shaken him, then gone on shaking him.

'And I told you you'd to do right by Hazel, didn't I? You shouldn't have kept her hanging on believing you'd wed her if it *was* me or anybody else you fancied. And you shouldn't have given her a baby, when you'd no intention of giving that child your name.'

'You don't think I meant that to happen, do you? I hadn't a thought in my head about . . .'

'About anything but your own excitement, is that what you're going to say? I bet it's the truth. Men like you make me feel poorly, only thinking of getting what you want with a girl.'

'It was what she was after. If you must know, it was her idea that time . . .'

'I don't want to know. I don't want to hear anything about it ever again. Your treatment of Hazel Wright was lousy. If I'd ever for one moment thought of you as a man to go out with, this would have killed all that stone dead.'

A great, quivering sigh ran right through her. I'm sounding like somebody in the talkies, she thought, and she couldn't stop herself. Somehow she had to convince Tim how much he'd disillusioned her.

'I'm going to see Hazel's mum and dad tonight, talk to them.'

Rhona gave him a look. She hadn't thought he had it in him.

102

'I love you, Rhona.' Tears were spilling down his cheeks from his bright blue eyes.

It might be true, she thought. And heaven help them both if it was. Whatever happened, she could never love him. There was only ever one man . . . 'Don't, for God's sake, tell them that! And don't dare mention it to me again. You don't know what love is – it isn't working a girl up until she doesn't know what she's doing, so's you can ease your feelings.'

'I love you. I need you, for the one I'll spend my life with. I knew that when you first came in here. I want to live with you.'

'I hope you don't think that's a compliment, Tim Brightstone! It makes everything ten times worse, a hundred times. How do you think you'd feel if . . .'

'I hardly knew what was going on. I only knew I was being driven insane, needing you.'

'So you slept with her, because she was willing. That is nice, isn't it? Is that the kind of goings-on . . .'

The telephone interrupted. Tim was in no state to answer it. Rhona didn't feel much better but she reached automatically to lift the receiver. She was shaking so badly with rage that the telephone stand wobbled. It was slipping off the edge of the desk when she clutched it.

At the other end of the line the voice was a man's, one Rhona didn't recognize. She was so disturbed that he had to give his name a second time before she took it in.

'Clive Ayntree, Rhona, Clive Ayntree. Thank goodness I've reached you. There's been an accident, I'm afraid – a terrible accident. At the reservoir. Phyllis is so distraught I don't know what to do with her. Father's in London, and Mother's still in the Swiss sanatorium.'

When he said there'd been an accident Rhona had begun feeling relieved, believing that people were interpreting Hazel's death as accidental. But now he was going on about Phyllis . . . She felt utterly bewildered.

'I'm sorry,' she said wearily. 'I can't quite understand . . .'

'It's Adrian, he's been killed.'

103

'Oh, God – God!'

'I can't make out what happened. Something to do with a mechanical digger, somebody wasn't taking enough care. Richardson had been driving them hard. Both Adrian and his father had been saying Richardson was going crazy to get the reservoir completed, that got worse today . . .'

'Poor Phyllis! She'll be inconsolable. I'll come immediately. Is – are you at her home, or . . .'

'Lavender Court. I brought her here as soon as I heard. She was just beginning to cook their dinner, when . . . Oh, Lord!'

When she'd replaced the receiver, Rhona closed her eyes for a minute, willing herself not to weep. This was all too much, far too much, on top of the bother here. Dazedly, she looked at Tim.

'More bad news, I'm afraid.' Her own voice sounded surprisingly steady. 'Adrian Newbold has been killed. I know his wife, Phyllis. I'm going to her straight away.'

Glancing through the window into the mill she saw the place was deserted, it was long past finishing time. In the middle of the quarrel with Tim she hadn't even heard the hooter go off.

'I'd promised your dad I'd see to things, but I must get off to see Phyllis as fast as I can. You'll have to lock up here. And do it right, think on. It's time you pulled your socks up and started taking responsibility, if only for your work.'

Every light at Lavender Court appeared to be switched on when Rhona parked the Morris Eight in the drive. Glancing around, she realized she was looking for the Richardson Daimler. It wasn't there. She couldn't imagine why she'd supposed it might be.

Mrs Bishop, tears trickling down her wrinkled cheeks, opened the door. 'Thank goodness you've come, love, maybe she'll listen to you. She won't have any of us near her. I've called the doctor, but he's attending a difficult birth. He'll come as soon as he can. I only hope he'll give her something to sleep her, there's no other way she'll begin to bear any of this.'

Mrs Bishop started leading the way towards the stairs. 'Mister Clive got her to go and lie down in her old room, but she wouldn't even let him stay with her.'

Clive was just in the doorway of the sitting room as they passed. He hurried out to speak to Rhona, his green eyes anguished. She wondered what his twin's eyes must look like. *Her* face, as well, would be ashen like her hair.

'Thanks for coming so quickly, Rhona. I didn't know any of Phyl's other friends I could rely on.'

'I'll do what I can.'

She became aware of someone beyond him in the sitting room, someone to whom Clive was extending the nominal hospitality of a drink but who was receiving no measure of warmth.

Hearing Rhona's voice, Wolf Richardson emerged. He took her earnestly by the shoulder. Through her dress, his hand was icily cold. His face seemed drained of every drop of blood, except for enough to generate the pulse vibrating at his temple.

'She refuses to see me, Rhona. Try to persuade her – *please*. I've got to tell her. This is my responsibility. It is my reservoir, I was the one pressing them to get the damned thing finished. But for me, well . . .'

'I'll see what I can do, Wolf. Don't – don't upset yourself.'

Phyllis was lying motionless on the bed, staring fixedly before her, clearly not seeing anything at all.

'You poor love!' Rhona hurtled across to gather her close; wrapped together, they lay there. She could feel her friend's nails digging into her back, clinging as if for life. Yet she sensed that at that moment Phyllis had no wish to live.

'You poor love,' Rhona murmured again, and then she was sobbing, all the tension of the past twenty-four hours increasing the distress caused by this latest tragedy. Phyllis was sobbing with her now, but relaxing, even as tears and the sheer relief of letting go began what, given a great deal of time, would be the healing process. Presently, she seemed to calm a little and was still.

'He's dead!' she screamed suddenly, just as Rhona was believing that Phyllis's weeping was over for the present. 'Adrian, Adrian, I want you, I want you!'

The sun had set long before Phyllis eventually controlled her tears. Drying her eyes, she sat up on the bed. 'I'm not very mature, am I? Sorry. I wish I could behave like an adult, but I can't, not with this.'

'No one expects . . .'

'Listen, please. His father was so calm about it all. He telephoned me, you know. From the hospital, as soon as – as soon as he – knew. I ought to have gone to their house, afterwards. But I – couldn't. His dad saw it happen, as well. But he's just getting on with things, for the rest of them. Adr – Adrian is – was the eldest, you see. His youngest sister is only ten. They have a housekeeper, she's been there since they lost their mother, but they need their father. He'll keep going, for them.'

There was another silence, interrupted only by Phyllis's jagged breathing. Then she sighed, a dry sob caught her throat. 'It – it isn't that I wanted Dad Newbold here, you know. Nothing can help, not really, not now. It's more knowing that so many people have been upset by – by what happened. And I'm not able to do a bloody thing to help any of them feel at all better.'

'There is one person you can help,' Rhona told her, after a few seconds' consideration. 'He's downstairs now, and there's only you can make him feel any different about this sad business.'

'Richardson?' Sighing again, Phyllis shook her head.

Rhona moistened her lips. 'He felt bad enough already today, after what happened last night, with them finding Hazel Wright drowned.'

'*Last night?* It was days ago, surely. Couldn't have been last night.'

'I'm afraid it was.'

'You were right, weren't you,' Phyllis said dully. 'That scheme is doomed.'

'Don't talk like that, love. It can't help, can it?'

Grimly, Phyllis drew her lips together and shook her head again. 'Nothing can.' After a while she said, 'I've nothing against Wolf, he was only doing something he believed in. Maybe he wouldn't have been putting so much pressure on today if he hadn't been perturbed about that girl drowning.'

'May I tell him that, from you?'

'If you like.'

Biting her lip, Rhona nodded. She was completely exhausted, wrung dry by trying to ease her friend's pain. She longed to go home but wouldn't leave Phyllis like this. If only the doctor would arrive.

'Rhona? You're thinking I ought to tell Wolf myself, aren't you?'

'I wasn't thinking about him at all. You can only manage so much. People understand . . .'

'You can tell him to come up. I don't know what the hell I'll say, but I'll see him.'

'I'm sure you can leave the talking to Wolf. He feels responsible, you realize that? Do you want me to come back up with him?'

'There's no need, thanks. I won't go for him. Haven't the energy, even if I was certain that was justified.' She grasped Rhona's arm. 'And thanks a million, Rhona, for coming. You'll come back tomorrow?'

'Whenever you need me.'

Rhona waited in the sitting room, trying to make conversation with Clive, until Wolf reappeared. She felt so tired she ached all over, desperate to get home to Gracechurch Street. As Wolf was coming downstairs the doctor arrived and Mrs Bishop hustled him upstairs to Phyllis.

'I'll be on my way now, Clive,' Rhona said. 'But I'll be back tomorrow. It won't be till evening, but I will come. Tell Phyl that, won't you? Take care of her.'

'Of course. Dad will be here anyway by morning. He's taking an overnight sleeper.'

'Good.' Rhona remembered she hadn't seen the Daimler outside, and turned to Wolf. 'How did you get here?'

'By cab. I was at the site when it happened. The Daimler's there still. I went to the hospital with Sir Reginald . . . Then I came straight here.' He held the door for her as they went outside. 'Not that it did any good, until you arrived . . .'

Wolf gazed at her, aching to be held, to be told that it wasn't all his fault. That people could forgive . . .

'I'll give you a lift, either home, or to the reservoir. I've got my own car now.' Wanly, she smiled. 'And I do owe you one or two lifts.'

Wolf attempted to smile back. 'Make it Farnley Carr then, will you.' He couldn't face that place again, could he, not today – if ever . . .

As she opened the door of her little Morris for him though, he changed his mind. It was the only way, wasn't it, to have her with him? To face, once and for all, that wretched site. 'On second thoughts,' he said, 'if you don't mind, it had better be the reservoir.'

Wolf didn't say another word as she drove up and over the moor. Rhona kept glancing sideways, conscious of his perturbation. She let him alone, reckoning he needed the quiet to recover some measure of control. He'd had a terrible two days, and must feel that he was the last person anyone would sympathize with.

The Daimler was no longer there, anyway; the site foreman told Wolf that Stimson had been to collect it.

'Sorry, I've had you make a wasted journey,' he began, getting back into the car.

'Doesn't matter.' Rhona had never seen the reservoir before, hadn't been near. Now she was desperate to see it all. The moon was full, silvering the lapping water, glinting from the frost that decked nearby shrubs and trees, shadowing the snow.

'How beautiful it is!' she exclaimed softly, enchanted.

'I never expected that!' Wolf felt choked by her unreserved exclamation. He swallowed. 'I thought you'd say the bloody thing should never have been built.'

'My dear, don't be idiotic. Your motives were sound. This was an accident. Yesterday – yesterday was a desperate girl who'd have killed herself, somehow, somewhere.'

'*Was* it suicide?' He was astounded.

Hadn't everyone known? Uneasy, Rhona got out of the car and walked towards the massive structure bridging the valley. The moonlight was sufficient to illuminate the huge concrete steps that strode down from the end of the reservoir and stretched from side to side of Vicar's Dale. She turned and looked the other way to the reservoir itself, full now, exquisite as any natural lake, peaceful.

Wolf was beside her now. She sensed his disturbance, and closed her eyes momentarily, yearning to help.

'If – if that girl's death is assumed to be accidental no one will hear otherwise from me,' he assured her.

'I don't suppose they'll want it advertised as suicide,' she said grimly. But she wasn't sorry she'd let Wolf know, he'd needed that knowledge. 'You've done a good job here, you know,' she continued, 'melding man-made with natural, creating something pleasing to the eye as well as useful.'

'Don't be too kind . . .'

'Kind? You get the truth from me, lad, haven't you learnt that yet?'

Wolf swallowed again, pulled her against his side, his arm across her shoulders. He didn't deserve anything like this. There'd never be quite so much hurt here, not while he could recall Rhona beside him, remember her words. Silvered, this place could be beautiful.

'Home, don't you think?' she suggested gently. 'You'll have to bring me again another day,' she added, before she realized she was committing herself.

'Did you get Phyllis to listen?' she asked in the darkness of the car.

'I didn't know she had so much courage. Yes, she heard me out. Thanks to you.' His glance flicked towards her. She was staring hard through the windscreen at the road. The little car rattled over the cobbles, jarring terribly when they crossed one of the tram tracks. The absence of smoothness felt strangely appropriate. As if he must accept discomfort. The hair shirt . . . ? If only to God it were that simple.

Rhona tried to clear her throat. It ached with unshed tears, tears for this man. And for them all. She wouldn't cry till she got home, she mustn't. Back at Lavender Court her tears had served their purpose. Here, they'd be a luxury she wasn't permitting.

'I've never been this helpless before,' Wolf admitted, his voice grating. 'For once, no amount of money will do a thing. The Newbolds aren't in need of financial compensation, there's no other kind, either, would have the slightest effect.'

'I'm afraid that's right,' Rhona agreed quietly.

'*You* can go there again,' he observed sharply. 'Phyllis will see you, and be glad you're there, caring. I'd only be an unwelcome reminder.'

Rhona hadn't realized how much Wolf needed to be of use to Phyllis and the rest of the Newbold family. 'There might be something you can do, in time. If there is – if anything she says gives me some idea, I'll let you know.'

'You're a good woman, Rhona.'

They'd almost crossed the moor. Farnley Carr was in sight now. She wondered why she felt so desolate.

'You'll come inside, won't you?'

Wolf's invitation startled her. It was anything but a social occasion. She glanced sideways, and saw how much he needed her to agree. And she'd believed she was aching to get home; she understood with a jolt that she felt this pain because she couldn't bear to leave him.

'Of course, if that's what you want.'

Stimson opened the door as Wolf was about to unlock it. She'd never liked the man before. Now she warmed to his sympathetic expression.

'You'll be needing something to eat, sir? And a drink perhaps? And for Miss Hebden . . . ?'

Wolf turned to her. 'We'd better try and eat. I think we both need something. Sandwiches, maybe, and soup . . . ? And a brandy. One shouldn't do you harm, even though you'll be driving, later.'

He watched Stimson walking towards the kitchen at the rear, then took her coat and hung it beside his own. 'This way . . .' he said, sliding a hand beneath her elbow.

Wolf closed the sitting room door behind them then swallowed, hard. Her sherry-brown eyes were seeking his, so anxiously that he might have been the one bereaved, not the perpetrator of that frightful accident. He didn't deserve her generous spirit, but couldn't contemplate existing without it.

'Rhona . . .'

She slipped her arms around him. Briefly, he rested his chin on the tumble of auburn curls. Was there affection in the way she leaned her head into his chest? Or was it only that she was exhausted?

'You'll have to stop blaming yourself, Wolf. It won't do a thing for anybody else. And it will eat into you.'

'It was because of that girl drowning, you know, that I was on at them today to get the damned thing finished. I wanted everything completed, to be shot of it. Perhaps so I could cut and run, then. I don't know.'

Shattered, Rhona stared up at him. She'd never contemplated that Wolf might leave Farnley Carr – leave *her*. She read in his grey eyes something of the distress he would feel if compelled to get away. Her own sudden bleakness choked her.

The weeping could be controlled no longer. His arms tightened about her, crushing her to his chest so that the thumping of his heart came louder than her own undisciplined sobbing.

The salt was sharp on his lips: first from her cheeks, then from the mouth he kissed. Beneath their lids, his own eyes moistened. He gathered her even nearer.

The surge within his body was entire shock, the last thing he'd anticipated. Yet Wolf recognized with a kind of joy the one way they might release all tension.

'Do you wish to sit down?' he asked gently, offering

111

her the opportunity to move away, to restore their former relationship.

'Not yet.' No time would ever be sufficient for communicating all she felt. And no means adequate for expressing her love of him. How could she not have recognized earlier what this emotion was?

Stimson brought their food. Even tonight, after everything, humour glinted in Rhona's eyes when Wolf hurriedly disengaged himself from her as footsteps approached. Thanking him, Wolf sent the man to his bed, then smiled as the door closed on him.

'Now, first — brandy.'

Rhona couldn't bear him to move even those few paces away. She went with him to the mahogany sideboard. She took her glass but remained immobile while Wolf poured and drank from his own.

'I don't think I've ever had brandy.'

His smile was tender. 'Taste it then . . .' Surprising her, he drew her to him once more, his head bent towards hers.

His lips tasted sharp from the keen spirit. He sipped again from his glass, again he kissed her. His probing tongue introduced a trickle of aromatic brandy. She sampled it and swallowed. Its warmth fired her exhausted soul as well as her body. Spreading through her, it seemed like a part of Wolf himself, given readily, healing.

'I needed that,' she murmured huskily.

Again, he sipped, again his mouth covered hers. She savoured his tongue. All yearning culminated in the hunger flaring from deep within her. Against her, Wolf stirred, his need undisguised. Rhona placed a hand at the nape of his neck, pulled his head down towards her once more, seeking his kisses. She had longed so fervently for hours to comfort and assure, to give herself in some way. There was no preventing herself pressing close, urging him to accept her.

He drank from the glass again, made her wait while he set it down, then hers beside it. Her face upturned, she stood there, lips already parted a little, eager.

112

The brandy took her breath slightly. With her gasp, his tongue plunged more deeply, savouring her as they shared the tang of the spirit. His hands were strong on her spine, holding her to him, one at her waist, the other lower. His touch more fiery than the lips devouring hers, he was willing her to receive him.

'I love you, Rhona. The time couldn't be more inappropriate, but I have to tell you. Since the day you walked through this door I've grown increasingly in love.'

It couldn't be so. Could it? That first day, his wife had only just left. She had seen her. Was Wolf simply another man talking of love because he meant . . . the other thing? A bit like Tim, in a way, too much like him?

What am I doing? she thought desparingly. How've I got into this? Standing so close that, though they both were fully clothed, they might as well not be. Kissing, exploring, sensing this was only the prelude. And only once had she been out with him. And she'd dared to be surprised at Hazel and Tim, who'd courted for years.

No matter how urgently she needed Wolf, or needed to give, she wasn't going to be like Hazel, or anybody else who let a man have what he was after, and no gold band on her finger. And with Wolf it was more complicated still. He was married, wasn't he, or had been. *A divorcé.* If he *was* free yet. She knew so little about him that she'd no idea of the situation. But she wasn't too besotted to know how she'd feel if they didn't marry afterwards.

'Don't . . . leave me, Rhona. Your mother would believe you were with Phyllis, she wouldn't be worried tonight.'

Rhona gave him a look. 'I'd know I was here, and I would worry.'

'I should have known.' There was no reproof in his tone, though she suspected she'd earned it. She'd not let him an arm's length away since the minute they'd come into this room! Was it because of the times she'd resisted that this attraction was so strong? Or because of the man Wolf was, so magnetic? And him starved of loving, just as she was . . .

'I am to be free, you know. Before all that long. There's nothing legal to stop us marrying.'

Rhona steeled herself not to heed him. For once in her life, her body had stopped her thinking, but not any more. 'Nay, love – don't you know me better than this?' Her voice cracked, she had to swallow. 'I've said before I don't hold with divorce, haven't I?' There – she'd said it now.

Grave again, Wolf nodded, and released her. He moistened his lips. She willed herself not to cover them with her own, not to put her arms round him. You can't have happiness just by taking what you want, she thought, and hoped she really believed it.

Wolf was frowning. He must have been wrong. Never once had she said she loved him. Some – some wishful dream must have prompted this belief that it might be love on her part, as well. And she had *her* dreams, carefully cherished.

'Naturally, you want an ideal marriage,' he said. 'Not a second-hand bridegroom. Some man, innocent as yourself, who'll explore love with you.'

'If I've thought about it all, that must be how I've visualized being married.' She had to say so, or she'd be in his bed tonight, she'd not stop herself. 'And you want somebody different, who'd be entirely happy about the way things are. I – I'd be expecting the impossible. I wouldn't make you happy.'

'I'd take a chance on it.'

'Thank you,' she said quietly, the lump in her throat choking her again. 'I'm sorry I can't. I really am sorry.'

She was weeping again, and had determined that she wouldn't. He was all kindness now, enfolding her, murmuring that she mustn't be so upset. She was overwrought, they both were. He understood. He would understand, always. He'd never try again to coerce her, by any means. He'd avoid these situations.

Avoid all proximity, she thought, would that make it all right? Was that what he thought? Didn't he know she couldn't be in the same room and not long to love him? No matter how many folk were there. That she couldn't

114

have him look at her without withering because she wasn't responding. That she couldn't live with this need searing through her, and not do something daft. Something they might both regret. She'd best try to live without him.

Rhona must have been exhausted. She slept that night, far better than ever she had hoped. When she awakened it was like coming out of a bad dream, then she remembered. A silent groan admitted the depression, new to her but slow to lift.

I'm bound to feel like this, she told herself as she quickly got out of bed. Hazel's death was bad enough, without Phyllis losing her husband so tragically the following day. She needn't look any further for the reason for her gloom. And she wasn't going to look; she wouldn't even let herself worrit on about Wolf! She'd never stop being thankful that she'd been there last night – but that was it now, finished. She'd wondered once before if she was scared of . . . yes, of sex. Well, maybe she'd every reason to be. Giving way to it had made a right mess of things for Hazel and Tim. No one knew better than her now that it could scarcely be ignored, and that it flared up between all the wrong people.

It was snowing the other side of the ice on the sash window. Holding aside the chintz curtain, Rhona realized that it must have snowed nearly all night, everything looked so different.

Even the little Morris looked unfamiliar, its roof pristine snow except for a row of arrowhead indentations where a bird had hopped. From up here she could hardly see the ridge of the hinged bonnet. Nothing in the street appeared the same, today – or was it . . . had *she* changed, so much that she'd never see anything as she had before?

Time I got on, she thought severely, going to have a wash and pull on her working clothes. If only everything didn't seem so bleak . . . I haven't died, I'm not even ill, she told herself. For me, personally, there has been no catastrophe. It wasn't even as if she was compelled to keep away from Wolf. He had spoken of there being ways in which their friendship might continue. Had he understood more than Rhona herself, and seen beyond the present to genuine cause for hope? Could she – could she, for today, while the hurting was so intense, believe with him?

Her mother was the only one around at home, the others were off to work before Rhona came downstairs. For once, she almost wished Eve wasn't there, she was in no mood for talking. Nor in the mood for anything.

'How was Phyllis?' Eve Hebden asked sympathetically. 'I half expected you might stay the night with her.'

Aye, Rhona thought, that was what Wolf said. 'She was beginning to calm down before I came away. There wasn't much I could do. And the doctor was going to give her something so's she'd sleep.'

'She'll need that, poor lass. She'll not know what ails her for many a long month. And her mother so poorly she's unable to do anything.'

'I know. It's a bad business. Makes you feel *that* helpless!'

'But you'll be seeing Phyllis again.'

'After work. I'll go straight there, don't get any tea ready for me. I'll just pop back to pick up the car.'

After the sharp cold of the snow-bound street, the smell of the mill hit Rhona as soon as she opened the door. She was used to the pervasive odour of wool and warm, well-oiled machinery and normally didn't notice it. The racket would begin in a minute as well. Today, that would seem oppressive. She cringed, thinking about all the clattering.

Tim and his dad were in the office; barely speaking, she could tell, though not quite so obviously avoiding one another. They both glanced towards her as she walked in, both began to speak, asking after her friend.

Briefly, Rhona told them what she'd found last evening. The dreary old office seemed crammed – with papers, ledgers, bobbins of wool, and the normal assortment of pieces from problem machines. And crammed also with the double tragedy affecting the three of them.

'Well, I'm glad you're in today, any road,' Bill said

117

with a tight smile that didn't alter his weary eyes. 'We're still having trouble with yon Noble comb. Some of these boxes want replacing. T'latest is they can't get spares over to us from Bradford.'

'But they were promised for first thing today.'

'I know,' Tim said quickly. 'The fellow who was bringing them skidded on the ice, bashed all the front of their van in.'

'Bradford's not far, couldn't we send somebody to pick the spares up?'

'Herbert Shackleton's the only maintenance man that can drive,' Tim told her, 'and we can't spare him, as yet. Why is it when one machine packs up others do the same?'

And you're not offering to go, Rhona thought grimly.

Timothy might have read her silent reproach. 'I've got to keep an eye on what they're doing to that experimental Gill box – the one for your knitting wools. The autoleveller isn't working properly.'

She turned to Bill, who was sifting through the post. 'Would you like me to run over to Fletcher's and fetch the things?'

He seized her suggestion, and Rhona felt relieved. She'd never felt less like being cooped up in the mill, she needed to get away with her own thoughts.

By the time Rhona had collected the car and was on her way to Bradford it was snowing harder than ever. Away from the side streets, the setts were bare of snow on the whole, though some of them seemed coated with ice.

The blizzard started suddenly, as she was heading out of the town towards North Bridge. Any other day she might have contemplated turning back. Today she was numbed to concern for her own safety, slowed down quite a bit, but continued driving on.

A woman was huddled into an expensive-looking coat, standing on the corner of the road, a suitcase at her feet. Evidently she had walked up the steep hill from the station. Rhona couldn't imagine why she hadn't got a taxi there.

As she neared her, the woman turned. Between the saucy little hat and the collar drawn up to her ears, black hair gleamed. Even from this distance, her eyes looked dark. It's Hazel, Rhona thought, bewildered, Hazel Wright! But how could it be – the girl's body had been found.

Drawing nearer, Rhona looked more carefully. It wasn't Hazel, though the woman had similar colouring, and she *was* familiar . . . What was more, she was urgently signalling for Rhona to stop the car.

Cautiously, to avoid a skid, she pulled in at the kerb.

Rhona realized then when she'd seen this person, and why she hadn't forgotten her.

'I am so sorry to trouble you,' the woman said as Rhona wound down the window. 'But I've waited interminably at the station, since then for fully fifteen minutes here, gradually freezing. Are there no cabs in Halfield?'

'It looks as if on a morning like this they don't expect much custom.'

'Can you tell me – is there any chance of finding a taxi if I drag my luggage further up the hill, into the town centre? I must find some means of reaching Farnley Carr.'

'I'll take you there.' Rhona wondered why on earth she was making the suggestion. 'It isn't all that far out of my way.' And I know it very well, she thought wildly, it's only a few hours since I came away.

'That is most kind of you,' the woman said, getting into the car. 'I am Beatrice Richardson, I'm trying desperately to reach my husband as swiftly as humanly possible.'

'Aye. Well, you'll know we won't be all that long.' Rhona was hoping they wouldn't have to keep up a conversation. She'd enough to concentrate on, trying to still the agitated pulsing of her heart. Fortunately, the blizzard seemed to be abating as suddenly as it had arisen, staring through the snow wasn't as difficult now.

'My husband's responsible for construction of the new reservoir,' Beatrice Richardson explained. 'I read in *The Times* that two tragic deaths had occurred there within forty-eight hours. Wolf and I might have had our differences, as they say, but that couldn't keep me away. I simply had to take the overnight train. Perhaps you know something of the accidents . . .?' Her sideways glance couldn't really be so searching as Rhona felt it to be. This had to be her own over-sensitivity, surely? Wolf's wife couldn't know of Rhona's connection with both victims, or of her connection with him.

'Yes. Both were terribly sad, I'm sure they've distressed everyone in Halfield.'

'Knowing Wolf as I do, he'll have taken it badly.'

'I'm afraid so.' Rhona immediately wished she'd kept silent.

'You know Wolf, then?' Again, Beatrice Richardson's dark eyes were scrutinizing her.

Rhona tried to appear as if she were giving her entire attention to road conditions. 'We've met.'

'Recently perhaps? At one or other of the celebrations when initial stages of the scheme were completed?'

'Er – yes. I was at the evening reception in the town hall.'

'I'm glad the reservoir received such acclaim. He deserves any acknowledgement that comes his way. Even if I couldn't see it at the time, Wolf's reservoir was much needed – and he certainly is just the person to bring such a project to fruition.'

'I'm sure,' Rhona murmured. Farnley Carr was in sight now, dominating the dazzling whiteness of the moor.

'I suppose I've matured in the past few years,' Mrs Richardson admitted, smiling ruefully. 'I was petty and small-minded about the whole damned thing. I must have been jealous – Wolf did give a deal of time and attention to that scheme.'

If Rhona had imagined herself meeting Beatrice Richardson, she'd have expected to dislike her. Here she was, though, empathizing with this frank admission of having been wrong, understanding that a different outlook didn't automatically prevent all affinity between them.

'I have a new respect for Wolf's determination, you know,' Mrs Richardson added. 'I just can't wait to be with him to share the concern because of these terrible accidents.'

Getting out of the Morris, Beatrice Richardson thanked Rhona effusively. All the while Rhona was breathing agitatedly, longing for Wolf's wife to stop speaking and close the car door so that she might drive away. She'd never felt less able to cope.

Continuing on towards Bradford, Rhona began shaking. Her hands on the steering wheel felt stiff with the effort of controlling the tremors attacking her entire body. And was her condition any great surprise? She'd been perturbed by mistaking Beatrice Richardson for Hazel. For what had felt like a very long time, she'd been bewildered, seized by an extraordinary sense of unreality. Nothing since that minute had lessened the trauma.

'I'm trying desperately to reach my husband,' Beatrice Richardson had said. *My husband*, not ex-husband. Never once during their conversation had she so much as hinted that a divorce might be pending. She'd made the trial separation sound insubstantial.

And the woman had travelled, in the depth of winter, all this way to the bleak moors of Yorkshire to be with him. Every word she'd spoken had expressed regret concerning past circumstances that had caused the rift between them. No matter what had occurred, a reconciliation appeared likely.

Last night, Rhona thought, *only last night*, she could willingly have slept with Wolf. She'd so nearly committed herself to him that she couldn't quite believe that their passion had been controlled before its consummation.

Approaching Fletcher's works at the far side of Bradford, the car skidded and almost hit a gas lamp. That's it, Rhona decided, enough! She would have to end this disturbance before it got more of a hold on her emotions. She would keep right away from Wolf. She'd been brought up to a firm belief in marriage. She would give his marriage every chance.

Dazedly she completed the business necessary for obtaining the combing machine spares, then dazedly drove back to Halfield. The snow had ceased now, but her vision seemed as indistinct as if through scattering flakes. Back at Bridge House Mill, she found that focusing on Bill as he walked between the spinning frames towards her required phenomenal effort.

'Are you all right, lass? You look fair whacked!'

'I'm okay, Bill, thanks,' Rhona assured him, with more haste than truth.

'Was there a thick snow over Bradford way?' he inquired sympathetically. 'Had a bad journey, did you?'

'It was a bit of a strain.' She was thankful to be offered some explanation for her strange manner. 'I expect I'll be fine once I get my breath back.'

Herbert Shackleton was pleased to have the spares for the Noble comb. He'd finished working on the Gill box that had been giving trouble. Rhona had noticed how he hated wasting time.

'It's a bit of a to-do, though,' he said, grinning, 'when one of the directors has to go running to pick up bits we need for t'job!'

Rhona managed a smile. 'From what I've heard, my father never hesitated over whether or not some task was beneath his dignity.'

'Tha's right there. And some of us old 'uns haven't forgotten him neither.'

That evening when Rhona went to Lavender Court, Phyllis seemed considerably improved, and was in the sitting room with her father and Clive.

'The doctor's given me pills for during the day as well as night,' she revealed. 'I never thought I'd have to take anything of the sort, but I'm only too glad to. Everybody is very kind, though, Rhona, most considerate. We had another visit from Wolf Richardson, this afternoon, and his wife.' Phyllis appeared oblivious to Rhona's feelings towards Wolf.

'Ah, yes – I understood that Mrs Richardson had returned,' she said very quickly, breathing deeply to check the flush rising from her neck.

'They offered to help with arrangements for the – the

122

funeral, but Dad Newbold already has everything in hand. You'll be there, of course, won't you, Rhona? It's to be midday on Monday at the parish church.'

'I – I'll have to see,' Rhona said awkwardly. Much as she wanted to give her friend any necessary support, she didn't think she could bear to see Wolf and his wife together there, not so soon.

It was because of another funeral that Rhona was prevented attending. Hazel was being buried on the same day. 'I'd be very grateful if you'd be there,' Tim said. 'Mother and Dad are going, but . . .'

Rhona still hadn't intended being present. Hazel's family hardly knew her, they wouldn't want her to attend. Especially if they'd heard any hint that Tim was too interested in her.

Their Stanley changed her mind for her, one evening just as she was getting ready to go out for a knitting class.

'You knew Hazel when she was little, didn't you, lass?'

Rhona waited, one hand, holding her hatpin, suspended above her head. 'And . . . ?' she prompted warily. She sensed already that she wasn't going to avoid that service.

'Well . . . none of the other fellows will be there, they'll be at work. Hazel's brother has asked me. We're not working that day, I'll not have that excuse. I tried to say no, but how could I? I know nowt about funerals, and such like, though. But . . .' Stanley paused, his brown eyes searching her face. 'Come with us, Rhona, please. You're used to church-going, and all that.'

Sighing grimly, Rhona stabbed the pin into the hat balanced precariously over one eye.

'It's going to be a bit strange, isn't it,' Stanley continued, 'with her taking her own life, and all that . . .'

'Aye.'

She had been afraid that Hazel wouldn't be buried in consecrated ground. The Wrights must have an understanding vicar.

By Monday all the snow had melted, and it was a bright day with a wintry sun turning the sandstone of St Peter's church a warm gold. Going through the arched doorway with Stanley, Rhona shivered. The interior was imposing. Its very size, rather than inspiring, made her feel slightly uneasy. Maybe with a large congregation the place would feel different. Today, especially since – so far – only about a dozen people had arrived, it felt grim.

Stan kept giving her a sideways glance as they walked slowly towards one of the oak pews near the back. Unfamiliar in a dark suit borrowed from one of his friends, he appeared even more uncomfortable than Rhona was feeling. Sighing, she slid to her knees and closed her eyes. She felt Stanley kneel beside her.

They had a long wait before Hazel's family and close friends arrived – too long, Rhona thought sadly. She could have done without thinking too deeply just now. Such a weight was pressing on her head and shoulders that she suspected she would never again walk upright, would never laugh, never talk of anything other than sudden loss, and funerals.

The coffin was oak as well, merging with the ranks of sturdy pews as Hazel was borne into the church. Rhona fancied that, somehow, the girl was becoming one with everything the Church represented. Had she been a committed Christian? How could Hazel's possible faith reconcile with her final desperation?

The flowers, covering the whole coffin-lid, were breathtaking – gloriously coloured, the only colour within the stark interior. It was Lent, the season of repentance, and all bright furnishings had been removed.

Even when she attempted to look away, those glowing wreaths drew her gaze again, forcing upon her the realization that a lass no older than herself lay in that polished wooden box.

'Such a waste,' Stan murmured at her side. 'Only a few years older than me, yet she'd had too much happen for it to be bearable.'

Swallowing, Rhona nodded. She glanced down at her black-gloved hands. She didn't want to watch the miserable procession walking behind Hazel. Her immediate family, closely followed by Tim, and Bill and Ellen Brightstone, all seemed so laden with grief that no one would ever reach them, let alone help them recover.

I could have been kinder to Tim, Rhona thought all at once, maybe he had been foolish rather than downright callous.

As the vicar turned to face them and the chief mourners filed solemnly into the front seats, the clock in the tower struck the hour. One o'clock. Across Halfield, another group of mourners would be trying to pull themselves into some sort of shape for carrying on, now Adrian Newbold's funeral was over.

I wonder how I continue believing in any of the things places like this represent? Rhona thought. If I *can* continue believing. Adrian Newbold didn't have to die, did he? And what about Hazel?

She wasn't really taking in what was going on near the choir screen, not deeply. On the surface, with a part of her mind, she was listening; sometimes looking towards the darkly clad congregation, repeatedly towards the coffin. But she wasn't letting any of it penetrate. I'm a coward, she acknowledged silently, and hoped that didn't show too obviously. I can't take any more. And it wasn't even really because of Hazel, nor of Phyl's husband, nor for the sake of the folk they both had left behind. It was because she herself couldn't risk the tears beginning. Tears for her own distress, for the man she loved who was just as lost to her as if he no longer lived.

There's no hope, she reflected: you might as well accept that, and get on without him.

Thankfully, Rhona followed their Stan out into the open air. Despite the draughtiness of the church, she'd hardly been able to breathe. Now they were outside, though, she had to face the reason for their being here. Both she and Stanley found there was no other place to focus than on the grave, and the box that would soon rest within it.

The wreaths had been removed now, the undertaker's men were preparing to lower the oak casket into the ground. As they moved, taking the weight, adjusting the coffin's angle, a glimmer of sun caught the brass of its handles, gleamed off the plate bearing Hazel's name. The light seemed to say something to her: Rhona was too disturbed yet to know what it was.

'Come on, let's see that our flowers are all right . . .' Stan had a hand on her arm, was urging her forward now that the chief mourners were heading towards the sombre black cars.

Their wreath was hard to find, there were such a lot of them, arranged all around on the narrow grass borders, some even on an old neglected grave nearby. Compared with many of the tributes, theirs was quite small. The flowers were nice, though, white carnations in the shape of a cross. Rhona had felt it had to be white. It occurred to her that that could have been because she'd frequently seen Hazel in tennis whites.

'She was such an energetic girl,' she murmured, and was compelled to turn away. Then she saw the wreath that she ought to have anticipated.

A magnificent dome of flowers, in every shade of bronze, and gold and palest lemon, so many blooms you had to wonder where they came from in February. The card was signed Mr and Mrs Wolf Richardson. The writing was a woman's, Rhona was sure. It seemed to her the final proof that Beatrice Richardson was re-established in her home.

Rhona was anything but sorry next morning when Tim greeted her with his intention of accelerating production of knitting wools.

'I've gone into it thoroughly enough and there is, in fact, very little difference between the machinery used for spinning worsted yarn and the kind for knitting yarns. The machines are modified, that's all – plus the addition of a roving frame that will twist the threads together.'

'And our mechanics ought to be able to understand how to keep it going.'

'Aye. You've come up with a winner, Rhona – we've

ordered sufficient machines already to set up production. Once we get going and turning out satisfactory yarns we'll increase the numbers. That'll mean another steam engine to give us enough power . . .'

Rhona frowned, afraid suddenly of the reality of the extra expenditure generated by her idea. Tim grinned, though, and for a second the devastation left his blue eyes.

'Dad's already accepted that we'll need more steam, the others on the board will listen to what he says. And, besides, I've heard of a right good Pollitt and Wigzell engine, second hand, but still going as strong as it did when it were built in 1910. It's a little family firm that's selling up – we'll get that engine, you'll see. Then we'll have it uprated, give it greater horsepower.'

'You're losing me, Tim,' Rhona confessed.

'Oh, aye?' He laughed. 'Don't tell me there's still summat you don't fully understand! Do you mean I can hold one over you regarding engines and steam power?'

'For the present . . .' Rhona smiled.

'Aye. I'll bet you'll be swotting up on it all now, so's you can reckon you know as much as the rest of us!'

Tim was speaking in his native vernacular, Rhona noticed, not using the elegant English he'd picked up at university. She suspected he was doing so for the purpose of convincing her that she stood as good a chance as he of mastering all there was to running Bridge House Mill. Today, she liked him for it; heaven knew, she needed some boost to her morale.

'You've brought a new lease of life to this 'ere mill, you know,' he complimented her.

Rhona raised an eyebrow. 'Oh aye?'

Seeing their first knitting wool coming off the specially modified roving frame was a tremendous thrill, though, and helped more than anything else in the struggle to put the past few weeks behind her. Here in the mill she never thought about Wolf Richardson.

Because of the differences in the processes involved, Rhona felt she was being stretched mentally in her daily efforts to familiarize herself with every aspect of wool production.

Introduction of an autoleveller on the Gill box and draw box automatically produced a sliver of wool that possessed a guaranteed regularity. From these two processes the wool moved on to the finisher which combined two ends then drafted them out to a suitable weight, and at the same time introduced a slight amount of twist.

Initially, of course, there were snags, with threads breaking at one stage or another during manufacture, but management and workers readily combined to sort out the problems. And somehow the difficulties only made the project more enthralling.

When the first good production run was completed, Rhona tried knitting with some of the new wools, and also passed on samples to the women and girls in her classes.

A week or two later they were coming up with suggestions for making Bridge House wool even better. Gradually, Rhona and Tim, working with their skilled operatives, had got the yarn as near-perfect as they might reasonably expect.

'I'm going in for designing next, you know,' Rhona confided to Bill Brightstone. 'Just you wait – one day we'll be the best-known supplier of knitting wool and patterns in the West Riding.'

The absorption with her work meant that Rhona was curtailing her other interests. There were only so many hours in every day. And even weekends flashed by. Now she was working on designs, she always seemed to have pen or paper in her fingers if she set aside her needles.

She was neglecting everyone, including Phyllis, although she felt no very deep guilt about that – the Ayntree family were rallying round Phyllis. She was also neglecting Auntie Norah, though, and she suspected the old lady would be missing her visits. Rhona resolved that as soon as she had drafted the first pattern for Bridge House wools to her satisfaction she'd see the old lady.

*

The dinner had been excellent, Stimson never let them down, but Wolf felt dissatisfied, restless, no more relaxed than he might in anyone's home but his own.

'And how is Charles?' he inquired, sipping his brandy, controlling a wistful smile as he recalled the brandy he'd shared, incredibly, only weeks ago.

'Very well.' Across the polished mahogany Beatrice gleamed, equally polished. If she hadn't always been so immaculate, he might have loved her more. Or might have loved her.

'You'll marry, of course, as soon as you're able.'

'Why not? You've made it plain enough during the past few weeks that there'll never be a reconciliation. You're tolerating me here, no more. There's someone else now, isn't there?'

Wolf stared sharply towards her. 'Why does there have to be? You've said often enough that I don't see beyond my work. Why shouldn't that remain sufficient?'

'I don't really know. There's something about you, Wolf, a new intensity.'

He willed himself not to react. 'You caught me at a bad time, arriving when I'd had such a harrowing two days.' And when I'd recognized, finally, that I was in love.

'Agreed, you weren't quite yourself. But that was no more than I expected, the reason I came. Now you're at least as composed as usual, if not more so. Careful to conceal . . .'

Wolf snorted. 'Oh, really! Just because I didn't fling myself at your bosom. That was what you wanted, wasn't it? To find me, just the once, unable to cope without you.'

'That's unjust – I genuinely did come to sympathize.'

'All right, sorry. But you have to admit you always did love to check my reactions with a massive surprise.'

'I should have learned my lesson. The response never was what I hoped. But so often shock was the only way of getting to you.'

'Let's not quarrel, for God's sake. The point of that went out of the window, long ago when you left. There's no going back.'

'Do you wish there were?' Her dark eyes boring into his skull, she was sitting very upright, her back rigid against the chair.

'You shouldn't have asked me that, Bea. I believe I shouldn't reply.'

'And if I insist?'

Her voice was even sharper than he remembered, she'd always been a determined woman, ruthless perhaps. Wolf understood how right he had been in supposing that she had thought to resurrect their relationship. Well, she'd invited the truth – there was no reason on this earth why he need mince words with her.

'Once I'd adjusted to your – departure, Beatrice, I saw all too clearly why our marriage hadn't worked. Why I was content to be rid of you.'

Her breath emerged swiftly, but her glance never wavered across the table. Beneath her perfect make-up, though, she blanched. Even she couldn't control the ebb and flow of blood.

Wolf continued, nevertheless, his tone level, devoid of cruelty. He'd been hurt once, but that was over and done, hurting was unnecessary and vindictive.

'If it had been merely that our relationship had foundered because of its monotony, and absence of common interests, I'd have held some regrets. But I didn't see until you had gone how utterly we were unsuited. I may have been intransigent about my work, and the time devoted to it – that is the way a business continues to flourish. But you are, and always have been, the most unyielding of partners. And about the one thing that might have put a fresh countenance on everything between us.'

'I never promised you a child.'

'Granted. And, foolishly, I never even questioned your willingness to bear me children.'

For the first time since she'd astonished him with her arrival, Beatrice looked uncomfortable. Glancing down, she toyed with an unused silver fork that lay beside the cut crystal wine glass.

'Women aren't merely machines for churning out heirs, you know.'

'Don't be trite with me.'

'They are intelligent human beings who need to be treated as such, and . . .'

'. . . I never treat you that way? Don't colour the truth just because it's viewed in retrospect. You know damned well I'd have shared with you each and every aspect of the business, if you'd shown one ounce of interest. Many's the time I've ached to share . . .'

'*You?*' she scoffed, all her colour returning now, and more with it, so that her cheeks more closely resembled the painted doll that he'd come to consider her. 'You were always intent only on proving how magnificently you could manage everything!'

'Because there was no alternative – *and* no other channel for my interest and enthusiasm.'

'And when did you ever share *my* interests – certainly not at all after you brought me away from London.'

'Interests? Parties, dancing, seeing how many titled people you could cultivate.'

'Wolf, my darling, you really are incredibly stuffy! We had fun, in the old days. Don't pretend they never existed.'

'Like a pair of children who had not reached maturity, and maybe never would. That is not my kind of happiness.'

'All you ever cared was to make Richardson's bigger and better, to prove you could exceed even your father's objectives. You ought never to have married.'

Briefly, Wolf smiled. There did exist the kind of marriage that would embrace all that he was doing, everything that he was about. And the right woman to complete that relationship. The last thing he intended, though, was permitting Beatrice one glimpse of his dreams. He allowed his tongue the freedom only to express the sentiments she expected of him.

'My father had built up the most competitive civil engineering business in this country. Do you suppose I would do other than everything in my power to further its success? You know as well as I do that that has meant keeping eyes and ears alert to any possible new developments. Roads, harbours, bridges, reservoirs and, these days, airports. Where they are needed is where you'll find me.'

'Like some little tin god, always too full of yourself to delegate.'

He made his expression impassive, determined to conceal that she had found a home for her words. 'That's the way Father worked, it's good enough for me.'

'And you keep more of the profits for yourself that way, too, isn't that nice?' Momentarily, she played with a strand of the exquisite black hair, tested it with her teeth, then smoothed it back into place.

She looked coquettish then, he thought, it no longer suits her. 'You did not once grumble about the profit I made. Doubtless you'll extract all you can when the divorce is finalized.'

'As you are aware, Charles has only his army pension.'

'You won't go short, you have my word.'

'And now you want me out.'

Wolf shrugged. 'It's a matter of indifference, actually. Farnley Carr is big enough for both of us, for a time. But the pretence is over. You and I shall not go out together, anywhere, again. If I'm not using the car, Stimson will have my permission to drive you where you will. Otherwise, you must go by hire car.'

And this truly is the end, finished, he thought. For a time he had permitted their joint outings, had allowed that she might have been motivated to return by sheer sympathy. Now he was certain she'd contrived a great deal in her last-ditch attempt at a reconciliation. Was it because he was more wealthy than Charles Ferris? Or because he was younger? More attractive even – no one could deny that poor old Charles was over-fond of a good table, and a full glass, with a figure that witnessed to indulgence. Wolf found he did not care about her reasons.

'I'm not sorry I came,' Beatrice announced. 'But I shall be glad to return to London tomorrow.'

8

One bright spring day Rhona drove out to Aunt Norah's cottage, smiling a bit as she recalled that first spring morning when she'd found the old lady installed there, and so happily. Ever since then Norah Lowe had improved, growing far less confused. Maybe because people had taken an interest in her.

'You've been working too hard, you look right peaky!' Auntie Norah exclaimed now, leading the way into the cosy living room. 'But you're only doing what your dad always did. I don't expect you're going to change, are you?'

Rhona grinned as she went to sit on the horsehair sofa. 'Happen you're right.'

'*Happen*? Of course, I'm right. You're tarred with the same brush as Paul Exton – not that there's much wrong with that, far from it.'

Norah settled into her rocking chair, and asked how the new line was going, nodding her approval when she learned that good-quality knitting wool was in production now.

'And are you going to ease up a bit now, then?'

'Ease up? Don't talk daft, Auntie, this is only the beginning.'

'Oh, aye – and what's to be next, then?'

'As soon as we get folk buying our patterns as well as our yarns, we're going after other markets. There's plenty of women's magazines have started up. That *Woman's Own* is well established now, there'll be others. They can print knitting patterns just as easily as they print recipes.'

'And you're going to convince them Bridge House designs are best, eh?'

'I'll see to it that they are best.'

'Ambitious, aren't we? And what about owt else? What about getting wed, bringing up bairns?'

Rhona looked away quickly, focusing on the *Monarch of the Glen*, trying to analyse the reasons for the picture's immense popularity.

'A splendid creature, so masculine, don't you think?' Auntie Norah challenged, a mischievous gleam in her brown eyes. 'You want a man like that, confident, far-seeing, protective of his own.'

'I want time to develop my own talents, thank you very much, that's all.' And the line of that antlered head was downright *arrogant*!

'Aye – well . . .' The old lady sniffed.

Rhona could feel the steady gaze still scrutinizing her face, but she didn't hang on. Was aware of the stag, formidable as those crags.

They were having supper when Auntie Norah announced, 'I had Wolf here a few Sundays ago. And his wife. She – seems quite pleasant.'

'That's what I thought,' Rhona said very quickly.

'Oh. You've met her then.'

'M'm. As soon as she arrived back in Halfield.'

'Is she here for good then?'

'She didn't say.' And I certainly wasn't going to ask!

'It seems as if their marriage hadn't gone as far on to the rocks as he'd imagined, doesn't it?'

'That's right. Wolf must be relieved.'

Again Auntie Norah was searching her expression. Rhona hoped to goodness she hadn't gone as pale as she felt. Every time she thought about Wolf, these days, blood drained from her.

'Happen he needs somebody on his side. Although I thought . . .' Norah sighed, shrugged, and stared into the fire. 'She's a nice-looking woman, his wife. A bit too smart, though, for my liking. Brittle, expensive . . .'

Rhona was compelled to smile. 'Wolf himself doesn't exactly live modestly.'

'No, but that missus of his is different, somehow. Not as sincere as him, nor as deep . . .'

When Rhona raised an eyebrow the old lady chuckled. 'Not that sort of deep, bless you – not devious! No, Wolf's not like that at all.'

No? Rhona wondered, and wished she could be sure.

Driving home that evening she felt even more depressed.

'You've had a visitor while you were out,' her mother told her, her sherry-brown eyes aglow with excitement.

Removing her coat, Rhona wondered why Eve was so surprised. 'Oh – one of the girls from the knitting class?'

'No – Wolf Richardson. He smiled when I told him where you'd gone.'

'But . . .' Frowning, Rhona realized that she was still holding on to her coat, and hung it behind the door. She'd been about to exclaim that Wolf wouldn't call now that his wife was living at Farnley Carr. But she'd mentioned nothing to Eve about Beatrice Richardson's return. Struggling to contain the emotions threatening to gag her, she swallowed. 'Was he on his own?' she asked, trying to sound casual.

'Oh, yes.' Clearly, her mother was astonished that anyone might suppose he wouldn't be alone. 'He wouldn't stay long, though I did invite him to, he said he'd telephone you some time.'

Disturbed as she'd been already, Wolf's attempt to see her completely bewildered Rhona. That night she scarcely slept. What *can* he want? she thought over and over again. How could he want to see her now that his wife was back with him?

Although feeling desperately tired next morning, she was thankful when daylight came. Everyone accepted that the Richardson marriage was no longer in jeopardy. She herself was the very last person to do anything to alter that. If Wolf believed she would consider seeing him now, he had totally misunderstood her.

Grimly she got ready for work and, frowning, walked swiftly along to the mill. The sooner she arrived, took his call, and put him straight the better it would be for everyone.

They were trying a new range of colours now – softer hues, made with natural dyes that Bill had discovered in an old book on spinning which he'd found in a second-hand shop. The first batch had just come back from dyeing, and when Rhona saw them she groaned.

'It's not so good, is it, Bill?' she said dejectedly as they sat either side of his desk, gazing down at the thick yarn slivers fresh from the vat. The colour was inconsistent, varying from a light rust red to a much deeper shade even within the length of wool they were studying. 'It's not even worth putting this through combing and finishing again.'

'It's early days yet,' Bill reassured her. 'There's bound to be a few problems with everything new that we try. Don't get discouraged yet, lass. We'll have another go, see if we can get a more even colour.'

'Did they, though – in the old days? Maybe folk were satisfied with this sort of stuff before chemical dyes came in.'

'I don't think that. According to that book, they were obtaining good results. And if they could manage it, all them years ago, we'll not be beaten.'

Wearily Rhona stood up. 'Ah, well – I suppose we've plenty to be getting on with, while somebody sorts this lot out.' Demand for the yarns which they were already selling was rising week by week. By the end of the month they'd have difficulty keeping production ahead of requests. And that meant working flat out, through every stage of production. Until she had established a solid demand in the shape of regular orders for Bridge House wools, they couldn't think of taking on more staff, nor buying more machinery.

'Aye.' Bill smiled. 'You go along and have a look at what's coming off the roving frame today.' He'd noticed how Rhona loved watching the finished product emerging. 'It's that blue you wanted us to try – now that *is* a great success, a right bonnie colour.'

Rhona managed a wintry smile. Today she felt unable to enthuse about her job or anything else. She sighed, squared her shoulders, and marched out through the office door. Work, that was it, work and more work. It was all that would keep her from brooding.

She was halfway down the gangway between the clacking mules when Bill called her back. When she turned round he was holding the telephone aloft and beckoning. Now, guessing who would be at the other end of the line, she was quivering with the same sort of violence produced by the mules that hemmed her in. Was the floor shaking with their vibration, or was she . . . ?

Damn him, damn him! she cursed inside her head. He's no right to get me into this state, no right at all. And I'll tell him so.

'Rhona?' Wolf asked. 'I tried to see you last evening, did your mother . . . ?'

'Aye, she told me,' said Rhona tersely. 'Whatever did you want?'

'To see you, of course. It's some long while since . . .'

'I wish I knew what you were playing at,' Rhona said agitatedly, her voice rising because even though Bill had closed the office door after him, the noise penetrated everywhere.

'There's no need to shout,' Wolf interrupted, quite sharply. Since last night he'd begun questioning the wisdom of telephoning Rhona at the mill, but felt compelled to fulfil his promise to her mother.

'Didn't know I was. But if you will ring me here you'll have to accept that there's an almighty racket goes on all the time. I can hardly hear what you're saying.'

'There's nowhere else I can ring you.'

'No. But I wouldn't have believed you'd have the nerve to bother me, anyway, not now.'

'Why now especially?'

'With your wife back at Farnley Carr.'

'Back? What on earth makes you suppose we're . . .'

'You can stop pretending,' Rhona interrupted. 'Who do you think gave her a lift to your home the day she arrived?'

'You mean – you . . . ?'

He sounded utterly shaken. Must be because he'd imagined he could keep quiet about his wife. Just for a minute Rhona ached to tell him it was all right, that there'd been a misunderstanding, that was all. Simply hearing his voice was creating within her massive surges of hope, and excitement; encouraging dreams . . . But she mustn't be soft, not for either of their sakes. She had to do the right thing, and stick by it, no matter how much that hurt.

For once, Wolf was at a loss. Because he'd never really contemplated any reconciliation with Beatrice, he hadn't realized how her return would appear to Rhona.

'We've got to talk about this, Rhona, when can we . . .'

'Talk? What good's that? Nay, you should know I'll not consider anything of the sort.' Hearing him was far more disturbing than ever she'd imagined, if she saw him again there was no way she could go on killing herself by stifling this love swelling up from her heart, pounding through her veins, *choking her*.

'I have to go now,' she gulped. 'And don't ring me again. There's nothing you're likely to say that I want to listen to.'

As she slammed down the receiver, she saw it was wet with sweat. I'm not surprised, she thought, it's a wonder I haven't passed out! She kept going hot all over, then cold, all too aware that she'd taken an irrevocable step. She felt as if she'd have to run off somewhere and have a good cry, get the man and what he was doing to her out of her system.

It's all right, she told herself silently, getting to her feet and walking unsteadily towards the office door. It's going to be all right from now on. Wolf won't contact you again, there'll be no need to explain, no need even to think about him and his wife. Only that thought didn't help, any more than any other. Trying to hurry so that the shakiness of her legs wasn't obvious to anyone, she strode through the noisy spinning shed again.

She felt sick now, desperately sick, and cold. Her heart had ceased thumping urgently, and atrophied into a leaden lump. Misgivings buzzed through her mind, misgivings generated by her growing deep intuition that she had finished with Wolf for ever, and without reasonable cause.

Nothing was right that day. Watching the blue yarn coming off in lovely thick hanks didn't satisfy her. It was a good shade, but that seemed not to matter any longer. After a while Tim appeared, walking through from the dyeing with another sample of the red they were trying.

Beside her, he held out the sample. The smell of moist wool filled her nostrils, seemed to flow right into her lungs. She didn't know how she controlled her revulsion and avoided vomiting.

'This isn't so bad, you know,' Tim said, apparently unaware of her distress. 'It's not nearly so streaky.'

'It's better than the last, I'll allow, but it's far from satisfactory.'

'But it is improved. You could sound a bit as if you appreciated that!' He grinned. 'You're a real misery today, there's no suiting you.'

'Oh, go on – it's all your imagination,' Rhona exclaimed, then turned and hurried away from him towards the Noble combing machine.

It was running very sweetly since the new boxes had been fitted. But she could have done without the reminder of that dreadful day when she'd driven over to Bradford. She closed her eyes for a moment. It's all over now, she told herself again, there's no need to go on torturing yourself. You've done the right thing, behaved the way you were brought up to behave. You've remembered that he's married. Just let them get on with it. And you've got a job here, lady, get on with that.

'Morning, Herbert, how's it going?'

Herbert Shackleton was attending to an old Gill box which seemed to break down very frequently.

'Ay, there's nowt no more I can do with this one! It's beggared – if you'll excuse me saying so. I wish you'd tell your board of directors that they can't only go spending out on new equipment for your fancy knitting wools. There's still orders for warp and weft, tha knows.'

140

'You want me to put in a word, do you, to get them to replace some of the machines that are worn out?'

'Somebody'll have to. It's time they understood that when a machine's had enough, that's it – finished. And I don't ever say nowt can't be done, unless it's so. I don't want any of you lot spending brass that might be coming into our pockets instead!'

Rhona grinned. 'Glad to hear it, Herbert. Actually, I've never doubted that you always do your best to make every bit of machinery last as long as it possibly will.'

Herbert grinned back at her. 'That's all right then.'

Restless, Rhona hurried back towards the office. She had her own desk in one corner where she drew up designs for patterns, and spent every minute she could snatch translating her ideas into knitting instructions. Still shattered, she was going to need all the concentration she could muster to work on even this favourite task.

Each time she attempted to express her sketches in numbers of stitches, and knitting and purling, her mind began straying. Instead of the yarn and completed garments, she was seeing a silver-white landscape, the reservoir by moonlight, and Wolf at her side. No matter that they both had been so deeply distressed that night, for the first – and, she was afraid, the only – time they couldn't have been more close.

'Why couldn't you have kept right out of my life now?' she murmured, agonized, while the office was empty. However would she learn, all over again, to remove from her head all the echoes of his voice? And how would she still the attraction that even now was like the source of a volcano churning deep inside her?

That night again Rhona hardly slept, but by morning she'd decided on something positive to oust Wolf from her mind. She approached Bill as soon as she arrived at the mill.

'We've got several designs to offer and quite a number of shades of wool. If you can spare me for a week or so, I'd like to go to London now. Show the editors of some of the magazines what we can do.'

'In a while – just leave it for a bit, will you, Rhona love? Only until we've got these new natural dyes to our liking. I need your eyes, don't forget, for that job.'

Rhona had forgotten. The constant checking of shades had become so much just another part of her routine that she had stopped considering how essential it was. Although compelled to agree, she resented being kept in Halfield when she needed so desperately to get away.

'It isn't as if I was planning a holiday,' she said to Eve one night as they washed up. 'It would be work – harder work than I've tackled so far, I'll warrant – them Londoners are tough business folk, and'll want some convincing that they should go for the stuff we're offering.'

'And you need to get right away from him at Farnley Carr, that's it, isn't it, love?'

'What makes you say that?' Rhona clung on to the plate she was drying, afraid that she'd give herself away by letting it crash to the linoleum. 'Have I said one word about him lately?'

'No. And happen that's the reason I've jumped to this conclusion. Ever since he called here when you were out there's been a noticeable silence. I'm your mother, love, and I'm not daft.'

Rhona gave a tiny snort and polished the plate as if to wear away the tea towel.

'Don't tell me if you don't want to.'

'There's nothing to tell. Wolf telephoned me at work, and I told him I didn't think seeing him was a very good idea.'

She didn't feel she could face explaining to her mother about Wolf's wife and was relieved when Eve confined her astonishment to a curious glance.

When her daughter didn't confide, Eve didn't persist. She'd never been all that happy about Rhona's friendship with that fellow, anyway. She could see the lass was upset, though, and experienced an ache in her own heart.

'Maybe a holiday is what you need,' she said sympathetically. 'How long is the mill shut down at Easter?'

'It'll just be the usual Sunday and Monday off, I expect, and Saturday morning if we're not too pushed.'

'Aren't you going to take a break, then?'

'I might. Or I might just use the opportunity to get down to working out more knitting designs. We've got some summer patterns back from the printers now, only just in time for this season. Now I've got to be thinking about winter or Bridge House will be late competing again.'

'You did very well getting any patterns at all out this soon.'

Rhona grinned, leaning against the wooden draining board while her mother covered the quart milk jug with its bead-fringed cover and put it to keep cool at the top of the cellar steps. '*You* might believe that, Mum. The only thing that counts out there is having stuff on show.'

'I only worry in case you're working yourself too hard.'

'You know what Auntie would say – "that never killed nobody".'

Eve's brown eyes twinkled merrily. 'Which really says . . .'

'I know – not what she'd mean it to! Don't you go all pedantic on me. I had to mind how I talked, didn't I, once.'

Regarding her daughter carefully, Eve paused before going through to the living room. 'Do you miss teaching, Rhona love?'

'Sometimes. Not that I have much time for brooding very often. And I always suspected I'd do something different from teaching just knitting and sewing, didn't I? Not that I thought of anything to do with the mill.'

Nowhere but the mill, though, could have absorbed her so completely, making her feel that she'd a place in the hub of production. And nowhere else would have provided such interest to spill over into her leisure hours.

To Rhona's surprise, Tim was the next person to try to get her to have a change of scenery over Easter, and to take that break with him.

'I'm going off to Bedfordshire,' he told her one evening

143

when they were tidying the office ready for going home. 'My Auntie Mabel runs a fish and chip shop down there. I pull her leg because their fish aren't a patch on what we get round here, but she only laughs. Anyway, she's asked me to go for the weekend. You could come as well – all above board, and that. Her family have all left home now, she has plenty of spare room.'

Consternation sent Rhona's pulse thudding. For weeks now Tim had been careful not to suggest anything between them. She'd been so relieved, certain that Hazel Wright's funeral had brought home to him the unreality of having any kind of relationship with her. She'd been so *sure* that she never again need worry about having to put him off.

'Thanks, Tim, but I've a lot of designing to get on with.' She was holding her breath, praying he wouldn't argue. She had liked Timothy much better these past few weeks when he'd been concentrating on work. And, by all accounts, he still spent a lot of time with Hazel's parents, something else that increased her liking of him.

'Fair enough,' he concurred easily, and Rhona began breathing again. As they were going out through the door into the street, however, he turned to her once more. 'You're doing too much, though, Rhona. Don't lose the habit of relaxing, if only now and again.'

'I'll relax, all right. When we've got our knitting yarns and patterns well and truly launched. When I've got all them smart magazines clamouring for our designs.'

It was to be two years before Rhona could make her planned sales trip to London; impatient though she was, she had to learn to bide her time. While Tim was staying with his Aunt over that Easter in 1936, Rhona received an agitated message from Ellen Brightstone. Bill had suffered a massive heart attack. He was admitted immediately into Halfield Infirmary, Tim was sent for, and Rhona kept Ellen Brightstone company as they desperately awaited any slight improvement in her husband's condition.

Within a week Bill was regaining consciousness, but the doctors remained gravely concerned about his health. The consultant said the upset of Hazel Wright's death could have contributed to the illness. And he wasn't helped by his inability to take things easy regarding Bridge House Mill.

There was no question now of Bill being fit to return to the mill in the foreseeable future, if ever. The long hospitalization would be followed by an even longer convalescence. And as soon as he could make himself understood, Bill had extracted Rhona's promise to stay in Halfield and help Timothy to cope. Her disappointment at being unable to surge ahead with all her plans was intense; only the relief in the old man's eyes eased her frustration.

It does always seem to be me who has to give up what I've set my heart on, though, she thought on a particularly wearing day. But I'll show them, when I get the chance! And she would use the time now to invent more unusual designs, and maybe even better yarns to go with them.

'Never mind, Tim,' she said, one day at the mill when he was depressed about the poor progress his father was making. 'One day – when your dad's right again, and we're back to normal here – I'll go off and make our name with all them clever folk in London. There'll be no stopping us after that. And we'll have such a celebration!'

9

The time had come at last, or the start of it all. Rhona was sitting in the London train. She was wearing a new suit – a very special suit, designed by Coco Chanel. She'd chosen navy blue because it would look business like, and with its easy-fitting skirt and jersey jacket it was comfortable as well. Her blouse was white crêpe-de-chine, but made of rayon. The silk crêpe-de-chine was in her suitcase, reserved for all-important meetings with magazine editors.

Smiling rather ruefully, Rhona eased her feet out of her shoes, but thought better of it and hastily slid them on again. She'd lashed out on these because they looked just like a pair worn by Ginger Rogers in *The Gay Divorcée*. They were so slim fitting and their heels so high, she couldn't imagine how anybody could have danced in them. But then Ginger Rogers wouldn't have been standing around Halfield station for half an hour.

Being so early was Tim Brightstone's fault. Not wanting to leave her own car at the station all the time she was away, she'd accepted his offer to drive her there. And he'd been far too soon picking her up.

If she hadn't been so elated, Rhona would have been quite cross with him for allowing her no opportunity for saying more than a hurried goodbye to her mother. It was the first occasion that she'd been away from Halfield on her own, and Eve surprised her by fussing.

It was Timothy's turn to fuss once they arrived at the station, and had such an age to spare. As they walked across the wooden footbridge he began asking her if she'd got her ticket safe, and was she certain she had enough money to last a week? Questions which he'd repeated over and over again as they stood on the draughty platform.

Rhona had tried not to laugh. She'd had too long to

plan this trip, hadn't she? How could there be anything she'd overlooked?

She wondered about taking her hat off, but decided it was safer where it was. She daren't contemplate placing it on the rack. Supposing somebody rammed a great heavy suitcase on top of it? The prospect alone made her feel ill. Determined not to be thought a country cousin from up north, she'd bought a Schiaparelli creation. It wasn't one of her more outlandish designs – just a neat little thing that perched on the front of her head, slanted over one eye with a bow and a lot of navy veiling that was stiffened to stand out all round.

As the train began chugging urgently and pulled out, Rhona smiled again, relieved. She was on her way! She opened the copy of *Vogue* that she'd bought to look at on the journey, but as the engine poured out more smoke and gathered speed for the gradient, she felt her heart racing and guessed she'd be too thrilled about what was happening to concentrate.

Tim would be on his way to the mill now. She'd got him to leave her as soon as she was settled in her seat. She wasn't used to saying goodbye to folk. Except for Bridge House Mill, she hadn't known what to talk about while they were waiting. And Tim had told her to stop going on about the place.

'Do you think there's only you who cares about the mill?' he'd teased. 'It'll still be here when you come back, and so shall we. Nothing will've changed, not here.'

His grin had faded suddenly, and Rhona realized he was jealous. Always, when they'd discussed her long-awaited visit to London, he'd appeared enthusiastic – until today. When she was the one who was setting off and he was left at home.

We couldn't both come, could we now? she thought, and wished – just for the moment – that they could have. Tim wasn't so bad, these days, not so bad at all. They'd been through a lot together, these past two years, crisis after crisis with his dad, panics about one thing and another at the mill. He'd had to get over whatever emotions he'd experienced when Hazel died, and get over them quickly. He'd grown up a lot, although he'd got his sense of humour back again and somehow he'd won Rhona round despite herself until they were the pals they'd been as children. And how he'd buckled to at the mill! There was nothing now that Tim wouldn't tackle, things were a lot different from the early days when he'd annoyed one or two of the old hands (and Rhona) by being frightened of muckying his hands.

It seemed as if all that work and responsibility had done something to him, altered a basic part of the man he was. He even looked better now. He'd been handsome before, but now he had more character in his features, was less the bonnie lad, more the mature man. An attractive man.

Attractive! Rhona thought and quickly turned a page of the magazine, trying to obliterate the image of Tim Brightstone that threatened to fix itself on her mind's eye. Was she going soft or something, feeling this way about him, just because they'd said 'ta-ta' for a few days?

It might have been fun having Tim come with her to London, though – nice to have somebody to discuss the day with in the hotel. He could be good company; if they could laugh at some of the traumas of the last couple of years, they'd have had a right good time together amid the bright lights! Aye, she thought wryly, and that wouldn't have done, would it? It was work she was coming all this way for, wasn't it? *Work*.

Rhona was sitting with her back to the engine, she wasn't risking smuts drifting in on to her new clothes. She could still smell the smoke, of course, not that she objected to that. There was a special excitement generated by the sulphury fumes, and the breathy chuffing of the engine. It took her back to seaside holidays, or days at Blackpool or Morecambe when she and Daniel and Stanley were all small.

And this is all so very different! she thought, a touch of fear increasing her exhilaration. These few hours were a kind of limbo, just a matter of existing until she arrived

148

in London. She had done all that she could in preparation, and prided herself on being thorough.

In her suitcase, along with knitted garments that showed to advantage all the varieties of wool they produced, were new patterns only yesterday collected from the printer's. And in case those weren't sufficiently up to date she'd sat up very late every night for the past three weeks, working on even more designs, doing sketches, and knitting sample squares to demonstrate how certain stitches would appear. If these magazine editors were not impressed, she'd like to know what they were seeking.

The unavoidable delay had meant that they had now perfected production using vegetable dyes. Rhona wondered if the subtle shades might be of more interest than some of the harsher colours obtained from modern chemicals. They specialized in fine, two-ply wools as well, some intended for baby clothes, but not all – she'd done a lot of this very fine knitting for herself, creating sweaters that were as thin and soft as the finest silky blouses.

Most important of all, though, were the suits. Rhona had taken for inspiration the easy lines designed by Chanel, but had created patterns that might be knitted by ordinary women who would never dream of owning even a poor replica of a Chanel outfit. She had made one up for herself in an exquisite dark green which even she acknowledged was enhanced by her red-brown hair.

She would show this, wear it maybe, for meeting the *Woman* and *Woman's Own* people, and pray that one or the other would feel it might appeal to their readers.

London was noisy: busy with the whistle of trains, clattering of thousands of feet scurrying from, and towards, carriages swiftly disgorging and re-filling. It hit her with a near-physical force that would have been alarming if she'd been less stimulated. As it was, Rhona only glanced around her all the more eagerly as she emerged from King's Cross station and hurried to join the queue for taxis.

An elegant middle-aged man in a dark suit and bowler

hat, complete with a neatly furled umbrella, stepped forward from just behind her as Rhona reached the head of the queue and began walking towards the approaching taxi.

'Excuse me,' she said firmly, stared witheringly into his cold grey eyes, 'it is my turn.'

She saw him colour and felt satisfied as he dropped back a pace or two. Clearly, she gave the driver the name of her hotel, and waited until he had stowed her luggage before nipping smartly into her seat.

. When the driver slowed to a halt outside the Bloomsbury hotel she'd chosen, Rhona took one long look at the immense building, its brickwork soot-darkened to a russet shade, and decided that this was quite imposing enough for her. Now for it, she thought, her heart quickening. Picking up her case, she strode swiftly up the few steps to the entrance.

Substantial revolving doors urged her smoothly and silently into the foyer. Glancing about, she smiled, her involuntary gasp just about contained. The multi-coloured Axminster carpet stretched as far as she could see, beyond the scattering of well-upholstered chairs and low tables of gleaming mahogany.

She'd received plenty of advice from countless people better travelled than herself, and recognized the formidable long counter as the reception desk where she must announce her arrival.

Nervously, she cleared her throat and began crossing what felt like an acre of luxurious carpet. To her it seemed that all the people sitting around paused, mid-conversation, to scrutinize this addition to their company.

And so what? Rhona silently demanded. She was as good as any of them – wasn't she. She'd nothing to be ashamed of.

'Good afternoon, madam. Can I be of service to you?' began the fellow behind the counter with a face as tight as his smart dark uniform.

'Oh, yes, I – thank you. I'm Miss Hebden, from Halfield. I've booked a room. I'm a bit sooner than I said in the letter, I didn't realize it's only a few minutes' ride from King's Cross.'

'Ah – yes. Miss Hebden.' He slid an open book across the highly-polished desk. 'If you would sign in please, madam. Room ninety-eight, you will be shown the way . . . Ah – Staggers, take madam to her room, will you?'

A boy, who didn't look more than ten but could have been nearer fourteen, had appeared as though by telepathic arrangement. Following him to the lift, Rhona tried not to grin. He was a dapper little thing, beautifully got up in a dark green uniform with gold buttons, but so very tiny her suitcase appeared bigger than the lad himself. Rhona nearly forgot herself and said: 'Here – let me take that.'

Once inside the lift he closed the gold-coloured gates with a flourish and pressed the buttons with an autocratic air. The lift was as nicely furnished as the rest of the hotel. The corridor where they emerged was no less opulent. At intervals between the ranks of closed doors were set small tables, all bearing exquisite arrangements of daffodils, tulips and forsythia. The carpet was a soft green. Half closing her eyes, Rhona could imagine she was in a long narrow garden.

'The bathroom is along the corridor, there – to your right,' the boy told her, his voice almost as grand as the reception clerk's. 'And here, madam, is your room.'

Deftly he inserted the key, turned it, then solemnly presented it to her. Still with a flourish, he took her suitcase through and placed it on the luggage stand. 'I trust that you will enjoy your stay with us, madam.'

He didn't leave, as Rhona expected, but remained, staring steadily straight ahead. Just for a moment, she felt disconcerted. Something was expected of her, and she wasn't quite sure what . . . She remembered then, only just in time. Feverishly searching in her smart new handbag, she located a shilling and handed it across.

'Thank you very much,' the lad began automatically, then felt the size of the coin, looked down, and beamed.

'Cor, thanks, miss – ever so! He gave a sharp little nod of a bow, and almost ran from the room.

Even before she had removed her hat, the telephone on the pale bedside table startled her.

'Hallo,' she began, rather breathlessly, noticing her palms were moist with perspiration, and she was clutching the instrument as though it might escape.

'Miss Hebden? I have a message for you, from the editor of *Woman* magazine.'

'What is it?' she asked anxiously, visualizing the cancellation of their meeting. She couldn't bear to have something go wrong with even one of the interviews that she had arranged.

'Their editor rang to say she regrets she cannot see you personally tomorrow. Her deputy will be pleased to meet you for luncheon instead – at Rule's Restaurant in Maiden Lane. If you ask the clerk on duty at the desk here, he can direct you . . .'

The news perturbed Rhona. Firstly, she felt deflated. She'd so looked forward to seeing the offices of *Woman*. Only a new publication, it surely must have very modern premises. Some of the other magazines, she had been warned, were in old buildings, anything but impressive. She was relieved, though, to learn her plans were merely amended, not cancelled or postponed. Seeing any London restaurant ought to prove interesting. But that was tomorrow . . . This evening offered its own interest.

Although a little apprehensive about dining alone in a London hotel, Rhona was eager to see more of the place. This bedroom was beautifully decorated in shell pink and cream, with a carpet so pale that she marvelled that she hadn't been asked to change into house-shoes or slippers. On the bedside table was an Art Deco lamp, with its twin beside the dressing table miror. A side table held ornamental figures of the opalescent glass popular a decade or so ago.

The restaurant was on the ground floor, so magnificent that Rhona had to draw in steadying deep breaths to give herself courage to walk through the double glass doors.

But she was greeted so smoothly, and conducted to a table covered in pale apricot damask, that she wasn't permitted to feel nervous. A waiter immediately presented the menu and left her to make her selection.

Thank goodness she hadn't chosen a hotel that was any more pretentious! Here, fortunately, the menu was in English and the dishes, in the main, familiar. She chose mock turtle soup to be followed by roast beef and Yorkshire pudding.

Hungry now, she discovered the soup was delicious. The beef, too, when it came was good, but the Yorkshire pudding was as flat as shoe-sole leather, nearly as tough. Were Londoners content to put up with this?

She gazed around at the high apricot-coloured walls, tall windows draped with gold velvet, and wall lights reflected back from splendid mirrors. Potted palms were spaced about the room, marble pillars supported the decorated plaster ceiling.

Though still entranced by her surroundings, Rhona did not linger over coffee. She was eager to get out and see something of London.

Leaving the hotel, she paused to gaze around her at the tall brick buildings, rows of enormous houses and several other hotels, set around a large square with a garden beyond iron railings in the centre. She walked on over wide pavements, careful not to catch her high heels in the round coal grates that she passed. And then she stood, motionless, looking towards a magnificent colonnaded structure.

I'm sure that's the British Museum, she thought. A glance at her street map confirmed that it was. She would love to have a look round, wished already that she were staying longer.

Determined on riding on the Underground, Rhona entered a nearby station. It was unlike anywhere she'd ever been. For a long while she simply stared around at the people hurrying purposefully in the direction of the ticket office, then descending on escalators deep below the city.

The tiled tunnels along which she hurried were very breezy. She had to grab her smart little hat to prevent it blowing away. The place was urgent with the distant swish of trains. As she arrived on the platform, a sudden rush of air and an exhilarating rattling thrust the brilliantly lit red train from the dark tunnel.

Rhona restrained an excited giggle as the doors slid open. She felt about sixteen, wide-eyed because so much here was new, never more alive.

Inside the compartment the seating faced inwards. Long upholstered seats divided by armrests covered in leather. The moment she had found a space the doors closed with a swish and the train went dashing onwards.

She got off at the Bank station and after a quick look at the map succeeded in finding the new Bank of England building where reconstruction was nearing completion. She had read that the massive structure should be finished within the next twelve months. Already it was most impressive, she was glad the Ayntree family had suggested that she try to see it.

Although she was feeling tired now, Rhona continued on in the direction of St Paul's Cathedral. Knowing that she had no appointments in this part of London, she was determined to see at least the outside of the building, and hoped she might return to view the interior.

She walked past the wide steps leading up to the main entrance, and crossed the street in order to pause and gaze at the magnificent dome. Regretfully, she decided she was much too tired to do anything but take the Underground again for her Bloomsbury hotel. Even though she found London so exciting, she must remember her business meetings, for which she intended to be in good form.

London suits me, Rhona thought next morning, feeling wide awake and alert after a night's sleep.

She assembled all her knitting samples, and the collection of patterns and sketches, before dressing in her navy suit and white silk blouse.

Setting out for Rule's restaurant, she walked through from her hotel. Passing through Covent Garden, she watched traders beginning to tidy their stalls after the rush of business, begun in the early hours of that morning. Heading towards the massive portico of St Paul's church, which she had read was a restoration of the original Inigo Jones design, she glanced hastily at her wrist watch, then stood quite still to look.

Here, she knew, George Bernard Shaw had set the meeting of Professor Higgins and Eliza Doolittle in his play *Pygmalion*. Picturing the flower-seller, she half closed her eyes, surrounded by the shouts of stall holders, the clattering of barrows, the smells of apples, oranges and bananas, and of flowers. It was easy to believe that a market had existed here in some form since the seventeenth century.

Smiling to herself, she gave a tiny sigh and walked on, carefully, so that when she left the pavement her high heels did not turn over on the setts. How much there was to see, she thought. She'd never have believed that, during her long-planned visit to London, the business she was so eager to generate might be overshadowed by this longing to explore.

Approaching Rule's, Rhona felt rather disappointed. Perhaps seeing so many impressive buildings had led her to expect the restaurant also might have a porticoed façade.

Entering, her misgivings evaporated. The scene might have been Edwardian, and seemed to conjure for her all the atmosphere that existed in coffee houses and inns where literary and theatrical people gathered. Around the walls were souvenirs of the theatre – a profusion of play-bills and prints.

'Miss Hebden, per chance?'

Before she'd had opportunity for more than an eager glance to left and right she was being greeted by this tall, angular woman, whose sharp blue, very alert eyes, had been watching the door.

'Yes, that's right.'

Her hand was seized in a powerful grasp. 'I am Miss

Delvoir, of *Woman* magazine. Would you care for a drink while we consider the menu?'

Not quite knowing how to choose, Rhona was guided by her hostess, and wished that she had some of the sophistication that enabled a woman to take charge of ordering so confidently, in one of the capital's most notable eating houses.

They began discussing designs before they were taken through to their table, then business conversation was suspended until they were drinking coffee.

'That was a lovely meal, thank you,' said Rhona, smiling. 'London is tremendously interesting, and coming here today is another exciting experience.'

'I trust that it compensates for not meeting in our offices. We're still conducting round parties from continental publications. That was the reason our editor could not see you herself.'

Rhona nodded her understanding, and suggested she should now show Miss Delvoir the samples she had brought.

Without exception they were admired, but eventually the sharp blue eyes sought her own. 'You will realize, of course, that we cannot take everything you are offering, no matter how interesting we might find the garments and your patterns for them. I do, though, like the idea of those wools created using natural dyestuffs. And I cannot resist this knitted suit. In the style of Chanel, isn't it?'

Rhona beamed. 'I'm thankful it's so apparent.'

'Oh, yes, indeed. And yet there are subtle differences in your design – sufficient to prevent any possible charges of having copied any specific Chanel outfit.'

'Hers are machine-made, anyway.'

'Quite so. I'm glad you have considered the fact that we must avoid any nastiness – not to say legal problems – if we are to carry this design in our magazine.'

They began talking terms; the figures they were offering sounded high to Rhona, but she tried not to reveal that in her expression. She even suggested that there might be some kind of guarantee that their interest would continue for the following season's designs.

Miss Delvoir's angular chin was raised slightly, and the blue eyes narrowed.

'Guarantee is too specific for what we are prepared to contemplate,' she told Rhona, but with a thin smile. 'I am certain, however, that if you wish to submit further samples of work turned out by Bridge House Mill we will view them quite favourably.'

Walking back to the hotel, Rhona needed all her self-discipline to quell the urge to skip along. If only the meetings with other magazines could prove nearly as encouraging, she'd return to Halfield welling over with success.

10

Rhona could hardly believe her eyes. She'd never seen so many shops as here in Oxford Street, and such massive ones as well. She was standing opposite the great Selfridge store and couldn't haul her gaze away. It must contain every mortal thing you could think of buying.

Once inside its large doors she felt that she could have spent days, never mind hours, in this one store alone. Dizzy with the different perfumes wafting from counters, dazzled by the range of colours of miles and miles of beautiful fabrics, she stood quite still absorbing it all.

She began wandering around, saw rows of hanks of knitting wool. I want Bridge House wools and patterns here, she decided immediately, and walked smartly across to the wool counter.

Learning that the manageress of that department knew nothing about their products, Rhona drew in a deep breath and asked permission to send samples of both patterns and yarns. Although the darkly clad woman told her solemnly that she must understand that willingness to see what they could offer in no way could be taken as obligation to purchase, when Rhona turned away she was feeling thrilled.

Time seemed to be racing away, however, and she had to bear in mind her afternoon appointment. Reluctantly, she left Selfridge's and continued along the street, but she couldn't resist gazing in windows as she went.

From the moment she'd arrived in London, Rhona had considered its traffic noisy. Here red buses, black taxi-cabs and innumerable motor cars made her head buzz. She'd not have changed a thing, though, no matter how loud the clamour. She'd never felt more exhilarated in her life.

Heading towards Oxford Circus, she kept looking at

first one side of the street then the other. Noticing a sign above a hairdresser's which advertised permanent waving for ten shillings and sixpence, she wondered if a perm cost that much in Halfield. Running a hand through her red-brown curls, she smiled to herself, glad that perming was something she needn't spend good money on.

Here, though, was something she did find tempting. 'The World's Largest Fur Shop' proclaimed the sign over Swears and Wells on the corner of James Street. For long minutes Rhona gazed and gazed, devouring with widening eyes the most luxurious creations that she might imagine.

If this trip's the success I mean to make it, I'll come back to London, she promised herself. And this is where I'll treat myself.

Rhona glanced again at her watch, she would have to hurry or she'd not reach the Lyon's Corner House at Tottenham Court Road with time to enjoy her luncheon.

She still couldn't resist slowing down, though, to admire the exquisite furniture in Waring and Gillow's window. She'd never seen such beautiful stuff. I could furnish a mansion here, she thought, if only I lived somewhere a bit better than Gracechurch Street. The beautifully made items displayed here would look magnificent in the right setting, somewhere like Farnley Carr maybe . . . She sighed over leather-upholstered easy chairs and couches, velvet-seated dining chairs, whose wooden frames were incomparably polished. Tables, sideboards, escritoires, all gleaming with mirror-bright surfaces. There was ultra-modern furniture as well but none, to Rhona, so wonderful as the more traditional.

Perhaps because so much that she had seen in the London stores appeared luxurious, Rhona was sorely disappointed by the magazine offices visited after luncheon. The only rooms that she saw were furnished severely, and their panelled walls badly needed either oiling or a good polishing.

They overlooked some kind of courtyard which was a conglomeration of dirty brick walls, rusting fire escapes and windows that looked as if no one ever gave them a thorough washing.

The woman with whom she had the appointment was no less dour. Although she was smartly dressed in black with touches of white, the outfit only reminded Rhona of the waitresses at the Corner House. And the 'nippies' had been far brighter, they had ready smiles! This woman's manner brought to mind her old headmistress. Rhona determined to employ some of the self-assurance needed when she first began to teach.

The interview was so brief that Rhona was very much afraid that she'd made no impression at all with either her samples or her own approach. Just as she was leaving, though, her gloom was somewhat dispersed.

'I see you are wearing a hand-knitted suit, Miss Hebden – one of your own creations?'

Rhona smiled. She'd been feeling so deflated that she hadn't even drawn attention to the suit. 'Yes, I made this to my own design. I've offered this particular pattern elsewhere, but I can easily provide a variation – using a different stitch, altering the line of the jacket just a little, or . . .'

'It's this suit I like, Miss Hebden, we wouldn't consider it at all if there were substantial alterations.'

'And nor would you if an identical pattern were reproduced in a rival magazine.'

Briefly, a wry smile softened hard lips. 'True. Well, allow me time, and I will think about your products.'

'How much time?' Rhona asked, hoping she didn't sound too difficult, yet unable to bear waiting for a decision. 'I'm leaving London on Saturday morning.'

'We have your Halfield telephone number. And your hotel number, in the unlikely event of our wishing to contact you before you leave.'

Later in the week, when she saw representatives of other magazines, Rhona was relieved that she hadn't known from the beginning how unforthcoming they would prove. Their common reservations about Bridge

House Mill's products made her doubt her own selling ability.

She wouldn't want to go home if she didn't get any more firm offers of doing business before the weekend. Although she'd loved her introduction to London, all that seemed spoiled now, and she felt too afraid of having failed to enjoy continuing to explore the capital.

By early evening on Friday she was feeling thoroughly depressed. It seemed now as though her only good meeting had been that first one, in Rule's restaurant. I shan't be able to face Bill Brightstone and the other directors, she thought, nor Timothy. Anybody else could have done far better than I have, certainly no one could have done worse!

The telephone was ringing as she went into her room to prepare for dinner. Something made her suspect it could be Tim Brightstone calling to ask how she had fared. Lifting the receiver took all her willpower.

Immediately, she recognized the voice of the woman who'd been the first to appear unenthusiastic about their designs and yarns. Cringing, Rhona listened.

'We have been considering the patterns and the samples that you showed me earlier this week, Miss Hebden.'

'Yes,' said Rhona tentatively, holding her breath and steeling herself to accept dismal news.

'And we like many of your designs. Your wool also appears to be of a quality which we might recommend to our readers. We spoke of the suit pattern which you claim you can produce. If we can have it within two weeks, as you indicated, we will feature it in one of our summer issues. Providing quality is maintained, we would consider publishing your designs regularly, with each new season.'

'Thank you very much,' Rhona exclaimed, smiling widely. 'I'll see you have that suit pattern long before your deadline. Have – have you any ideas on the kind of garments you might like to follow it?'

'I will leave that to you entirely. Just remember that we try to remain ahead of every season, and that we go to press well in advance. But I'm sure you're well aware already of the need for such forward thinking.'

Their terms exceeded those of the first magazine. 'I'll press my board to make a deal of it,' said Rhona, sounding cautious, even though everyone at the mill would be as ecstatic as she herself was. When she replaced the receiver, she controlled the urge to race, whooping for joy, around the exquisite room. She felt certain no other occupant had experienced such a tremendous thrill of satisfaction.

The telephone rang while she was changing into her pale cream crêpe-de-chine gown for celebrating her success. For a long moment she stared at the receiver, afraid of hearing that the previous call was a mistake.

She need not have troubled. This was yet another magazine interested in their patterns and yarns. Rhona was so delighted she scarcely knew what she was doing. She would return to Halfield elated by her excellent progress, could hardly wait now to tell everyone.

Tim met her at Halfield station. Rhona couldn't believe it was only days since they had stood there beside the other track, saying goodbye.

'How did it go?' he inquired immediately, seizing her suitcase.

Rhona had planned to tease, having him on that she'd not achieved a thing. But she was too thrilled to keep the news quiet.

'Three, possibly four, magazines wish to take our designs, and they'll recommend our yarns. Getting them to agree was far harder than I expected though. Right up to last night I was terribly afraid I'd only interested one of them.'

'But we've done it!' Tim almost shouted. He plonked down her suitcase and pulled her to him for an enthusiastic kiss.

'You're a genius, love. I'm right proud of you.'

Rhona was too elated to mind about the kiss. In any case, it seemed a long time now since there'd been any real need to hold Tim quite so far distant.

And when he stopped the car in Gracechurch Street

and invited her out to celebrate that evening, she discovered there was nothing she'd enjoy more. Or nothing
that was likely to come her way.

Tim had decided it should be a grand occasion. He'd
booked a table at the Devonshire Arms near Bolton
Abbey. Rhona could have hugged him: anywhere else that
was modern and glossy might have compared badly with
some of the places she'd seen in London. Here, she was
conscious of being back in Yorkshire, and back to an
unfolding life that she'd only dreamed might be possible.

'You've worked that hard,' said Tim, his blue eyes
aglow, while they sipped sherry before ordering their
meal. 'You deserve a good time now, and a bit of a fuss
making of you.'

Sitting, after their meal, in the cosy lounge while they
drank coffee, Rhona couldn't help noticing how attractive
Timothy had become. His eyes smiled again as well as his
generous mouth, and his hair with its glossy fair sheen
made him look very appealing. He seemed now fully recovered from Hazel's death, and she was glad for him.

'You've done so much for the mill, Rhona love,' he
said, threatening to embarrass her with seemingly ceaseless praise. 'Neither me nor my dad would have thought
of producing knitting yarns, let alone have had the least
idea where to begin on patterns; or selling any of it!'

'But you might have had your weaving sheds by now,'
she suggested, wondering if he ever thought longingly of
his original plans.

Tim grinned. 'Aye – I might, and all! But I'd not have
been working so close with you, would I?'

This once, she wasn't in the mood for warning him off.
It had been a good week, and tonight a fitting conclusion
to all the satisfaction.

'I liked London a lot,' Rhona confided. 'But I don't
think I could live there. Where would I be without the
Dales to escape to?'

When they left the hotel Tim surprised her by turning
in the opposite direction from the car. 'How about a bit
of a walk to give our dinner a chance to settle?'

Smiling, Rhona agreed. It had been a lovely meal, but more filling than she needed when she'd spent most of the day sitting in the train.

The night was fine; chill – as spring evenings were this far north – but so clear there seemed to be millions of stars in the navy-blue velvet sky. Rhona found it hard to credit that this was the same sky that had looked so different from among the city's tall buildings. There's so much space here, she thought, breathing deeply as they walked along the road.

After a few minutes Tim led the way through an opening in the wall beside them, than caught her arm so she would stand still and look. Over the hillside was a half-moon, illuminating the ruins of Bolton Abbey on the river bank. Alone, she might have found the pastel-grey ruins eerie. With Timothy, they were mystical.

'It's fair grand!' Rhona wished she were more articulate. I'm too tired, she thought, too tired to find the right words. She was glad to be here though, very glad.

'And I've a grand lass with me!' Tim murmured, his voice suddenly husky.

He drew her against him, his jacket rough through her flimsy dress, and his chin scratchy when they kissed. His lips lingered over hers, but made no attempt to part them. Something inside her said that Tim was learning. Briefly, she felt half afraid, wondering where his new wisdom would lead.

'Do you never think, Rhona, that we get on very well, these days – that we might see more of each other? If only like this, as pals, for a night out.'

'I'll admit when I was setting out for London I wished for a minute or two that you were going, and all.'

'You never said.'

'There wasn't a lot of point. We couldn't both go off and leave your dad to cope on his own. Is he all right, by the way?' She was horrified to find that she'd been too full of her own success to even ask.

'Not bad – a bit cantankerous when he can't get as

much done as he'd hoped. And when he was missing you! The mill hasn't been the same without you.'

'Get away with you, I've only been off for a few days!'

'It's felt like longer. And you haven't really answered what I asked, about us going around together.'

Rhona smiled in the darkness. 'You've picked a fine time to suggest that, haven't you, Tim Brightstone! You'll have to hold your horses a bit, won't you? I've come home with orders, haven't I – enough to keep me busy every spare minute – aye, and minutes that aren't spare and all.'

'Are you just continuing to make excuses for not letting me take you out?'

She considered for a moment. 'Do you know, I don't believe I am, not now. You'll have to be patient for a while, won't you, my lad? Bide your time, I promise I won't jump down your throat if you put it to me again when I've less on my plate.'

As Tim was driving them back to Halfield, though, Rhona smiled again to herself. Coming out like this had been exceedingly pleasant.

Rhona couldn't get used to how tiny the house looked. Ever since she'd walked across the yellow-stoned step when she arrived home from London, she'd been sharply aware of how small and cramped the place was. And for five people! At first, she told herself it was being away that had done it, making her see everything afresh. She'd waited then for the images of splendid London squares, of spacious rooms with large windows, to fade and leave her with normality.

Her memories of the capital had faded, sure enough, within just a few days of her return. But this new impression of her home hadn't changed. Each day when she came in from work there was some reminder of how inconvenient the house was. She hated having to use the outside toilet, and getting washed in the kitchen. She didn't like the way her mother had to prepare meals for the whole family in a kitchen that was no more than a tiny scullery. They had to boil all the hot water needed, either in kettles or in the enormous copper. While she had all that money she'd inherited, sitting there in the bank earning a few pounds interest, but otherwise doing nothing.

If they purchased another house, somewhere larger, more modern, they could replace some of the old furniture with up-to-date pieces. Nothing ostentatious, mind – not as fancy as the stuff she'd admired in Waring and Gillow's – but good sound stuff, to go with the solid house she had in mind.

She mentioned her ideas to her mother, one hot summer day when Eve had been baking.

'You look tired out, Mum, have you never thought of having a bigger kitchen, one with its own door you could open to let in more air, and to let out all that heat from the oven?'

Eve snorted. 'What would I want with a bigger kitchen? I manage very well in this one.'

'And look like a rag at the end of the day! There's no need for that, Mother, you know there isn't.'

'What's got into you, all of a sudden? Am I looking that old now? I know I've got a few grey hairs, but . . .'

'Don't talk daft, you know that isn't what I mean. What I'm saying is it's time we were thinking of getting a nicer house, somewhere where Stanley and Dan didn't have to share the attic. You know how hot it gets up there this sort of weather.'

'They don't complain.'

'No, and they aren't in a position to do anything about it. *I* am – you know I've more than enough to get us somewhere decent . . .'

'I see,' Eve flared, her eyes glittering. 'Not decent, is it? I'll have you know, lady, that I've made this a comfortable home ever since we came here. And you're the first, and the only one, who's ever had any complaints!'

Rhona sighed. 'Mum, I didn't mean it like that. I want to make things easier for you, anybody'd think I'd suggested something that'd make them harder.'

'I've never asked for an easy life, I'm not starting now.'

'Maybe not. But you'd be wrong in your head to refuse to have somewhere nicer, wouldn't you? You can't want to spend the rest of your days in Gracechurch Street.'

'There's far worse places.'

'And better, that's what I'm telling you.'

'Oh, *telling* now, are you? I won't have it, do you hear? If you try to push through this idea of yours, I've done with you. How do you think Dad would feel, having you turn round and say the home he's provided isn't good enough?'

At that moment the door opened and Jack came in.

'Hallo, Eve love, Rhona . . .' But his blue eyes didn't light as they usually did, he was too astute to be unaware that they were arguing.

'What's all this then? Don't say you two are falling out?'

'We shan't, just so long as Madam here remembers what I've said.'

'No, Dad – it's nothing.' Leaving the kitchen as he came through to wash his hands, Rhona caught hold of his arm, gripping it fiercely. 'It is all right, really.'

'Oh, aye?' He turned away from her, and she'd never heard more disbelief in his tone.

Rhona realized now why she'd approached her mother while no one else was there, and felt rather ashamed. She'd known in her heart how her stepfather would feel about moving, and hadn't wanted to admit to herself what her suggestion could do to him.

'I think I'd better know what this is all about, don't you?' he prompted, carefully rinsing soap from his hands under the running tap before drying them equally meticulously. 'If it's upset your mother, it is my concern.'

'Well – come and sit down first, have a listen to one of your favourite records, there's that new Gracie Fields. I'll wind the gramophone . . .'

'Gracie Fields, my foot! I will not be sweet-talked by you, our Rhona, you ought to know that by now. Out with it, lass – what's to do?'

'I only wanted to help out more, I'm earning good

money at the mill, you know. And – well, there's that lot sifted away, doing nothing.'

'And . . . ?'

Rhona swallowed, watching him heading for his favourite shabby armchair, seeing him glance with satisfaction at the table laid ready for their meal.

'Since she seems to have lost her tongue now you're here, I'll tell you,' Eve declared from the kitchen doorway. 'Our home isn't good enough for her ladyship any longer, not since she's been to London. She wants a bigger house, and I don't suppose it'd stop there either. It'd be a whole lot of flashy new furniture after that, and every new fangled gadget she could lay her hands on.'

'It wasn't just for me, drat you!' Rhona couldn't help flaring back, choked because her ideas were causing such ructions.

'Don't you dare speak to your mother like that!' Jack sprang from his chair, unaccustomed rage making his thin face white. The blue eyes appeared staring now, hard as diamonds. 'You might consider yourself grown up but, by heck, if you're not careful you'll get a leathering!'

'Jack! Don't you get as bad as her. There's no cause for any of us to lose our tempers. Happen Rhona did think her suggestion was for the best. Well, she understands now how we feel, we'll say no more about it. She knows we're not thinking of moving from here to accommodate her fancy notions.'

After she had calmed down Rhona recognized something admirable in the way her mother had refused to contemplate giving up the home that her husband had provided. Eventually she apologized for distressing them both, and hoped the matter would be forgotten.

Jack Hebden began thinking it over, though; one Sunday during dinner he mentioned Rhona's proposal to her brothers. '*If* the idea came to anything, you'd both be affected, you've a right to have your say. You might be longing for a bigger place than this, somewhere more modern.'

Dan's eyes widened. 'One of them semi-detached

168

houses maybe? With a bathroom at top of t'stairs and three bedrooms.'

'Four or five happen – if that's all that'll satisfy Madam here,' said Jack heavily.

His sarcasm was wasted on his sons on this occasion. 'Five bedrooms!' Stanley exclaimed. 'Nay, that's proper ridiculous for folk like us.' He turned to Rhona. 'You *have* got a good opinion of yourself, just because you've been to stay in London. I didn't realize how far short of what you consider proper we lot were. We've always been happy here, and never ashamed to bring any of our friends home either. There's nowt no more that anybody can want, so far as I can see. And you must have kept your eyes shut in London if you didn't notice any of their slums.'

Rhona felt sick. Ever since the day of Hazel Wright's funeral she'd felt a special affinity towards their Stanley, now all that seemed destroyed. And she'd caused the destruction.

'I did say we ought to forget the idea, Dad,' she said miserably.

'It's a great pity it ever was raised.'

Unfortunately Dan was too young and too enthusiastic to let the subject rest. From time to time he'd give Rhona a dig, trying to get her to bring the suggestion out into the open again. 'We could all discuss it, couldn't we? See what the benefits of moving would be . . .'

Oh, no, she decided. If they lived in Gracechurch Street till they were carried out feet first, she'd not be the one to make things any different. She'd stirred up nothing but trouble. Stan was speaking to her only when he couldn't avoid doing so, these days.

Working to forget the uneasiness at home was no difficulty. Orders were pouring in. Since her trip to London she'd had repeated requests for more patterns. *Woman's Weekly*, which had been established since 1911 and seemed intent on keeping abreast of newer magazines, was particularly interested in all that she could offer. And each design published became its own advertisement for their yarns.

Rhona still visited Auntie Norah, and increased her visits while she felt rather unpopular at home. One Saturday they were sitting out in the little cottage garden, enjoying the scent of the roses which the warm sun was drawing out.

'What's up, Rhona lass? You're not your usual cheery self. I hope you're not sickening for something.'

'I'm all right really, thank you, Auntie. It's just that I've made a bit of a mess of things . . .' She told Norah Lowe about her attempt at getting her family a more convenient home. 'I only meant to make life easier, less cramped – and now look how it's turned out!'

The old lady sympathized when Rhona explained the ins and outs of it all. 'I'll bet there's times when your Mum thinks back to how things were at Exton Hall. She's bound to, we're all human. You mustn't take on so, love. We can't help it if our best intentions are misunderstood. It'll all blow over, you'll see.'

'I certainly hope so.'

'And I know how they must feel, don't I? Nobody could have resisted change more than me. Yet look at me now – isn't this garden a picture? I've never been more content than I am with my little home.'

You're much better in every way, as well, Rhona thought, and wondered if having Wolf take responsibility for housing her had removed a secret anxiety that originally was creating Auntie's lapses into confusion.

'What you need, Rhona love, is taking out of yourself. It's a pity you didn't call last night. I had a visit from Wolf.'

Rhona suppressed a groan. How would that have helped? Seeing him and his wife?

She watched a butterfly diving from one delphinium to the next beside the grey stone of the cottage wall, and willed Norah Lowe to change the topic.

'He was asking after you. Was very interested in your

business trip to London – and delighted that you're doing so well.'

What could she say? How *could* she be glad that he still cared? Hadn't she shut her mind to him, and shut up folk like Bill Brightstone and Norah if they mentioned his name? Because he was married.

'Time he concentrated on his smashing-looking wife.'

Norah scrutinized Rhona's expression. 'You've listened to nobody, have you! It's nigh on two years since she walked out on him again.'

Something inside her head was screaming. How could I not have known? Except by avoiding Wolf, and everywhere that he might be. She'd been very thorough. And he had his pride, he'd not have broadcast the news all round Halfield. A failed marriage might make him appear less than successful. No, that's not fair, she thought, aware that the split would cut deep, would feel raw as well.

'You can't know she won't be back again, on and off, on and off! How can they live like that? At least, they don't spoil two houses.'

'He's not like that, and you know it. Stop blinding yourself, Rhona. This time that divorce is definite.'

'Oh, aye? Did *he* tell you?' It was no good pretending indifference, not when she'd the opportunity to get at the truth.

'No. He hasn't said a word for long enough. But one of the ladies from the chapel told me at the time. Her brother-in-law drove Mrs Richardson to the station the day she left. According to him, she was full of plans for getting wed again. To an ex-army chap – colonel or summat.'

'I'll believe that when it happens.'

Rhona was deeply shaken. The sunny afternoon no longer felt peaceful, Auntie Norah had ceased to be a reassuring person whose company eased the tensions of business and of Gracechurch Street. She made some sort of excuse, hurried to the little Morris and drove away.

She headed up Moorland Road, in the opposite direction from the town. In the distance she could see the reservoir, glinting beneath the blue of the cloudless sky. She warned herself not to look in that direction. Where was the sense in reminders?

When the gleam of water had been passed, she realized how tense her neck and shoulders were, that her fingers were clenched savagely around the steering wheel. While inside her head thoughts and impressions were whirling ceaselessly, as fruitless as a busy gerbil treading its tiny wheel.

She was in no state for driving. Dully, she drew off the road and closed her eyes, resting her forehead against the wheel. This makes no difference, she told herself urgently. I haven't seen Wolf for month after month. Yet I've managed without him. I'm making something of my life, winning respect in my career. I'm getting Bridge House wools and my designs – *mine* – known all over the country. If I keep going this way I'll have something to be proud of long before I'm thirty.

It's over and done with, long since, over and done. If he'd cared tuppence for her he'd have been in touch ages ago, would have made sure that she understood the situation.

He'd made no attempt to contact her, she must accept that, no attempt at all. And then she remembered. Wolf had telephoned, hadn't he, and she'd hardly given him a chance to say a thing. Because he disturbed her, she'd shut him up. Whatever he might have said had gone unheard and – oh God, how would she bear it? – so it must remain.

11

Tim was motioning to her from the office doorway, miming something. Holding a telephone receiver to his ear? Her heart lifted, and lurched back down again.

This wasn't the first time. On the rare occasions when she had received a private call since learning that Wolf was alone now, she had experienced this same reaction. Try as she might, she couldn't rid herself of hope, nor of the longing to have him telephone her – to be granted the opportunity to re-live that previous conversation, and revise all her words.

Tim grinned as he handed over the receiver. 'Your friend,' he told her. Again, her heart surged, again she couldn't permit any elation.

The call was a surprise, nevertheless, and a pleasant one. Young Amy Lightowler had got a job serving on the knitting wool counter at the Co-op.

'I was busting to tell you, I hope it's all right phoning you.'

Rhona congratulated her, saying how pleased she was. And for a time she was reassured by the thought of girls settling into ordinary, peacetime jobs. It made her feel they were justified in the ecstasy with which Chamberlain had been greeted, after landing at Heston, waving the agreement achieved at the meeting in Munich.

Not long after that day, though, newspapers and wireless were carrying disturbing items that emphasized the reality of impending conflict. Looking back, wondering how much she had chosen to ignore, Rhona recalled how, last March, car manufacturers had ceased production and had gone over to providing spare parts for aircraft.

Uneasily, time passed and by November, Sir John Anderson had taken charge of Air Raid Precautions, and begun preliminary plans for evacuating children, blind people and expectant mothers. Once they were into 1939, men and women began volunteering for Civil Defence.

That March, a year after he had made the move against Austria, Hitler invaded Czechoslovakia. Rhona cringed, hearing the news, picturing what this must be meaning for the citizens of yet another country.

There seemed no way now of holding back the certainty of war. In April in England the Ministry of Supply was set up, and conscription of men aged twenty to twenty-one was introduced. Rhona could picture their small family decimated by the absence of her brothers.

'They'll not get me joining up,' Stanley announced firmly.

'You'll *not* . . . ?' Jack Hebden demanded, giving his elder son a sharp glance. 'What's all this, then – I didn't know we had a conscientious objector in our own home!'

'I've a right to my own mind, same as the rest of you. I've been going about a bit, haven't I, to meetings, for quite some time. You've all got it wrong. You can't fight evil with evil – killing and so on, to get your own back on t'others, simply because they pick the quarrel.'

'Ay, love –' Eve said fervently, her golden-brown eyes glistening with the concern that suddenly was impossible to phrase. 'Are – are you sure you know what you're saying? Doesn't all this mean anything to you, don't you want to keep it as it is?'

'I'm sorry, Mum. It's not quite how you make it sound, but I have studied this out. That's what I feel. I'm stopping over here.'

'Nay, lad, they'll never let you,' Jack put in, trying to conceal the extent of his alarm. 'You don't want locking up, do you? That's what'd happen if it does come to a war.' Sadly, he shook his head, he'd never thought a son of his would turn out this soft.

'Nay, I'll not go to prison, that'd help nobody,' Stanley responded. 'I have thought this out, you know. I shan't be sitting on my backside. I shall go down the pit. They'll not be able to get enough miners once this lot starts.'

Afterwards, when Stanley went out to the snooker club,

(if that *was* where he went) Rhona tried to console their parents. Sitting either side of the fire, they were dreadfully quiet.

'If they do need a lot of miners,' she said, 'they'll be glad there's folk like Stan thinking the way he does.'

'Well, you needn't upset yourselves about me,' young Daniel told them. 'I'll be joining up, soon as they'll have me. You needn't fret, Dad – Mum, you'll have one hero to be proud of.'

Right up until the last, Rhona kept trying to believe the war would make no substantial difference to her career. But by that August, when Ribbentrop and Molotov were signing the non-aggression pact between Germany and the USSR, Bridge House Mill was preparing to go over to spinning yarn for uniform cloth. Any knitting wool produced would be navy, air-force blue, or khaki. Rhona was desolate.

She had worked as hard as she knew how to build up business for their new knitting lines. With this bloody war she might as well never have bothered.

'I just don't understand,' she confided to Tim. 'What have I done wrong that makes my success always disappear overnight?' She couldn't help feeling bitter. She'd ached to go on studying, she hadn't wanted to give up teaching to work at the mill. But she'd set aside her own inclinations and had done her best, only to have this happen.

She felt sickened when she listened on the wireless to news of Poland being invaded. Perhaps, after all, she should think herself lucky. Four out of every six schools in London were being commandeered for other purposes. Most of the children and expectant mothers had gone already, evacuated, miles away from their homes. It all made the compulsory carrying of gas masks and the desultory preparation of shelters in and around Halfield seem very half-hearted.

In Yorkshire, those first few days of the war felt even more unreal than in some parts of the country. Rhona,

175

along with many a thousand others, began believing there would, after all, be few other disturbances in their lives.

And then she opened the *Courier* one night and read thick black headlines that made her shudder. Alarm sent the hairs rising at the back of her neck. By the end of the article her alarm had turned to indignation, and fierce disbelief.

HALFIELD INFILTRATED BY ALIEN

Do you know your neighbour? Do we know *ours* . . .? In these uneasy days, it is merely sensible to be cautious. It was with the interests of the citizens of Halfield at heart that our reporter visited Farnley Carr to question its owner, Wolfgang Richardson. Since Mr Richardson declined to comment upon information which we have received, we can only place before you – as is our duty – the facts, as we have been made aware of them.

As none of our readers can have failed to notice, Wolfgang Richardson came to the area some six years ago, intent on making money. We do not question the benefits that have resulted from construction of his reservoir, but those among us who, at that time, entertained misgivings concerning his motivation, may have reason to feel they warranted a more serious hearing.

Mr Richardson never attempted to conceal the profitability of his civil engineering empire. Farnley Carr itself, his staff, the family limousine, witness to his solvency. Anyone conversant with the size of profits attainable within the construction industry will be aware that all these are but tokens of his wealth. The question we should be asking ourselves is where the money that was made here, in our midst, is being deployed.

It has been brought to our notice that Wolfgang Richardson is Austrian-born, a compatriot of the dictator determined to seize the whole of Europe and beyond. Nurtured by a mother who is of Hitler's stock, how can this man, who infiltrated our local society, fail to experience loyalty towards the Fatherland?

According to our source of information, Richardson already is financing schemes to facilitate the movement of German forces. For all we know, he has originated construction of the very roads over which enemy armies now progress, as they ruthlessly savage our allies whose only provocation was in existing upon land that Hitler deems should be his . . .

There was more, and it was no less inflammatory. It's only rumour, Rhona thought, diabolical rumour, put about by someone who disliked Wolf.

Empty rumour or not, though, it was spreading too rapidly to ignore. Next morning's *Yorkshire Post* carried an article which, if somewhat more circumspect, was no less perturbing. That evening letters applauding the piece appeared in the *Courier*. Rhona could not remain silent.

Over the years, many times, she had been uncertain about Wolf. This time, through the depths of her being, she had no doubts of his integrity.

Have we become so indoctrinated by warmongers, her letter began, *that we have ceased to believe in the freedom which is an intrinsic part of being British? Are we so eager to fight, that we seize this first, fragile hint that we might have located an enemy? Can we not pause to consider what Wolf Richardson has done, and is doing, for our area? As a governor of Littlewood School he gives freely of his time – time in which he might otherwise be increasing the profits which seem to cause some people inordinate alarm. He also has continued, to this day, to visit those who were re-housed following development of the reservoir.*

Where is the great British freedom for which we are prepared to fight – shouldn't we allow others the same facility as ourselves – to be judged by how we appear to those living around us?

Many of Mr Richardson's compatriots have left their home-land following the German invasion. Witnessing the grief and hardship that many Austrians are suffering, we cannot question their total aversion to all that Hitler represents. Are we to condemn, unheard, the one of them in our midst?

She could have worded some of it a bit better, if she'd had more time, but she couldn't delay trying to get this into print. Taking the letter to the *Courier* office was quicker than the post. And she wanted to emphasize that it must appear anonymously.

The elderly man on the desk was rather old-fashioned in a wing collar and a suit shiny with age. Reading through her letter, he smiled, his pale grey eyes glinting behind thick spectacles.

'About time,' he said. 'Halfield shouldn't be seen as full of prejudice. And I'm glad *you've* spoken up – Miss Hebden, isn't it?'

'Yes,' Rhona confirmed, rather puzzled. She was certain she'd never met this man before.

'You've forgotten to sign this, I see,' he observed, frowning.

'No, I haven't forgotten. I'd rather remain anonymous – for personal reasons.'

'Oh.' Disappointed, the man looked from the letter to her, then back. 'I – er, if you would excuse me for a moment, Miss Hebden. I will see what I can arrange.'

He disappeared through a highly polished walnut door, leaving Rhona anxiously considering what he had said.

The door swung open again, admitting a heavily built gentleman whose demeanour suggested authority. Rhona was not surprised when he introduced himself as the editor of the *Courier*, Christopher Wellington.

'I'm delighted to meet you at last, Miss Hebden. I knew your late father well, I'm coming to respect you as a worthy heiress to his ability.'

'But . . .' she began.

Smiling, he raised a large hand that looked more suited to a butcher. 'No, we have not met previously, but you

178

have made your mark in Halfield with your foresight and diligence.'

Flabbergasted, Rhona gazed and gazed at him. Mr Wellington took out an exquisite gold pocket watch.

'And now – to this present business. You are to be commended for this admirable letter. We are going to press at the moment, I shall ensure it space, in a prime position. Contrary to popular belief, we do aim to present a balanced view. No one could have better expressed the right, and fair, opposition to the rumours we investigated. The only question is to how this will be presented.'

'How? I . . . ?' Rhona didn't quite understand.

'I am sorry you do not wish to append your name to this letter. Even if you are unaware of it, Miss Hebden, you're admired locally for tenacity, common sense and sheer hard graft. You should be straightforward about your opinion, by aligning your name to the cause of truth.'

Although he'd spoken at length, allowing her opportunity to recover from learning that *her* name might influence anybody, Rhona still was too stunned to say very much. Christopher Wellington was smiling encouragingly, one eyebrow raised.

Contrary to her intention and against her better judgement, Rhona acquiesced. Thanking her, the editor came round the long walnut counter and escorted her to the office steps, where he shook her firmly by the hand.

Rhona walked dazedly along the street. Suddenly, she had difficulty recalling her reasons for not having her name appear below that letter, but changing her mind seemed significant.

Somewhere deep inside her stirred a strange exhilaration. Her heart was pounding in her chest, yet alarm was draining from her. She'd never imagined that she possessed much courage but, just this once, she felt satisfied that she'd found a bit of courage from somewhere.

She pictured Wolf reading what she had written and visualized him smiling to himself – if not entirely without amusement, at least with some pleasure. And he would know that she no longer snarled as she had that time over the telephone.

The first reactions to publication of Rhona's letter were from her family, and surprised her by being cool, if generally approving. They said so little, in fact, that by the morning following its appearance she was feeling disappointed. If no one takes any more notice than they have, she thought, I might as well have saved myself some time. Even though she had been so astounded that the *Courier* editor might think she would have some influence, suspecting that he was wrong didn't go down very easily. That morning Herbert Shackleton waylaid her.

'You're being a bit venturesome, aren't you, Miss Rhona? I hope you know what you're doing. If that man does turn out to be a Nazi, you're going to cop it, and no mistake.'

'I'll worry about that if it happens, Herbert. I don't for one minute consider that he might be.'

'All t'same, I don't think you ought to be sticking your neck out like that. You could get us all involved, tha knows. We could lose a lot of custom if he were a Jerry, and they turned against his friends.'

Briefly, Rhona felt like telling him to leave such anxiety to Bill Brightstone or the board of management. But she wouldn't say anything of the kind, not to Herbert, who was a likeable chap, and a loyal employee. And, although neither Bill nor Timothy had mentioned the letter, she ought perhaps to clear the air with them by bringing up the subject.

As it happened, they were both in the office, so she wasted no time.

'I've just been told off by Herbert Shackleton for not considering the mill before I wrote to the paper. Happen I'd better find out what you two think, so I know where I stand.'

Hesitating, Bill looked up from his desk. Tim, standing beside his father's chair, had no reservations.

'As a ploy to get back into favour with Richardson, I daresay it'll succeed, admirably . . .'

'As *what*?' she demanded, furious. 'That was the very last thing I was thinking about when I wrote that letter. As a matter of fact, I wasn't going to allow them to put my name to it. It was only because the editor of the *Courier* was so insistent that I allowed them to print my name.'

'Phew! Sorry, old love,' Timothy began, about to take her arm and apologize.

Rhona shrugged his fingers off the second they brushed her sleeve. 'Forget it! It doesn't matter.' She moistened her lips. 'What about you, Bill, what did you make of it?'

'I can't believe for one moment that Richardson would support Hitler, and when I read what you'd said, I wished I'd had the guts to write that myself. Speak as you find, that was one code your dad lived by. You won't go far wrong if you go on as you are.'

Despite her reluctance to hear him out, Timothy followed her from the office.

'I've done it now, haven't I?' he said contritely. 'It was jealousy, of course, that must be obvious. I didn't want you getting thick with him again, not now we get on well together – or did get on.'

'I suppose we still shall,' Rhona admitted, smiling slightly. 'But you'll have to learn that I'm not going to keep myself to myself just to stop you fretting. You shouldn't be like that about Wolf Richardson, though, you daft hap'orth, I haven't seen him for many a month, have I?'

When she got home to Gracechurch Street that evening, she discovered that it wasn't uninterest that had muted her family's response to her letter. Dan was standing on the hearthrug, back to the fire, his face aglow with a strange excitement. And she sensed that Eve, Jack, and their Stanley, as well, were concentrating on him.

'What've you done now, Dan?' she inquired.

'Only what he's been threatening for the past twenty-four hours. He's signed on, hasn't he?' her stepfather told her, managing to issue a warning in his eyes, that too much shouldn't be said in front of her mother.

'For the navy,' Dan announced, and exchanged a smile with his father.

'Never a Hebden in the past has thought of putting to sea,' Jack informed them all. 'But I'm sure he'll do us credit wherever he goes.'

'Well, our kid,' Stan said, gravely, going to stand beside his brother. 'You know what I think about fighting, I'm not telling you again. But I hope you don't have any cause to regret your decision. Take care on yourself, think on!'

'Dinner's a bit late,' Eve said abruptly and rushed into the kitchen. After the strangely quiet meal which no one had really enjoyed, Eve spoke again. 'It wouldn't be so bad, Dan, if it weren't one change on top of another. First, there's your dad having to adapt to producing munitions, then there's Stanley making plans to go down the pit . . .'

'I shan't be going all that far away,' Stanley reminded her cheerfully.

'Then there's you, Rhona,' her mother continued. 'Having to forget all your plans.'

'It's only until the war's over,' Rhona said, trying to sound philosophical. 'We'll all adjust to what must be. And help others to adjust, and all – like Dad's doing at the works.'

Someone knocked very loudly on the door, and they all appeared to start. Rhona saw Eve glance towards Daniel, as if she half expected somebody had come already to take him away to sea.

'I'll see who that is,' Rhona offered, reluctant to leave the table, though, as if it might begin the breaking up of the family group.

'Don't forget to switch off that light before you open the door,' Jack Hebden reminded her. Precautions might be overlooked in their concerted anxiety. He reckoned he was as much in control of himself as anybody, yet it was taking all his willpower not to break. Dan was their little lad, wasn't he? The youngest, and the first to go.

Let this not be a stranger wanting to come in, he

thought. Leave us be, just for tonight. We've had enough, all of us. And this flaming war's only just beginning!

12

It was pitch black out in Gracechurch Street, so dark that she could see only a pale blur where the man's face would be.

'Rhona . . .'

'Oh.' Just the one word had been sufficient. She would know that voice anywhere.

'You – you'd better come in.'

He was immediately behind her as she turned to switch on the light again, so close that the once-familiar tang of the soap he used sent her heart pumping agitatedly.

'It's Wolf,' she announced awkwardly, and superfluously – all the others had turned, and could see well enough for themselves.

'What a nice surprise!' Eve exclaimed, rising to welcome him. 'I'm afraid we've only just had our dinner. We were a bit late tonight.'

'Please – don't worry on my account. I only came to . . .' Smiling, he glanced sideways at Rhona. 'To thank you.'

'It's my fault we're all at sixes and sevens tonight,' Dan announced unable to keep quiet about what he had done. 'I'm joining up – in t'navy.'

'Good for you,' Wolf approved, still smiling. 'The country needs energetic young men like you.'

'We don't all look for glamorous uniforms, though,' Stanley said, for once eager to let his intentions be known. 'I'm going down the pit as soon as they'll take me.'

Wolf grimaced. 'Now that's something I really could not contemplate. You have my deepest admiration. On the rare occasion that my work has taken me underground, I've found the experience grossly claustrophobic – and that was in somewhat better conditions. But there, I shouldn't put you off.'

Stanley grinned. 'You'll not do that. My mind's made up.'

'And you, Mr Hebden?' Wolf inquired, turning to Jack. 'Is the war enforcing changes in your work also?'

'I suppose I'm lucky really. The basics won't be all that different, we're going over to making munitions.'

Pensively, Wolf nodded. 'There'll be changes for all of us. I've been approached to assist with various projects, some confidential. Mostly, they're concerned with development of airfields for military purposes. There's some talk also of providing underground headquarters for leaders of the government, and of the forces.'

Wolf sat there easily, talking with her family. Rhona steadily grew more composed. When he drew her aside and suggested they might go out somewhere so that they could talk, she agreed readily.

It was strange sitting beside him in the Daimler again, and even more odd because its dimmed lights increased the feeling of being isolated together.

'Interested though I am in your people,' Wolf confided as he drove, 'it was you I came to see. There's no way I can thank you enough for taking the trouble to write to the *Courier*, my dear.'

'I couldn't let them get away with what they were saying. I was blazing mad! Really incensed. It's just typical of some folk, that narrow-minded they won't even stop to consider that the truth might be very different.'

Wolf didn't comment. She could feel the warmth of his appreciation all around her in the car, though, compensating for the dreadful blackness beyond its windows.

'Why didn't you speak up for yourself? You were given the opportunity, weren't you? *I* would have, if it had been me accused like that.'

'Partly, my lips had to remain clamped, because of the nature of the work I'm undertaking. Contracts affecting national security aren't to be aired around simply to make one person live more comfortably.'

'And have you still got folk over there?' she asked,

wondering what anguish Wolf might be suffering on behalf of family or friends.

'No one very close, but there are those who must be considered. We know it isn't only people over here who read our newspapers, don't we?'

'Well, let's hope there'll be fewer criticisms of that sort flying about now. I couldn't bear to think of you being victimized.'

Her emphasis had been on 'you', and Wolf was encouraged. He smiled to himself. 'At least, you gave me courage to approach you again; I – hope you're not sorry.'

'Why on earth . . . ?' Embarrassed, she checked. 'Oh, well . . . I did go on a bit, didn't I, that time you rang me at the mill. Do – do you have any idea why?'

'A pretty shrewd idea.' He didn't mention what it was, though, and Rhona didn't probe further. She was tingling to the tips of her fingers and toes, alive with awareness that Wolf was so near.

'I don't know where we're going,' he admitted. 'With all cinemas and other places of entertainment closed, there isn't a lot of scope.'

'That doesn't matter.' How could he think it might? 'There'll be plenty to talk about. What have you been doing since I saw you last?'

'I was planning another reservoir, not far from here – over towards Wakefield. I'm afraid the war has put an end to that. But I was going to ask about *you*. From what Bill Brightstone has told me, your wools and patterns have taken off with a vengeance.'

'Aye, they weren't doing so badly. Oh, Wolf, I'm so terribly deflated – the war's stopped us producing any fancy yarns.'

'You're deeply disappointed, that's natural. You've worked so very hard.'

'It seems as though everything I touch goes wrong, or comes to an abrupt halt. Going into the mill wasn't my idea . . .'

'But you did it – and you've triumphed. You will again, Rhona, once this wretched war is out of the way.'

'And how long do you reckon that'll take?'

Wolf sighed. 'Longer than most people expect, I'm afraid.'

'You're a great help, aren't you!' Worrying that he might take her remark seriously, she laid a hand on his arm. 'I didn't mean that. I know you have to be realistic. It's just . . .'

'You've had too much realism, maybe – giving up teaching, abandoning your plans for going to college.'

'I suppose Bill's told you all about that.'

'He filled in details following what you told me. He was so relieved and delighted, though, that he couldn't appreciate how much you were sacrificing. But I think I could, Rhona, and – *liked* you all the more for it.'

She knew he'd substituted liked for something else, for a word she'd been aching to hear from him for a very long time.

'Are you going to drive around all evening?'

'That would be an extravagance when petrol's scarce! No, I'm taking you somewhere where you once said you'd return with me.'

The reservoir was barely visible, with nothing but a gleam from the heavily masked headlamps and a tiny sliver of moon.

'And a lot of good bringing me here is!' Rhona teased. 'I can't see a darned thing!'

Wolf laughed quietly. 'I can assure you it's fully completed, and has been for many a month.'

'I had heard. Anyway, happen it'll be better to concentrate on getting to know you again. Though it doesn't feel as if we're strangers.'

'So far as I'm aware, I haven't left too many gaps in learning what you've been up to over the years.'

'It sounds like Bill *has* been busy talking!'

'Or Auntie Norah.'

'She'll have done her share! Has she talked about herself as well, though – telling you how much better she's been? Whatever else, you've revitalized Norah Lowe, Wolf – made her lose that awful confusion, given her fresh confi-

187

dence to get on with living again.' She paused. 'I wish –
oh, I wish I could start all over again, if you must know.
That I could take back all I've said to you that's been less
than justified, less than – the truth.'

'What's to prevent that? We're here, both capable of
making what we will of opportunity . . .'

'You never bear grudges, do you?'

'I've never seen reason to, with you.'

They both reflected. 'We've wasted enough time, don't
you think?'

'Aye, I think you're right.' The outbreak of war,
however unreal it might feel, had given some kind of
urgency to life, and had given her a realization that she
was too old now to be afraid of saying what she felt.

When Wolf drew her to him, Rhona found his mouth
hungrily, her own lips moist, eager. The excitement of
simply seeing him again had grown into a relentless tremor
that was pulsing through every nerve.

'I'm free now, Rhona my dear,' he told her huskily,
between urgent kisses. 'Free to love you. Make time for
me in your life, give me a place . . .'

'Do you think I haven't? How can you not know! I've
hardly stopped thinking about you since that day we met.
I've told myself over and over that I was being daft, but
I couldn't stop caring.'

'And – wanting?'

She had to give him the truth about this as well. 'Why
do you think I kept away when I believed . . . But let's
not talk about that. You – you *are* free, aren't you?'

'Yes, my love, yes.'

Her lips traced the line of his cheek, his eyelids as they
closed, then swiftly returned to his mouth. Fevered by
her desire, Wolf crushed her against him. There was no
disguising the massive need she generated by being close,
and no longer reason for any caution. For six years he'd
waited, never touching another woman, because this was
the woman he needed.

Through the silky texture of her blouse her breast was
firm beneath his fingertips. Tiny gasps interspersed her

kisses, leaving no doubt of the attraction she was feeling. Her tongue as well as his was exploring, exhilarating . . .

He found buttons on her blouse, and her fingers aided when his own seemed clumsy. Her skin was silkier than he'd imagined, a hundred times more enticing.

Against his mouth she smiled. 'Wolf, Wolf,' she murmured, stirring with a passion so fierce she suspected it never would be stilled. She ached to press him close, to go on pressing until no substance kept them apart. She'd tried to fight this undeniable force, to contain it. The years of withholding were sufficient, she needn't pretend any further denial. He was free, *free*. They would marry quickly, as soon as humanly possible. All these glorious emotions must be allowed expression.

Suddenly being with him after all this time had released her. Her fingers tingled with the need to touch him, and to hold, to learn to know him entirely. And he was no less eager to know her. His hand was warm through the thin material of her skirt, caressing, generating even more urgency.

The dismal wailing carried eerily across the water, echoed from the bleak moors, and startled them both.

'Not the siren, it can't be!'

'There's no mistaking that,' said Wolf ruefully. 'We'd better get moving.'

'No, Wolf.' She couldn't contemplate anything that might change this. 'It – it's bound to be a false alarm, all the others have been. We don't get air raids here, do we?'

'So far. I'm taking no chances. Out here there's no cover whatsoever.'

'Where'll we go?'

'Farnley Carr, of course. It's near enough, isn't it?'

Oh, yes, she thought dismally. Suddenly she felt sickened. She hadn't been near his home since that morning his wife came back from London.

'Let's hang on here for a bit.' She didn't want to see the furnishings that woman had chosen, the chairs where she had relaxed, mirrors where that immaculate face had been reflected.

189

'That's senseless, Rhona.'

She heard marching feet then, approaching through the darkness behind them. A platoon of Local Defence Volunteers reached their car, divided ranks to pass on either side. Two lads who couldn't have been more than fifteen peered in at them, sniggered, turned for a final stare.

Appalled by the gnawing frustration deep inside her, Rhona struggled to fasten her blouse.

'I think we'd better move on,' she said grimly. 'What're that lot doing out here?'

'Mobilizing, I suppose, making for their headquarters.'

'Where on earth's that, in the middle of nowhere?'

'They have use of my outbuildings.'

She could hardly concentrate on what he was saying. God, how she needed him; and to have them belong to each other, even more than to merge with his body.

Starting up the car, a smile was in his voice. 'We'll soon be there, my love.'

And all those men, those lewd youngsters, would be there as well. Watching through the night as Wolf drove up, as they went indoors. Some of them might be folk from the mill, or from the church.

'Can't we go somewhere else?'

'There is nowhere,' Wolf told her sharply. He'd not take her back to Gracechurch Street, not like this, while he was desperate to love her. 'What's wrong with my home?' he demanded, driving along.

'Nothing.' Everything. 'It'll be surrounded by the LDVs.'

'Only outside. And most likely well away from the house. You're ashamed of knowing me, aren't you?'

'No, Wolf, never, never. It's just – it's been so long.' She felt awkward with him again. 'Why did you leave it so long?'

He sighed. 'To give you space, a chance to meet someone who had no previous marriage. And chance, maybe, for you to come to terms with the real world.'

'What's that supposed to mean? What're you suggesting?'

'Only that you're a shade unrealistic, expecting an ideal situation.'

They had covered the short distance over Moorland Road, and he slowed in the drive of Farnley Carr. Grimly, he moistened taut lips. 'Are you coming in?'

As the car neared the house they heard the men, grouping over near the old stable block, receiving orders. Wolf felt Rhona stiffening beside him.

'It's time you reached a decision, Rhona. Mine was made years ago, in the first few months of knowing you. I've waited ever since . . .'

'Not quite,' she interrupted. 'Your wife's been back since then.'

'So? She stayed only a matter of days.' All at once he understood what Rhona had been supposing. 'Do you really believe that's how I'm made – that I can't have a woman under the same roof without having sex with her? If I haven't been sufficiently circumspect with you to convince you, I don't know what the blazes you do expect!'

From the way she had spoken in the past, he had believed she understood. Didn't she know how desperately he had wanted her, needed *only her*? Had she felt none of the emotions that he had experienced?

'Are you coming in?' he repeated, hating the suspension of his breath with which he anticipated her reply. When in his life before had he let one person's response so affect him?

He strode around the car and opened her door. Still, Rhona did not make a move to get out. He sensed her eyes, watchful in the darkness, swivelling past him towards the approaching platoon of men.

'Yes, they've seen us,' he said swiftly, shut her door again, and returned to the driving seat. 'That's the difference between us, isn't it? Pity I was too blinded to notice before. While I want the whole world to witness what I feel for you, you're frightened – either of caring for me,

191

or having someone find out! And whichever it might be makes precious little difference.' He needed assertion that she was his, couldn't continue wondering if she might be committed elsewhere. There was speculation enough on that score – and had been for several months. Had he been the one who could not see, because he'd no desire to, had he blinded himself to Timothy Brightstone seeing her off to London, meeting her train again in Halfield, taking her to celebrate . . . ?

The town lay below them, blacked out, the way he loathed. Because the inability to see its light had spawned his fear of never seeing her again. Well, now he'd made that long-awaited plunge. Thank heaven he couldn't have foreseen the unutterably depressing consequence.

Distantly, as if it came from another world, he heard the all-clear floating over the valley.

'There's the all-clear,' Rhona murmured beside him, terrified by the inexorability of their parting.

'There's no going back now.'

They both know he didn't mean only to Farnley Carr.

'Goodbye, Rhona,' Wolf said as he stopped outside her door.

Rhona couldn't reply. Without even glancing over her shoulder, she raced into the house and straight up to her room. Vaguely she was aware of the startled expressions of her family as she hurried through the living room to the stairs, but was incapable of speaking.

For several days afterwards Rhona contemplated telephoning Wolf. But there seemed nothing to say.

Their quarrel had arisen because of Beatrice, how could she do other than fuel it if she telephoned to explain how she had felt? It was solely because of Beatrice that she hadn't contacted Wolf before, because of *her* that she'd wished to avoid visiting Farnley Carr this time, just as she now could understand that it was because of her that she had closed her ears to all conversation about Wolf. It was her own determination to avoid the subject which had ensured that she did not know his marriage was over.

There was another problem, as well. Wolf had told her that he'd left her alone to give her opportunity to meet someone who had *not* previously been married. If she were to get in touch again, when the only explanation of her behaviour was this ridiculous inhibition, he would be certain it confirmed her inability to cope with the situation.

One evening the following week Rhona was walking along Gracechurch Street to post a letter. It was dark, she was only just able to see the tall, handsome woman in a khaki uniform getting off the bus. In the dim light the woman appeared to be smiling in Rhona's direction.

But I don't know anybody in the ATS, she thought, although the person in uniform did seem to be walking straight towards her.

'Don't tell me you haven't owned me!'

Astounded, Rhona stared and stared, trying to link the familiar voice with this person.

'I've slimmed down a bit, I know, thank goodness – that was the training. But I didn't think I'd changed that much!'

'Amy! Amy Lightowler!'

The girl laughed, sliding her arm through Rhona's. 'At last! I was getting quite worried, thinking there was summat up with one of us. Not so sure now that there isn't – you *have* missed me this last few weeks, I hope – found there was an enormous gap in your knitting class? In both senses of the word!'

'I certainly didn't believe I knew anybody in the ATS. Are you old enough, anyway, for joining up?'

'How old do I look to you? I had to do something, hadn't I? All my brothers have, and my dad. Mum's joining the WVS and all – learning first aid, then she's going to teach it, so she says.'

Rhona smiled to herself, trying to picture tiny Mrs Lightowler summoning enough presence to teach anybody anything.

'I know,' said Amy, sensing what Rhona was thinking.

'But she's changing a lot already, having everybody going off to do their bit.'

'And when are you off, Amy love, or are you stationed somewhere round here?'

'I wish I was, but we're going down South. I'm home on a forty-eight-hour pass. Not that I mind being away like that, in some ways. I've made a lot of friends already. Though I'll miss folk like you.'

'Well, I'm delighted you've come to see me. You'll have a bit of supper with us now you're here, won't you?'

Seeing Amy going off to war shook Rhona. And made her feel somehow old, and useless. Whilst she knew she had to remain at the mill alongside Bill Brightstone, to keep up production of raw materials for uniforms, she felt left out of everything.

At home, things were different already. Her stepfather was working long hours, frequently seven days a week. Daniel was away training for the navy, and Stanley had gone to stay with Cousin Helen and her husband near Barnsley so he'd be handy for the pit. Like Mrs Lightowler, Eve Hebden was involved with the WVS and spoke of helping with the Red Cross also.

Determined to assist the war effort, Rhona began teaching raw beginners to knit – women and girls who never before had attempted to handle a pair of needles. They began on scarves then progressed to making gloves. One or two developed enough aptitude to master turning a heel so they could knit socks.

Guiding other women into producing items for the forces' Comforts still didn't seem sufficient to Rhona.

'I wish to goodness I could do more,' she confided to Timothy one evening when locking up. 'I know the stuff we make here is vital, but I can't get it out of my head that I could be doing something more constructive.'

Tim nodded understandingly. 'I know exactly what you mean. Although we've had to change our products, our methods are still the same, so we're not experiencing most of the adjustments inflicted on other people.'

Rhona grinned. 'I was afraid you'd be telling me not to

talk so daft. I just feel sometimes as if I'm not taking this lot seriously enough.'

'But through no fault of your own.'

'At least, you can see that.' Rhona was looking at him, noticing how grave his lovely blue eyes were, that he seemed to be turning over something in his mind, wondering whether to speak. 'Is that what you've been feeling as well, Tim?'

'And more. That's the reason . . .' Sighing, he gave an awkward shrug. 'I suppose telling you won't hurt, but you must promise not to hang on, to Dad, till he has to be told. Till it's definite. I – I've volunteered, Rhona, for the RAF.'

'You . . . ?'

'I've been thinking about it for a long time. I know I don't have to go, with what we're doing here at the mill. But you'd always keep this place running – with Dad, of course. And he's so much better now.'

'Aye – he has been,' Rhona said grimly, sickened by Tim's news. 'And how long do you think he's going to stay that way, with you in the forces, giving him and your mother endless anxiety?'

'He'll be all right, I'm sure of it.'

'Nay, nobody can be sure. Worry's the last thing he should have to undergo.'

'All right, Rhona love, I know – I do really. But I have my life as well, I owe it to myself to live it the way I think I should.'

'Aye. Aye.' Wearily she shook her head. All at once she felt abominably tired, and so close to breaking down that she wanted to run out of the mill and home.

'What's up now?' Tim asked concernedly. 'Fed up because you can't get away and join up as well? Your face's fallen a mile.'

'Happen that's it. Happen . . .' Sighing again, she shook her head. 'Oh, never mind.'

'No, Rhona, what is it?'

He pulled her against him, still holding her gaze with his, and then he drew her even closer, a hand gentle at the back of her neck as he pressed her face into his shoulder.

His jacket smelled of the mill, of processing wool; she supposed her own clothes did. But the smell was familiar, safe. Just as Timothy was a familiar part of her life. And very dear.

'You shouldn't have done that,' her muffled voice told him. 'You'll have me blubbing all over you!'

'So . . . ? That's what we're about, Rhona, surely. You and me – pals that have seen the worst as well as the best of each other. How long is it since you came to work here?'

'I'd have to reckon up to be able to tell you, it passes that quickly.'

'And so will this – the war.'

'For you, maybe – learning to fly aeroplanes – or are you applying for ground staff?'

'I'm flying, so long as they'll have me.'

'I was afraid you would.'

'You'll keep an eye on Dad, stop him worrying too much.'

'Oh, I will, will I?' And who'll keep an eye on me? Who'll stop my imagination running riot and picturing your plane crashing?

'You won't be getting into a state yourself?' Amazed, Tim held her a little way away so he could scrutinize her eyes.

'What do you think, you daft bat! How will I know from one minute to the next whether you're all right, or not?'

'You'll know. You'll think about me – providing you spare me a minute – and you'll sense that I'm all right.'

'You're as daft as a brush, Tim Brightstone! But you're a plucky 'un for all that. There's some fellows would have seized at the chance to stay at home.'

'Well, at least it's done one thing for us,' he said, smiling down at her.

'Oh, yes? And what do you reckon that is?' Rhona was

trying to match his cocky tone, but deep inside her a leaden weight was hurtling around.

'Made you let on that you do care what happens to me. It's nice to know.'

'What good does it do, though? Answer me that. You'll be off in no time, and it could be for many a year.'

'Who says so? Who says the war'll last that long?'

Wolf says so, Rhona thought, felt herself colouring, and managed yet again to make her mind almost a blank. She didn't think about Wolf any longer, much less mention his name.

'All right, happen they were wrong. I hope, for all our sakes, that they were.'

'You'll keep in touch, won't you, Rhona love? Let me know how things are going here, how you are.'

'I suppose so.'

'If you'd rather not . . .'

'Don't be silly. Of course, I'll keep in touch. It's just that everybody's going, everybody but me. Even Amy Lightowler's lied about her age and is in the ATS.'

'All the more cause to believe we'll soon have Hitler on the run. With that many joining up, how can we fail?'

'All right, Tim, all right.'

'It won't be all work, not at first, any rate. There'll be leaves . . .'

'And you down South, like everyone else – Amy, our Daniel . . .'

'You don't know where I'll be sent. But you could come to me, for a weekend or something. Have you ever been down South?'

'You've soon forgotten! I went to London, didn't I? But no, I've never been anywhere else down there.'

I wouldn't want to travel in wartime, either, Rhona thought that night when she was mulling over everything Tim had said. It'd be horrible in dark, overcrowded trains – with no knowing when a bomb might come hurtling down.

When the time came, Bill Brightstone took the news of Tim's signing on far better than Rhona had anticipated.

'You and me will manage very well,' he assured her the day before Tim was due to go, and made her wonder if he had secretly regretted having so much responsibility taken from him.

Tim asked her to drive him to Halfield station; in return for him seeing her off on the London trip, he said, making a joke of it. But she knew on the day that he wanted her there because of the friendship grown so strong between them.

'I was waiting for you when you came back,' he said, trying to laugh away all seriousness. 'I'd like to see you standing on that platform over there when I come home.'

'You're not bothered about the bit in between then – I thought you said there'd be leaves . . .'

'There'd better be, only . . .' Timothy drew her to him, his eyes very serious. 'Well, of course, I shall want to see you. But I've a nasty feeling things are accelerating that swiftly there won't be all that many chances of coming back to Halfield.'

'I see.' He'd chosen a right time to mention this!

'Don't say anything to Dad or Mum, will you? Don't let on. It's just a feeling I have. Could be wrong.'

'And good old Rhona's the only one to be upset, is that it?'

'You'll survive – we both will, I'm sure.'

I wish I thought so, Rhona reflected miserably, willing herself not to cling to him and go all weepy. But *everybody* was going away, everything was different. For some unaccountable reason, for the first time in aeons, she was back as a small child. A small child helpless and afraid; out of her mind with fear because grown-ups were crying. 'Your daddy's gone to heaven,' she heard somebody say, and experienced again the bewildering ache that was loss.

'Here's the train.' Tim was hugging her closer. Aware of her trembling, shocked by the terror in her eyes. 'Oh, Rhona love . . .'

His kiss was full on her mouth, the pressure of his lips crushing her own against her teeth until she tasted blood. Deep in her throat, she moaned, anguished. His kiss deepened, his lips stirring over hers, his tongue separating her teeth.

The train was at the platform. All about them carriage doors were crashing open then slamming to again. And still Tim went on kissing her, and she was responding, fiercely, willing him to come home safely. Willing him to restore the life they had known, which only now she knew had been very special.

His chin was grinding against hers, threatening to crack her jaw, yet nothing would make her move one fraction of an inch away. Nothing but that train, and the necessity for Tim to clamber aboard.

'You'll have to go,' she said distractedly when they paused to draw in air. Smoke from the engine drifted between them, making her throat raw. The harshness seemed, in some twisted way, welcome.

'I know,' Tim groaned.

For one last time he held her to him, closer than ever before, his kiss devouring her mouth. Through both their coats she felt him hard with longing, and deep in her own body an answering need was surging.

13

Rhona had never thought of Halfield as a bright place. Now with so many people away in the forces and many of those left behind working overtime in essential industries, it seemed duller than ever. At the mill she was busier, now that Tim had gone. His father, though, was making the best of the situation, living for Timothy's rare letters, proud that his lad was learning to fly. He was also enjoying taking more of a hand in running the mill.

'Just you see, Rhona,' he told her, with a frequency that threatened to grow wearisome, 'we'll manage to give the government all they ask for as long as this war lasts. Then when Tim comes home we'll all pull together and get back to producing the stuff we want . . .'

'He doesn't seem to realize how long this war is going to last,' Rhona confided to Eve one evening as they sat either side of the bit of fire they were permitted, both knitting navy-blue socks for all they were worth. 'He talks as if there'll be hardly any changes by the time Tim comes out.'

'No doubt that's the way he *has* to think, love,' Eve said sympathetically. 'Him and Ellen. Tim's all they've got, and there's no sense in dwelling on the present.'

'I know. I do know really. Both of them are getting on, and we should just be glad he isn't making himself ill with anxiety.'

'Only *you* are . . . ? her mother prompted.

'I don't know. It's just – well, sometimes, Mum, I think I'm the only one alive who realizes that we could be in for year after year of conflict. And that means there'll be lots of our lads killed as well as Jerry's.'

'And you're missing Tim.'

'Aye, I am that! I was sorry to see him go, I won't

pretend I wasn't. But I didn't realize. He's a rotten letter-
writer, and . . .'

'. . . You want to know how he is, what he's doing.'

'I always knew before, didn't I? Well, for the past few
years, anyway. Happen we were too much in each other's
pockets – too much for seeing each other clearly. But
we've been pals for a long time, Tim and me. When we
were kids, then since . . . if not all the time we've worked
together, certainly since I came back from London.'

'And Timothy grew up, didn't he, with that sad business over Hazel Wright.'

'You saw it, and all? You never said.'

'I don't always say what I'm thinking. And nor do you.'

Rhona grinned, laying aside her knitting for a few
moments. 'About Tim? I've hardly known what to think.'

'Nor what you feel?'

'Feel? Well, it's not love, that I do know.'

'Oh, yes? Are you sure?'

'Mother? What makes you say that?'

'You've been subdued since he's joined up.'

'I've been subdued before.'

'Usually over some man that's upsetting you. Except
that one time, giving up teaching, for the mill.'

'This is different, this is wartime, everybody's under a
certain degree of strain.'

'Especially when their menfolk are away, and there's
no spark of attraction to keep them going!'

'Tim's just a friend.'

'Doesn't he attract you?'

Rhona busied herself with the sock again, her red-
brown hair, worn longer now, swinging forward to conceal
her eyes.

'Your dad,' Eve began, stopped, and corrected herself.
'*Jack* was a good friend to me, a very good friend, when
your father died in the last lot. He was kind, considerate,
somebody to rely on, always there.'

'Yes, well – there aren't many like Jack Hebden, are
there?'

'And are you being too choosy? Looking for someone

who'll be your ideal? I could be choosy as well, you know. And very determined. After I'd lost your dad. I can only be very thankful Jack was persistent – I've never had cause to regret it. Men can't be persistent when they're busy fighting a war.'

'There's nothing like that between Tim and me. I've told you, we're only friends.'

'There's worse reasons for getting married. Like not being able to get enough of each other.'

Rhona raised an eyebrow without glancing up from her needles. 'You're getting very outspoken, Mother.'

Eve smiled. 'I *am* forty-seven. Isn't it time I stopped pretending I'm naïve? I'd like to see you happy, Rhona.'

'What's that? I thought that particular emotion was suspended while we get on with this war.'

'There's still men and women, dear – still with the same needs. And maybe needing each other more because of what they have to put up with.'

'Well, if it's Timothy you're worrying about, I imagine he'll be having a high old time. If he isn't chasing all the WAAFs, he'll be after the local girls.'

'Where did you say he was – Kent?'

'Yes. Somewhere near Maidstone, a little village.' She didn't really wish to talk about it. Tim hadn't been back, not even on an overnight pass. He wrote sketchily and infrequently, it hurt far more than she would have believed.

When Timothy telephoned, at last, it was to the mill. After speaking with his father for ten minutes or so, he asked for Rhona.

'Dad's giving you a long weekend,' he announced. 'How about us spending it together?'

'You're coming on leave! About time . . . ! Oh, Tim, thank goodness . . .'

'Actually – I can't get up there, love, not this time.'

'But you never have, you could make the effort. We haven't seen you for ages.'

'So you *are* missing me. Good. That's why you're

coming to me. You can have Friday off, we'll have the whole of Saturday together, and . . .'

'Oh.' Rhona didn't know what else to say. She had longed to see Tim, with a longing made more acute now just by hearing his voice, but . . .

'It's hell without you, Rhona.'

'Some hell, what about all those WAAFs?'

'Brawny as anything, with brains to match.'

Banter or not, their conversation was the first in what felt like eternity. She could picture him very clearly, his blue eyes glinting, his glorious fair hair aglow beneath the lights of this office. And she could feel the rhythmic attraction, strong as it had been during that dreadful parting on the draughty platform at Halfield station. She couldn't not go.

Tim met her at the station nearest to his billet. Her journey had been appalling, long and wearisome, with frequent stops in between stations. She had been crammed into the corridor on the train down to London, wedged between khaki and blue uniforms, and filled with guilt because she was daring to travel and take up their space. The train out to Kent had been less packed, but had stopped just as often and, in gathering darkness, had felt isolated from the rest of the world.

Suddenly, though, seeing Tim and being drawn close in to him, neither discomfort nor misgivings were of any consequence. Tim was kissing her again, savagely, and her entire being was responding.

'Welcome, welcome, welcome!' he exclaimed, releasing her only to pull her towards him again for another tremendous hug. 'God, have I missed you!'

'It's been pretty quiet without you as well.'

Tim beamed, seized her weekend case and flung his other arm around her shoulders. 'Can't waste time now – you're staying with the Coopers, same as me. I've been billeted on them for a while now. They farm. There's Ma Cooper and her daughters – three of them, great hulking women, make two of me, each of them!'

He had a car outside, a 1920s Austin Seven. 'Borrowed it from one of my mates.'

Tim drove the way he was speaking, swiftly, with enthusiasm, despite the age of the car. Rhona was glad of the feel of him beside her. Warmth emanated through the rough cloth of his greatcoat, and with it pulsing vitality.

'They're pleased with me here,' he told her, off-handedly. 'Seems they're short of university types. I'm working for my wings – there's a chance I'll gain them in record time.'

'Halfield's going to be dull for you afterwards.'

'Different, not necessarily dull – all depends on you.'

'On *me?*' Her own startled voice made her laugh, and Tim guffawed.

'What's the joke?'

'No joke – just joy, my love, to have you here.'

'Sure that's all? I sense you've something up the proverbial sleeve.'

'And if I have – if I've had one or two good ideas, would you object very strongly?'

'I know you too well to say I'd have no reservations, don't forget that! As if I'd commit myself to any of your notions before hearing all about them! And don't forget either that working at Bridge House has given me a taste for shaping my own future.'

He was slowing the car. Moments later he had drawn off the road into the entrance to a field. His arm went round her as soon as he switched off the engine. It was nearly dark now, the line of bare trees on a distant Wealden slope hardly visible against the cobalt sky.

'I can't wait any longer,' Tim said huskily. 'Anyway, back at the farm there's always too many people. I have yearned for you, you know, little Rhona Hebden. My pal, the one who's known me since I was a nipper, the one who represents home to me now.'

His kiss began gently this time, savouring her lips until they parted. And then his tongue explored her mouth, thrilling her with the intensity of the emotions it generated. A great surging eagerness, wild almost, because it was so insistent.

'The life here is good, you know,' he said breathlessly. 'I love the activity, learning, stretching out to achieve something so totally different, being challenged. But it'd all go to pot if there wasn't some kind of anchor – like this, us.'

Rhona smiled. 'You've not been too busy for thinking about me, then?' she asked lightly.

'Not all the time. And – and there was always this reminder, even while my mind was occupied, some part of me needing to have you, to hold . . .'

His lips scoured hers, inflaming her, conjuring within her a need so strong that she grew alarmed as much as excited. 'Tim . . .'

'Don't be scared, sweetheart, there'll be nothing you don't agree to. Pity this car's so damned tiny, though!'

Rhona laughed, and he took her mouth while it was open, tasting, teasing a little, testing her teeth with the point of his tongue, until she was kissing him back, hungry for love. Never had she been more alive to her own body, and what it was willing from them both.

'Better get on our way,' Tim said at last, ruefully. 'There's a dance in the village tonight. I was looking forward to showing you off to everyone.'

Now, though, he thought, I'm not certain I can share this time with anyone; can share *you*. Almost, he blurted out right away the need to make her his; to seal the relationship developing since before either of them could recall, making it his cornerstone in a shifting world.

Mrs Cooper was a large lady, with capable hands that jerked Rhona's up and down in the warmest of greetings. Her eyes were grey, so pale they were almost silver, but they glinted with merriment, unclouded by the war that had taken her man away to sea. Hearing that Rhona had a half-brother in the navy, she declared they would have plenty to talk about.

'That's if Tim here doesn't commandeer your whole stay.'

'I'm afraid Tim's likely to,' he warned them, his steady blue gaze riveted on Rhona.

Meg, Di and Bertha, Mrs Cooper's daughters, came in from milking, washed at the sink of the huge farmhouse kitchen, and sat down to supper with lots of laughter and some ribbing for Rhona. She'd never met such exuberant young women, was glad that Timothy had been placed with such an easy, extrovert family.

Agreeable surprises continued when they arrived at the village hall for the dance. Most of the men from the air-force base appeared to be present. And Timothy Bright-stone very evidently had found he belonged among officers as well as the ranks. Continually smiling, watching how popular he was, Rhona was soon enjoying the evening. People constantly gravitated towards the pair of them, their attitude towards her witnessing to the magnetism drawing them to Tim.

'I didn't expect you'd be unpopular, don't get me wrong,' she confided when at last they moved away to dance, 'but I didn't know I'd have to fight for your attention!'

Tim laughed with her. 'You'll never have to fight for that. But what about you, Rhona – did absence make you fonder of me, or of somebody else?'

'There's no one else,' she said very quickly, wondering if she was being incautious, recalled then how much she had missed him. And who else was there, now? 'Happen this war *has* done us a bit of good.'

'Teaching you that you might look elsewhere and fare a hell of a lot worse, perhaps?'

'Perhaps. Just – don't rush me, Tim.'

'You're asking a lot. Do you know how much? I've wanted you, *loved* you for many a year, and you've known that. And now you can't pretend any longer that you don't want me – if only in some ways.'

He was using the attraction which she could not deny – especially while dancing like this, locked together in a sensuous foxtrot. Somehow, though, she could neither hold him off, nor condemn her own eager body. She could only remain close against him, aware of his desire for her, thrilled by his passion.

'There could be only this weekend, you know, for many a week. You do understand that, Rhona? Here in Kent, men are in the skies the moment they're trained, almost before that. They go out over the channel, and beyond . . .'

'Don't . . .' It was a sort of blackmail, did he know she'd pay the price he was demanding? Because she'd lost so much, and couldn't contemplate him going out there, and not returning. He was so very alive, vital, charismatic.

'This time,' he said huskily into her ear, 'I haven't been my usual irresponsible self. I do want you, Rhona, but I wouldn't just take you, I want us married.'

'Married?' she echoed. 'There's a war on . . .'

'By special licence. I do have one. I've spoken to the local vicar, it is possible.'

'But . . .' She wasn't saying no, she was simply thinking – of the marriage she had pictured . . . of Eve, and Jack Hebden giving her away, Stanley there, their Dan . . .

'I do know, Rhona. War does funny things to people. And sorts a few priorities. Like do you need a fine white gown, and a crowd of folk there, or do you wish just to dedicate yourself to someone, simply, solemnly . . .'

Rhona didn't answer. How could she, while he was making her throat ache because he was so sincere? And while all her nerve-endings were vibrating with this *hunger* that overwhelmed her.

'I ought to send you away, you know, Tim Brightstone – to the far end of this room. This way, I can't think straight.'

'Me neither.'

'You've done your thinking! I came away unprepared – totally unprepared for any of this.'

'Was nothing inside you hinting what you needed?'

'Oh, aye – there's always that. And what do we do when the passion's sated, Tim? Tell me that – what'll there be for us?'

'A home, lass, after the war. And, God willing, bairns in it.'

'You sound just like your dad!'

'What's wrong with that? You've always had a soft spot for him.'

Was that why Tim was talking this way? Was he so calculating? And so much in love he was desperate to convince her . . . ? How wrong was it of him to try every way he knew to make her want to marry him?

'You'll not get an answer yet, you do know that? It's too serious for deciding in a rush.' And with a drink inside her. The inevitable bar had been set up in one corner, she'd been persuaded into having a port and lemon. It was making her talk, animatedly, to complete strangers, and did not assist thinking.

'I'd better not have much more to drink,' she admitted to Tim when he had led her off into a rapid quickstep.

He laughed. 'Nonsense, it's doing you good. You've not been so gregarious for a very long time.'

'Oh, haven't I? And how do you know, Mr Clever? You haven't been around.'

'M'm.' Briefly, his humour faded. 'And isn't that the very reason why I want to see my ring on your finger? For too long, we've known nothing about how the other was feeling . . .'

'All right, love.' She looked at him and smiled. Wasn't this *her* complaint about Tim's absence? 'I would consider that, you know – an engagement ring.'

'Engagement's neither here nor there, something and nothing.'

'Depends who's involved, how seriously they take things.'

'And how much would it mean to you, if we were engaged? What difference would it make from – well, from as we are?'

'I'd be waiting for you, wouldn't I? Promised to you, till this lot's over and you come home.'

'But you wouldn't be mine, would you?'

'Course, I would. I just said, I'd wait.'

'Aye. And waiting's what we'd have to do, wouldn't we? You'd no more be mine, than . . .' Shaking his head, Timothy sighed. 'Well – would you?'

'We'd belong together. Everybody'd know that when I wore your ring.'

Abruptly, Tim stopped dancing, led her off the floor, and out through a side exit. It was cold in the open after the heat generated by dancing, but he didn't give her a chance to feel the chill. Before she could protest, he'd slipped his uniform jacket around her shoulders.

'Do you really want me, Rhona?' he asked gravely. 'I have to have the truth – don't go being kind, or even sympathetic because of all this and me being in the RAF.'

'Oh, Tim . . . at this moment it's hard to be certain. Being with you is exciting, you've completely gone to my head tonight. I've missed you such a lot. Had almost forgotten . . . well, you must have noticed what your kisses were doing to me.'

'Want another reminder . . . ?' he suggested, his lips tantalizingly close to her mouth.

Rhona pressed the flat of one hand at his chest, holding him a little away. 'Heaven's above, don't start that again just now! I want you too much, don't you see? You've got me so confused. And we were *friends*, Tim . . .'

'And that's the way you want to keep it.' His voice was stony, his blue eyes frozen.

'Not necessarily.'

'It is because of Hazel? Haven't I paid yet, on account of her, will I always be punished . . . ?'

'Nay, lad! Don't talk so daft. This is nothing to do with her, nor with anybody but us two – and if we're going to be right for each other.'

'We could – give it a try. See how we make out together. They all go to bed early at the farm. And anyway, my room's over the stables.'

'You *have* thought this out, haven't you? You're taking a bit of a liberty, aren't you? Expecting friendship to develop this fast, into – the other thing.'

'I think it's developed long ago, only one of us won't

admit it. You were greedy for me that day I left Halfield. In my case, there's been no means of appeasing what I feel for you, for many a long year. And I'm not ashamed of what you do to me . . .'

'Ashamed? Is that what you think I am, of – of having feelings.'

'Aren't you? We're two adult people, Rhona. I'm prepared to commit myself to you, for life.'

He pulled her towards him, enfolding her in the jacket while his arms prevented her escape. The cloth was warm from him, bore his masculine scent, inflamed her senses. Through her skirt she felt the rough texture of his service trousers, and could feel him also, pressing close, alerting within her the exhilarating urge to belong.

'I need you for a part of myself, Rhona. Just the way I need to be some part of you.'

'Oh, Tim . . .'

'You've said that before. It tells me nothing. I've been direct with you.'

Despite conflicting emotions, she smiled. 'Very! And happen that's what's wrong. I didn't expect you'd suggest marriage, nor the other . . .'

'I'd take care of you, you know. I'd not risk giving you a youngster.'

'It's not that, I . . .' Amazed at herself, Rhona gazed into his serious eyes, suddenly aware that children had been crowded out of her life, for too long. These days, Tim would be a good father. 'I only . . .'

'. . . Need time? I know.' He sighed. 'Come on, inside . . .'

Back in the hall, they danced again, repeatedly, and very close. The five-piece band had switched to smoochy numbers. All around her Rhona could see uniformed men and their girls, clinging as if this night might be their last, kissing overtly, because it could be.

Even over the sound of the band, the dismal siren penetrated. Amid a lot of rueful laughter, catcalls and groans, they trooped from the room without any fuss, down stone steps into the cellars.

The air smelled musty and was damp. Like other girls, Rhona made a face, shivered. The jacket she'd returned to Timothy was thrust about her once more; gratefully, she hugged it to her.

'Over here, love . . .' An arm across her shoulders, Tim guided her away from the crowd. A low stone shelf ran along the wall here, where the cellar narrowed.

'At least there's a seat.'

Rhona grinned. 'Of sorts – it'll be freezing cold.'

'That's not your worry.' Swiftly he sat, then drew her down on to his lap. 'That, surely, is one hell of a lot warmer!' he murmured into her ear.

Across the other side of the cellar the others were clustered together, laughing, talking, some of the lads with drinks in their hands still, some of the girls as well. Candles were being lit and set on any available surface. A young woman crossed towards them, placed a candlestick nearby on the stone slab. As she walked away, Tim reached over and snuffed out the candle.

'Happen you need to get used to me again, Rhona love.'

'Happen so.'

His breath was warm against her ear, and then across her cheek. His lips brushed her own, tentatively, making her conscious of a new Tim Brightstone. 'Yes . . . ?'

His mouth against hers, Rhona couldn't feign indifference. Deep inside her she was screaming for his kisses, and for more. It'd take somebody harder than this rock surrounding them to tell him no.

'Yes, love, yes,' she gasped.

Still Timothy held back. It was her lips that did the searching, her tongue that probed until his teeth parted, her fingers that opened his shirt, found the hair on his chest.

At first unaware, she was stirring, urgently, the mouth greedily devouring his the symbol only of her longing. Eyes closed, she'd grown rapidly oblivious to everything except Timothy.

'Darling, Rhona darling,' he whispered against her

211

mouth. 'You're sensational, better even than I dreamed. It's going to be so good, sweetheart.'

'I know, I know,' she agreed breathily, 'oh, Tim!'

Beneath his jacket she was feverishly hot now, fired by his heat which seemed to envelop her entire person. His hand slipped over the satin of her blouse; rhythmically, he caressed her breast.

Her cry of ecstasy was strangled as she contained it within her throat. Softly, silently, Timothy chuckled. 'That's nothing up to what you're doing for me, darling. I just want to hold you here for ever, right where you are. At least, until we can be alone . . .'

Should she be letting him talk like this? Shouldn't she be putting him in his place? But then he did wish to marry her, and this was wartime.

On cue the roar of an aircraft taking off shattered her into forgetting her emotions. Another followed seconds later, then a third, a fourth . . .

'That's our lot,' Tim announced, smiling.

'The – the aerodrome's quite near, then?'

'Just the other side of the hill. Ten minutes by car. When we're trained of course, fully operational, we'll live on the base. That's one reason the lads make the most of their freedom now.'

The planes setting out to cross the channel changed everything. Even after the all-clear had sounded and they went back for the last half hour's dancing, Rhona was very quiet.

She wasn't much more talkative while Tim was walking her to the Coopers' farm. It was dark inside the large, old-fashioned living room, yet when Tim reached towards the light switch after closing the door, her hand checked his.

She stepped closer to him, putting her arms around him, locking them, then raising her lips for a kiss. His need of her was just as strong, making her press into him, firm breasts taut against his chest.

'Have you really seen to getting a licence?' she asked, solemnly, when the need for air checked their kisses.

'I really have – we only have to speak to the vicar, just to confirm.'

'Tomorrow . . .'

'Today now, it's past midnight.'

'It's a big step.'

'Aye.'

His Yorkshirism made her laugh. 'You sound like your dad again.'

'The solid, steady part of me that'll make you a good husband. Not, mind, that I really believe I deserve you. You're a fine lass, Rhona Hebden, making your way in the world. Going further than most women.'

Once she'd have ribbed him, laughed him out of that sort of talk. Today she couldn't. And she suspected he'd never say anything like it again. And if he did seem to be paying her a lot of compliments? Happen there was a grain of truth in what he said.

'Can we make a go of it, do you think?' Could *she* – by letting go of Wolf, entirely, emptying her soul of him as well as her head?

Quietly, Tim was laughing. 'I've just told you I think you're marvellous. Do you mean I'm not up to much?'

'I mean I'm being my usual cautious Yorkshire self. And I suspect this is the wrong time for that. You need somebody at the back of you, Tim Brightstone, don't you?' And I need someone who shows they want me.

She half expected he'd joke about it, say that wasn't where he wanted her. Instead, he was totally serious. 'More than ever. And I've never stopped saying you're the one who belongs with me.'

'Go on then, we'll have a go.'

Tim crushed her to him in a massive, breath-seizing, hug. 'You'd better get off to bed then, love. Or I won't be doing this the right way, at all.'

Any doubts and misgivings that she'd been experiencing evaporated when he didn't expect her to share his room. As she undressed Rhona heard the planes coming back, one by one. I've done it now, she thought. Having given her word, nothing on this earth would make her retract.

213

Her last night as a single woman – how unreal it all felt! Would tomorrow feel any different, would *she*? She'd surprised herself by how fiercely she'd longed to make love with Timothy, how fiercely she still longed.

Daybreak in a strange room with cocks crowing beyond its blacked-out windows awakened her to the contrast with her home. And to the significance of the event ahead. Everything felt so unreal still that she could scarcely believe this would be her wedding day.

When she went down to the farmhouse kitchen Tim was just walking in through the door. His glorious golden hair was wind-tossed, awry, his face flushed with hurrying, but his blue eyes glittered with happiness.

'Hallo, love!' He came across the quarry-tiled floor in two or three strides, seized both her hands and kissed her full on the mouth. 'I've seen the vicar, and it's ten o'clock.'

'Ten?' She'd never be ready.

'It's all fixed, we're having just a short ceremony, and that was the only time he could fit us in. There's lots of people getting married in a hurry.'

'All right then, good. You'll have to take me as I am, though, I had been hoping to get something new to wear . . .'

'It's you I'm marrying, not a clothes horse.'

Thank goodness she'd thought to bring the Chanel suit. 'But I haven't got a hat . . .'

A hearty chuckle made her swing round. 'I'll bet our girls have something that'll do. They don't go in for hats very much, not for dressing up in, but between them they'll be able to fit you up.' Filling the doorway from the hall, Mrs Cooper was beaming. She was also holding something in her hand, something that she passed furtively to Tim.

'That's a beauty,' he said, looking down into his palm. 'Are you certain you wish to part with it, Mrs Cooper?'

'I'm sure, all right. What did I tell you?' Noticing Rhona's curious look, she winked at Timothy. 'Are we going to let on to her?'

'Why not? Rhona will be thrilled.'

'What'll I be thrilled about now?'

'This ring. I hadn't a chance to get you one, had I, not with you only arriving last night, and . . .'

'. . . You springing a wedding on me!'

'Well – yes. I was asking Mrs Cooper if there was a jeweller's anywhere near when she offered us this.'

'It was my mother's, dear.' The farmer's wife was beaming, her large face aglow. 'There's no hope of it going anywhere near even my little finger. She was a neat body, you see, not built for comfort like yours truly.'

'Let's have a look . . .' Rhona smiled as she gazed at the ring. It was a broader gold band than was fashionable these days, but it did appear tiny. Would it fit?

'We'd better try it.' Taking her left hand, Timothy slid the ring as far as the knuckle.

'Careful, don't get it wedged or you'll have me getting wed with the ring in place!'

Trying to come to terms over the price, Tim followed Mrs Cooper into the scullery. She'd wanted to make them a gift of the ring, he couldn't let her do that.

'Maybe you couldn't have worn it,' Rhona heard him saying. 'Well, we couldn't get married without it. Fair dos – I'm going to give you something.'

Mrs Cooper was insisting on putting on a spread for them, after the service. Tim had invited several of his mates, and two of the officers from the camp, to the church. There would be wives and girlfriends as well, and all would be welcome afterwards at the farm.

'It'll be early for lunch,' Mrs Cooper observed. 'I'm going to lay on bacon and eggs, and lots of home-baked bread. It's no good being in farming if you can't put your hands on a bit of bacon when you need it special.'

She offered Rhona her share of bacon now. 'You want something decent inside you beforehand. You'll be too excited afterwards to have much of a meal.'

'I'm too excited now,' she exclaimed. 'Or scared – wondering what I'm letting myself in for! Some bread and marmalade will be fine, thanks.'

'I thought you and young Tim had known each other for years?'

'So we have. But you don't think of marrying somebody just because you've grown up with them.'

For once Mrs Cooper's expression grew thoughtful rather than jovial. 'Perhaps you've grown into each other, though, dear.'

Tim had been listening without saying anything. He came to stand behind Rhona's chair, placed a hand on each shoulder. 'I never thought I'd be glad about the war, but today I'm thankful it's accelerated things. Rhona knows how many years I've wanted to make her mine. Well, that's only the beginning – by the time this lot's over she'll have got a home together for us, we'll be a family. And there's nobody in the West Riding will make a better wife and mother.'

'I'll try and make up to you for having to wait so long.'

Tim chuckled, leaned forward and kissed the side of her neck. 'Don't worry, love, I'll see you do that, all right!'

When he'd gone to get changed, Rhona hastily swallowed the last of her breakfast and stood up, about to go to her own room.

'What are you wearing, dear?' Mrs Cooper asked, following her up the stairs. 'If you'd just show me, I'll see what sort of hats the girls have got.' Her daughters were busy somewhere about the farm; evidently, they rarely came indoors while it was daylight.

Mrs Cooper admired the Chanel suit. 'Our Bertha's got a navy-blue hat – a right smart one that she got off the vicar's wife.'

Just in time Rhona contained her smile, and avoided asking if the vicar might recognize it. What did the age, or the history, of the hat matter? This was an abnormal wedding, in difficult conditions, she must simply remain thankful that Timothy was determined on there being a ceremony.

After a considerable amount of muttering and rustling of tissue paper from the next bedroom, Mrs Cooper reappeared. 'Now, isn't that lovely – might have been made to go with your nice suit.'

The hat was a Garbo-style slouch. When Rhona tried it on, it threatened to slide down over her ears and engulf her. Yet she knew already that she would wear the thing, no matter what. Mrs Cooper had literally taken her to her heart.

'It's just the shade,' she enthused quickly. 'Isn't that lucky! You're sure your daughter won't mind lending it?'

Mrs Cooper laughed. 'It hasn't been out for many a month, dear. My girls don't need no hats for milking, do they? Nor for ploughing, and the like.'

Glancing at her watch gave Rhona a nasty jolt. It was nine o'clock already, she'd never be dressed in time. And, for once, she'd have to fluff out her hair, somehow, instead of smoothing it down – otherwise she'd not see out under that brim to find her way down the aisle.

One of Tim's friends was to be his best man. Another, Frank Hewitt, had agreed to give her away. He was a nervous twenty-five-year-old who looked all of eighteen. When they were left together in the farm living room after the others had departed towards the church, Rhona tried to make him feel more at ease.

'I understand you're from Yorkshire as well,' she began, trying not to rivet her attention entirely upon the clock. There was only one available car, the one in which Tim had picked her up last evening. Barry Sinclair, its owner and Tim's best man, was ferrying everybody to the church.

Rhona wondered how long she could keep this up with Frank being so unforthcoming. 'Do you like the life here? Timothy seems to have settled in very well.'

'He wanted to join up.'

'And you didn't?'

'It was Father's idea.'

When he didn't seem inclined to enlighten her further, Rhona prompted him: 'He thinks it's a good service to be in, does he? Flying's the thing now, isn't it? The air's where this war's going to be won, or so they say.'

'I'm supposed to set an example, to the lads back home. Father's . . . Well, actually, he's a Lord Lieutenant.'

Rhona was astounded. '*That* Hewitt . . .'

'He farms as well.'

'On a somewhat larger scale than Mrs Cooper.'

At last, something made him smile. 'Er – yes.'

'It's lovely, anyway, to have somebody from home with us today.'

'I wish I knew what I was supposed to do.'

Rhona grinned. 'That makes two of us. But I think you only have to sort of hand me over. Give me shove, or something.'

'At least I don't have anything to say.'

'Did your father choose the air force for you?'

'He preferred it to having me go down the pit.'

'*Would* you have?'

'I couldn't contemplate hand-to-hand fighting. And I'm a rotten sailor.'

'So, this is the lesser – or the least – evil?'

'It was. Might develop quite a liking for flying. Actually, away from the old man, I might like a lot of things.'

'If you can stick around Tim, I'm sure you'll manage to enjoy most of the experience.'

'Oh, Tim's all right. Knew him at Cambridge. He was a few years ahead of me, but the same college. Not a fellow you can miss.'

Rhona recalled Tim last evening, surrounded by his friends, local girls, contemporaries. Even the officers from the station appeared drawn to him. It seemed she was being very fortunate.

A car was heard approaching up the narrow lane.

'You've got a new reservoir then, to serve Halfield,' Frank Hewitt said, out of the blue. 'Richardson's a family friend. A good bloke, no side, very straightforward. I like him.'

Rhona nodded. She couldn't speak, was too shattered, just by hearing his name, and knew words would not conceal the deep ache inside her.

Outside in the tiny Austin, Barry tooted for them to hurry.

Somebody had filled the Kentish ragstone church with winter-flowering blossom. As she went in a watery sun turned the greyish stone to gold, and highlighted the fragile blooms.

I never thought about flowers, Rhona sighed inwardly. She'd nothing to carry, no bouquet.

'I want you to have this – to keep. It was Mother's, from her confirmation.' In the shadowy porch, Mrs Cooper pressed a prayer book into Rhona's hand. Its cover was fine white leather, she'd pinned a white chrysanthemum to its marker.

'You're so good, so very good.' Suddenly Rhona was overcome, a part of her aching for her absent family, the other part bewildered by the warm-heartedness of these strangers. 'Thank you.' She hugged the older woman.

'I'll be sitting on his side, but I'm here for you both. There's no way I can share myself between you – even if I'm big enough!' Mrs Cooper stifled a laugh. Her frankness reminded Rhona of Amy.

She watched as the farmer's wife strode away towards the front of the church. The vicar was coming to meet them and conduct them in. He encountered Mrs Cooper halfway down the aisle and they performed the ritual dance of two people sidestepping wrongly, attempting to avoid each other. 'Sorry,' each whispered urgently. A subdued titter rustled around the church.

'What a funny wedding,' Rhona remarked, somewhat bemused still.

'And that's before I get cracking,' said Frank ruefully, then offered her his arm.

Happen it's a good thing it's such a strange affair, thought Rhona as they began following sedately behind the vicar. I'm not having much opportunity for thinking about all that this involves. This may not be right, not what people would expect, but it feels as if it's the only way I'd get to that altar. Somewhere at the back of her mind, she was growing aware of this being less than the entire truth. But before she could further analyse the circumstances and her reaction to them, she saw Timothy.

She'd thought yesterday that he looked grand in uniform. Now, as he turned to gaze when she was almost level with him, the sun slanted down on to his gleaming hair, and he looked splendid. Grave now, his eyes were more beautiful than she'd seen, like still water.

She wanted to drown in them, to drown herself in him. I've never really known you, she thought, never appreciated. When he appeared solemn like this, she could see his dad in him, though there wasn't much family resemblance. Those eyes, though, reminded her of someone . . .

Jack Hebden, that was it, wasn't it? She'd thought so before, hadn't she, years ago. If only Jack was here now to give her away. And Eve . . . God, but she couldn't marry anybody, not without her mother here! But what was it Eve had said, only so recently? About herself and Jack, about Rhona and . . . Tim, yes – *Tim*.

'I'm wild about the hat!' Tim whispered when they stood shoulder to shoulder.

'Ssh!' He'd been looking so serious, what was he doing making a joke now?

'You *can* smile then . . .' Tim murmured.

Facing them, the vicar contained his own amusement, cleared his throat, and adjusted his spectacles. 'Dearly beloved, we are gathered together here . . .'

14

Rhona was ravenously hungry when they reached the farmhouse. In the great kitchen Meg, Di and Bertha were frying eggs and bacon as if cooking for the entire air force.

'That smells good!' Tim exclaimed.

'It certainly does,' Rhona agreed eagerly. 'Have we time for a bacon sandwich before the others arrive?'

'Getting your strength up, are you?' Meg teased, glancing over her shoulder, a beaming smile dominating her round face.

'Everything go off all right?' Bertha inquired, leaving their youngest sister, Di, in charge of the eggs while she began buttering great wedges of home-made bread.

'Very well – I think.' Rhona was still experiencing this strange detachment. This couldn't be *her*, married, and suddenly feeling so famished that nothing else mattered. 'Oh – thanks for the hat, by the way. Where shall I put it?'

'Aren't you going to keep it on for a while, make sure everyone sees it? It looks far more dashing on you than ever it did on me.'

'Well – all right then, thanks again.'

'Here you are – there's an egg in there as well.' Bertha handed each of them a plate.

Rhona eyed the massive sandwich, oozing egg yolk and the odd dribble of bacon fat. 'Just take my jacket off first, then I can enjoy myself.' If the worst happened the blouse, at least, would wash.

Tim was seated already at the scrubbed deal table, wading through his bacon and egg, his eyes half closed in delight. 'Just what I needed after that ordeal.'

'Ordeal, was it? It was your idea, remember!'

He swallowed a mouthful, leaned across and gave her an enthusiastic kiss.

The door was flung open and Mrs Cooper bustled in, removing her hat – an ancient sepia cloche – as she crossed towards the stove. Beyond the window the vicar was leaning a rusty-framed bicycle against the wall. As he came in Rhona and Tim stood up.

'Ah – my dear Miss . . . er – *Mrs* – er, Brightstone. May I say how charming you are looking. I do so admire your hat, very modish! My dear lady wife has a very similar model. Never seems to wear it now, can't think why.'

Tim thanked him for organizing the ceremony at such short notice, and Rhona added her own thanks. And wished secretly that she'd been married in her own church, with her own vicar. She felt as though she'd never come out of this dream. Yet she appeared to satisfy everyone with the responses she was making.

Most of Tim's friends were arriving now. Gathering platefuls of food, they spilled over into the downstairs rooms; the parlour that Rhona hadn't seen earlier and the living room. Hand in hand, she and Timothy wandered among them, pausing to laugh and to chat.

Someone had provided wine – white as well as red, and flagons of cider. She never quite emptied her glass before it was filled up again. 'This doesn't look like wartime,' she told Mrs Cooper who was smiling broadly as she supervised the feast.

'The wine's been in the cellar donkey's years. My husband's very partial to wine. Can't abide the taste myself. This is my tipple, and the girls'.' She raised her tumbler of cider to them.

Eventually Barry managed to quieten everyone sufficiently to be heard speaking as best man. He was rather long-winded and filled his speech with so many double entendres and innuendos that Rhona soon gave up the attempt at working them out. I ought to feel ashamed, she reflected. The service went through in a sort of haze, because of being hustled into it, now I'm scarcely aware of what's going on. And it all was in her honour. Hers and Timothy's:

'Have you got everything packed?' Tim asked her urgently as soon as he'd replied to the toast.

'Packed?' Her heart plummeting, Rhona wondered rapidly how much she had missed. This was still Saturday, surely? She wasn't going home till tomorrow.

'Didn't I tell you? A great stroke of luck, old love – while I was seeing the vicar first thing this morning, I happened to mention we'd only the one night. And nowhere to go. He's got a brother lives over at Folkestone. He's a parson as well, but he's just joined up as a chaplain. His vicarage is empty . . .'

Rhona swallowed, gazing at him, perplexed. She didn't want to go off to some cold, empty vicarage on the Kent coast, in the middle of winter. Why couldn't they stay here? There were two rooms, weren't there? And they only needed one. Now. She stifled a sigh.

'Just throw a few things in your bag then, it's only overnight, worse luck. We'll have to be back here early tomorrow, anyway. I have to report before midday. You can pick up the rest of your things then.'

Dully, Rhona went up to her room. The mirror was old, a lot of the silvering had worn off its back. Her reflection didn't look much better. A smile might have helped, but she felt as though her smile had been worn away. She'd done nothing but grin since getting up. Most of the smiling had been from her heart, deeply appreciative, she acknowledged, looking at the prayer book Mrs Cooper had given her. The white chrysanthemum was turning brown at the edges now, its petals curling all the wrong way. Carefully she unfastened it from the bookmark, found some tissue paper in her case, and pressed the flower between folded layers.

Suddenly, she grinned at herself in the mirror, amused despite her momentary deflation. That hat certainly was some creation! Slowly she removed it, took out the lavatory paper that she'd used as packing to make it fit, and went on to the landing to set the hat on a polished chest.

She couldn't fault the Coopers, they hadn't spared themselves in providing a magnificent, if unconventional, wedding breakfast. And they hadn't withheld one ounce of warmth. She couldn't fault any of Tim's friends either, they had rallied round to make their day memorable. And nor could she fault Tim, really. Even though she'd have preferred being consulted about tonight. She didn't suppose he would have felt easy with her, in his billet.

'Are you ready?'

He was at the door of her room, coming in now, his keen eyes assessing her lack of preparation. 'We've got ten minutes, that's all, love. Be sharp, will you. Barry's dropping us at the station.'

She waited for him to leave, allowing her to select the personal items she might need, to find underclothes, her nightdress.

Tim remained where he was, motionless, staring. And he has every right to, Rhona realized, extensively shocked. If it weren't for the abnormality of war, he'd expect to be included in most of her private moments from now on.

Hastily she found the few things she would need to see her through to the morning, bundled them anyhow into her case, and slowly closed the lid.

'Right then,' she said, and made herself smile at him.

It was different once they were in the train – better. Every compartment was packed, they ended up in the corridor. Fortunately there were fewer passengers here. Tim located a small space where they could actually stand without being crushed by other people, or overheard.

'It was strange, wasn't it, our wedding,' he confided, one arm steadying her against the lurching of the train. 'Didn't seem quite – real, somehow. Unfamiliar church, lots of folk, but some I hardly knew . . . must have been worse for you.'

'I – didn't mind.' Rhona swallowed, willed her eyes not to fill. God, what an anticlimax! This is my wedding day, she thought. My one and only . . . !

'I'll make it up to you, I do mean that.' His voice was husky. When she looked into his blue eyes she knew she needn't have contained her own emotion, and was shattered. 'When this lot's over, Rhona, we'll have a –

well, some sort of blessing or something. In Halfield, in the church you've always gone to, with your folk all there, and my mum and dad.'

'It's all right, really, I . . .' Again, she swallowed. 'That – that would be grand, though. I might feel married then.'

'You think it'll take that long, then . . . ?' Mischief lit his eyes again, quirked the corners of his lips. With the back of his hand he dashed away all signs of emotion. 'You've been a brick, darling, you truly have. I hardly dared hope you might agree. I'll take infinite care of you, you'll have no regrets.'

He drew her against him, leaned with her, pressing close while the juddering carriage at her back turned from icy cold to warm.

Rhona closed her eyes as his lips tenderly found her own. He slid his hands around her beneath her suit jacket, holding her firmly to him, the masculine scent of him filling her senses, familiar, reassuring.

The empty vicarage stood exposed on The Leas at Folkestone, battered by winds wailing in from the channel. Inside, though, the downstairs rooms were aired by log fires lit by the absent vicar's daily, a gaunt woman who lived nearby and had handed them the key.

She'd left food for them in the old-fashioned larder: mutton chops, a cabbage that would serve six, potatoes, and a ready-baked apple pie. They hadn't eaten since late morning. Rhona removed her jacket as soon as they'd explored the rambling house. 'I'd better prove I can cook you at least one meal.'

'Not yet, you don't.' Tim's grasp was firm, pulling her sharply into his arms. His mouth covered hers, his tongue plunging immediately, deep between her lips.

'Aren't you hungry?' she asked when he allowed her to breathe again. Wasn't her own hollow feeling hunger?

Shaking his head at her, Tim smiled. 'I'll not answer that one. Come on, love . . .' Gently this time, he kissed her again, then smiled once more, leaning down towards her, his forehead touching hers. His golden hair felt silky to her brow, cool. She freed a hand, reached up and touched the glossy waves. Tim's look was tender again, his eyes dark with emotion. Smiling back, she ran tentative fingers over his cheek. He caught her hand, cupped it, filled her palm with kisses.

Rhona slid her arm through his and walked with him up the stairs. In the doorway of the master bedroom he drew her to him once more, smiling, his glance caressing her.

'You didn't suppose I'd wait, did you, not when the sirens could go, on and off all night, interrupting.'

'Off course, there is that. I never thought.'

'There's never any air raids in Halfield.'

There have been quite a few – and one that I'll always remember, thought Rhona grimly. Couldn't she exclude Wolf, if only for today?

The ample Victorian bed was surrounded by sturdy walnut furniture. The entire room reeked of mothballs. In the ugly fireplace, behind the mesh of its guard, a pathetic cluster of low-grade coal struggled to produce dismal smoke.

Rhona shivered as she methodically removed her white silk blouse, then slid off her navy Chanel skirt.

'Just a minute . . .' Timothy went to rummage in his kitbag, then he went from the room while she was finding her nightdress. He came back from the bathroom with a couple of substantial tumblers.

'This'll warm you up for a start.'

He'd half filled the glass from the bottle he'd brought with him. As she went to sip the glowing amber liquid, Rhona sniffed. She'd smelled this before, a long time ago. She gazed, hard, at Tim's lips, waited . . . He'd taken a drink from his own glass, now he swallowed. She blinked, returning herself to today.

The powerful spirit caught her throat, but she gulped it down, deciding it was time to let go, to begin liking her wedding day. 'It can't be rushing through my veins, but that's how it feels!'

'That's the way brandy's meant to feel. Drink that, then have some more . . .'

He was sipping carefully, savouring each mouthful. He'd been warned by some of his pals what too much alcohol might do to him. But there was no mistaking Rhona's need of something to untangle all those inhibitions. He'd read in her eyes, at the farm, her abrupt loss of privacy. He knew her well enough to expect she'd experience a keen sense of invasion.

'Come on, love, it'll warm you up no end,' he coaxed, willing himself to hold on before permitting even his eyes to devour that gleam of skin around and beneath her slinky white petticoat. 'Haven't you tasted brandy before?'

'Oh – yes. As a matter of fact, I could acquire quite a liking for it. Though I doubt if wartime's quite the moment to go in for such things.' She was beginning to babble, not because of the drink, but she hoped Tim might suppose it was. 'Happen you'll have to think up some other means of keeping me warm.'

She drained the glass, nevertheless, before setting it aside. Let that make me forget, she thought. And smiled yet again at her husband.

'Anybody'd think you were the one feeling the chill, anyway,' she remarked wryly, and crossed the few paces of linoleum to his side.

Silently she removed his jacket, folded it and placed it over the back of a cane-seated chair. His tie was next, then she began on the buttons of his shirt. And all the while Timothy was watching her, smiling to himself, moving only sufficiently to permit her to continue with her task.

He wasn't wearing any vest, and as soon as she stripped him of his shirt she felt the pulses awakening deep inside her own body. He was a lovely shape, neither so skinny that his ribs showed nor covered with surplus fat. Masses of fair hair curled down the centre of his chest, eventually disappeared into his blue-grey trousers.

If I have to, she thought, *if* I have to I'll have them off him, and all. I can do it. Tim's been so determined that we'd get wed, he had this all worked out, without any prompting from me. He's brought me away, so's we can be alone. He'll not be disappointed.

His bare torso looked literally statuesque, perfectly formed, creating within her an astonishing feeling of awe. She needed to touch, to learn that he was real, to feel his skin beneath her fingertips.

She stepped closer, slipped her arms around him, her hands sampling skin, tissue, the hard line of muscle. Now his fingers were on her, sliding straps from her shoulders, gently caressing one breast. Fiercely, they clung, mouths searching, locating, tongues sharp with brandy exploring each other.

His fingers went to his waistband. Swiftly he discarded trousers and pants, then pulled her to him again, breathless now, desire groaning deep in his throat.

'Tim, Tim . . .'

Her cry seemed to echo his need.

He was pressing at her while she was straining to be close, ever closer to him. Her petticoat slid to the ground, his hand anchored on her spine forcing her against the stirring of his body.

Ripples of glorious sensation soared right through her from every inch that he was touching. 'More,' she heard a voice insist, and knew it was her own. I'm feverish with love for him, she thought, glad there'd be no pretence. And glad also that it did seem to be love as much as wanting.

The hand left her spine, dragged her knickers over her hips and thrust them out of the way. Briefly, he struggled with one of her suspenders, then chuckled. 'They'll have to stay as they are.'

He followed her down on to the bed, the length of him fitting to her, his mouth bruising her lips, fingers tracing the top of her silk stocking, progressing over her thigh.

She had become one tremendous need, conscious only of this man who would be part of her, and she of him, complete . . . Thank God we came away, she thought, astounded by her own desperation to have his touch . . . everywhere. Most of all, though, to belong.

228

Timothy was trying to think, to consider, to *slow*. She was his, and this was new for her, he must not scare . . . Gradually, willing some restraint, he permitted his fingers to travel on again. Gently – was it gently enough? – he enticed her to accept him.

'More,' she breathed again. This time he was certain of what he'd heard.

Rhona felt tremors concentrate from every pulse-point towards the touch of him. Her silk-clad legs slid over the icy sheet as he pressed nearer. Prepared for pain, she stiffened, but only for a moment. Her own relentless rhythm superseded other responses. Eyes closed, she gasped, savouring sensation, willing him to remain there always, uniting them.

Straining him to her, her fingers thrust deep into his spine. She was shattered by her own urgent need to continue this glorious closeness. You've waited a long time for this, she thought, realized with a start that she didn't mean only Timothy . . .

Abruptly, the tempo of their harmony slowed. Relaxing against her shoulder, his lips were motionless, kissing her no longer. Gilded lashes lowered, his eyelids now were still. A sleepy, contented sigh tingled over her bare skin from a mouth tender from tasting her.

Rhona smiled. She might be unpractised, but it seemed she'd achieved everything required of her. For somebody who'd left home only yesterday without any thought of marrying, that wasn't so bad. Whatever else their wedding might have lacked, she'd given enough enthusiasm.

Inert though, Timothy felt heavy, crushing her into the lumpy flock mattress. She was compelled into a sudden stillness which, somehow, did not feel quite right. It didn't hurt to admit to herself, but only to herself, that she'd hoped . . . Well, she'd loved the sensations, they might have lasted a bit longer. Now, she – well, she'd keep as still as she was able, just to let him sleep.

When Tim moved eventually, his lips covered hers possessively. 'You gorgeous woman!' he murmured against her mouth. '*Wife.*'

Rhona smiled into his eyes, returning his kisses eagerly, thankful she had this means of delighting him. She was sore now, her only need less romantic, if no less urgent.

'You're going to have to shift to one side a bit,' she told him ruefully. 'I'll have to go spend a penny.'

Was it ridiculous, in that ornate old bathroom, to be aware of Tim only the other side of the landing, and that he might hear? I can't be silent about it, she thought and reproved herself for being irrationally embarrassed. After what they'd been doing.

She lingered briefly afterwards. The gilt-framed mirror revealed eyes that were enormous gleaming jewels – how different she looked! The hair that she'd fluffed out that morning was ablaze, haloing her glowing face. And the rumpled pink corset suspended wrinkled silk stockings.

I'd look better without that lot, she decided. And it is rather late to worry about covering myself. But did women walk about wearing nothing, even on their honeymoon?

She couldn't see Timothy when she returned to the bedroom. That was all right then, he'd not have the chance to disapprove of her nakedness. Her nightdress was where it had slid, almost under the bed.

She was padding across the chilly linoleum when she heard him behind her. One hand slipping down over her stomach, the other locating her breast, he held her to him.

'Where were you then?' she asked, trying to sound unsurprised.

'Behind the door, where else?'

'Thought you'd gone to put the kettle on or something.'

'Can't you think of anything but food and drink?'

'Evidently, you can!'

'You did make me wait half a lifetime, love. I'm only human.'

They were on the bed immediately. He held her curved into him, his caresses reawakening her. Leisurely kisses travelled over the nape of her neck, he nibbled at her earlobe. Rhona trembled with a thrill that couldn't be disguised. Tim was stirring again, their bodies beginning to harmonize.

Slowly, sensuously, he moved over and across her, making her moan again with renewed yearning. Timothy groaned ecstatically, buried his face at her throat. She felt his teeth on her, moaned yet again, increased his urgency, was exhilarated by his excitement.

It couldn't be wrong of her, could it, to like what they were doing – to wish him to take his time now, so that their loving lasted for hours?

Tim was kissing her neck, kissing and, by the feel of it, biting. I wonder if that'll leave a mark? she thought then reproached herself for caring. He'd slipped a hand beneath her and was kneading her lower spine, intensifying her response. Clutching his shoulders, Rhona surrendered to waves of desire stronger than stormy seas.

Timothy was grunting now, throaty sounds, expressing need of their intimacy. She smiled tenderly. He was like an adorable puppy, eager and excited, panting.

The panting ceased in one exhausted sigh, once more he stilled against her. She kissed the corners of his lips, his lowered eyelids. She'd never felt so tenderly about anyone. Being a part of someone else was wonderful.

Timothy awakened when she finally got out of bed.

'This time, I am going to make us something to eat, no arguments,' she told him firmly. 'Looking after you is part of marriage as well.'

'Who's arguing?' He smiled luxuriously and stretched taut arms above his head. 'Give us a kiss first, though, love.'

His mouth was affectionate over hers, deeply tender again. 'God, but you're marvellous! I'm almost glad you did make me wait for this, Rhona, you're magnificent.'

'You're not so bad yourself.'

'You could develop a taste for this, then?' he teased.

'Like the brandy, yes. Just wait till we've got this war over with, we'll make up for everything.' Suddenly she felt cold, though, so terribly afraid she might have to wait as long as that before experiencing their lovemaking with any regularity.

She went to have a hurried bath, and could hear

Timothy whistling to himself. Again, she was glad she was the one who'd made him happy. It made everything seem better, didn't it? What mattered, anyway, even when the bath water was lukewarm and she'd brought only a hand towel with her?

'Run one for me, will you, love,' Tim called as she tried vainly to dry herself quickly.

'I'm not so sure I should. I'm not your slave, you know,' she called back lightly.

'Have I even hinted that you were?' He came to the doorway. 'I shan't get too spoiled, I'm sure, in the few hours we've got left.'

'Sorry, I . . .' All at once she was choked with tears. 'Ay, love – I am sorry! How'll we ever say goodbye?'

'We won't, ever. Don't hold with it. It'll just be take care of yourself, till next time . . .'

Rhona gulped, swallowed, forced a grin to her lips. 'Aye. T.T.F.N., like they say in ITMA.'

Again, he held her. Again, sweet kisses lingered over her mouth. 'Go on then, Wife, get cracking on that dinner.' Or I'll take you here in this old-fashioned bathroom, he thought, because I can't get enough of loving you. Because there's no way on this earth that I can know the longing, the waiting are ended. Because I'm so bloody scared that I shan't survive to even see you again.

She was starting to prepare the cabbage and potatoes when the siren curdled her blood with its unearthly wailing. It seemed much worse here, because of the cliffs and the sea perhaps. Rigid with apprehension, she clenched her fingers over the rim of the wooden draining board, her eyes wide and wild as she ordered herself to find self-control.

Tim found her like that after hurtling downstairs, trying to pull on his shirt over his still-damp body.

'I thought so . . .' He pointed to the large table in the centre of the adjoining breakfast room. 'See that – he's had the top reinforced. Improvised shelter. Better get in there sharpish. Here on the coast, we can't take chances.'

'But . . .'

'Had you got the dinner on?'

'No – worse luck. The blighters could have let us have a meal first. I'm fair clemmed!'

Glancing swiftly around, Timothy noticed the apple pie, seized it with one hand and Rhona's wrist with the other.

'Are you certain this is necessary, or even good?' Crouching down then crawling into the space beneath the table was an experience she'd rather have missed. The worn carpet smelled of old dog.

'It's better than having the house crashing down through our skulls if the worst happens. Have a look – the old boy's been thorough, had some corrugated iron fastened underneath this table top. And the wood itself's a couple of inches thick.'

'Wouldn't we be safer in the cellar?' It couldn't be this claustrophobic.

'I had a scout round soon as we arrived. Looks like the cellar's been bricked up. Well, there's nothing for it but to have our pudding.' Grinning, he broke off a piece of the apple pie and handed it to her.

'We can't, not here.' Although absent, that dog was so intrusive.

'It's meant for us, agreed? You surely can't pretend we're standing on any ceremony, crammed together under the blessed table, and might be for many an hour.'

'Don't say that.'

His blue eyes lit. 'You'd have preferred the cellar, would you? Liked what was happening to you in the cellar of the village hall last night?'

'Timothy!'

'Don't answer if you don't like to, you don't have to tell me anything. I only know what you were doing to me, and that *wasn't* because you were an ice maiden!'

'What's made you start talking this way?'

'It doesn't upset you, does it? We're man and wife, Rhona, there's nothing forbidden between us.'

'All right. I – happen I just need time to get used to the idea.'

'I'll try and spare your ears. I'm just so glad we're wed,

that we belong and . . . well, you're just as exciting as I knew you would be.'

Rhona was pensive. She'd never imagined she might be all that attractive. That Tim would want her so much. Suddenly, emotion filled her again. It mattered a lot, already, being the woman this man of hers needed. That there was all this for them to share, before they had to be apart.

'More pie?'

She giggled, taking another portion, beginning to eat hastily. 'No one can say we're not original, sitting under a table dining off apple pie – and nothing else, on our honeymoon!'

'Like us, unconventional. Marrying before any real courtship. But we've grown into being so right together, haven't we, love? And because it hasn't all been sweet music, this seems *more* romantic.'

'M'mm . . .' She wouldn't think too carefully about that one. But she smiled, kissed him lightly on the cheek.

'Had enough to eat . . . ?' Tim was taking another piece of pie, had noticed Rhona's frown.

'I was ready for something more substantial. Never mind. We're not going to starve.' She sighed. 'I could do with a cup of tea. Do you think . . . ?' She moved only slightly, and Tim grabbed her arm.

'Don't you dare get out of here.' He was livid. He hung on to her as though terrified she'd move out of the makeshift shelter.

When Rhona gave him a look, he shrugged. 'Go on, tell me you're used to looking after yourself. But this is serious, love. They don't have sirens going down here when there's none of Hitler's planes about.'

'But I can't hear a thing, no planes, nothing.'

'You're neither trained nor equipped for doing so. And right here on the cliffs we're the first that'll know when they're across the channel. With hindsight, maybe I shouldn't have brought you here. But there was only Folkestone on offer, and no time for thinking it through.'

And you were only considering your need to be on your

own with me, Rhona thought, and kept silent. Should I be glad about that, or what, she wondered. Oh, what the heck – this is our honeymoon!

'You were thinking for us,' she said, was surprised that her voice was husky.

They were there for what felt like hours, with still no sound of activity anywhere beyond the vicarage walls. And still Timothy would not agree to their emerging. He felt responsibility heavy upon the head that should have been airy with happiness. He would do everything in his power to protect her. If he was being irrational, unwarrantedly cautious – hard cheese!

'It's a bit draughty down here, isn't it?' Rhona remarked eventually, although she'd been determined not to say one more word about their situation.

'Can't even remember whether I left my jacket upstairs or somewhere down here. Still, can't be much longer, surely. Come here . . .'

He drew her to him, wrapping his arms about her, his lips pressed into her hair.

Don't smother me, she thought, and hated herself for being so unappreciative. After a short while, though, her leg went into cramp and she was compelled to say something.

'Hang on, we'll lie down – more comfortable,' he suggested.

'In my best Chanel skirt? Heaven knows when we'll be able to get any decent clothes again.' Suddenly she laughed. 'Listen to me! Grumble, grumble, grumble! Sorry, love, I don't seem able to stop fussing.'

Tim grinned. 'You're used to being careful with your things. Take the skirt off, then.'

That made sense. It was all she had for travelling back to Halfield in.

'Oh, Tim – I shan't want to go back, I know I shan't.'

'And that's what's making you on edge. But you'd not be happy for long in Kent, specially when we're living on the station.'

'Will that be soon?'

'You know how brilliant your husband is – be trained in record time!'

It was best to make a joke of it, like that. He knew he'd soon be in the air, that they were pushing them all into the skies as fast as they could learn what to do with the machines they were given – as fast as those machines were assembled and rushed to the airfields.

'Anyway, who'd run Bridge House with Dad if you didn't get back? At least you'll have the fun of telling them all our news.'

'I wonder whatever they'll say!'

'Dad will beam from ear to ear and say "About time too!" or something of the sort. Mum won't say a lot but she'll give you a great big hug. She might tell you she's always wished she had a daughter. And she has always thought well of your dad.'

'If I get back in time I'll go round and see them as soon as I've told my own folk.'

'And how will they take it?'

Rhona laughed a little, half to herself. 'Mum was hinting that I ought to settle down with you, not so long since.'

He squeezed her shoulders. 'Remind me to thank her, when I do get leave to come up to Yorkshire.'

'Might that be soon, how are you fixed for leave?'

'Depends how things go. There's so many factors that are unpredictable as yet. Still, I'm sure Dad will be willing for you to take a bit of time off to come down here.'

'I'll be thankful when this lot's over and we can start getting a home together.'

'You can do that now, keep you occupied. You could start looking soon as you get back there.'

'I don't like that idea, not on my own.'

'I'd like to think of you in our home, love.'

'Happen so, but how do I know what sort of place you want?'

'I'm not bothered, so long as it suited you. Two up, two down, a mansion, anything . . .'

'A great help, you are!'

'You'd enjoy looking, you know you would.'

'I'll bet there aren't many houses on the market now.'

'There must be some, if only from folk that have pegged out.'

'Cheerful!' Rhona grinned. 'It'd have to be near the mill, I suppose.'

'Not necessarily, you've got the car.'

'Aye, and petrol's scarce, hadn't you heard?'

'There'll always be an allowance for business folk.'

'If I find us somewhere to live – and I mean *if*, you'll have to put up with my taste. Or in so far as I'm able to find what I want. You don't know what you're letting yourself in for, Timothy Brightstone. I've got plenty of ideas, you know, of how I'd want my home to look.' She paused, growing to like the prospect. 'It's a good job I've got some brass behind me, so's I can buy . . .'

'Here – wait a minute,' he interrupted, very quickly. 'You're not using your money. I won't have that. I'm providing the home.'

She concealed her smile. 'Don't talk so old-fashioned. It was all right a minute ago for me to be running the mill. Now, all at once, it's all wrong for me to be spending what I've got.'

'Do you think I want people believing I can't provide for you?'

'Who'd know, besides you and me? Ay, you do talk daft! My way's much more practical, you know. Tell you what – if it makes you feel any better, we'll do as I say, but only *pro tem*. As soon as you're out of the air force afterwards we'll sort out whose money pays for what. I promise I won't make a fuss.'

Timothy took her by the shoulders, turning her to face him. 'I could shake you, you know! Trying to get round me like that . . .'

Her sherry-brown eyes glinting, Rhona raised an eyebrow at him. 'Better not, love. You're the one who's determined on having me see to a home for us . . .'

He crushed her to him instead, suddenly afraid that any difference of opinion was a threat to their relationship.

Afraid as well that this wasn't quite real, and by morning it would slip away. Rhona was real enough, though, warm from contact with his body, yielding as her silky petticoat clung against his service trousers and slithered up her stockinged leg.

Her breasts felt firm against his chest, her hair was fragrant as it brushed his cheek, and with every sense he recognized her beauty. The surge of desire almost made him smile. Good though it was to make her his this way, it couldn't really express more than a bit of what he was feeling.

'Not here . . . ?' She bit her lip, furious with herself for failing to contain her astonishment. But she'd been surprised that he could be needing her again, even rather alarmed now that he was easing her petticoat upwards.

His thumb negotiated her elastic, and at once she was stirring, bemused by her own wild body that was so swift in response.

'Sweetheart, I want to love you in every place imaginable. Why's the bed such an acceptable spot? I'd want you on a moonlit beach, beside a lake, on our own moors . . .'

'I hope you'd pick a warmer time of year, then!'

He laughed joyously, holding her even more firmly to him. 'Or take your mind off everything!'

'Aye, lad, you seem to manage that . . .'

His mouth stopped her speaking while he tore at his own buttons. So eager now that she could hardly wait, Rhona was ready for him when he moved above her. If this is desperation because we've so little time together, she thought, somewhere beyond their urgent stirring, we seem to be agreed it's necessary.

Thinking surrendered to being and to feeling, to knowing he was a part of her. Relaxing to allow her emotions their will, she gloried in their possession of each other.

Her eyelids closed, she could see the moors he'd mentioned, the old carpet seemed to take on the rough contours of heather-clad earth, the table leg against her ankle felt rough like the bark of a sentinel tree. Her

238

nostrils flared, as though to the scent of peat and a breeze fresh from a tarn.

But the breeze was his breath, heated and moist on her neck. 'I love you, Rhona Brightstone,' he gasped, hardly able to speak. 'I'll go on and on proving how much. And there'll be more to us than this – you have my word.' He paused, drawing in great, hasty breaths. 'Though this surely is a marvellous beginning . . .'

15

'You couldn't have pleased me more, you know that, don't you!' Bill was grinning widely, his face flushed with delight, as he pumped Rhona's hand up and down. 'You'll be the making of our Timothy – he'll calm down a lot, and . . .'

'I think he has calmed down,' Rhona interrupted, smiling. 'Quite some time ago. But I'm glad you're pleased, Bill.'

Her mother and stepfather hadn't been so unreservedly enthusiastic, but that was natural. Eve, particularly, had felt deprived of organizing the wedding. 'I just don't like to think that some other woman had to lay on a spread for you.'

'Mrs Cooper was only too pleased.'

'I daresay. But you're my daughter. And Dad's always expected to give you away just as if you were his own. Haven't you, Jack?'

'Aye, that's true. But you shouldn't let it bother you, Eve love. Our Rhona did what she thought was best, in the circumstances. And if we're a bit disappointed, at least it's about the wedding itself, not about who she's married.'

'There is that,' Eve agreed. 'In fact, happen I'm partly to blame. It's not long since I was on at you about marrying Tim, is it, love?'

'Quite. And we'll make up for it when he manages a long enough leave to come up here.'

'You'd better tell him I expect him to stay with us, think on. We need time to really get to know him,' her mother said quickly.

'Aye – tell your Tim we won't take no for an answer,' Jack Hebden added. 'We want the opportunity to show him he's one of us now.'

Her first few days back at work passed rapidly, and

quite pleasantly. So many people were to be told of her marriage that Rhona was prevented from feeling too deflated about her husband's absence. And Tim had telephoned the mill on the Monday morning, to check that Rhona had arrived safely in Halfield, and to speak with his father.

Hearing his voice had brought back to her all the excitement of the weekend, increasing her eagerness to pass on their news. Auntie Norah must be one of the first to know, she decided. She would also have to tell Phyllis. For some reason she couldn't quite identify, Rhona felt uneasy about confiding in her friend. And yet Phyllis now was, as far as one could see, recovered from Adrian's tragic death.

Mrs Ayntree was back at Lavender Court after her long stay in a sanatorium. Her improved health, however, was somewhat overshadowed now by the family having to adjust to Clive's absence. And Phyllis, more than anyone, seemed to miss her twin very greatly. She and Rhona had smiled quite recently, though, over the strange coincidence by which he and Dan Hebden had met up during training, in the navy.

Clive was expected home on leave the Friday after Rhona's return from Kent. When Phyllis heard a car in the drive of Lavender Court, she went racing to open the front door. Excitement turned to perplexity when she saw who was standing on the step.

'Oh – good evening, Wolf, do come in,' she said hastily, her fair skin flushing as she hoped she was concealing her disappointment. 'I trust nothing's wrong?'

Since she'd recovered from losing Adrian, she'd more or less forgotten Wolf Richardson's existence. Following completion of the reservoir he also had dropped out of her father-in-law's conversation.

'In here . . .' she said, leading the way into the living room. 'We don't use the sitting room, these days, it requires all that additional heating. It makes one wonder why such large houses were built . . .' She checked abruptly, recalling how much larger Wolf's home was.

241

Although his grey eyes did not light he smiled, and gave a shrug. 'Yes, I do agree, so many places couldn't have been utilized fully for many a year. Actually, I've offered Farnley Carr for use by the armed forces, but to date they haven't considered it suitable. I know it's very remote . . .'

'Clive's joined the navy now. In fact, he's due home on leave. I thought you were him arriving.'

'Sorry.'

Smiling, Phyllis shook her head. 'Don't be. And sit down, please – better make it over there, near what bit of fire there is. Can I offer you a drink?'

'No, thank you. I won't impose on too much of your time. It's just . . . well, frankly, I couldn't think of anyone else who might help.'

'Help?' How on earth was she expected to help Wolf Richardson? Come to that – what help could he require of anybody? Wasn't he so magnificently self-sufficient?

Wolf felt no less awkward than Phyllis herself. Yet he was here, at last, he would force himself to speak of his reason for coming. 'It's about . . . you're a close friend of Rhona, aren't you?'

'Of course. Whatever's wrong – she's not ill or anything, is she?'

'No, nothing like that. It's – look, I'm afraid I'm expressing this very badly, maybe I'd better start again. This is very personal – I would appreciate your discretion. The fact is – some while ago, Rhona and I had a disastrous evening together, when it was meant to be the opportunity for – for cementing the relationship between us.'

Phyllis tried to disguise her smile. She was surprised, but not displeased, to discover there was something between Wolf and Rhona. 'Oh, if that's all, I'm sure it'll blow over, and turn out all right. Rhona's the last person to bear grudges, isn't she? Know what you want to do – as soon as you get home, ring her up.'

'As a matter of fact, I did try that. I telephoned Bridge House Mill last Saturday morning. She wasn't there.'

'That's unusual. I thought she worked all the hours God sends! She wasn't ill, or anything?'

'Bill Brightstone said she was away for the weekend.'

'Well, then – you try again.' Phyllis paused, looked at him again. 'Or have you lost courage?'

Wryly, Wolf met her glance. Was it that obvious? 'I'm not aided by only being able to telephone her at the mill. I know Brightstone, but not well enough to wish him involved in personal matters.' And not while he's the father of *that person* . . .

'I see.' Phyllis felt strangely flattered that Wolf had chosen to confide in her while he hesitated to reveal any hint of all this to another man. And she wasn't sorry to have the opportunity to help. She'd felt sympathetic when Beatrice Richardson left him that second time. Having somebody die was appalling, how must one feel if they simply chose to go right away? And marry again with indecent haste.

'What do you wish me to do?' she inquired gently. 'Like me to have a word, find out . . . well, how she feels?'

'No, I . . .' Grimly, Wolf sighed and met her glance levelly. 'You see the way it is. Don't know why I came here really, except . . . No – no, I don't wish you to say anything at all to Rhona. But – well, I suppose I hoped *she* might have said something in the past, of her regret, perhaps, about our quarrel.'

'Sorry, I don't know that she has. Not anything concrete. At one time, though, she was quite – *interested* in you . . .' Her voice died away. It seemed years since Rhona had even mentioned Wolf. 'She doesn't confide in anyone very much.'

Hastily Wolf stood up. He should never have come here, whatever had possessed him? 'I must apologize for troubling you.'

Before he'd got himself out of the room the telephone rang. 'Excuse me, you don't mind, do you? Please sit down again,' Phyllis said quickly.

As she lifted the receiver, she grinned, her green eyes

lighting. 'Great heavens, Rhona – hallo! What an extra-ordinary coincidence – are your ears on fire? . . . oh, I'm fine – and you . . . ? Good. And what have you been up to, I understand you've been away? Have a lovely time?'

Wolf was unable to contain his smile. For so long he'd hesitated over the wisdom of coming to see Phyllis. All at once it seemed he'd made a most opportune decision. In a few moments she would mention to Rhona that he was here, that he wished to contact her. Everything then would be up to him. Since he'd rehearsed and re-rehearsed all that he intended saying, even this abnormal nervous-ness would not ruin a thing. He would apologize, briefly, for any misunderstandings, and assert firmly that they were not going to throw away happiness by being intransigent.

'Oh . . .' Phyllis's strangled gasp made him look at her again. Suddenly her face was the shade of her hair. Even from the other side of the room like this he saw the light go out of her eyes. 'Yes,' she was saying, 'er – naturally, I wish you all the very best. I hope you'll be happy, Rhona. It's just – well, you have rather taken the wind out of my sails.'

Something was very wrong. That was patently obvious. His elation was expiring, the familiar gnawing ache returning between his lower ribs. He longed to stride over to Phyllis, take the receiver, and demand to be told what was amiss. Dread, more than his customary good manners, kept him where he was. When she eventually replaced the telephone nothing in Phyllis's appearance could be called reassuring.

'*Is* Rhona ill?' he demanded immediately.

'Ill? Oh, no.' I can *not* tell him, she thought wildly. And knew that, somehow, she would have to give him the truth.

'Is she joining the forces now?' he suggested, anxiety deepening.

'No, it's not that either.'

He sprang to his feet again. 'Have I no right to know, Phyllis? Why are you holding out on me? You must be

244

aware, from what little I've said, that I do care very deeply about Rhona. If there's some disturbing news, then I . . . What is it?'

Phyllis got to her feet again. She seemed to sway a little, and looked so fragile that he was afraid she might faint. 'You know Bill . . .'

'Yes, yes,' he said hurriedly. 'And that he suffers poor health, if . . .'

Numbly, Phyllis swallowed. She inhaled deeply, trying to find courage to say what must be said. Her legs leaden, she crossed to him, grasped his arm. 'It's not Bill Brightstone. There's no easy way to tell you this. And you have to know, sooner or later. I'm afraid sooner's kindest, in the long run. Rhona – got married on Saturday, Wolf. For your sake, I'm desperately sorry.'

'Brightstone's son?'

Phyllis nodded gravely.

Feverishly, he wrenched his arm free of her hand.

'No, Wolf – wait. Don't go yet . . .'

He was out of the room, though, striding through the hall. The front door slammed to behind him, his feet crunched over the gravel of the drive. His car door shut with a bang, the engine revved, he drove away.

He had sat in the car for hours, staring through the blackness that was the reservoir and surrounding moor. There wasn't a single star in sight, no glimmer of moon, no light of any kind. Appropriate. The only thought to console him was that if Rhona was so deeply involved with young Brightstone, he himself hadn't been entirely responsible for wrecking any potential relationship before it had really begun. He needn't go on cursing his own ineptitude. Whatever he had done or said on the evening that had turned out so abysmally, she had been committed to that fellow, and wouldn't have responded to *him*.

The fact that she *had* responded he tried to dismiss. There had been no denying the sexual element attracting them to each other from the beginning. He had believed their affinity founded on mutual understanding, respect and affection. Was desire so important to her? The cause of their parting had been her assumption that sex would have driven him to sleep with Beatrice immediately the opportunity was presented.

I have been totally wrong about the girl, he told himself time after time. Remaining unconvinced was regrettable, but it was also irrational.

As the wintry dawn was painting the sky primrose above the horizon of gorse and heather, he drove reluctantly towards Farnley Carr. Should I get right away from here? he thought, desperate to rid himself of every association with her. But the work in which he was involved tied him to his company, and the company was here in Yorkshire. He could scarcely uproot all his employees in order to avoid the girl he loved.

That morning Wolf tried again to interest the Ministry of Defence in his home. Given good reason to get out, he might find a smaller place, some way from Halfield. The day he heard they still had no wish to take over his residence, too far away from civilization for their purposes, he grimly set his teeth, silently challenging life to do its worst. No Richardson gave in under circumstances, no matter how unpalatable. His one consolation was knowing that Phyllis alone was even partially aware of the depth of his interest in Rhona.

Enjoying her new status, Rhona wrote daily to her husband. Somehow, she felt much more a part of the camaraderie generated by the war. Telling him about what was happening at the mill, production of yarn for uniforms became more substantially a part of the war effort. And she was happy to pass news on. The only matter that she avoided mentioning was her own condition. Even when, in time, a visit to the doctor confirmed that she was expecting, she still hugged the information to herself.

Concealment was simpler than it might have been – she remained reasonably well, and experienced no morning sickness. Happen it's because I keep myself too busy to dwell on every little funny feeling inside me, Rhona thought, and didn't pause long enough to ask why she persisted in filling her day so completely.

Apart from the infrequency of Tim's letters to her, she had no grounds for complaining about him. When he did write he always told her how much he loved and missed her.

As she found her waistband growing progressively tighter, she marvelled that her mother hadn't noticed her increasing weight. I'll have to tell her soon, she decided – definitely when I'm four months. There would seem less of an age to wait by then, maybe she'd be ready for sharing the anticipation.

Auntie Norah was the first one to remark on Rhona's changing shape, one Saturday when they were out in her tiny garden. Rhona had offered to do some weeding for the old lady, but a delighted laugh surprised her.

'Nay, Rhona lass, I think I'm in better fettle than you for suchlike, don't you?' Norah Lowe observed, winking mischievously. 'Or is it a new exercise or summat for mothers-to-be?'

'I didn't know you could tell –'

'I might be lacking some of my faculties, lass, sight isn't one of them! And why didn't you come straight out with it and tell me then – do you suppose you'd be the first with a honeymoon baby? There's plenty as will envy you the peace of mind of knowing folks can count up t'weeks to their hearts' content and find nowt wrong!'

'You are a naughty old lady talking that way!' Rhona reproved, but failed to hide her amusement.

'And what does the bairn's father think, then? I'll bet he's like a dog with two tails!'

'As a matter of fact, Timothy doesn't know yet.'

'I see – planning to celebrate, are you, when he comes on leave?'

Rhona smiled. 'How did you guess?'

'His mum and dad aren't in the picture then, you're not afraid of them letting the news out?'

'No one is, except the doctor – and you, you sharp-eyed old love!'

'You must be keeping well if your own mother hasn't put two and two together long before you were showing. You are still living with them?'

'Yes – haven't found a suitable house yet. And if Mum has guessed she hasn't said.'

'I seem to remember she didn't have too bad a time when she was carrying you. Happen you'll be the same. It's to be hoped you are; knowing you, I don't expect you'll give up working before you have to.'

'I don't suppose I will.'

'You'll have to take things a bit easier somehow, love. And you can start by sitting yourself down this minute.'

After what Auntie Norah had said, Rhona felt guilty about not confiding in her mother. And yet now she was set on celebrating when Timothy had a long leave, telling her mother and stepfather at the same time seemed a good idea.

It was Timothy again, though, who thwarted all her plans for his next leave. 'I can only get a forty-eight-hour pass,' he told her over the telephone. 'I've spoken to Dad and your taking travelling time again is all right with him. With your coming to Kent, we'd have far more time together . . .'

That made sense, but didn't ease her disappointment. And nor did it do anything towards helping her family to get to know him better. Rhona began uneasily to wonder if Timothy might prefer Kent to Halfield now, if he'd be reluctant to come to Yorkshire even when he could manage longer away.

When it came to the weekend in Kent, Rhona found Tim's welcome sent all her misgivings and disappointment floating away. He hugged her close the minute she stepped off the train, kissing her eyelids, her hairline, then finally her lips, with such infinite tenderness she felt a smile expanding from deep inside her.

'I'm torn apart when you're away from me, Rhona love – aching to be with you. I wish sometimes I *could* be torn apart, as well – that way there could be a part of me with you all the time.'

248

Rhona couldn't help laughing. 'Well, in a way, you've managed that,' she told him. 'Though this wasn't how I pictured you hearing about it. A rickety railway bridge is hardly the most romantic place!'

'Eh – ?' What was she on about? 'To hear what?'

'What's wrong with you these days, you're as thick as a plank? And you used to be that quick! I'm having a baby, of course.'

Of course? Speechless, Timothy stood quite still on the footbridge, while people pushed by impatiently on either side of them.

'A baby,' Rhona repeated, then hugged him. He looked so bewildered that he didn't seem much more than a child himself. 'You needn't look so astonished, love,' she whispered into his neck, 'you did enough to make one happen, didn't you!'

'Well, I'll go to heck!' He sounded just like his father. 'I never thought . . . not the first time.'

'*Times*,' she corrected him with a knowing look, and chuckled.

'Have you been all right then, travelling all this way? I mean – you should have said; I could have come to you, only that'd have been wasting hours and hours that we might have spent together.'

'I am all right, Tim. And I do understand. We're together now, that's all that matters.' And that was true enough now. She'd been proper daft to be perturbed about not seeing him for so long, and for caring where they met.

'And what does Dad say? I'll bet he's hightly delighted.'

'Do you think I'd tell him before I'd said anything to you? There's only Auntie Norah knows, and the doctor.'

'Doctor? Have you been feeling poorly then?' Consternation robbed his glorious blue eyes of their light.

'I've told you, I'm perfectly all right. But I wanted to be sure, and to find out what to do for the best. This youngster's going to have the finest start imaginable, war or no war.'

Rhona had wished to keep their news to themselves, but Tim was so thrilled he told first Barry, who had brought the car to pick her up and drive them to the farm, and then Mrs Cooper.

'You've wasted no time before proving yourself, Master Tim!' the jovial farmer's wife exclaimed. 'I hope they pays you well enough in the RAF to support a wife and family.'

The entire weekend boosted Rhona's spirits. Afterwards, she arrived back in Halfield infected by her husband's exhilaration. She immediately told her mother about the coming baby, and was rather surprised to have confirmed that Eve hadn't even suspected.

'I thought you were putting on a bit of weight, but I reckoned that was because you were more contented.'

'And I suppose I am – I mightn't have planned to have a baby this soon after getting wed, but now it's on its way I think I'm going to enjoy being a mother.'

'You've picked a right time, though, to be expecting!' Eve remarked. 'With food rationed. Where's your quarter pound of butter a week going to go, and as for meat – one and tenpence worth won't do you a lot of good!'

'I think there'll be special provision for women in my condition.'

'Think? Haven't you found out, lady? Rhona Heb – *Brightstone*, I'm ashamed of you! You'd better get down to that food office as soon as they open tomorrow. I'm not having my grandchild deprived of anything.'

Rhona laughed, and crushed her mother to her. 'I'm not really that irresponsible, you know. But I'm only just nicely getting used to the thought myself.'

'You have to say that, don't you? I suppose you imagine it excuses keeping your own mother in the dark.'

'If I know you, you'll get as fed up of waiting as I will. You'll be thanking me for not telling you before this.'

'When's it due, love?'

'Not till November.'

'So the poor little blighter'll have its first few months in the cold. We'll have to find some means of keeping this house warmer before then.'

'Well, actually, Mum – Timothy and I are after a place of our own.'

'Not – not down there, in Kent, love?' Dread curdled Eve's anticipation.

Rhona shook her head. 'I couldn't if I wanted to, could I? Who'd keep an eye on the mill if I moved away?'

'You intend continuing work, then?' Eve's disapproval was evident in her frown and the clouding of her eyes.

'As long as I'm able. I'm perfectly well, and I'm better occupied. We all have a job in wartime, mine's taking Tim's place here.'

'But you will look after yourself?'

'Have I ever given you cause to think I'm daft, Mother? I want this child – maybe more than ever I've wanted anything, there'll be no chances taken.'

'And when the baby's here, what then? Who'll take over from you at Bridge House Mill? If your job's so important, I mean . . .'

'We'll just have to wait and see, won't we?'

'Oh, yes? And will you be coming, smiling, to me, asking me to look after the bairn while you go back to that place?'

'It was my dad's mill, you can't blame me for feeling some concern that it keeps going.'

'Trust you to think of that one! You certainly take after him in more ways than one.'

'Would you consider looking after the baby for me?'

'Consider, happen – promise, no. I don't hold with women working when they've become mothers.'

'But you don't hold with war either, and you wouldn't stop me doing my bit.'

'Don't you be so sure, not if it means my grandchild has to suffer.'

'Suffer? With you for a grandma he, or she, will have far too much fuss made of him.'

During the next few weeks Eve Hebden frequently wondered if Rhona was being as circumspect as she ought. The search for a house had proved to be less prolonged than feared. A neighbour of the Ayntrees, an old man of ninety, died and the house in Apsley Road was put on the market. Rhona took both her mother and stepfather to view the property with her. Jack was the first to voice his enthusiasm.

'It's a grand place, Rhona love. You want to snatch it up. With things as they are, folk are staying put. Especially up here, well away from the bombing.'

Rhona grinned, glancing round at the old-fashioned dark wallpaper, the drab brown paint. 'You can see as well that I might be able to make something of it, then? And what do you think, Mum?'

Eve smiled. 'When you told me where it was that you were after a house, I thought it seemed right, somehow – that you should settle a few doors from where you were born. It wants a lot doing to it, and that won't be easy with all the shortages, and you having to take care.'

'But I'll make it a lovely little home,' Rhona concluded, already picturing some of the décor she wanted.

'*Little*?' Jack echoed, and laughed. 'Did you fancy somewhere bigger than this place, then?'

'You know her,' Eve remarked, 'always has had big ideas.'

'Nowt wrong with that, so long as folk don't get above themselves, and our Rhona never has done.'

'So far!' Rhona observed, and laughed with them.

Having found a house, she realized she was more than ready to move into her own home. She was eager to have the transaction completed so that she could get to work on the place. Tim managed to wangle a seventy-two-hour pass and added his enthusiasm to her own.

'I suppose I shan't be able to prise you away now, to spend the odd weekend in Kent with me,' he teased.

'Oh, I don't know,' she said, trying to keep a straight face. 'Depends how fed up I get of cleaning it out and decorating.'

'You won't go doing too much, will you? Promise me . . .' He was alarmed by the possibility of Rhona jeopardizing her own health or the baby's.

'You're as bad as Mum. Does everybody think I'm potty? I take care of myself, I'll have you know. And look how well I am – expecting seems to suit me.'

Rhona was too thrilled with all that was going on to be any worse than rather tired by everything she was tackling. And Bill had insisted that she slightly curtail her hours at the mill. He and Ellen were so elated about their prospective grandchild, he'd employed a girl of fifteen to act as Rhona's assistant.

'Learn all you can from Mrs Brightstone,' he'd told Joyce Naylor the day she started at Bridge House. 'You'll need to carry on with some of her work when she goes into hospital, you know. I hope you're bright enough to keep things ticking over with me till she comes back to work.'

'I take it you are coming back to work as soon as you're able, are you, Rhona lass?' her father-in-law asked one day when she was having tea with him and Ellen.

'You have a cheek, Bill,' his wife reprimanded. 'You might at least let Rhona have the bairn and enjoy it being here, before you start on at her about the blooming mill!'

Rhona smiled. 'It's all right, I've been into all this already. My mother's itching to get her hands on a baby again. The arrangement is that as soon as I want to go back to work I shall leave him – or her – with Mum at Gracechurch Street, It'll be ever so convenient, I'll be able to pop along there at feeding times, and so on. And my mother's glad it'll give her good reason to stay where she is.'

Ellen Brightstone nodded gravely. 'Aye, there's a lot of talk of women her age with no young 'uns to look after being sent all over the country to work in essential industries. I'm thankful I'm too old for that.'

'I know,' Rhona agreed. 'If all that's rumoured materializes, there's masses of families going to be split up before this lot's done. And there'll be thousands like my mother, only too willing to do their bit, helping with the WVS, or Red Cross, but very reluctant to leave their menfolk to fend for themselves.'

'I think it's wicked, you know,' Ellen went on. 'A woman's place is looking after her man. I know when they've joined up like our Timothy there's nowt a lass can do, but while they're at home, they should be taken care of.'

'Certainly, this war's taking its toll on my stepfather,' Rhona acknowledged. 'He puts on a cheery front, he's not the sort to grumble, but he comes home worn out. And he can't be sure of getting even one day a week off.'

'Disgusting, what are their management thinking of!' Bill exclaimed. 'No matter how vital the war effort, there's no necessity for that. And how long's it going to go on, that's what I keep asking? There's only so much people can take. They'll start cracking up if they're pushed as hard as that for any length of time.'

'Well, let's hope it's brought to an end sooner than we fear,' Rhona said, determined not to permit the war to dim the joy of having a child. 'It'll have been on well over a year by the time our little one arrives.'

16

Christine Eve Brightstone came squalling into the world in October 1940. Although premature, she was a good weight, a healthy child, so beautifully formed that Rhona immediately forgave her the strenuous labour, and the fright of arriving early.

'Thank God she's all right,' she kept saying over and over again to the nurses. She'd been terrified that insisting on working so long had caused the premature birth; when it seemed so prolonged and so damned hard, she'd wondered how on earth she would face Timothy if everything wasn't as it should be.

By the time he appeared at the hospital Christine was beginning to thrive already, and now she had rested Rhona was glowing with happiness.

'I was afraid you wouldn't get leave,' she exclaimed, hugging him when he embraced her rather gingerly. 'She's so wonderful, darling, I'd have burst if I had to wait any longer to share her with you.'

'I twisted a few arms to get away,' Tim said, proud of his ability to be there now she needed him. 'You helped, by having her ahead of time. You *are* both all right, aren't you?' he added anxiously.

'See for yourself – I'm coming round nicely now. And there's your daughter . . .' Rhona had been ever so slightly pleased that he'd come straight to her bedside rather than first making for the cot at its foot.

'She's very tiny, isn't she?'

'Not according to the hospital. She's big for her age – only an ounce or two below the ideal birth weight, despite her being early. And there's nothing wrong with her breathing or anything, or they'd not have had her in the ward with me.'

'And is she good?'

'She does holler a bit sometimes, mostly when she's hungry.'

'Are you – er, feeding her yourself?'

'You bet! Sister says that gives them the best start. And I wanted to, anyway. Saves messing about mixing up feeds. You know I'm all for an easy life!'

'That's a laugh!'

'Well . . .' Their glances met, and grasped. She'd never felt as close as this to Timothy before. She believed she'd never felt happier. She was enchanted with her daughter, and thrilled that Tim's repeated looks in the direction of the cot revealed that he might be equally besotted.

'Have you been up to the house?' she asked after a while.

'No, came straight here from the station.'

'You are staying there, though?'

Her husband looked uncomfortable. 'Actually, Mum and Dad want me to sleep at their place, they don't see much of me.'

'Oh.'

'What's wrong, love? It'd be different if you were there, wouldn't it?'

'All right. I just wanted you to see how it's coming along. Up to this last couple of weeks when I wasn't getting around too well, I'd done a fair amount to it.'

'I told you not to.'

'I've done it bit by bit. And I've had help – Phyllis. She's got a good eye for colour, and she's not frightened of muckying her hands.'

'Give her something to do.'

'Something *else* to do. Phyl's working now – training to be a nurse. They're crying out for nurses, and she loves the job, can't wait to be given a bit of responsibility.'

'Good for her. And what's that brother of hers doing?'

'Clive's been in the navy for a long while. Trained with our Dan, as a matter of fact, didn't I tell you? Don't know if they're still together. Dan's due home on leave any time now, so we'll know more then. His first real leave. Good job he's not wed.'

Tim smiled knowingly. 'He must have had some time off. Maybe he's got other interests, keeping him away. He's said nothing . . . ?'

'Our Dan's the last one to make a habit of writing home – and even less likely to tell us about a girl he might have met.'

He shrugged. 'Anyway, we've been giving your family plenty to think about, especially this last day or two.'

'Mum and Dad came in last night. You should have seen him with young Christine! Mother was delighted, naturally, but his face was a picture! He insisted on uncovering the poor mite, as well, checking she had all her toes.' All at once, Rhona's eyes clouded. 'You will look in on them while you're on leave, won't you?'

'I thought Jack Hebden was that busy at the engineering works nobody could catch him at home?'

'All the same – it'd be nice if you'd try to see him. And Mum's always there some part of the day. They're both disappointed this war's preventing them really getting to know you.'

'The situation's far from ideal for anybody. I'm not here indefinitely, you know, and I shall be trying to spend all the time I can with you.'

'All right, love.' She mustn't let herself feel disconsolate: she had an exquisite baby, and her husband had managed to come and see them both. I'm not disappointed in Timothy, she told herself. And I'm not going to be.

'Well, look who's here – the proud papa!'

Glancing away from each other, they smiled as Phyllis walked lightly down the ward towards them. She was out of uniform, but the assurance in her manner reminded Rhona that her friend was very much at home in the hospital.

Recalling that Phyllis had never met Tim, Rhona introduced them and smiled to herself as her friend gave him a mischievous wink. 'So, you're the clever chap who's helped Rhona produce such a beautiful infant. I can see now why she fell for one straight away!' Laughter lighting her green eyes, she turned to Rhona. 'You didn't tell me how handsome he is, did you? I'm surprised at you for making him wait so many years!'

Timothy was grinning, making no effort to conceal the satisfaction generated by Phyllis's unsubtle flattery.

'You'll give him such a swelled head he'll not get his uniform cap on! And he'll be murder to live with when you've finished . . . Not that it'll take me long to bring him down a peg or two! Handsome is as handsome does, my mother always says . . .'

'And she's a wise woman,' Phyllis added, still laughing.

'Is she now?' a male voice asked from just behind Tim and Phyllis, making them jump and swing round to stare.

Rhona gazed and gazed, a lump rising in her throat and tears suddenly filling her eyes. 'Dan! Ay, lad – I hardly owned you!'

Daniel, his navy-blue uniform immaculate, looked years older than he was, no longer her youngest brother but a near-stranger. A precious stranger, though.

'Hallo, Rhona.' He strode past the other two and leaned over to kiss her. 'Are you all right, love?'

'Improving with every day. Having both you and Tim arrive today is just the tonic I needed to set me up.'

'You've not said hallo to your niece.' Phyllis, her hair a long pale cloud about her face and shoulders, was bending over the cot.

Daniel turned away from his sister. She noticed he was several moments before he moved; moments in which he was gazing at her friend's gleaming hair. And she *is* lovely, Rhona thought. She'd grown accustomed to Phyllis with long hair, and to seeing it pinned up securely and concealed under her nurse's cap.

'Do you know our Dan, Phyllis? He's the youngest – though nobody'd think so to see him now.'

Her friend murmured an awed 'How do you do?' and offered a slender hand.

Taking the hand, Daniel remained almost transfixed. His husky echo of her words emerged as little more than a sigh. And he continued to look at Phyllis as though he'd seen no one more beautiful.

Phyl herself was no less conscious of *him*. Her scrutiny was more practised, though, her appraisal all-encompassing as she examined the frank, open face with those very direct brown eyes which were threatening to shake her composure. 'You know my twin, don't you – Clive Ayntree.'

Daniel nodded, cleared his throat, and drew in a breath. 'I do indeed. But he never said how . . .' Suddenly, he shrugged, smiling at himself, the flare in his cheeks showing even through the tan.

'You still haven't looked at your niece,' Phyllis reminded him gently, but her own smile was as much at her reaction to the meeting as at Daniel's. She'd never been smitten like this before. With Adrian it had been a slow-growing relationship that deepened into love. This gorgeous creature in his dashing navy blue was affecting her instantaneously. I want him, she thought, and immediately was afraid. Wanting someone too much was a mistake she didn't make twice.

'She's got blue eyes like you, Timothy,' Dan was saying now. He hadn't spent all those weeks away from home without learning command of himself. 'And your fair hair.' Involuntarily, his glance slid from his brother-in-law to Phyl's glorious head. He made himself turn and include his sister. 'So, she's not landed with your ginger mop!'

Phyllis intervened. 'Rhona's hair isn't ginger, is it – be honest, Daniel! It's a lovely shade. And, anyway, baby's hair will probably change, it often does. Eyes, as well. They're all born with blue eyes.'

Dan grinned, not caring that she was correcting him. 'You seem to know all about it.'

'Phyl's nursing now,' Rhona explained. 'She's always astounding us with her knowledge.'

'Really?' He took the opportunity to scrutinize this enchanting woman who, it seemed, was also skilled.

Phyllis laughed. 'I really am nursing, though only training as yet. About astounding everyone I'm less certain.'

I'm not, thought Rhona, or about astounding one person. She felt quite elated as well as amused by the overt attraction between the pair.

'I'm not well up on babies,' Dan continued, smiling again towards Phyllis. 'And although I'm glad she's arrived and everything's all right, her timing could have been better. I was planning on spending this leave at Rhona's new home. Haven't seen it yet, and I quite fancied enjoying a bit of space around me.'

'You were the one on my side, weren't you, when I wanted the family to find a bigger house,' Rhona remarked, thinking how long ago that seemed. 'Happen I'll be out of here before you have to report back, I'll look forward to showing you round. You'll have to stay with me for a few days.'

'Or you could take a quick look now,' Phyllis suggested, glancing at her watch. 'That's if Rhona doesn't mind.'

'Why should I?'

'I'm in charge of the key, it's just along the road from where I live – when I'm not here in the nurses' home.'

'If you cut along with Phyllis I wouldn't mind a bit of time on my own with my husband, since it's his first day,' Rhona said, even though she envied anybody who was going to be showing her family round her new home.

'Yes, you cut along,' Timothy said very quickly. And Rhona realized that he'd been standing there, contributing very little.

Daniel glanced towards his sister. 'You don't mind if I push off for a while then?'

'It won't be for more than an hour,' Phyl added. 'I'm due back on duty.'

Still, Dan hesitated. Rhona smiled at them both. 'Get along with you – Phyl's entitled to deputize for me, she's done more than her share of work on the house.'

The attraction between Daniel and her friend proved more enduring than Rhona had anticipated, and allowed Timothy and herself to concentrate more or less uninterrupted on their daughter and each other. When not taken up with their own future, though, they shared their surprise and amusement over the way Phyllis always seemed to appear on the ward when Dan Hebden was visiting his sister.

Because she was so fit and the hospital authorities were trying to free all possible beds for military personnel, Rhona was discharged before Timothy's leave ended, and they savoured a brief taste of life with their daughter in their own home. Daniel visited them one evening, rather grave-faced as he asked to talk to Rhona alone.

'Ay, lad, of course. Tim'll welcome a few minutes when he can spoil his little girl without me breathing down his neck!' she exclaimed and led the way through into the sitting room.

'Sit down, love, make yourself at home,' she said, trying not to let his serious expression worry her. 'It's not as cosy as the living room, I know, but I want you always to feel at ease in our home, Dan.'

'Thanks. I – well, as a matter of fact, I want you to play the older sister, for once, and give me a bit of advice. I – er, happen you've noticed how Phyllis and I are – well, drawn to each other. I – that is – I'm serious about her, Rhona. I'd like her and me to get wed. But . . . well, you know how it was when she was widowed that young. I daren't ask her, don't know how she'd react. We've had a wonderful time getting to know each other, but . . .'

'And you haven't given her any hint, no clue at all?'

'I'm torn, Rhona, torn right in two. Of course, I can't disguise all my feelings, not when we're together. But nor can I show how deeply I really feel about her.'

'What a pity! I think you ought to try, Dan – take the risk.'

'When I can't imagine why she'd even look at me? He had money, hadn't he, Adrian Newbold? His father's a sir. And she's not without brass herself.'

'And you're an extremely personable young man, even though you are my brother.'

'Young, aye. Don't remind me!'

'Yes – she's my age. And in some ways, now you've

been away from home, you're more mature than she'll ever be. You needn't tell her I've said that, mind.'

'As old as you . . .' Dan looked horrified. His brown eyes appeared wide with alarm.

'I'm not quite doddering yet. And I'm certain Phyl isn't.'

'Will – would the difference matter?'

'If you let it – now, by doing nowt. Or later, by making her feel old – by reminding her the difference exists. All it amounts to is whether you're in love. If you are, the problems won't be insuperable. If you aren't – well, I'd rather you didn't let this attraction get out of hand with my best friend.'

Daniel glanced down at his hands, thought for a moment, then grinned at her. 'I have learned a bit about sex, you know, while I've been away. I can tell when it's something more lasting.'

'Then you'd better be quick and ask her, hadn't you? It'd be nice if you both knew where you stood before you go back off leave.'

Daniel didn't find courage to say anything, though. And suddenly it was the last day of his leave. Phyl had finished her shift at two that afternoon and they came straight to Rhona's. She pressed them to stop and have tea with her. Timothy was back on duty in Kent, the big house was very quiet.

'I'm almost sorry young Chrissie's such a good baby,' she admitted with a grin. 'Sometimes I'm tempted to stick pins in her or something just to have one other person awake!'

Phyllis laughed. 'You'd better not do that, not to my god-daughter! Can't you just talk to her, anyway, even when she's asleep?'

Rhona laughed with her. 'How did you guess? I do that all the time.'

'You'll be thankful that she is good, soon enough, when you have to leave her with your mother. When did you say that'd be, how soon are you going back to work?'

'The doctor said six weeks. If I've anything to do with

it, it'll be sooner than that. So long as Madam, here, is only just along the street.'

'I'm surprised you haven't suggested to Bill Brightstone that you have a cot rigged up in a corner of the office.'

'Nay, Phyl, don't talk daft! The racket at the mill'd scare her half to death! And don't forget he's her grand-father – there'd be nothing done at all, by either of us!'

'Well, don't forget I've offered to do my share of sitting with her.'

'I won't forget.'

Rhona began undressing the baby. She'd filled the bath and set it in front of the living room fire. 'I hope you understand this is only because of the war, young Christine,' she told the child with a smile. 'I haven't established us in a lovely big house only to do as they would in Gracechurch Street! But it's warmer here than upstairs. And I'm not risking you catching a chill.'

She'd only just lowered the infant into the bath water when the telephone rang. 'I'll bet that's Tim. Will you take over, Phyl love, while I go to answer it?'

Phyllis sponging the exquisite tiny form was more than Daniel could take. Her wonderful pale hair had swung forward gracefully, the way it always swung when she leaned over, but not sufficiently to shield her eyes. There was more tenderness than he ever recognized in her normal cheery manner; a gentleness to the curve of her sensitive mouth which choked him. He didn't know what to say, hadn't known all afternoon. He was all knotted up inside by dread of going back from leave, and with the knowledge that it was up to him to say something. And he knew that if he did, somehow, he'd not retain control. He'd never felt like this before – not all emotional, not that he was in serious danger of making a fool of himself, *blubbing*.

Men don't cry, they just . . . don't. He hadn't for many a year. The only occasion he could remember was that dreadful night out at the reservoir.

'You're quiet today, Daniel.'

So she hadn't been totally absorbed by the infant, nor

in conversation with his half-sister. She *had* been aware of him. *How* aware he wasn't certain. Never had been, since the day they'd been introduced. The attraction was there, he knew, *that* kind of awareness. That had been acknowledged, in repeated glances exchanged, in the kisses that were something he couldn't have withheld.

But all that had been light-hearted: at first, a bit of fun. I just wish I was the one that was older, experienced, he thought. I wish to heaven I knew how to handle this.

'It's – that sort of a day,' he admitted ruefully. 'One minute, all your leave's in front of you; then tomorrow you've got to go back.'

'I know.'

Dan gave her a look. She sounded choked as well. Was it possible . . . ? There was no being sure with Phyl. She was so vital, glowing, how could you tell if she even cared?

And I've got to find out, he thought despairingly. Today, because it's all we have. Awkwardly, he stood up, feeling lost like he had that first day in the navy, rather apprehensive.

'Phyllis . . .'

Their Rhona came back in, smiling, though rather sadly. 'Tim's got some kind of promotion – they're having a binge in the village hall there. He sounds a bit tipsy already.' And already she'd forgotten the rank giving him so much satisfaction – because she was afraid it increased his danger?

'He's done well, hasn't he?' Phyllis remarked, watching her friend's eyes, willing herself not to mention the greater hazards Timothy could face.

'Tim would,' Rhona said briskly. 'He's that sort, these days. And the air force suits him. I don't think he got enough of a challenge here at the mill with his dad.'

'It's to be hoped he settles again all right, after the war,' Dan said, and felt Phyllis reproving him.

Rhona smiled, without her brown eyes lighting. 'He'll have plenty to think about then, getting to know Chrissie all over again. We'll keep him occupied, as well as the mill. And his dad will be coming up to retirement before long.'

Phyllis had lifted the baby out of the water and was holding her, enveloped in a snowy towel, on her lap.

'Are you going to take over now?'

'You bet I am!' Rhona gathered the infant to her. 'You won't be sorry neither, she's due for a feed. Whatever else, she possesses a strong pair of lungs!'

'I shan't have to stay much longer, anyway.' Phyllis glanced at her watch. 'I can't come up here without looking in at Lavender Court. Even if my parents are in London, Mrs Bishop expects me to call.'

When Phyllis was ready for leaving, Dan rose as well. Rhona smiled, concealing the ache of another parting. 'Off back to Gracechurch Street then, young Daniel? You'll be needing an early night if you're off to sea first thing tomorrow. Tell Mum I'll bring Christine round to see her in the afternoon.'

Still holding the baby wrapped in her towel, she drew Dan to her in a massive hug. 'Just look after yourself, mind.'

'You'll come with me to Lavender Court, won't you?' Phyllis suggested as soon as they had left the house. 'We can go back into Halfield together then. Did you say what time you'd be at your mother's?'

Awkward yet again, Dan glanced down at his feet. 'Actually, I didn't say. They're not expecting me for a meal. I think Mum assumed I was going to spend the last few hours of leave with Rhona.'

After they had visited Mrs Bishop and Phyl had picked up one or two items from her room, they emerged into the cool, autumnal air.

'If you're not expected anywhere for supper,' Phyllis said, smiling, 'you're welcome to take pot-luck with me, in the nurses' home. I do a smashing corned-beef hash.'

Daniel grinned. 'Sounds marvellous! They allow you to take folk – er, *men* in then?'

She gave him a sidelong look. 'Strictly forbidden,

naturally. But I must be the only inhabitant who's never even tried to. There's a rear entrance.'

The nurses' home was an enormous ugly Victorian building opposite the hospital. The gates had been removed for scrap iron, and at the back the space was boarded across.

'We climb that,' Phyllis announced. 'I've seen the others. There are plenty of toe-holds between the wooden slats.'

Wryly, he grinned. 'That wouldn't suit our Rhona, she's always on about her stockings.'

'We take them off,' Phyllis informed him. 'Don't look!' She didn't wait, though, for Dan to turn his head before she swiftly unfastened suspenders and drew off her black regulation stockings. Her gaze met his, and held on. 'Thought you'd be over that fence by now – or on top ready for helping me up . . .'

'Er – yes.' Compensating for staring fixedly at her long, elegant legs, Daniel hastily scrambled up to sit astride the rough fence, and stretched down a hand to help her.

Her hand grasping his, Phyllis led him through a neglected shrubbery and up towards the house. When he began heading for a glass-panelled door, Phyl shook her head and drew him with her in the direction of a large ground-floor window.

'Maggie's room – we always leave the window open a fraction.'

Pushing up the lower half of the sash window, she climbed neatly over the sill and into the room. 'Come on . . .'

'What happens if she's in bed when one of you comes in this way, or – or getting dressed?' Dan asked, following her inside.

'Ah – wait till we get upstairs, then I'll explain.'

Cautiously Phyllis opened the door slightly and glanced out into the corridor. 'Coast's clear.'

She was enjoying this. Daniel was less happy. But they made it up a narrow stairway and, eventually, into her room. Her green eyes were glinting with suppressed laughter. 'Your face!' she exclaimed. 'Do you never do anything you're supposed not to?'

'It's not that. I just didn't want to walk right in on the girl.'

'Better than walking into Sister Tutor. Her office is beside that rear entrance. And you wouldn't, anyway. Maggie's madly in love with one of the registrars. Off-duty, that's where you'd find her.'

'You mean they're – living together?'

'Till his wife finds out. She's a doctor as well, over in Leeds.'

'You – you don't *approve* of such goings-on?' Daniel was appalled, couldn't equate this worldly Phyllis with the woman he thought he knew.

'There is a war on.' But then she stood gazing very directly into his perturbed brown eyes. 'As a matter of fact, I don't automatically condone that, no. Depends what the circumstances are. I gather that his wife can't be all that concerned, or she would have made more effort to hold their marriage together when they weren't both on duty. He evidently seemed very lost, before Maggie came along.'

'Even so . . .'

'Are you a bit of a prude, old love?' she asked, smiling, not at all dismayed by the idea that he might be.

'Old-fashioned, do you mean?' Daniel shrugged. 'Didn't know that I was, despite my upbringing.' The few months in the navy had shown him the nature of that. 'But it was more that I didn't like to think of you . . . what was your word – "condoning" affairs.'

'I don't.' Her steady green eyes were wide, concealing nothing. 'If someone was being hurt by what their partner was doing, I wouldn't be able to bite my tongue – my business, or no. But I do try to be a realist, Daniel. Life isn't easy, at the best of times, and war is anything but the best.'

And what about you, yourself? he wondered, still unable to frame the words. What if you really cared again, for – somebody? *Could* you care? Or will it always be Adrian Newbold, even after all this time?

'You don't have a girl somewhere then, Dan?' Phyl asked seriously. Time was remorseless, and she sensed his difficulty. 'Not someone you've met while you were training?'

'Me – ? No!' He laughed. 'I wouldn't hang on, not to just anybody, but I became rather intimidated by some of them girls down South. Give me a Yorkshire lass, now . . .' He hesitated, sighing again wistfully. A girl with pale hair, lustrous green eyes, more than a hint of mischief in her smile.

'And do you see yourself settling down, when this lot's over?'

'There's times when I envy our Rhona and Timothy now. I reckon they did the right thing, giving each other an anchor.'

And a home, he thought, picturing the house which his sister had made so comfortable, with its warm-toned walls, curtains dyed a warm toast-brown to disguise their fading, and well-polished furniture gleaned largely secondhand.

'You don't think there's any harm, then in being committed, even when circumstances force you apart?' Her lovely eyes were still seeking his, making thought difficult, let alone speech.

Dan cleared his throat. 'Partings are far from ideal, aren't they? Like you, I try to be realistic. I've always believed in loyalty. Take my mum and dad, for instance. There's nobody would split them up, even if they were miles away from each other. They belong. Folk either do, or not . . .' And, God help me, he thought, I'm too much the coward to even try for where I want to belong.

'Know something?' Phyl murmured huskily, stepping closer towards him, slipping her arms around him beneath his jacket. 'I'd like to be the person where you belong, Daniel. If you think it's forward of me saying so, too bad. All the time we've been together, that's been all I could think of. And I never believed I'd . . . oh, never mind.'

'Ay, lass!' His arms came round her, pressing her to

his hard body, while hungrily his mouth sealed her lips. He'd never been more thankful than now, because Phyl had come out with what she was feeling.

'Marry me, Dan – as soon as you come home again.'

'You knew I'd never dare ask you, didn't you? Even though I fell for you the minute I saw you.'

'We'd better do something about it then, hadn't we?'

'If only I wasn't going back in a few hours.'

'Certainly the ceremony will have to wait, that doesn't mean . . .'

'Phyllis?'

Her smile tender, she paused. 'I said – I want you, Dan. And you needn't try pretending you're not aroused.'

Daniel grinned, bent towards her again, savoured her lips. Phyllis was leaning fiercely into him, her breasts an exquisite pressure through his shirt, the rest of her warm, yielding . . .

She moved away only long enough to lock the door and draw the heavy blackout curtains. Grasping him firmly by the arm, she steered him through the darkened room until they reached the bed.

'It's only a bed-sitter, plus a bathroom shared with a couple of girls whose room is the far side. If you use the bathroom, you remember to lock both doors, theirs as well. Otherwise, it's all self-contained, everything I need.'

Everything he needed. Sitting on the edge of the bed, he pulled her close into his arms, kissing her feverishly, all the desire that he had disciplined for days surging with the glorious knowledge that they would marry. He just wished he didn't feel so naïve . . .

'I've never – at least, you're really the first, Phyl. I've never done more than kiss and cuddle with a girl.'

Against his lips, she smiled. 'You seem to be catching on fast!'

Laughing, he parted her sharp white teeth with his probing tongue. One hand located her small, firm breast.

'Just one second,' Phyl interrupted, swiftly unfastening her blouse. She did something to the strap of her bra.

His fingers slid readily inside. 'Lord, but you're

269

wonderful!' he exclaimed, kissing her again deeply. 'I want to touch you all over . . .'

'I think you may count on that.'

His dread of seeming inexpert evaporated as soon as he realized that *her* experience was a relief to him. Her fingers were busy with the buttons of his shirt, he felt them stealing across his chest.

Daniel drew her across his lap, kissing her throat, her ears, eyelids, and then again her mouth. Her hand was warm upon his knee, searing through the cloth, alerting pulses which he hadn't known existed.

'If you don't stop that,' he told her gruffly, 'I'll not hold out much longer.'

'Well, this is the bed.'

'And what if I give you a kiddie?'

'If he or she is as gorgeous as Chrissie, I'll be delighted.'

'You surely looked perfect holding her. Made me want – well, you don't need explanations now. And to *mean* what I was longing to do with you, to mean it should last.' For this to be a part of him, this total knowledge of her, to be the memory carried across dark seas. Into the unknown – the only true reality, in that strange world of unfamiliar vessels, throbbing engines, and the silence beyond the metallic hull. Silence that concealed the enemy. The killer.

17

Christine adored her grandmother, Eve. After one apprehensive morning, while Rhona wondered every hour about her daughter, she was happy to accept that the arrangement permitting her to work again was admirable.

Bill Brightstone was delighted to have her back at Bridge House once more, and Rhona herself was anything but sorry. Chrissie might be an enchanting youngster but, as yet, she wasn't much company. And didn't begin to take Rhona's mind off the more alarming aspects of the war. At the mill, especially now that her assistant, Joyce Naylor, had settled in, there was always something going on. Joyce was a nice young thing, pert and blonde, and willing.

There was the dinner hour as well, when Rhona rushed along Gracechurch Street to feed the baby, enjoying the opportunity to talk with her mother, catching up on family news.

Stanley appeared to have adapted to working down the pit and living away from home. He was doing a lot of overtime, though, and rarely came to Halfield for weekends.

'I know we're all supposed to do what we can for the war effort,' Eve confided anxiously. 'I just hope he isn't going to make himself run down.'

'Our Stan? Nay, Mum, he's fitter than any of us, he'll be all right.'

'You haven't seen him for many a week, have you?' her mother persisted. 'He's lost a lot of weight, I thought he was looking peaky.'

'He's staying with our Helen, isn't he? They'll see he's all right.' Her cousin was a good little cook. 'It's not as if he was with somebody we knew nothing about.'

'At least our Dan was looking very well while he was

home on leave. He seems suited with the navy. Just so long as he comes home safe at the end of all this lot.'

'And not only for our sakes. Phyl mustn't have to face up to losing somebody else.'

Eve smiled. 'I don't feel as uneasy about Dan, somehow. As if I'd been assured he'll come through as right as rain. And I'm glad about him and your friend Phyllis. I wondered what was going on when he was off out so much while he was here.'

Rhona smiled. 'They had me on for quite a while. I ought to have guessed straight away, I saw the way our Dan was looking at her!'

'But you'd plenty to think about, without him, hadn't you? With Madam here only just arrived on the scene, and Timothy coming on leave. How is he, by the way, have you heard this week?'

'Not since the day he rang to say he'd been promoted. Before Dan went back. I'd written saying I was going back to the mill, thinking he might have something to say about that, but Timothy's no letter-writer.'

'Well, I'd forgive a lot for this grandchild he's helped you produce.'

'Aye. Little does he know that's what's stopping my complaining about not hearing how he's getting on.'

'Everything is all right between you two, though, isn't it, love?'

'Ask me again when this war's over. It can't be all right while we're living this far apart, can it?'

'I suppose not.'

Eve quelled a sigh. She was concerned about Rhona and Tim – not worried exactly, concerned. There was no doubting that Rhona was thrilled with her daughter, but there had to be more to keep a couple happy, didn't there? To a degree, Eve felt responsible, she had encouraged Rhona to think of Timothy that way. Still, she couldn't regret anything that had brought Chrissie to brighten life for them.

And she knew Rhona, didn't she? Her daughter had

never been one for issuing glib assurances like some folk, just because they were what you wanted to hear.

Eve looked at the clock on the mantelpiece. 'Isn't it time you were getting back to work?'

'You'll not be so eager to have her handed over when the novelty's worn off! And when she learns the power in having a good yell!'

Eve laughed. 'You think she will, then?'

'You may bet on it!'

Rhona was content to have her mother share the care of her baby, and although delighted with her own home she still enjoyed visiting Gracechurch Street. Quite often of an evening she would stay there for a while, accepting a share of their meal, then replenishing their rations with items from her own storecupboard.

Seeing more of her stepfather was good, as well. And even though he generally arrived home exhausted he always found time and energy for playing with Christine.

'You're spoiling her, you know,' Rhona told him one day, feigning severity. 'She's going to turn out that precocious with the attention you give her.'

'Only because she's the image of you,' Jack asserted evenly.

'My hair's not as light as that, I only wish it was.'

'It'll probably darken,' he prophesied, 'then it will be your shade.'

'Poor little beggar!'

He grinned. 'You've never been vain, any road, I'll say that for you. But her eyes are like yours now, and your mother's, you can't deny that.'

'And she knows how to use them, even at six weeks! One glance from her, and she winds me round them tiny fingers.'

'And I wonder who she gets that from?' Jack Hebden inquired, smiling wryly.

Rhona grinned back at him. 'I don't know what you mean.'

Being a mother's grand, though, she realized. Now she'd established a working routine again. An entire new dimension had developed in her life. And, being married into the Brightstone family, her ties with her career were strengthened rather than dissipated by motherhood.

One day, she hoped, they might have a son – a lad who'd go into the business, following in Tim's footsteps, and Grandpa Brightstone's. Strangely, she never considered that Christine might grow up to follow in her own.

Rhona was at work when the news came. It was a Friday afternoon. For once, she'd been watching the time. They were into summer now, and she was actually going away for the weekend. Cousin Helen had kept sending messages with Stanley that she wanted to see the baby again. Rhona had hung on long enough to feel using some of the petrol she'd saved was justified.

When the motorcycle drew up outside the mill, somehow she noticed over the clattering of the spinning frames. Immediately she was so alarmed that she was ready for the telegram boy before he came through the door. She made certain of getting to him before Bill could.

The buff envelope was addressed to her, anyway. One of her neighbours in Apsley Road had directed the lad here. Sickened, her heart thudding, she tore open the envelope. He was missing. He wasn't dead, she kept assuring herself over and over again, *missing*, that was all. It was more than enough. And she had to find some words for telling his father.

Bill had reached her now, coming out of his office while she was oblivious. He was staring dazedly towards the words jumbling hazily across the white paper.

'It – it could be worse, Dad,' she said, her voice so unemotional that it sounded cold. 'It's only that he's gone missing, nothing more than that. And we understand that they have to let us know. It's not that they aren't giving us any hope. He – his plane could have come down quite safely, even this side of the channel. It could be that he's not managed to get word back to them yet.'

'Aye, it could.' Bill was calm, taking the news very

well. 'Are you all right, lass? Hadn't you better come and sit down for a bit?'

Wanly, Rhona smiled. 'I was just going to say something similar to you. Happen we'll get Joyce to rustle up a cup of tea.'

Rhona stood aside, waited for Bill to begin walking towards the office, then she followed. She couldn't let him take her arm, or touch her at all, that way she'd break. Her fragile self-control might never be regained.

'I don't know how ever I'll break it to his mother,' Bill confessed. She always looked on the black side, these days, she'd be bound to think he'd not be coming back.

'Want me to come home with you?' Rhona offered. She couldn't feel much worse, no matter how many folk she had to tell.

'Ay, Rhona love, it's us should be looking after you. He's your husband, father of your bairn.'

'I'm just that glad we have Chrissie. Whatever happens, we'll keep going, because of her.'

'Aye, aye.'

Numbly, Rhona telephoned her cousin, cancelling all arrangements for the weekend, asking her to explain everything to their Stan. 'I'd better just get along to Mum's,' she told Bill afterwards. 'I'll have to tell her. Will you hang on here, just for a few minutes? I'll drive you home then, and we can have a talk to Mum Brightstone, together.'

As soon as she got outside the mill, Rhona discovered she was shaking. Walking along to 46 Gracechurch Street required concentrated determination.

'Whatever's wrong?' Eve asked immediately Rhona walked through the door and stood, her face like paper against the flare of her hair, while she leaned against the door frame. 'Is it Timothy?'

'He's missing – not dead, missing. Oh, Mum, I don't know what I ought to do. I said I'd go home with Bill to tell Tim's mother, he's so afraid she'll take it badly.'

'You don't look fit for anything. How's he taking it?'

'He's – all right. Shaken, same as me, but all right.'

Eve put her arms round her daughter, hugging her to her breast. 'Ay, love, I am sorry! This bloody war! Still – at least, there's a bit of hope.'

'Quite a lot, actually. We've got to think that way. He could have come down anywhere – they're taught to cope, aren't they, after all? How to land where there's no runway, even how to bail out, if they have to . . . Where's Christine?'

They both turned. Rhona noticed her stepfather then, on the hearthrug, playing with the child; there when he was needed.

'Oh, Dad . . .'

Rhona hurtled across to kneel beside him. He pulled her against his side, pressed his lips to her temple.

'Ay, lass . . . It's a bad do, is this.'

She could tell by his voice that he wouldn't be able to say much more.

'You're not going anywhere, Rhona love,' her mother announced suddenly. 'You stay with your dad, he'll see you're all right.'

He always had. Her eyes glistening, Rhona squeezed his hand.

'I'll go with Bill,' Eve continued firmly. 'I know I've never seen a lot of Ellen, but we've always got on. And she might need another woman, just for a while.'

'Get a taxi then, won't you – don't let Bill go driving.'

Christine started crying the minute her grandmother had left the house. Secretly Rhona was relieved, though she wished for once that the baby hadn't been weaned. She ached to hold her to her breast.

Her hands outstretched to draw the child to her, she checked. Grimly, she willed herself not to pick her up. With strange clarity, she saw herself spoiling Christine, because she was growing irrationally afraid that the infant was all that remained of Tim.

'Try and stop her grizzling, will you, Dad? While I go get her tea.'

When Eve came home, an hour or more later, her eyes were red-rimmed, her nose glowing. Why can't I weep?

Rhona thought, and knew that somehow there was too much emotion, that it was too complex to express itself that simply. And there was Christine to consider, it was no use upsetting the child.

She was persuaded to spend the weekend at Grace-church Street. After work on the Monday, though, she insisted on going home. She couldn't give up on the life that she and Tim had planned, nor give in to the longing to remain in this cushioned existence which felt so unreal.

Following his initial quiet acceptance of the news that his son was missing, Bill Brightstone changed. His face gravely set, he sat for hours at his desk gazing, without really seeing, far into space.

'It's Ellen,' he told Rhona repeatedly. 'She's taken it that badly I can't stop trying to see what's become of our Timothy, so's I've something to reassure her with.'

Whether for his wife or himself, her father-in-law certainly was worrying so much that his mind wasn't on the job. The only good thing about it was that Rhona was fully occupied, compelled to assume more authority for the running of the mill.

Herbert Shackleton was one of the first to notice. He'd expressed his concern about Timothy on the Monday morning, by Friday afternoon he was looking incredulously at Rhona as she finished handing out pay packets to the work force.

'I hope you don't mind me saying, Mrs Brightstone,' he began, 'but your father would have been right proud of you. Proper stoical, you are, and no mistake.'

'That's as may be, Herbert. I only know I've got to keep this place going, and keep myself going for Christine.' And I daren't let up, she thought, dare not let myself begin to feel.

'Well, I just hope there's some better news for you afore long.'

There was no news, however, and the days went by nevertheless, gradually extending into two weeks, four, six. Dully Rhona went through the routine of leaving the baby with her mother, coming to Bridge House Mill, collecting Chrissie, returning home. Every time a telephone rang, she started, expecting to hear something – word that Tim was safe. Or otherwise.

People were rallying round. Stan had come home that first Sunday, then for a weekend to stay with her. He appeared bigger even than before he'd gone down the pit, a reassuring person to have around. She wondered how her mother could have imagined he might be losing weight.

Phyllis became a frequent visitor, dropping in for an hour or more whenever she was off duty. She was wearing a ring Daniel had sent to her just before putting to sea. His ship was escorting a convoy to some unnamed destination. Nobody asked where.

'We were getting married next time he comes home,' Phyllis told Rhona one night. 'But if there's no good news about Timothy, by then, we can always postpone the wedding.'

'Thanks, Phyl love, but no,' Rhona said, managing a smile. 'You have your lives as well, Tim wouldn't want you holding them up for us, any more than I do. You get wed as soon as you're able, I'll be there, cheering you on.'

She was delighted about Phyllis and Dan, they seemed well matched. Having Phyl as her future sister-in-law deepened their friendship.

Despite Rhona's resolution, Christine was growing accustomed to a fuss being made of her. She was a bonnie little girl, even Rhona's determination to be rational about her didn't prevent her recognizing the loveliness of her golden hair that glinted with red tints in the sun. Now, perhaps because her father was missing, everyone seemed to rush either to pick her up or play with her as soon as they appeared.

'As you can see, I'm no better than the rest of you!' Rhona exclaimed one Sunday afternoon when Phyllis called and found her on the floor, hugging the child while Christine was giggling away and tugging at her mother's hair.

'Does it matter?' Phyllis asked, tucking her long elegant

legs beneath her as she joined them on the rug. 'There'll be time enough for getting tough with her later on, when there's less strain on you.'

'*If* that day comes,' said Rhona dismally. 'I get scared, Phyl – scared that I'll never hear one way or the other, whether he's dead or alive. Couldn't take not knowing. Not for ever, this is bad enough.'

'He might have come down somewhere where the French Resistance are hiding our lads, you know. Could be they're only waiting their chance to get him back across the channel.'

'Happen.'

'It's been a long time, hasn't it, old love,' Phyllis sympathized, her green eyes misting. She was watching Rhona now, as she gathered the baby to her. She might have been about to crush the breath out of her, she was squeezing her that hard.

'It's not very easy, specially weekends. Housework never occupies your mind, does it? Or it doesn't mine. All I keep thinking is all the things his dad has said during the week, all their anxieties that he can't stop passing on.'

'If he keeps on about it so much, can't you sort of point out to him that he's making you more upset?'

'How can I? He's getting old, is Bill – older than ever now this has happened. Maybe talking about his fears eases it for him.'

'It's such a shame this should come just now, when you've started getting your home as you want it, and you were all so happy.'

'Aye, Bill's besotted with our Chris. I ought to go over and see them more often now. I haven't done so since just after we heard, and I know that's wrong.'

'But you can only take so much,' Phyllis observed. 'You need different company. What about Norah Lowe, have you seen her recently? If you like, I could come with you – either to the Brightstones' or to visit the old lady.'

'Thanks, love.' The trouble was she felt she ought to take Christine on her own to see Tim's mum and dad.

And as for Auntie Norah – she'd never enthused about Tim, anyway, had she?

'Happen I'll go and visit Mum Brightstone some time when Bill has to go out of an evening. He still has meetings he has to attend.'

Breathing deeply, as if he might clear his entire body of the stress of the evening, Wolf strode through Halfield, and turned up the lane leading home to Farnley Carr. It had been a bad day, he'd awakened that morning with grim foreboding pressing him down into the mattress until getting out of bed required a massive effort.

Once he was up, though, and bathed, shaved and dressed he'd felt his customary assurance that he might cope with whatever occurred. At his desk, however, he'd found nothing untoward awaiting him. Construction was going ahead on various air bases up and down the country, all seemed to be proceeding to schedule, with no more than the usual headaches over supplies of materials. And such problems, anyway, were more the concern of his sub-contractors.

The meeting he'd left ten minutes ago had gone smoothly as well. He and his fellow governors of Little-wood School had gathered to discuss final details of its handing over, for the duration of the war, to the army. Its fee-paying scholars dispersed, the school was requisitioned as a military hospital. Dormitories were being turned into wards, staff rooms would serve medical personnel instead of teachers. But, as Bill Brightstone had observed, wounded soldiers would have less scope for causing havoc than their more able-bodied brethren who, some reported, were none too careful of premises they had taken over. They envisaged few problems over their school.

Bill Brightstone. Yes. Wolf quickened his step, hurrying uphill with scarcely any increase in his heart-rate, no perceptible change in the quantity of air inhaled. He was fit, these days, fitter than for many a year, since he'd adopted the habit of walking.

He would not dispose of the Daimler, but he would and did limit its use. To someone in business like himself, obtaining sufficient petrol for all his requirements presented no difficulty. Not using his full entitlement had become his unpublicized private war effort. He'd surprised himself by enjoying the exercise along with the satisfaction of making his personal contribution.

This evening was one of the rare occasions when he wasn't either thinking through some company project, or gazing about him at the subtle changes of the surrounding countryside. He found a great deal of pleasure, and his own peace, in the meadows and moorland between Halfield's blackened stone and his home. *Not*, though, on this occasion.

Wolf sighed wearily, anything but pleased with the knowledge that he could not discipline his emotions. Nothing would have made him consider quitting the board of governors of Littlewood School, but each confrontation with Bill Brightstone became harder than the last.

It had begun months ago now, when Brightstone somehow managed to get hold of a film and came along with his snapshots. Sitting at the glossy table of the school's staff room, Wolf had taken hardly any notice of the pictures being passed around. Bill did harp on, and they should all have been thinking of completing their business and getting home before the blackout.

And then there she was, looking if anything younger and more vulnerable than when he'd first seen her. Such a girl herself, she surely could not have borne this infant.

'Don't you think young Christine's like her mother?' Bill had asked them all and, Wolf suspected, himself in particular. 'Our Timothy's that thrilled he didn't know where to put himself when he came home on leave. You should see her hair now – it's a magnificent combination of his colouring and Rhona's. The missus says it'll darken later on, but just now it's a lovely gold with just a hint of red that gleams, especially when she's just been bathed.'

There had been other photographs as well. Wolf hadn't

looked. To satisfy the proud grandfather, he'd faked interest, but had stared instead at the polished table top.

At each subsequent meeting Bill had held forth at length on some aspect of baby Brightstone's progress, and who could blame him? With his son away, little social life, and everybody at the mill no doubt sated with the child's doings, where else could he air his enthusiasm? Each time, Wolf had come home aching from the reminder he had not needed.

I can't go on! he thought repeatedly. In his exquisite master bedroom, he struggled for hours against the pain, physical and mental, that was becoming his especial torture. Would time never dull wanting her, never complete his resignation?

Tonight, he liked himself less than ever. Although still glowing in accounts of young Christine, Bill had been sobered by a distress already shared by many families. His son, Timothy, was missing. Evidently his squadron had gone out: several aircraft, including young Brightstone's, had not returned.

I *did* say how sorry I was, Wolf silently assured himself. He felt almost as certain that he had sounded sympathetic. Why then was he experiencing this self-disgust, generated because Tim Brightstone's disappearance might have been arranged for his sole benefit?

He felt jaded to death. Stimson was away and he was missing him. With less chauffeuring to occupy him, the man had become a venturesome cook, creating all kinds of interesting meals. From corned beef, leeks, various sorts of meat which Wolf preferred not to attempt to identify – even, he suspected, whalemeat. Things which normally would never be permitted in the Richardson home.

In Stimson's absence, Wolf felt the more keenly having lost other members of staff who once had contributed to the smooth running of Farnley Carr. They had gone, one by one, to munitions work, the forces, or the land army, and had been replaced by two cleaning women who fitted visits to his home around caring for grandchildren, enabling their daughters to work in factories or on buses.

Tonight Wolf had no appetite, preparing something felt like too much trouble. He would make the effort, however, depended too much on himself and his ability to keep going. Maybe tomorrow there would be word from Stimson. He had expected him back long before this.

Stimson had been ill, hospitalized with a stomach tumour. From what he heard, Wolf supposed that the operation could have involved more than Stimson was admitting. He insisted that it had been some minor obstruction, completely removed, without too much difficulty. Wolf was less sure. Much as Stimson preferred his old role where driving predominated over domestic tasks, he wouldn't normally take so long away from his job.

After finishing his scratch meal, Wolf cleared the dishes into the kitchen to leave for one of the daily women, and went through to his study. He felt restless still and, although there was paperwork which might occupy him, or that morning's *Times* and *Daily Telegraph* as yet unread, he could settle to nothing.

He sat instead at the window, looking out over the edge of the moor in the direction of Dale Reservoir. From this side of the house the plantation of trees surrounding the water was visible. On a pleasant summer evening like this, the sky cloudless and sunny still at almost nine o'clock, he even fancied he could see the gleam of gently lapping water.

That was fancy, though; he knew well enough that the folds of the intervening hills made such a sighting impossible. And surely that did not matter? Who was more familiar than he with every foot of the reservoir's structure – who better able to visualize every detail of its undeniably satisfying contours?

During the years since its completion Wolf had succeeded in consigning to the back of his mind the two deaths that had so disturbed him. The place now had become his favourite of all the projects in which he had been involved.

When this blessed war's over, he promised himself, there'll be another reservoir. Hadn't he found just the right situation, out near Wakefield? But that lay well into the future, so far ahead beyond the unknown of this major conflict that one could not envisage work unconnected with fighting.

At least, here in this part of the West Riding, they were fortunate in avoiding the worst of the confrontation. He ought to be utilizing to the full this benefit of absence of heavy raids.

Precisely on cue, the wailing siren sent his heart sinking in the way that he never quite controlled. Sighing, Wolf turned from the window, gathered together a few of the vital papers on his desk, and hastened towards the door leading to the cellars. Carved out of the rock of the hill itself, they had been declared suitable protection, anybody would be far safer here than in any man-made shelter. Anyone with a quarter of his professional expertise would verify that.

In any case, he thought, as he crossed the flagged ground to the chair and table he'd installed there, the raids here were singularly brief in duration. And singularly uneventful.

He was fortunate to have chosen this area for his home, they were *all* lucky to be living here. All? his innate accuracy queried, and he thought again about Bill Brightstone, and others like him, whose anxiety for their kin weighted their days and interminable nights.

Rhona would be experiencing all that, he realized, wondered then why something so obvious hadn't occurred earlier to him. He was filled with such an overwhelming need to offer the comfort which he knew in his heart neither of them would permit, that he felt a lump growing in his throat. A moisture that he would have denied blurred his vision.

With sheer force of will he directed his attention to the documents before him on the square table. Estimates, drawings, surely amongst these he would find something to absorb his wayward attention. Before he had reached the foot of the page Wolf heard the distant all-clear, collected everything together, then ran up the stone steps and across the marble floor towards his study.

Again, he gazed from the window, filled with wordless thanks that they were spared the ravages suffered by other parts of the country, by other countries . . .

The noise of an aircraft engine forced him to scan the blue of the sky, frowning slightly, puzzled by what might be different about its sound. Why did he experience this ominous sinking, why feel so cold that he might already have received news sufficient to strangle his pulse-rate? Standing there, unaware of any reason for holding his breath, Wolf suddenly let air emerge in a gasp of undiluted horror.

Just coming into view, its fuselage alight, was an aeroplane. Dropping rapidly, smoke spiralling, its spluttering engine finally silenced, it was heading straight for the reservoir plantation. God, those trees! For several days there had been no rain, the sun had burned down constantly. The lot would go up like kindling!

Checking his pocket for his keys, Wolf ran out of the house towards the garage. Swiftly unlocking its doors, he flung himself through and into the Daimler. Perspiring yet shivering, he turned on the ignition. The engine refused to fire. How long had the car stood here, unused – a week, ten days, longer . . . ? And with Stimson away nobody had bothered even to turn the engine over.

Desperately, he tried again and again, picturing the trees surrounding the reservoir ablaze. Should he have stopped to alert somebody else – the fire service? He prayed he wasn't the only person who'd seen the blazing aircraft.

When at last the car started, Wolf swung it out of the garage and swiftly down the curve of drive. The iron gates were long since sacrificed to the war effort, he was out on to the road after the merest halt to check for approaching traffic.

Heading across the rim of the moor he allowed himself to glance away from the road. There was no sign yet of conflagration among the trees, only the faintest trail of smoke drifting into the now-darkening sky witnessed to the wrecked plane.

Maybe it hasn't done too much damage, Wolf thought, hope rising a little as he stamped hard down on the accelerator, racing to the vicinity of the crash. Repeatedly he checked his rear-view mirror, expecting to see either the fire brigade or the Auxiliary Fire Service, summoned to attend. There must be others who had seen this lone aircraft. He couldn't be the only one.

Nearing the wooded slopes surrounding the reservoir, Wolf began breathing more easily. There was no hint of fire anywhere that he could see. Perhaps the plane had burnt itself out before touching the ground, it could have landed in one of the areas of parched earth where vegetation was too sparse to fuel the blaze. Almost there, he was able to glance down and sideways at the reservoir itself. Initially, he saw nothing untoward, relief rushed over him to replace his panic. Driving alongside the reservoir now, only a few hundred yards from its edge, he began believing that the shattering sight he'd anticipated all the way here might be avoided. He even began to wonder if he could have imagined that plummeting aircraft.

He was almost level with the massive concrete embankment bridging the valley when he noticed the water it contained. Currents were appearing, lines resembling the wake of some giant vessel. He looked more carefully towards the retaining dam. As he watched, the central section of bridging concrete slowly shattered, tumbled, roaring out of sight, over the edge.

Heedless of possible damage to the car, Wolf drove over the tussocks of grass till he reached the service road. Within seconds he had driven as close as he could get and was gazing, appalled, at the wreck of the Messerschmitt embedded in the gigantic concrete steps which, crumbling, now released ton upon ton of surging water.

The water had extinguished the blaze, but the devastation he'd imagined if the plantation of trees should catch fire was nothing compared with the destruction this tremendous force would cause.

The fuselage had been thrust into the upper tiers of the retaining dam. Inexorably, the rush of water was easing it free. Like a trampled tin toy, the plane was crushed, splintered into metal fragments, first submerged then lost completely beneath the turbulent suface.

'No, God, no!' Wolf murmured aloud, hypnotized by such horrific demolition. As if it were no heavier than a cork, the bulk of the fuselage emerged again, flopped around briefly, then was lost in the torrent.

Sick with shock and the enormity of the catastrophe, Wolf staggered out of the car and leaned, shaking, against its door. Some distance away a man was waving urgently, then cupping his hands to shout over the roar of water. Wolf recognized the reservoir keeper, was too shattered even to recall his name.

'I've opened the sluice gates,' the man called. 'But that won't divert more than a trickle compared with that lot!'

'I know, I know.' Despairingly, Wolf pressed whitening knuckles to his forehead. Was there nothing they could do, no way on this earth to stop the raging flood? Could they only stand and gape as destruction tore down through the valley?

'At least there's no houses down yonder,' the man shouted, 'and if that poor Jerry bugger weren't dead when he came down, the impact would finish him.'

Grimly, Wolf nodded. He was trying to force his numbed brain to function. There must be some way they could lessen the havoc. They couldn't simply do nothing.

'Where you off to?' the man called after him as Wolf flung himself back into the Daimler and started her up. Back he drove over the rough grassland, taking the shortest way to the main road. He set off down the valley, intending . . . well, he didn't know. Only that remaining immobilized was more than he could endure. Who could even contemplate what he might find there? Or how far he would get, he thought grimly, as he saw the water spreading out, a widening, thundering lake.

Fifty yards ahead the road turned sharply to the left, dropping steeply with the gradient of the hill, and disappeared below the swirling surface.

'Oh, Christ!' He was done, finished. Had that fellow been right – he himself couldn't even think! Was there no one living further down the valley? Would this gigantic mass of water eventually ease into a river, containable by the narrowing vale? Might it prove less devastating than he feared?

Feeling too demolished to act, after stopping the car Wolf switched off the ignition, then waited. To his left several blocks of concrete from the dam had been ground into the hillside, remaining like some child-giant's building bricks. Pieces of twisted grey Messerschmitt, one bearing a scratched swastika, had been hurled by the torrent into a patch of gorse.

It was obscene, revolting.

Wolf heard screams, one thin, high-pitched, others child-like; most blood-chilling of all, the screams of a man.

Scrambling from the driving seat, he peered through gathering darkness towards the opposite hillside.

Briefly, he saw them – a family, two adults, a boy and a girl. One moment they were gazing horror-stricken as surging water advanced down their pathway, the next swept off their feet. All four were tossed like celluloid dolls over and over, bobbing around for seconds, and then no more, out of sight, drowned.

'They hadn't an earthly, Mr Richardson. N'body could have got to 'em. N'body.'

'But . . .'

'I've alerted the police, they're clearing anybody down in the bottom out of t'road of this lot. They're stopping all trains running along the other side of the valley there, the last one through were half an hour since. They've put blocks on all the roads, keeping everybody well clear.'

Wolf swallowed, nodded, tried to speak but no words

came. Why hadn't he thought to do that? Warning people, keeping them away? Why hadn't he, right at the beginning, planned for this contingency?

'It were a stray Jerry, by the looks of it. Somebody must have taken a pot shot at it, somewhere . . . You couldn't have known.'

Wolf shook his head, turned aside abruptly and vomited, violently, into the ditch.

'The level of the reservoir has sunk quite a bit now, Mr Richardson. Another few minutes and it'll be below the breach in the dam. It'll stop coming over then.'

'So long as there are no cracks running down from the place of impact,' Wolf said gravely, blowing his nose, wiping his mouth, then his watering eyes.

'Look yonder – see, the flow's nearly been checked. You can see the concrete again, just about.'

'It's darkening fast, will be black as pitch in half an hour.'

'Aye; we'll not be able to do much more afore morning.'

'We'll have to drain her off.'

'I've seen to all that. Don't you go fretting. Before I come after you, I saw to all the valves. Now it's stopped coming over the top, it'll be draining off gradual, like. Safely. I've got Sir Reginald Newbold on his way here. Him and his men'll see to it that the structure's safe enough to leave till daylight.'

And I'm the only one doing nothing, thought Wolf.

The road beyond the car was still flooded. Wearily, he rejected the possibility of proceeding any further. 'I'll see you at the keeper's house. Unless you want a lift there . . .'

'You're not fit to drive, sir.' Was he too far gone to understand that?

'Can't leave the car here. It's blocking the road. Once the water down there subsides, people will need to get through.'

Wolf reversed up the narrow lane till he found a spot wide enough for turning. Grimly, determined to keep his shaking foot on the accelerator, he negotiated the service road to the reservoir keeper's premises.

He found the man in the control room, nodding approvingly over the gauges. 'That should do it now. I reckon we've got it contained.'

'*We?*' To his last hour, he'd feel he'd failed to do anything.

'Could have been a hell of a lot worse.'

'Didn't you see them? And hear . . .!' Wolf swallowed again. 'They were only a young couple, and their children. Boy and a girl.'

'Aye – I saw.' He paused. 'They'd know nowt, you know. Nowt at all. It'd be that quick they'd be under in a trice and . . .'

Inconsolable, Wolf walked away, out into the night. Instinctively he gazed around, looking for lights from distant farmsteads, from his own home which should just be visible on the brow of that far hill. Then he remembered the blackout. And felt that daylight never would come. As if the tragedy of the bursting dam had inflicted permanent darkness on them all . . . on him in particular. Wasn't it all his fault?

'You're not driving home like that?'

As Wolf reached the car he became aware of the other man watching him, concerned, from the blacked-out window.

'Eventually, not for a while. I – need to walk, think.'

'You've done enough thinking, I reckon. Come back inside, Mr Richardson, if you're not going home yet.'

'No, I – thank you, but no.'

The breeze was chill off the water remaining in the reservoir. His thin summer shirt felt hopelessly inadequate. The flannels flapping about his legs might have been drenched by the water, though they were not, only clammy and cold.

I can't endure this, Wolf thought, cannot accept it. When he'd walked as far as the main road again he stood immobilized. He heard a car approaching, stepped automatically aside when he saw its shaded lights.

18

The car did not pass. Wolf turned away, concealing his face; the darkness that he'd regretted only so recently couldn't sufficiently disguise his emotions.

'Wolf . . .'

It was *her*. She was out of the little Morris, its door slamming after her, as she hastened towards him.

He set his lips tightly together, willing himself not to break.

'Wolf,' she said again, huskily, nearing him now. Her hand touched his shoulder. 'I was driving home from Mum Brightstone's, he'd been out to a meeting. I saw it all – the plane coming down, crashing, the – all that water . . . !'

'I couldn't do a bloody thing!' He spoke without facing her. He couldn't let her see how devastated he was, how *useless* he felt.

'They're all out now, doing what they can, police, the Auxiliary Fire Service, the lot. I could see them from the road I was on. It's under control now, Wolf, there's nothing you or I can . . .'

'That's it – rub it in!' His own voice was savage, unrecognizable.

'Where's the Daimler?'

'What . . . ?'

'Your car, Wolf, where've you left it?'

Still not looking at her, he jerked his head towards the reservoir keeper's house.

'Good. And Tommie Kitchen'll keep a careful watch for further signs of flooding . . .'

'So?'

'Come on, love, let's get you home.'

'I can't just walk away. An entire family was swept off in the torrent, don't you understand?'

Biting her lip, Rhona nodded. 'I saw it all.' But she had *known* Wolf would be here and – well, here she was. 'Come on,' she said again. The catastrophe might have been infinitely greater. Though that wouldn't help him.

Wolf shook his head. 'Stimson's away.' He couldn't tolerate the emptiness of Farnley Carr. Could not live alone, even for the one night, with his thoughts, his responsibility.

'All right,' Rhona said slowly, considering. 'I can give you a bed, for the few hours that's left.'

Numbly, no longer capable of argument, he got into her car. Dimly, he sensed something odd, unexpected, about her continuing in this direction, but was too perturbed for coherent reasoning.

Only as Rhona turned into the drive of the detached villa, one of several in an avenue overlooking Halfield, did he understand. She didn't live in that friendly little house in Gracechurch Street now, with Eve and Jack Hebden. She was a married woman, married to Brightstone.

'No – I'd – rather not. If you don't mind, I'll . . .' Wolf shuddered. He was cornered, trapped between his desolate mansion and – learning how skilled a homemaker she was. 'Oh, God!' he breathed.

He had known she would be capable. How much so, he'd never truly understood, until he was inside her home, a glass of brandy in his ashamedly trembling hands. Somehow, he was secured in an enveloping armchair, gazing while she put a match to coals laid ready in the grate.

'That's better,' Rhona approved, smiling at him, her tired eyes glinting as the fire began to blaze. 'Just stay like that while I fetch Chrissie in from the car.'

'Chris . . . ?' he murmured, but she was gone.

Wolf's unease increased. The child, the Brightstone child, had been there all the time, in her car. The sense of having someone intrude on his distress was so intense he wanted to escape, to run. But running would have required effort, far more effort than he might summon.

When Rhona came in with the carry-cot his hands were

over his face, his head sunk in misery. Aye, lad – they're bad times, she thought. For some reason she didn't analyse, she whisked the sleeping baby upstairs to her room.

Wolf was sipping the brandy when Rhona returned. He appeared composed. Strangely, she felt more disturbed rather than less – he ought to let go. Men ought to be free to cry. She knew how desperately she'd wanted that release when she first heard about Tim.

'You'll have to get busy now, won't you?' she said briskly, pouring a drink for herself. 'There'll be no time now for other projects till you've got that reservoir reconstructed.'

'Never!'

'Oh, you can say that, tonight. Don't think I don't understand. The shock was bad enough for me, you must have felt it a hundred times more keenly. That reservoir's needed here, Wolf.'

'No, no! Keep quiet, you don't know what you're saying.'

'Oh, I know, all right. You made sure my comprehension was complete. And there'll be more industry needed in the area now there's a war on. Here, because there's so many places where they'd be bombed to smithereens. Factories to provide munitions for the lads out there, uniforms, radios and telephone equipment.'

'Hasn't that bloody thing killed enough people, even with tonight?'

Wolf gulped, sipped the brandy, choked and coughed.

'Here . . .' Kneeling on the carpet before his chair, Rhona took the glass and set it on the nearby low table. She grasped his wrists then, and his agitated pulse seemed to steady a little beneath her fingers.

'You brought new life to this town, Wolf – creating work by starting construction of Dale Reservoir, enticing new industry that dragged a lot of our folk out of the slump.'

Sighing, he shook his head, his eyes tightly closed.

'And when the war's over, what then?' Rhona continued

sharply. 'What's going to happen to all the lads coming back, and finding their workplaces closed down? What'll become of them when there's no point in businesses starting up afresh – because there'll be insufficient water. When every piddling little stream has to be clarified for drinking. What'll become of Bridge House Mill when the dyeing plant can't carry on, when we've no water providing steam to drive our machines? They'll take what we've got there, you know, divert the mill-race, like as not, so's folk have water for their homes.'

'You'll find other sources . . .'

'Other sources, my foot! They weren't there before, they'll not just magically appear, to save you a few reminders! You always take everything on yourself, don't you? Can't you see – somebody shot down a stray German plane, it happened – just happened to come down where it did. How can you blame yourself?'

'That thing was there. And I built it.'

'All right, love, all right.' She drew his hands towards her, kissed his clenched fists, held them against her cheeks.

Wolf felt her cool glossy hair brush his chin, sighed, and buried his face in her curls. Releasing his wrists, Rhona reached upwards, her arms sliding around his shoulders, gathering him to her. Leaning into her, he remained motionless, warmth from the fire and from each other began easing the pain.

'You want to try to sleep,' she told him quietly after a while.

'As if I could.'

When Rhona moved Wolf shivered. 'There are calls I ought to be making.'

She showed him where the telephone was, went from the room while he spoke with the police, verifying that the one family alone had been lost. He felt no real relief when they told him that the flood waters had been diverted by the narrowing of the valley, the contour of the hills forcing it to drain away along the original river bed. It meant nothing when they said his design had enabled the reservoir to be drained effectively as soon as humanly possible. He made another call then to the reservoir keeper. He'd felt he'd never face Tom Kitchen again, but he'd taken too much for granted.

'You did a magnificent job, Tom, that won't be overlooked. You acted calmly and promptly, controlling a situation which, with anyone else in charge there, might have been far more devastating.'

He was back in the chair when Rhona returned to the room. She saw him shiver again, sat on the floor in front of the fire, and extended a hand to him.

'It's warm enough down here.' Smiling slightly, she drew him down to the carpet. 'I'd laid the fire before going out. Nappies have to be dried, even when you've been at work all day. I always mean to get them done and on the line before setting off for the mill, doesn't always work out.'

Hearing her talk like that, of the little domestic details of her life, made him ache to have a share in her. Wolf crushed her to him. Her back was to his chest, his arms encircled shouders that felt too thin through the stuff of her dress. Stretching his legs to one side, he leaned his head against the chair, Rhona leaned against him. She was pressing to him, closer than close. For the first time with her, this closeness generated no physical reaction. All senses seemed chanelled into the one despairing need, for understanding.

Through the rest of the night, neither spoke very much, and nor did they sleep. The hours, paced by the oak-cased grandfather clock, slid away harnessed with Wolf's troubles. A strange half-peace overtook his exhausted soul. He'd never misjudged her, never over-valued their relationship. The affinity was greater than desire, and it did still exist. God help them!

His kiss was fleeting, and in her hair. Briefly, he squeezed her shoulder. 'I won't ever forget, my dear.'

He was gone then, stretching before he opened the outer door, then walking swiftly away down the drive. Not looking back at all, he strode away along the road.

She was leaving for the mill when the postman brought the letter. Timothy was alive, his plane had come down over occupied France, he was in Germany now, a prisoner of war.

Rhona's next news of Wolf was only partially a shock. When her father-in-law spoke of him enlisting in the Royal Engineers, she realized she'd been expecting something similar. He would be glad to get away. And she shouldn't be praying with all her heart that one day he would return.

Rhona busied herself more conscientiously than ever at the mill, concentrating all her energies on increasing production of warp and weft for uniforms.

In what spare time remained, she dragged the baby along to knitting bees, where she drilled housewives into producing 'Comforts' for the forces, introducing folk with more enthusiasm than skill to the intricacies of turning heels, and producing gloves with the required number of fingers.

Slowly, Tim's letters began coming through, yet somehow they made the situation all the more strange, distanced from her. Each time Rhona wrote back, she quelled her consciousness of the necessary effort. This was her husband, why couldn't she write more freely to him?

Christine thrived on days in her grandmother's care, and evenings of being taken about in Rhona's blue Morris. She slept or prattled away to herself while her mother took the knitting classes, and on visits to Norah Lowe wallowed in the old lady's attention. Auntie Norah's very evident joy on hearing that Timothy was alive had made Rhona overcome all misgivings about the old lady's attitude. Her love of children was plain in her affection for Rhona's offspring.

'You've got a bright little lass there, Rhona love,' she enthused while the youngster hauled herself up by the prickly black horsehair sofa. Her delight was complete when, eventually, Christine managed to say 'Nantie Nornoh'.

I just wish there was someone else who shared her progress, Rhona thought, bewildered by the knowledge that, for all their interest, her mother and stepfather did not fulfil that need.

Rhona had been shopping for a few remnants of material to make up dresses for her rapidly growing daughter when she saw him striding towards her. The surrounding grey of Halfield's walls and pavements could in no way dim the magnificence of the uniformed figure. Immaculate khaki, perfectly pressed and gleaming with brass buttons, never suited anybody better. Tall, slender, but still with powerful shoulders, Wolf personified the dynamic English officer.

'What's all this then? she exclaimed as he drew level with her, and she pretended she'd heard nothing from Bill Brightstone of Wolf's rapid progress to the rank of captain. 'That doesn't look like a private's battledress!'

Wolf grinned, his grey eyes lighting in a way that drove off all memories of the night the reservoir was destroyed. 'Er – no. Someone seemed to hold the opinion that I *might* be more use shouldering a bit of responsibility!'

Wryly she grinned back at him. 'Aye, well – happen they've heard how you like them shoulders to be as broad as they appear! You look well on it, anyway, Wolf. I'm pleased for you.' If not pleased for myself, because this looks like our parting, at least for the duration.

'Thank you, Rhona. And how are things with you? I hear your – your husband has been located. I hope they aren't treating him too badly.' That you're not too hurt because of his being a prisoner of war. If only to God there were some way that I might share what life is doing to you . . .

'Difficult to tell. Tim says he's all right – not that he can be too forthcoming, their letters rarely arrive intact. But I reckon, knowing Tim, he'd find some way of getting it across if there was too much to grouse about.'

'And you manage to get letters back and forth without too great a difficulty?'

'It's all rather hit and miss. You don't hear for ages, then you receive a batch of letters. But, actually . . .' Mid-sentence, Rhona stopped abruptly, gulping back her words. What on earth was she thinking about, she'd nearly admitted to Wolf that the hardest part was knowing what to write to Timothy.

'He could be worse off,' Wolf remarked pensively, willing himself not to speak of the idea that had formed and refused to let him alone. 'Are you – do you have any spare time just now? I'm only in Halfield for the weekend, embarkation leave. I thought, that is – could we have tea, or something, together?'

The little café was nearly empty. The tea she poured with a hand requiring all her will to keep it steady was drunk but hardly noticed. All her attention was on this splendid officer who was telling her how he'd risen to the rank of captain, and of his mingled excitement and dread generated by heading overseas.

It was as they reached the sunlit street afterwards that he suggested she see Auntie Norah with him, he was going there to say goodbye. Standing so near that the ferny fragrance of his soap was alerting all her senses, Rhona was commanding herself *not* to press her side against the khaki cloth. The arms she was longing to feel about her were forbidden, not her husband's arms. She had no right to experience this exhilarating quickening of each nerve-ending, this strange dizziness; no right to wish they might belong. Prolonging this was an almighty temptation.

'Sorry, Wolf – Mum's only looking after Christine for a couple of hours and that's nearly up now. And besides, I saw Auntie Norah only last weekend. Give her my love, though, tell her I'll call again soon.'

'Sure.' Wolf was preoccupied. When she dared meet his glance, the grey eyes were a shock – searching her face, while he clearly searched his brain for words, the right words for something vital.

'I'm going to miss – er, Halfield, my dear. I wondered – will you . . . will you write to me, Rhona? *Please*. Keep me in touch . . .'

'I – don't know.' Her words were as halting as his, her own mind equally disturbed. Both uncertain of the rights and wrongs of what he proposed, both were equally sure of what they needed. Rather ruefully, Rhona smiled. 'I suppose I might as well. I don't imagine Stimson will write you many letters.'

And there's no one else, she thought, but could not say that. For she, perhaps more than Wolf himself, felt hurt by there being no one. 'Aye – go on, give us your address. You'll have to put up with my spelling and Yorkshirisms, mind. We haven't all had your education!'

He clenched his hands down at his sides. It was the only way he might avoid hugging her, in the middle of the town, in broad daylight. 'Look forward to hearing from you then . . .' He turned abruptly, and walked away.

Rhona waited for over a month before she did as Wolf had asked. Her first letter to him was brief but friendly. His reply, although no less friendly, should not have caused such disproportionate elation.

Dear Rhona,
How good it was to hear from you, many thanks! Army life is proving as different as anything could be from my normal existence, making this link more vital than even I believed. Fortunately, we're occupied for ninety-nine per cent of the time that we're awake, permitting little opportunity for brooding.

As it happens, most other officers in this outfit are regulars, and don't enthuse too greatly about those of us who aren't! The only good in this is that it forces fiercer effort from the likes of myself, keeping us even busier. If there were time for considering, I'd be wondering at my own decision to enlist. The way things are, I learn daily to accept this life here.

Have you perhaps ever experienced life on more than one plane at some given moment? I repeatedly find awareness of my work dimming to accommodate brief thoughts of Halfield, and my friends there – and thoughts of some that prove anything but brief. For a while, such reflections and memories grow far more real (surely more significant) than all the practi-

*calities of war which surround me. They are my sanity, maybe,
certainly they sustain me.*

*Enough of myself. Though selfishness sparked this corre-
spondence, I never intended it should nurture self alone. Write
when you can, Rhona, and when you do, write of your life
there – of what you are doing. It seems to me you well
understand choosing the way one should, rather than the way
that most entices. You, who never have sought ease, deserve
a more fulfilling life and freedom from anxiety. There must
be days when you feel depressed by all that the war is doing,
by being denied opportunity to expand the Bridge House business. Do, please, feel free to unload your troubles on me –
there must be some truth in the cliché about halving them!*

Yours,
Wolf

It seemed to her like the one release she'd been seeking.
It never had felt right, somehow, to bother her mother
with the things that upset her. Eve was a cheerful stoic –
admirable, but just fractionally daunting, especially when
a general dissatisfaction, rather than distress, was her
daughter's complaint.

I've struggled for so long, Rhona thought; to rear Christine on her own, to drain herself at the mill, enduring
Bill's constant though understandable misery concerning
Timothy, and all the while ensuring optimum output from
the spinning frames. Even the evenings teaching knitting
were a chore now, she was so weary, and the garments
they made so utilitarian.

She had to will herself not to write back immediately
to Wolf, not to pour out her heart. She owed Tim a letter.
His last, a scrawled note, gave her nothing to respond to.
He was unutterably bored; they were fed, but uninterest-
ingly; they were lousy (which he despised). He did not
ask after Christine, much less Rhona herself.

You're expecting too much, she told herself in the big
silent house, once Chrissie was settled for the night. How
would *she* react to an enemy prison camp, to the depri-
vation, indignity?

She wrote telling him of their daughter's progress, though not of her own bitterness because that progress wasn't truly shared with him. She mentioned his parents, how they were reasonably well, despite their concern for him. And she told him how, on a recent leave, Dan had married Phyllis. She added reminiscences of their own hurried wedding and then quite suddenly, she couldn't write another word on the subject. She hated herself for resenting Phyllis's and Dan's very evident joy. She had felt her smile was plastered on her face throughout their wedding day. Could she really be wondering why it had to be *her* husband in Germany, imprisoned? Surely, she wouldn't wish this on anyone else? If only they'd had more time, though, time to *feel* married before he was removed. The short leaves that had seemed to pass in a whirl would be luxury indeed to them now.

Liking herself less than ever, Rhona completed the letter, sending all her love, that it might compensate for her inability to write more than a page or two. As if it might outweigh her resentment of circumstances.

For days Rhona refused to permit herself to answer Wolf's letter. Maybe on the following Monday, she promised herself, if she'd completed all the chores she planned for the weekend. Before the weekend had begun, however, she was surrendering to despair.

Friday was an abysmal day. Ellen Brightstone had called in at the mill while she was out shopping, and Rhona was appalled by the way in which the relationship between Bill and his wife appeared to have deteriorated. Normally, she'd considered them a typical north-country couple, never wasting words over a lot of sentiment, but warm in their affection and respect for each other. Now, Bill seemed to have changed into a grousing old man, who scarcely had a civil word for his wife.

'It's because he's worried sick about our Timothy, I know,' Ellen, close to tears, confided to Rhona when she walked her to the mill door. 'I just wish he'd realize I'm no less anxious, and I haven't a job of work to occupy me, have I?'

Rhona could only agree, give her mother-in-law's shoulders a squeeze, and resolve to try and do more for her.

'I'll bring Chrissie round at the weekend, shall I? That might give Bill something else to think about – you, as well.' She was fond of Ellen, couldn't bear to see this happening.

That evening Christine began playing up. Looking back, Rhona recognized that her daughter had grown increasingly demanding. But with Eve and Jack Hebden, Phyllis and, for a short while, Dan making a fuss of her, Rhona herself hadn't been left to cope.

Today, Christine threw a tantrum because Rhona insisted on taking her home for tea instead of remaining at Gracechurch Street. Working full time and with a house to follow, evenings and weekends were precious and somehow she'd to scrape together time for the promised visit to Tim's parents. Having got a protesting Christine home, however, she wasted over an hour calming the child and coaxing her to eat. Only the threat of sending her to bed without anything eventually persuaded her to cooperate.

'You're spoilt, young lady,' Rhona told her. 'And that's just what I swore you wouldn't be. There's too many folk run round in circles trying to please you, it's a pity they can't see what you're really like, how naughty you can be.'

Christine looked at her then, and gave a shrug; her mother's opinion might have been of no consequence. Rhona raised her hand ready to land an almighty slap on her bare arm. Horrified, she checked. If she began walloping the kiddie, she wasn't certain she could stop.

'But we're landed with each other, aren't we, Christine, we'd better make the best of it. We'll have a bit of fun together while you have your bath, then I'll tell you a story before you go to sleep.'

'Don't like your stories. Grandad Hebden tells the best stories.'

'Grandad Hebden gets tired, though, he can't be doing with you every night.'

'He's your daddy, isn't he?' Christine said plaintively. 'My daddy's gone away, he's been locked up. That's why he can't come home.'

'That's right, love, but only till the war's over. And we've got to be very sensible and patient, until then.'

'But I want him here now. He could tell me stories. *Now*. I might be too old when he does come home.'

And so might I, thought Rhona glumly, too old for everything. How many months – *years* – was it since they'd made love, since she'd felt she was a woman? How long had she gone on, working, caring for Chris, just existing . . . ?

Christine was nearly two. Incredible though that seemed, life had continued. Without Tim, or almost without him. Without her career, for who could pretend the work she was doing now provided much satisfaction?

When Christine was at last in bed and asleep, Rhona began tackling the ironing. She'd done half a dozen items when she caught her hand on the iron, burned it severely.

'Damn and blast everything to hell!' she swore, wrapped her hand in a newly laundered tea towel, and unplugged the iron.

Dear Wolf,

I really was going to get some work done tonight! I was determined to get the ironing out of the way, now I've burnt my hand. I'm feeling right sorry for myself – I hope you meant what you said about off-loading my problems! I expect I'm grumbling about something and nothing. Just remember, though, whenever you need a jolly good moan, pick up your pen.

It was good to receive your letter, word from another world. Yes, I feel, like you, that I'm living on more than one plane. I thought it made me peculiar in some way (not that I'm suggesting you are!) but it's often the only way I survive.

This has been one of those days, with me not liking anybody very much, certainly not the people I spend much of my time with. I wouldn't admit this to anybody else, but Bill is getting me down. Sorry you have to endure my complaints, but I know they'll go no further. And he is becoming a cantankerous old so-and-so. Even with his wife, and she's such a nice little body. Don't know how women put up with domestic chores and nothing else. But then, I'm not truly domesticated. As you would gather, if you could see this place.

It's funny, when I found this house and was getting it ready, I was thrilled to bits. I wonder why I'm so dissatisfied, always longing for something different? These days, it's mostly wishing this war was over and done with.

Happen it's better when you're doing something constructive. Is it? Are you glad you're . . . wherever you are, working your guts out to bring some kind of peace? Is it great to be compelled to give your mind (or most of it) to something so much bigger and more important than oneself?

Do you know what scares me most, these days? When I look to the future, I dread discovering that I'm not satisfied with anything any longer. That, when we're permitted at long last to produce the yarns we wish, I shan't be able to care sufficiently about them. Happen I look ahead too much. Or not enough . . . ?

I do go on, don't I? Did you want somebody to cheer you up? I can't believe this is what you anticipated. This weekend I'm taking myself in hand. I've got to see Bill and Ellen, I promised. And I'll visit Auntie Norah. She seems well enough, though I do wonder how much longer she'll keep that way – she must be ninety-six. She doesn't seem anything like that, but I've been thinking she ought to have a telephone. Before the winter sets in.

I'm also going to make time to go to the library. Reading's kept being crowded out. Now, it might keep my flagging brain relatively alert.

Do you enjoy a good book? I'm sure your taste would be far more intellectual than mine. I tend to go for the latest Agatha Christie. Another author I love is Nevil Shute, but like a lot more writers he's had to suspend creating fiction while he either helps fight this war or reports its progress.

Is anyone today doing the job they chose?

I do ramble on, don't I? I've just read through from the beginning! Don't judge me too harshly, I am jaded to death.

Don't forget you're entitled to write at similar length, about the life you've been thrust into. That should do me good: at least, I sleep in my own bed, don't I?

Take care of yourself,

Yours,
Rhona

How disappointed she was with the letter she'd written! She wouldn't have been at all surprised if Wolf hadn't replied. Men at the front needed something to give their morale a lift, didn't they? When she'd first agreed to their correspondence, she'd visualized her letters being sparkling, even clever.

Wolf's answer came so swiftly that she was astonished as well as delighted when she recognized the assertive handwriting.

Dear Rhona,
How is the burn? I never thought you would be so careless! Someone who shall be nameless once told me: 'You haven't even the sense to look after your own hand!'

Anyway, your disability (I hope it proves temporary) was my good fortune. I always look for your letters, and whatever their content am cheered by their arrival.

He'd been touched by her lack of pretence, the very ordinariness of her letter brought her so very close. And her evident need of comfort made him thankful he'd initiated this communication between them.

Yes, of course, being compelled to do all that is expected of one here is more satisfactory than remaining where you are, on the sidelines. And, I would remind you, I came here as an escape! A good reason for doing nothing about matters too disturbing for consideration. That has not changed, which is why – unlike you – I prefer to think, if not solely of 'here', most certainly of 'now'. (I might add that some aspects of army life do rather encourage this. There seems to be an inordinate amount of what, for your tender ears, I will call red tape. Being commissioned, one fortifies its necessity, unquestioningly!)

One day, when we see some action, its existence should be justified. Certainly, no exercise in discipline ever comes amiss. But how can I, formerly accustomed to doing my own will, presume to mention this to you? I'm sorry that you're not more contented. The only consolation I may offer is that life is changing very rapidly, radically as well. I don't believe any of us may assume that we can prophesy the future.

I suppose what I'm trying to say is that none of us should be too careful of what lies ahead. I can recommend the suspension of visualizing which is necessitated by my own situation. Coping with one day and then the next, as they arrive, can be remarkably liberating.

He'd wondered here if he appeared to contradict some reflections from his earlier letter. But she wasn't to know the near-physical pain of contemplating his eventual homecoming. She must not be allowed to guess how determinedly he would evade all thought of her family life, and his inevitable exclusion.

And as for Bill – knowing you will not quote me, I dare say that he does tend to grow wearisome. I feel for you, and feel sure also that your understanding will avert many an altercation . . . even before it arises.

There was more, all of it in good heart, making her spirits soar, making her laugh. And laughing was something she'd almost overlooked. Somehow, the knowledge that Wolf shared her private opinion of her father-in-law generated increased tolerance. Her days at the mill felt easier, she minded less about spending some of her free time taking Christine to Timothy's parents.

The only disadvantage of keeping in touch with Wolf was its constant reminder that she did not know where he was, what he was doing – whether he was in serious danger. And not knowing proved to her how much she did care, desperately, that he should survive.

He's only a friend, she reminded herself regularly, and I am a married woman. But I am concerned about Tim as well, she assured herself. He's the father of my child, the man who'll make a home of this house when he returns, and will make a family with me.

19

During the next six months, letters from Wolf became her lifeline. Christine was developing swiftly, by turns a winning child and a precocious one. She'd been an early talker – doubtless, the result of Rhona's habit of speaking to her so much. Now there were days when Chrissie's ceaseless chatter grew exasperating. Each time that happened Rhona felt contrite, ashamed of her over-tiredness even, because it prevented her compensating for the child's absent father.

And yet she never mentioned Christine when writing to Wolf, nor mentioned Timothy either. Wolf was a part of her life far removed from family, removed also from the drudgery of her day-to-day existence. After that first occasion she never again referred to her feelings about Bill Brightstone. Somehow, though, if only obliquely, Wolf always managed to convey his sympathy towards her situation. And convinced her that one person, at least, took time off from the horrors of war to care.

It was only during the long dark nights that she felt guilty. I write to Timothy just as frequently, she reminded herself, and always at greater length than he writes home. Even to herself, she would not admit how obsessed by Wolf's safety she had become. Repeatedly she willed herself to care less about him. Each time she awaited a letter from him, she vowed the correspondence would cease. Too much importance was attached to the arrival of an envelope with his handwriting.

And then his letter would come, illustrating their rapport, perhaps emphasizing his need of this anchor. She'd assure herself that severing this link to placate her over-active conscience would be unkind, and was unnecessary. After all, she and Wolf alike were meticulous in permitting no space for affection, much less sensuality.

Their letters took nothing from anyone else, harmed no one.

The cable came one Saturday morning when Rhona was busy trying to fit her wriggling daughter for a dress she was making. Her lips full of pins, she answered the door, felt her heart plummet. It's happened, she thought, because I've grown too attached to him. Because it wasn't allowed, I was too weak to resist and have to be punished. Wolf has gone, and now I am desolate . . .

She spat the pins on to the floor; gulping, she tore open the envelope. Tears thickened her throat already, pricked at her eyes. Numbly, she read and re-read the telegram. It wasn't Wolf who was dead.

'God, what have I done!' she screamed.

Christine came running out of the living room. Because of the child she must not faint, couldn't find blessed oblivion, escape. Somehow, she got herself and Christine away from the front door, across the hall, and back into the room. She staggered over yards of carpet and flopped into the nearest chair. All at once the homely room had changed, appeared immense, while she herself was tiny; very, very frail.

Timothy was dead. He'd been ill, the cable said, dysentery. Weakened by months of prison-camp food, he'd possessed no resistance with which to fight the illness. If she personally had drained his strength she couldn't have felt worse.

Grief was a silent agony in her chest and the swift-formed tears were unshed. Rhona couldn't remain immobile. Leaving the chair, she began prowling the room grown massively unfamiliar. Back and forth she plodded, back and forth, an echo of the guilt hurtling about in her agitated mind.

Christine came to her, seizing her hand and tugging, until she eventually looked down. 'Do you hurt, Mummy, does your tummy ache?'

'No, love, no. It's all right. Just be quiet, go and sit down . . .'

Shaking her head, her daughter remained, leech-like,

attached to her perspiring fingers. A contact Rhona felt she didn't deserve, and ought to avoid. If she let this continue, mightn't she break, soften . . .

'I didn't mean this to happen,' she murmured, aghast. 'I didn't, I didn't!'

Hours later, Christine began fussing because she was hungry. Rhona had ceased walking, at some juncture, was huddled in a chair again. Her daughter, still holding her hand, was perched on its arm.

It couldn't be six o'clock in the evening! Whatever had happened to the intervening hours? Had she been lost in madness, simply lost . . . ?

'I'll have to tell somebody,' she muttered, glancing about the living room that appeared no less large, and like a stranger's. Locating the telephone, right beside the chair she occupied, took more than a minute or two. She struggled to recall the number of the telephone Jack Hebden had had installed.

'Oh, Dad!' she exclaimed, so relieved that he at least sounded recognizable. 'Thank God you're there. It's Tim, I've had a telegram . . .'

He and her mother were there quicker than she'd believed possible. Unable to speak, she handed them the cable. They took over, just as they had that first time. Again, Eve went to break the news to Tim's mother, also to his dad. Making a game of it, Jack took Christine into the kitchen and got together her tea.

Rhona sensed his repeated appearances at the living room doorway, checking on her, was thankful he didn't fuss, or even add to his initial sentence. 'Rhona love, I'm that sorry!' he'd exclaimed, coming into the house.

Her mother returned as Christine was sitting down to eat. As it happened, Timothy's aunt from Bedfordshire was staying with the Brightstones, she would look after them.

'And what about you two?' Eve asked, lovely brown eyes awash. 'Will you come home to us for a while?'

'I – don't know.' She needed space, for thinking, couldn't bear the prospect of having even concern invade her privacy. She pictured herself at Gracechurch Street, walled in with the eyes which, however loving, would see through to her truth. Panic tightened her aching throat even further. 'Could – could you stay the night here? I might know my own mind by tomorrow.'

She doubted that, the power of deciding had been interred, deep beneath the mound of earth within her soul. Earth which she had accumulated, by failing so hopelessly. I only need have endured, she thought that night in bed, I was not expected to risk my life, I only needed to remain totally committed.

When she tried to close her eyes, she saw his face – alert, alive, his blue eyes glittering, his glorious golden hair radiant as the sun. He isn't *dead*, her personal demon insisted, he can't be!

Sunday came, stretched unendingly ahead, then gradually diminished; its entirety was nighmarish, eerily subdued. By Monday morning, though, when her parents got up early so Jack could be in time at the engineering works, Rhona was resolute. She was going to the mill. She couldn't be certain Bill would be up to working. And anything was better than this place, furnished with mind's-eye pictures of having Tim live there with them.

Bill was at Bridge House, but a shattered Bill, his eyes unashamedly red-rimmed, his voice rasping. He grasped her shoulder when she walked in, tried to speak, and couldn't. Rhona nodded, sighed, touched his cold hand with hers. They both worked frenziedly, willing clattering spinning mules to drown out feeling.

Taking time off only for the service they held for her husband, Rhona refused to let up. With Christine, she made an effort to return to normal life; away from her, she retreated into her own self. Leaving the church, scarcely aware of her parents and Timothy's, she made her vow. Never again would she write to Wolf, there'd be no more excusing the letters that ought not to have begun. Too late, she would be single-hearted, committed to a memory.

*

Dear Rhona,

Would you believe that I'm hospitalized? Not a casualty of enemy action, but ignominiously the victim of an intestinal infection! You, I am sure, will appreciate the irony.

The doctors are pleased with my progress, although they refuse to suggest a date when I may return to duty. It seems by ability to pass this on to the rest of my unit – if not the entire regiment – far outweighs my possible usefulness back in uniform!

As you will imagine, I am unutterably bored. You must know by now that I am not much given to inactivity. I don't believe I am geared for over-much contemplation.

I think of you frequently, especially now that I have time for a great deal of reading. I re-read a Nevil Shute yesterday, mean to approach something less easily devoured, but the library here seems to go in for escapist literature. As you might guess, I've been posted back to England until I'm cured, front-line hospitals have enough work treating casualties.

Do please write quickly (if only briefly) and save my sanity!

Yours (desperately),
Wolf

Rhona felt panic screaming through her long before she'd read to the end. Not Wolf, not now. No! NO! *NO!*

Nothing could happen to him, *nothing must!* She couldn't bear that – knew, if she wouldn't admit it, that there'd be more than this dull, unreal ache if she were to learn he had died. Her guilt increased, as did her anxiety.

That night she didn't sleep at all, spent the hours weeping – silently, so she wouldn't disturb Christine just the other side of the wall. No one must intrude, no one must search out the reason for her distress, and recognize her long-term neglect of her husband.

And yet she couldn't *not* write to Wolf, couldn't wait, unknowing. She must keep in touch, learn that he was recovering . . . *pray* that he was.

At four o'clock in the morning, huddled into her dressing gown, she was sitting at the living room table.

Dear Wolf,
*Yes, it is ironic! It also is very unfortunate that you should
be ill; I do so hope that by now you are greatly improved.
Take care of yourself, won't you? Do everything they tell you.*

Come through this safely, she thought, for God's sake!

I wish I had some books I could send you.

I wish, oh how I wish, that I could visit you.

*But I never made a habit of spending money on books, not
with a good library in Halfield. That would have gone against
my careful Yorkshire soul!*

But have I always been careful for the wrong things, she
thought, aching again. Caring for you, while my handsome, engaging Timothy died, far away from me?

*Perhaps you can persuade some pretty young nurse to acquire
some reading matter that would be more to your taste?*

Just don't let there be too many pretty nurses, nor any of
them too pretty. Don't use up all those rare smiles of
yours . . .

I wish I had some good news to brighten you up.

And wish with all of my heart that I could tell you my
news, could warrant your sympathy. Closing her eyes, she
shuddered, then seemed to feel Wolf's arms about her, to
hear his voice, reassuring. And she knew, in that moment,
she'd never speak of Timothy to him.

*I must confess I haven't seen Auntie Norah for a few weeks,
I'll rectify that soon.*

I'll cram my life to the limit, and beyond. There must be
less time for thinking, reflection, yearning . . .

You were right, by the way, about Auntie refusing to have such a newfangled item as a telephone! I did try, anyway. She certainly appears well able to cope as she is, for the present.

She's far better equipped for coping than I am! Would you even know me, my dear, in this strange desolation? Would you recognize this great inertia that requires so much concealing?

The local hospitals here are filling up with wounded men. We see them about Halfield in their special blue uniforms. Phyllis works long hours, but seems almost exhilarated by the need she fills. I'd give anything to feel justified in giving up my drudgery at Bridge House Mill for nursing.

And if, by some miracle, I could be spirited away to where you are . . .

How could I leave them? she thought, appalled – how could I leave the fair-haired spirit who dwells in my home, and how could I even contemplate leaving Chrissie!

Two at a time she raced up the steep stairs, along to Christine's room. The child stirred with the opening door, murmured, and slept again, peacefully. You're mine, my love, my child, and safe here, I'd not desert you. Forgive me, Lord, for being torn. And I won't desert.

You'll notice I still bemoan my lot! If only I weren't so weary of it all, if some small part of it captured my imagination. Yarn for uniforms is so dreary.

Life is so grey! Insubstantial now, with a future I can not picture and a home from which purpose is slowly evaporating. And there's no hope of a Daimler driving up beside me, a chance meeting that would change everything.

Sorry I haven't provided more to sustain you. Happen you'll understand I can't dredge much out of this present existence.

Maybe by the time you receive this you'll have recuperated,
anyway; you always appear so self-sufficient.
Look after yourself,

> *Yours,*
> *Rhona*

And, she resolved, addressing the envelope, self-sufficient
is the way he will have to be. As soon as she learned he
was recovering, that would be it: no more letters. This
was an indulgence she no longer could permit herself.

Tomorrow she'd volunteer for more duties for the
WVS. There seemed to be an increasing load on them,
with so many servicemen brought to Halfield for treatment
or convalescence. There were some men, she knew from
Phyllis, too ill or incapacitated for writing to their loved
ones. She might help there, and perhaps with organizing
transport to and from hospitals. Some of that could be
managed taking Chrissie along with her, whenever Eve
wasn't available of an evening.

Dear Rhona,
Many, many thanks for this most welcome of all your letters
which was received on the day I transferred to a convalescent
ward. The next move will be a short spell of leave, which I
shall take hereabouts.

I could not take seeing you, you understand, knowing you
belong elsewhere, to him. For this reason only, I will
myself away from you. For this, my eyes are full as I
write, my throat as well, and heart. I would not have you
recognize the guilt written all over me, because of needing
this contact with you.

I rather suspect the leave will be curtailed, anyway. Things
appear to be hotting up, as the saying goes, even officers have
their uses – despite what my men would claim! I can imagine
their faces when I am restored to them! They would be
surprised by the depth of my concern to keep them with me,
intact, to see this war out.

And how much more surprised would you be, my love, to learn my concern for you, my deep abiding affection? I'm afraid you would be appalled to know my love is enduring, that it did not surrender to your marrying Tim Brightstone. That it never will yield to any circumstance, any more than before my own misgivings.

Your anxiety regarding my health reminded me of my mother; which is, perhaps, an inevitable sequence of your maternity. No doubt your daughter is growing rapidly, and delighting you with her vivacity.

There, I've said it now – placing her between us, irrevocable, real – as real as the relationship creating her. This Brightstone child is yours, and will be there for all future years. This barrier. This person whom you have borne, who isn't my flesh. This living individual, who is not – and never can be – the child I would have given you. The child for whom I have longed, and increasingly since knowing you. If you could only know how fiercely I am aching to give and go on giving – to place myself within you, respectfully as much as in passion. And in love greater than desiring . . .

I take your not mentioning your father-in-law as your acceptance of his foibles. I trust that before too long you all will be reunited, a family in the true sense of the word.

By which time, assuming I've come through this war alive, I shall muster some of the self-sufficiency that you imagine I possess, to get myself right away from you.

I smiled to myself over your persistence in trying to encourage Auntie Norah to accept a telephone. Still trying to prove you can do better that I? That you know better? I'm glad you haven't changed beyond recognition! You need not worry that you might be diminished by what the war is doing to you. And I, for one, am unendingly grateful for the time you spare.

Please do continue this contact. These hostilities surrounding us do drain even the most 'self-sufficient' of us of our serenity! Yours, in eager anticipation of your next letter,

Wolf

He might have been warned that she intended ceasing to write. And, with his usual skill, was ensuring what he wished. Or needed . . . ? She could not, would not, let his needs matter.

Somehow, though, Rhona seemed to have less control over her own will since Timothy had died. People were considerate: Eve and Jack Hebden, her two half-brothers, Phyllis, all cooperated to ensure that she no longer relied quite so completely on her own resources. No matter what she determined, her resolution softened. Although she never mentioned her bereavement to Wolf, she didn't find the will to stop writing to him until they were into 1944.

Bill Brightstone would have just given up, had it not been for Christine, the grandchild he and his wife idolized. Since her own mother increasingly was involved with WVS work, Rhona accepted her in-laws' offer to take charge of Chrissie of an evening, or sometimes at weekends. Even though she was denying herself some time with her daughter she knew she was delighting Tim's parents. She never could do enough for them.

Her own life was crammed to the limit, as she'd intended, now that she was doing voluntary work at the hospital as well as helping organize transport for wounded men arriving in Halfield. At Bridge House Mill there was little pretence, these days, that Bill was in charge. Nominally he was still mill manger, but most of its running was organized by Rhona. Fortunately Joyce Nayor had proved adaptable, well able to shoulder some of the administration, leaving Rhona more free to cope with difficulties as they arose.

During the course of the war their board of directors had been depleted by illness, deaths, and the resignation of two men who felt they'd better employ their skills involved in production of munitions. Two only of the board existing at the time when Rhona went to the mill remained in their seats.

The numbers had been made up by local businessmen, now retired from their own companies, and the entire board seemed to accept Rhona's control of the mill as a part of the strange wartime role assumed by women.

'I don't believe they really understand how much I did before the war,' she confided to Auntie Norah one day. 'But so long as they don't start opposing me yet awhile I'd best not grumble.'

'Well, you won't, anyway, will you, lass – grumble, I mean!' the old lady remarked, smiling warmly. 'I never hear you carrying on about anything, nowadays.'

'There wouldn't be much point,' Rhona admitted ruefully. 'All my complaining's done inside my own head. Everybody has their own worries, why should they think mine deserve attention?'

'You're not happy, though, are you, Rhona love?' Auntie Norah said, her brown eyes concerned.

'What's happy – with a war that's gone on this long? I'm not really *un*happy either, you know.' I just exist in some kind of limbo, she thought, *waiting*. For what, she couldn't imagine. Maybe that was the trouble – imagination, dreams, long since had been sacrificed to living. Or existing.

'Happen we'll all be better once this lot does come to an end. Even up here, where we don't have to face all that bombing like them poor beggars down in London, everything feels so dreary.'

'Aye.' Rhona sighed. 'We can't even make ourselves look brighter, these days. Make-up is so hard to come by.'

Auntie Norah sniffed. 'Never approved of all that paint, any road. And you don't need it, with them beautiful eyes, and all that glorious hair.'

Rhona laughed. 'Glorious? Unruly, more like. Still, at least I don't have to resort to winding it up over an old stocking in a Victory roll, like girls with no curl in theirs.'

'Suits some of them like that, and it does keep it tidy now nobody can get hairpins for love nor money.'

'We'll have a field day, won't we, afterwards – when stuff like that starts coming back into the shops!'

The old lady snorted. '*If* I live that long, I don't suppose I'll be too concerned to pretty myself up. But I would be glad of a decent pair of shoes, instead of them cheap, wedge-heeled things. As long as I'm around, I intend being able to go out a bit. If only in summer time. A couple of new frocks wouldn't come amiss either, I'm sick of make-do-and-mend. Every time an advert appears in t'paper with that Mrs Sew-and-Sew's brilliant notions, I want to tear the thing up.'

Rhona nodded. 'I wondered last year when Italy surrendered if we might not be too long before things started looking up. But that's six months ago now, and it's going to take something dramatic to turn the corner for us.'

It's so utterly depressing, she thought, and not only because of having lost her husband. The pain of that was waning, and she was fortunate to have Christine, someone to plan for and an interest beyond her work. Everything seemed so grey, though, the only brightness was when their Dan came home on a rare leave. He and Phyl never left Rhona out of things. Stanley was less bright company when he came home for weekends away from the pit.

Stan Hebden's earlier political interests had intensified, making him appear very serious, dour even. He was full of what he and like-minded citizens would do after the war, how they'd insist on better conditions of employment, a shorter working week, some kind of health care for everybody.

On June twentieth Rhona's thoughts were on London, as she had known it during her visit. That was the day she heard about flying bombs, the dreadful pilotless planes which were the new weapons the Germans were using. It was a Tuesday, and when Rhona called to collect Chris from her mother that tea time her alarm was so obvious that Eve insisted they stay and have a meal with them.

'I'm not going out tonight. I did my stint at the WVS

last night. You and Christine spend too much time on your own in that place, you know.'

Rhona suspected her mother would be only too thankful if she gave up the home in Apsley Road and moved back with them, but she'd never do anything of the kind. And they *weren't* in particularly often anyway.

'All right, thanks. But we were out at the weekend, on Sunday.'

'At Ellen's and Bill's, wasn't it?' Eve said with a wry smile. 'I'll bet that cheered you up no end!'

'Tim was their only one,' Rhona reminded her, a touch sharply, wondering if her mother perhaps resented the time she and Christine spent with the Brightstones.

'I know, love, I know. It's just that I'd like to see you a bit chirpier.'

'Not sure we're entitled to that – specially when we have it so easy up here. You have heard, I suppose, what Hitler's doing now – sending over some kind of . . . well flying bombs is what they call them.'

'Aye, we heard,' Jack Hebden said grimly. 'On the wireless.'

Christine had grown up a lot during the past six months, could behave nicely at the table now, drilled by both Rhona and Eve into curbing her exuberance until she'd finished a meal.

Rhona caught herself watching her daughter, smiling at last, delighted by the pleasant, attractive child who was developing from the frequently precocious one. There are times, she thought, when I can hardly take my eyes off you, young Chrissie, when I want to hug you to me the whole time!

While she was looking at her, Christine's head began drooping forward sleepily.

'I suppose it's time I took her home,' she said ruefully. 'Trouble is, once she's in bed I start thinking, worriting on about first one thing then another.'

'Why don't you take yourself round to see Phyllis, she's not on duty evenings this week, is she?' Jack suggested.

'Your mum and I will be glad to see our Chris is all right for a couple of hours.'

'I know, and that you keep my old bed made up for her, so she can go to sleep in comfort. But if I go out tonight it won't be for a chat with Phyl, it'll be to do summat that's a bit of use.'

She couldn't get out of her mind the awfulness of what was happening elsewhere in the country, and to their men overseas.

Her parents exchanged a glance. Getting Rhona to let up was next door to impossible.

'At the WVS?' Eve said. 'Well, if that's what you want, you can still leave Chrissie here. She's not going to need much rocking, is she?'

Rhona hadn't even switched off the engine of the little Morris outside the centre when one of the other women came rushing up to the car.

'Didn't know you were on tonight, Rhona. Thank goodness you've turned up! I've nobody to meet the train. There's several lads to go to the hospital, and it's due into Halfield in ten minutes.'

'Using the jeep? I've never driven that! Not that I mind having a go, if there's nobody else. I only hope the men I'm picking up aren't too badly injured, or my driving'll likely make them worse!'

The jeep was very different from the Morris Eight but Rhona managed to keep the engine running, and was beginning to familiarize herself with the gears by the time she arrived at the station. There was no sign of the train yet, which wasn't unusual.

Her footsteps echoing over the boards, she walked through the darkened ticket hall as far as the barrier.

'I'm from the WVS – meeting the train that's bringing wounded for the General Hospital. It hasn't come in yet, I suppose?'

'It'll be another quarter of an hour or so, running late. You can wait here, if you like, then if any of 'em need a bit of help you'll be to hand.'

'Okay, I will,' Rhona agreed. It was the first time she'd

done the actual driving to the hospital, instead of being at the desk, but she'd gathered from Martha and the others that the term 'walking' wounded could apply only loosely to the men they met.

An air-raid warden crossed towards them, and began speaking with the elderly ticket collector. Rhona walked away a little to stand alone, waiting, suddenly chilled by her thoughts. How different everything was from that time she'd set out on her selling trip to London. She'd been so excited then, had returned so elated. And how different again from the day she'd come here to see Timothy off when he was joining up; different, as well, from her mingled dread of the journey and looking forward to seeing him on her arrival in Kent, when they were spending his leave together.

How unsuspecting she'd been of the way that one weekend would turn out, and that she'd be returning here married! Why did it all have to go wrong in the way that it had with Timothy, who'd been so very *alive*, dying – and not really a casualty of battle? Why was she limited to helping the war effort in a mundane way like this, when she ached to be more use, to do something nobody else could? And why did she never feel satisfied, not even for more than a few hours at a time, why experience this intense longing for change? It wasn't only the need everybody had for the end of this war. Somehow, she knew even without thinking it through that there had to be more, for her, than an eventual return to peace. I wish I understood, she thought wearily, I wish I understood what I was aching *for*, why I felt I was waiting for something to happen.

She seemed miles away, deep in reflection, when the train steamed in. Doors slammed in the darkness on the platform, she heard male voices, an isolated curse, and the unmistakable tapping of sticks and crutches.

They were a sorry crowd who came into sight the other side of the barrier. One lad who appeared no more than seventeen had heavily bandaged eyes, and was being guided by a man who looked at least fifty and had one leg in plaster. Another two were on crutches, one with an ominously folded trouser-leg; the other seemed to have both legs encased in plaster. The next man had a savagely gashed face, with fresh blood seeping through the dressings as if nothing would contain the bleeding. The one behind him had an empty sleeve and was limping. Towards the rear of the party she glimpsed an officer's cap. Well, she couldn't hang around for him to catch up, on the off-chance that he wanted to say something. Her first priority was getting his men in to the jeep and, as fast as she could, to hospital.

Rhona was dreadfully afraid that she was taking far too long getting them installed, but they were patient, on the whole, glad to be near the end of their journey.

'Got a cigarette, by any chance?' the blind lad asked, once most of his mates were aboard.

'We keep a few in here specially,' Rhona said, thankful that one of her jobs at headquarters, stocking the vehicles with cigarettes and matches, was appreciated. 'Light one up for him somebody, will you?' she asked, handing the pack over her shoulder. In her rear-view mirror she was watching the officer clamber aboard at the back of the jeep.

'Everybody on?' she called.

He wasn't the one who replied. ''S right, darling,' a Cockney voice answered from immediately behind her. 'Just you get us to our beds, smart as you like.'

'It'll only take five or ten minutes,' she assured them. 'For which you'll be extremely thankful! It's the first time I've driven one of these things. I'll try not to make every gear-change diabolical for you.'

Between coping with the strange vehicle and the blacked-out roads, Rhona was fully occupied. The men were talking occasionally between themselves, and she was glad. She wasn't certain she could have managed reassuring conversation as well if it had been needed.

When they arrived at the General Hospital she drove straight up to the entrance then asked them to remain where they were, just for the moment.

The man on duty in the porters' lodge soon confirmed that the men were expected, and beds had been allocated. 'All non-commissioned, right? And all just about walking cases?'

'There's an officer as well,' she told him. 'Don't know his rank, I'm afraid. He was right at the back of the jeep, hasn't said a word.'

The man shrugged, moved some papers around; for the first time Rhona noticed his paralysed arm. 'Haven't got no officers down here,' he said, checking against a list. 'Happen he's only escorting them.'

'Happen so.'

'You can wheel 'em in, love.'

'Right you are.'

'Are there any needing wheelchairs, or stretchers?'

'There's a couple on crutches, depends how independent they are – might prefer their own steam.'

'Aye – lots of 'em do.'

Rhona assisted some of the more gravely disabled out of the jeep and into the wide hospital corridor. Her eyes misting, she gazed after the little party for a moment as they struggled away in the direction of the wards.

Pensively, she walked back to the jeep and got in behind the wheel. She was deeply moved, faced afresh with the reality of war, shaken. How dared she feel so dissatisfied with her lot! About to let go and lean her forehead against the wheel, she sensed that she wasn't alone. Glancing back over her shoulder, she could just discern the outline of an officer's cap, motionless, in the farthest corner.

'Oh – sorry. I'd almost forgotten . . . Were you simply accompanying the lads? Where are you for now, sir – the barracks, the station . . . ?'

'No, home, please.'

'Oh, you're local!' Her voice warmed with delight because someone was getting something out of this distressing business, if only one night in his own bed.

'Where to then, love, is it Halfield itself or the outskirts?' she asked, switching on the ignition and letting in the clutch.

'God, I didn't know I was that unrecognizable!'

'Wolf!' Startled, she let her feet shoot off both clutch and accelerator. The jeep juddered violently, and stopped. 'I never even got a proper look at you, did I?' she said, her heart thudding agitatedly.

'Okay, okay.'

'You might as well come and sit up front.'

'I'm all right as I am. Just drive, will you? To Farnley Carr.'

'Sure. Of course.'

Somehow, Rhona summoned sufficient composure to get the jeep moving more or less steadily. Her breathing was still rapid, shallow, even when she reached his home. The house was well blacked out, not a glimmer of light showed at any of the windows. Stimson must be his normal efficient self.

Wolf had alighted by the time she walked round to the rear of the vehicle. Rhona was desperate for a sliver of moon, anything, so she might be able to see him. As it was, she could make out his shape, that was all.

'Thanks,' he said curtly, sounding not at all like anyone she knew.

'Wolf? Are you all right?'

'Yes. Er – thank you.'

'You don't sound it. Want me to come in with you . . . ?'

'No, no. No, I'll be fine.'

20

Christine had insisted on coming with her, had refused to remain with her grandparents, and now she was asleep. Parking the car, Rhona glanced ruefully behind her.

'Chrissie? Come on, love, we're here . . .'

Sleepily her daughter opened one eye, sighed with all the aggrievance of a cross three-and-a-half-year-old, and stared out of the window.

'Don't want . . .'

'I know. And you didn't want to stay with your gran and grandad either. You'll have to put up with what I want now.'

'No.' She rubbed chubby fists into her eyes, tried a tentative wail.

'You know I don't stand for that.' Getting out of the car, Rhona tilted forward her seat, reached inside and hauled Christine out by one arm.

'Hurts,' Christine muttered reproachfully.

'Not as much as the smacked bottom you'll get.'

Her daughter whimpered.

'And I can't bear little girls who do nothing but cry! It's time you learned that when you choose to do something you've got to put up with . . .'

'Why do I always have to put up with something?' Christine demanded.

Rhona tried not to smile at the soulful eyes, regarding her so solemnly from a face rosy with sleep.

'Because that's the way life is, my love. Sorry.'

Christine turned from gazing at her to studying the house towering before her. 'I not been here before, Mummy. Will I like . . . ?'

'Of course you will,' Rhona responded quickly. And wished she thought she herself might like something, anything, about the next few minutes.

With a little tug she encouraged Christine on. 'This is quite an adventure for you, you know. When I was your age I didn't even know houses as big as this existed.'

'Might get lost,' Christine suggested plaintively.

'Not if you do as I say.' Was she threatening her, blackmailing? Tactics she normally abhorred. Did the situation, and the alarm enveloping her own spirit, justify such measures?

The doorbell didn't appear to be working. After waiting a couple of minutes Rhona clattered the brass knocker. That was tarnished as well. Whatever had come over Stimson?

A woman opened the door. Rhona knew her by sight, she lived in one of the houses not far from Norah Lowe's.

'Good evening,' Rhona began. 'I've called to see how Mr Richardson is.'

'I see. You'd better come in then, although I don't rightly know that . . . well, come in, anyway. You're Rhona Brightstone, aren't you? Jimmie – my lad, worked at Bridge House till he was called up.'

'Not Jimmie Rawson?'

'That's right. Fancy you remembering.'

Rhona smiled. She ought to be asking about the lad. Maybe afterwards . . . At the moment she was far too concerned about the imminent confrontation. And about Christine, yawning extensively and pulling on her arm.

'I wonder –' Mrs Rawson began, 'your little girl – happen it'd be best if she waited here. There's a nice, comfy settle.'

Rhona nodded. 'Good idea, so long as Mr Stimson wouldn't object.'

'Eeh – didn't you know? He's been gone twelve month or more. A tumour, not the first he'd had, there'd been other operations.'

'No, I didn't know. I'm sorry.'

'That's why I come in for a few hours, two or three times a week.'

And who will cope the rest of the time? Rhona wondered, perturbed. 'And how's Mr Richardson today?'

The woman raised blue eyes towards the ornate plaster-work ceiling. 'Not himself, not at all. Could be the journey still, I suppose. I gather he only arrived last night. I wasn't here yesterday.'

'Was no one else?'

'No one else what, Mrs Brightstone?'

'Here, with Wol – Mr Richardson.'

'Ay, bless you, there's only me, these days. There wasn't any need, was there, not with the place shut up most of the time.'

'No, well – is it all right if I see him?' She wanted to get the encounter over, felt just as nervous as that first time she'd come here.

'Well, he's not doing anything; if you're afraid of inter-rupting owt, you won't. He's hardly stirred at all ever since I got here this morning. And a right turn he gave me, I can tell you, just being here when I came in! No word, nothing, no bed aired . . .'

'I imagine he's slept in far worse, of late. If at all. And he appeared too exhausted to care.'

'You saw him then?'

'Brought him here. I was driving for the WVS, picked him up at the station, along with his men, for the hospital.'

'You know what to expect then.' Mrs Rawson walked briskly across the marble floor, rapped on the sitting room door and opened it.

'There's someone come to see you,' she announced, and turned away, as if afraid.

After a hasty glance to check Chrissie who was sliding on a cushion from one end to the other of the polished settle, Rhona had followed.

'I won't be long,' she told the woman quietly. 'I hope you don't mind keeping an eye on her.'

Wolf, dreadfully haggard, didn't rise from the leather armchair when she entered, and Rhona realized swiftly that whatever she'd once disliked about him it hadn't been bad manners. She recognized now, though, that it wasn't lack of grace so much as absence of interest anchored him in the chair. And the thin features didn't relax even for a minute into anything resembling a smile.

'Rhona,' he said, and nodded to himself, dispiritedly.

'If I'm intruding . . .' she began, suddenly feeling even more uneasy than she'd anticipated, 'I'll just inquire how you are and . . .'

'Go? Wouldn't the waste of petrol disturb your careful Yorkshire soul?'

'Happen so.' Sadly, she smiled a little. 'And you don't care, do you, whether I stay or not?'

'I wouldn't say that,' he said, then shrugged hopelessly. 'I wouldn't say very much about anything, would I? Because I – don't know, Rhona, not what I want, or what I'm – *doing*. Nor who I am. God, it's all so . . . bloody!'

He was staring hard into the empty fire grate, swallowing repeatedly, avoiding her. He was wearing an old army shirt, without the tie, and an even older fair-isle pullover that clashed terribly with the shirt. They showed too much of his stringy neck and the Adam's apple working agitatedly up and down. Rhona, recalling the broad-shouldered man she'd met on that first occasion here, and his ruggedly healthy face, tried to reconcile memory with this wreck of humanity, and failed. She almost wept.

'Why did I come back?' he demanded huskily. 'Why?'

'This is your home, where you belong.'

'Do I?' Wolf snorted sharply. 'I didn't mean that – why did I survive, when all they – the lads . . . didn't.'

'Some of them, surely – in whatever shape. They were with you last night.' Had this war unhinged him? Didn't he remember?

Grimly Wolf shook his head. 'They were from a different outfit altogether. They bundled me into the train with them. Not much use any longer, you see . . .' His voice trailed away.

'Do you want to – tell me?'

'No. Yes. I – don't know.'

'When was it? What – happened?'

'D-day.'

Oh, God! No wonder. 'I see.'

'You don't. No one does. Not if they weren't – there. It was grim, bloody . . . and not one of my men got out.'

'Mummy!' Christine's shrill little voice interrupted. Startled, Wolf gazed across the room to where Rhona was still standing just inside the door.

'Yours?'

She gave him a look. He couldn't have forgotten about Chrissie. 'Yes – I had to bring her. Mum would have baby-sat, but Christine had other ideas.'

'Mummy, Mummy!'

'Can't that be stopped?' His grey eyes glinted furiously, sharper even than his tongue.

'It can, and all! I can take her straight back home, happen that's the way you want it.' Christine's cries intensified, making Rhona just as impatient, embarrassed, and eager to get her out of the house.

'No – er, no. Just try to curtail the screaming.'

Wryly, Rhona smiled. 'You don't know what you're asking. Christine hasn't responded well to the upbringing the war's ensured for her. I'm afraid my mother spoils her quite a bit, so does Dad. Unfortunately she comes under my thumb for only a portion of her time.'

'Don't you indulge her, then?' Wolf challenged, hating the unseen Brightstone child, the one of whom he'd made this barrier.

'I most certainly do not,' she told him, raising her voice above Christine's yells. 'Look, if you want us to get out, you've only to . . .'

'No – I told you.'

'Then I'm afraid you'll have to let me go and calm her down, or bring her in here.'

Wolf swallowed again, trying to contain his urge to shout that he couldn't take any noise, nor any reminders of Rhona's other life, *with that man*. And nor could he allow her to take herself out of his sight. Why, she could be long enough – might even decide, after all, that leaving was best.

'You'd better bring her in, there's no real alternative, is there?'

Rhona apologized to Mrs Rawson for the fuss her daughter was making.

'That's all right, love. I suppose her daddy's away in the forces, eh?'

Rhona didn't put her in the picture. Christine had stopped yelling, and Wolf was waiting.

The child was incredibly like Rhona. Far older than he'd imagined, dressed in pale yellow, a silky dress that enhanced the glorious hair so similar to her mother's. Tears hung on long coppery lashes, and misted sherry-brown eyes enlarged with apprehension.

'Say "hello", Chrissie, go and shake hands . . .'

Frowning slightly, the little girl obeyed. 'Hallo,' she greeted him gravely, and offered a freckled hand. 'What're you called?'

'Wolf.'

'Ugh!' Christine shivered. 'Like in "Red Riding Hood"?'

The faintest of smiles hovered over his thin lips. Wolf shook his head, squeezed the warm little hand which, despite his name, wasn't withdrawn.

'Not in the least like that Wolf. You ask your mother . . .'

Rhona snorted wryly. 'More like a bear, these days.'

Briefly, over the child's flare of curls, their glances held. '*Touché*,' he murmured.

Emphatically Christine shook her head, the exquisite eyes scouring his features. 'But bears are 'normous, fat and big and hairy.' Without hesitation, she pressed the hand grasping hers to her cheek.

The lump enlarged in his throat.

'And they hug you to death.' Still pensively, Chrissie gazed at his hand, then experimented with her lips in its palm. 'You're not hairy.'

And I could hug you, thought Wolf, his eyes stinging. And go on hugging you, because of the mother who bore you, and this near-sacred resemblance.

331

'Don't let her be a nuisance.' Rhona was on edge, afraid of where all this might be leading.

'She's not yelling now, is she?' He sounded smug because of his uncalculating ability to quiet her child.

Rhona suspected he believed she didn't know how best to handle her own youngster. She said nothing. Eve always maintained that Chrissie behaved more badly for her own mother than for anyone else. It's only because I subconsciously try to compensate, she thought, for the hundreth time. Because I'm all she's got – and half the time I'm torn in two because of the mill. And because of the caring devoted – *elsewhere*?

Christine was continuing her inspection. 'That's a soldier's shirt, isn't it? Are you going away to fight?'

Wolf shook his head. 'Not – not for a little while, anyway.'

'Have they hurted you? Are you wa – *wounded*? Mummy helps the wounded soldiers when they're being made better, sometimes. Like Auntie Phyllis. When she isn't too busy.' After a pause Chrissie placed her head on one side, trying to puzzle out what he was doing, just sitting. 'Are you always busy? Mummy is . . . Might you have time for me?'

'Christine, that's enough.' Rhona made as though to cross the room and whisk the child away.

Wolf's arms went around the small, firm body. The stuff of her dress felt deliciously cool, reminded him of something . . . 'Don't, Rhona. She's fine. Fine.' He could hold the child, relax with the contact with this small person, where he never might touch her mother. The tenderness in his expression told Rhona there was no cause for concern, or none regarding his interest in her daughter. No matter what, she could entrust the child to him. Always. And Wolf as well as young Chris was passive now.

She felt a massive need to talk, of something, anything to prevent her dwelling for too long on the remarkable ache of love engendered by seeing Wolf with her baby.

'I made that frock she's wearing out of an old evening dress of mine. A very old dress.'

'Your careful Yorkshire soul again.' Do you suppose I wasn't sure this cloth was the same, that I'd ever forget the effect of its shade with your colouring, now reproduced?

'You can't pretend that's a fault in wartime.'

'I can't pretend anything, can I? Try to obliterate, yes. Perhaps.'

'Have you got a little girl?'

The faint smile returned when he glanced again towards Chrissie. But then he was compelled to swallow. Briefly, he closed his eyes. 'No, dear, no.'

'A little boy then?' She needed a playmate, wanted excuses for coming here again.

'No.' Again, Wolf swallowed. He stroked the gleaming curls.

'Aren't you anybody's daddy?'

He could not answer. Or not with any degree of composure. If he had pictured for a million years, he couldn't have visualized a girl so like her mother, so like the child he might have fathered. *Granted that choice.*

Appalled, Rhona was immobilized, staring at her offspring, unable to check her chattering, agonizing over its effect on Wolf. It was very evident that he couldn't cope with emotions.

'The Germans tooked my daddy away.' Christine confided, looking up at him again. Her grave little face increased the lump in his throat. He couldn't have spoken if he'd had anything to say. Should he be suggesting that the war would soon be over, that her daddy would be home . . . ? And where'll all this be then . . . ? Where'll *I* be . . . ?

She scrambled all over his feet then, determinedly, on to his lap. She looked across at her mother. And so did Wolf.

'Rhona – for heaven's sake! Are you going to stand around all evening?'

'I was brought up to wait to be invited to sit.'

'God, you should know better than to expect refinements now!' He grinned slightly, though his grey eyes didn't light. He indicated a brocade-covered sofa.

'Come and sit here with me, Christine,' Rhona said firmly.

But Christine was gazing up at Wolf, her eyes wickedly amused. 'You said a bad word!' Suddenly she started singing. 'Who's afraid of the big bad Wolf, the big bad Wolf . . . Who's afraid of the daddy Wolf.' Shrieking with giggles, she turned into him, flung her arms about his neck. 'Who's afraid of the daddy Wolf!'

'It would seem there's one who isn't,' he observed quietly, using his delight to taunt the child's mother. Smiling blandly as he looked across the room.

Initially, Rhona was cross with them both. Could have marched over, hauled Chrissie away and given her a slap for showing off. And told him he should know better than encouraging precociousness. I'm jealous, she thought – of him, because my baby's showing such blatant preference, and of her, for getting him to smile.

Did it matter, though, really? Whatever the trauma Wolf had endured following the D-day landings, he did need someone to make him think, if only for a few minutes, about something else. And wasn't Christine, engaging like this, infinitely better than the whining child who'd arrived?

She caught herself smiling. 'We try ignoring her,' she told him softly. 'Sometimes it works.'

'And sometimes she hits me,' Christine added. 'Hard.'

'That's enough, Christine,' said Rhona sharply. Her eyes had blurred with tears, she couldn't feel more foolish. And all because this was the man she loved, whom she'd loved always. And he must remain nothing to her, and nothing to her daughter.

'If little girls are naughty they have to be corrected,' Wolf said seriously, though his eyes lit as he looked down into the small face. 'Even with a smack.'

Mrs Rawson knocked on the door and asked if she should make tea or coffee. Wolf began to inquire which

Rhona would prefer, but she was standing already, shaking her head.

'Some other time, thank you. We can only stay a few minutes longer. It's high time Madam, here, was in bed.'

'She's always saying that,' Christine informed Wolf in a loud whisper. 'When she's busy, putting me to bed gets me out of the way.'

Rhona was astounded, not only that Christine had comprehended this much, but that she was capable of expressing it. And I used to be proud of her command of words! she reflected.

'Your mother knows you need sleep to give you all this lovely energy.'

'Lovely?' Rhona asked him ruefully, but she was smiling. He wasn't so bad really: if she didn't take care, Christine wouldn't be the only one in his thrall. 'Come on then, Chris, say goodnight nicely . . .'

'You'll bring her again?' Wolf asked, his grey eyes turned to silver by his need.

'I wouldn't be at all surprised.' She wasn't making any promises. She hadn't forgotten his initial reaction to *her*. His responding to Christine instead wasn't exactly a boost to morale. And there was a limit to how much she could take of seeing the two of them besotted with each other.

'Goodnight,' Christine said, 'we will come again.' She studied his face, where already the eyes were veiled, the mouth grown unsmiling. Impulsively, she kissed his cheek.

I ought to warn her about being over-affectionate towards men who are unrelated to her, Rhona thought. But not tonight. As if resolved to prove her impeccable behaviour, Christine walked sedately across the carpet and slid her hand into her mother's.

'Take care, Wolf,' Rhona said quickly, and turned away before the distress gradually overtaking his face prevented her leaving.

The next time Rhona set out for Farnley Carr she was alone. She had left Christine with Tim's parents, and hadn't breathed a word to anyone about where she was going. The past few days, since her previous visit, had been uncomfortable. Christine, enchanted by him, had spoken of nothing but Daddy Wolf who lived in a big house, and liked her.

'So he's home, is he?' Eve asked Rhona. 'Wounded?'

'Not physically,' she had replied. 'This kind seems harder. He was at D-day, lost all his men, from what he says.'

'I thought D-day had been an unqualified success?'

'Maybe that was what we were meant to think, propaganda. Or maybe Wolf was unfortunate.' She didn't say any more about him then, had discovered she couldn't steady her voice, even to say his name.

I'm going to explain to him, Rhona thought, tell him how since Timothy died Christine has been desperate to find someone to be her daddy. It doesn't really mean very much – she'd tried calling Daniel daddy, hadn't she, and their Stan. It should be no harder explaining to her that Wolf might be called uncle, just as they were.

He opened the door himself, this time, it appeared it wasn't one of Mrs Rawson's days at the house. He had shaved, Rhona could tell, but his hair needed cutting and, from its appearance, a comb wouldn't come amiss.

He glanced towards her side, pointedly. 'Come in,' he said tersely. 'On your own then?'

'Yes, for once. I thought we ought to talk.'

'Oh?' Wolf shrugged, but led the way nevertheless into the sitting room, gestured towards the brocade sofa. 'Take a seat, won't you?'

He went to his own chair, as though unable to remain standing for more than a few seconds. Looking intently at him, Rhona wondered if he really could be seeming worse than previously.

'Your daughter's very like you,' he announced suddenly. 'An enchanting child.'

'While she's getting her own way.'

'I wouldn't know about that. I only know I envy you parenthood. I always wanted a family. Beatrice – didn't.

I'd have thought more of her if she'd told me that right from the start.' He swallowed hard.

Rhona tried not to focus on the tears in his grey eyes. But this wasn't quite the time for saying all she'd intended.

'She was good for me the other evening,' Wolf continued. 'I want you to know that. With Chrissie there – there's no possibility of dwelling for too long on – on what happened there, in France.'

'I suppose that's true. She doesn't permit anything else claiming your attention. I didn't realize that could be an advantage.'

'So – I was thinking – when you can spare the time, maybe you wouldn't mind too much . . . er, from the security of your family life, sparing me a little . . .'

Security? He most certainly hadn't heard then, didn't know that they weren't a family any longer. That Timothy wouldn't be coming home. He'd defeated her again, however unwittingly, and she didn't know what on earth to say next.

'I lost all my men, Rhona, every one,' he told her savagely. 'In the landing on Gold Beach. Working alongside frogmen, we'd cleared a narrow way in between the enemy's underwater obstacles. I was moving the lads to another sector when I glanced back. Through the constant firing, I spotted an amphibious tank, off course, heading straight towards a mass of submerged pylons and concrete cones.

'Hoping desperately to clear the obstacles in time, I ordered the lads back into the water. The – the tank kept on coming, it struck something that was mined. The lot went up – my men, as well.'

He paused, then sought her eyes again. 'I – for days, I've thought I was going insane. Who can say I won't! But for those few minutes . . . Can – will you share just a small part of your daughter with me? Just temporarily . . .'

She was shaken out of all preconceived ideas of what she would do or say. 'You know I will, don't you? Or I hope you do.'

'You have your own life, I do understand that.' He had some pride left.

'But so have you; one day, we'll get busy reconstructing it.'

'*We?*'

'It wasn't to give Chrissie an outing that I came the other day.'

Wolf nodded.

'Have you seen a doctor since you came home?'

'Doctor? What the hell for?'

She sighed. Wasn't his pleading for anything sufficiently unlike the old Wolf Richardson to alarm him? 'To – check you over, I suppose.'

'He'd find nothing wrong.'

'If you say so.'

'That is precisely what I say!'

Rhona felt whipped. He still possessed the greatest capacity of anyone on this earth for hurting her. If she cracked she'd be useless; to him, as well as herself. Rapidly she turned, strode towards the door. Something made her look back.

Tears were pouring unheeded down ashen hollow cheeks.

She sighed. 'Wolf . . .'

He was shaking his head. 'Get out, you'd better get out.'

Rhona made her busy life even busier; driving everybody and herself at the mill, working with the WVS, spending hours with servicemen at the General Hospital. And thinking about Wolf. She decorated her bedroom – a very pale cream distemper – made Chrissie two new frocks out of an old one given her by Eve, started an additional knitting class. And worried about Wolf.

There was no way she could keep away. She took Chrissie with her.

Looking no healthier than he had days ago, Wolf opened the door.

'Daddy Wolf . . . !' Christine threw herself at him.

With energy that he'd been disguising successfully, he swung her high up in his arms. 'Hallo, Chrissie – I've missed you.' Just in time, he remembered to smile towards Rhona, if only with his lips. 'Thanks,' he murmured. 'Well, come in, won't you . . .'

With Christine high on his shoulders, he led them to the sitting room. Discarded newspapers were strewn over the luxurious blue carpet near his chair. Three dirty cups and saucers had been left around the beautifully furnished room. A quantity of unopened mail was heaped in separate piles on the sideboard. Several envelopes looked official, from what Rhona could see, military.

'Have you got any biscuits?' Christine asked solemnly. 'I'm hungry.'

'Chris . . .' Rhona began warningly, then shrugged. 'She's always saying that, take no notice. How've you been, Wolf?'

'Okay,' he lied, while his eyes told her differently.

She wasn't going to mention a doctor ever again. 'How – how long's the leave you've got?'

He snorted. 'Leave? How neat! Do you suppose anybody got around to discussing *leave*?'

Christine began to fidget.

Relieved, Wolf drew the child down from his shoulder, gave her a quick hug, and set her down on the carpet. He took her hand. 'The kitchen's this way . . .'

From behind, as Rhona followed across the chequered marble hall, he might have been quite normal: a friendly uncle taking his small niece to find goodies. Or a father even . . . Hastily, Rhona blinked. Only when he started, astonished to discover she was with them, did she understand quite how urgently he was trying to escape. From *her*? Or only from reality?

The kitchen was no tidier than the room they'd left.

'Mrs Rawson isn't in today.'

Rhona grinned. 'Really?'

Very briefly, his grey eyes were amused.

You're still there, she thought, somewhere interred

339

beneath the Normandy offensive and all that it did to you.
She ached with the distance between them.

'Have you eaten today?'

'I – don't know.'

He wasn't prevaricating, she could tell. 'I'll see what I
can find.'

She scrambled dried eggs, and heaped them on toast.
Christine, her chair drawn up to the table as close as
possible to Wolf's, adored him with her eyes, while he
shared eggs and toast with her.

'What about you, have you eaten?' he asked Rhona
eventually.

'We have, good corned-beef hash. You must make
allowance for my gannet of a daughter.'

'What's a gannet?' Christine demanded.

Wolf smiled down at her. 'A delightful sea-bird.'

'That's your version!' Rhona exclaimed, but smiling.
She couldn't but love his treatment of her child.

Her appetite sated, Christine beamed around, leaned
her head affectionately against his arm. 'Do you really live
here all by yourself? Isn't there a Mrs Wolf?'

'Not any longer.'

'Oh.' Christine considered for a moment. 'Did she die?'

'No, she simply went to live somewhere else.'

Christine drew in a deep breath. 'My daddy's . . .'

Go on, Rhona silently willed her: tell him. Get the truth
into the open, for I can not.

'. . . locked up somewhere. Germany, I think.'

'That's sad.'

'M'm. Why don't you live with me and Mummy, there's
lots of room.'

'I don't believe your daddy would think that was a very
good idea.'

'But Daddy's . . .'

Tell him now, Rhona willed her again. You know the
truth, I've explained to you often enough. That he won't
be coming home . . .

'. . . a prisoner.'

At a loss, Rhona began splashing water into the sink,

dunked the pan and other utensils she'd used, collected the dirty cups from the room across the hall. If Wolf is disturbed, I'm not much better, she thought. She couldn't simply blurt out that Tim was dead, not like this, while Chrissie seemed to have disregarded the fact. And Wolf didn't, for one moment, suspect.

As she returned to the kitchen her daughter was holding forth again. 'Shall we sort of pretend you're ours?'

Watching Rhona, her back to them at the sink, Wolf inhaled deeply, several times. What the hell do you imagine I'm pretending, child? And loathing myself because of it. Where is the sense in any of this? Where is sense at all . . . ? What right have I to long for a home, family, a wife – when all those men, every one, are denied living?

When he didn't respond, Christine thrust a warm, slightly sticky, hand into his. 'Don't be sad. I love you. And Mummy does as well. It's only that she's busy. *Again*.'

Wolf couldn't avoid smiling. God, but she was pure enchantment. As her mother would have been . . . If only Rhona would say something. Her silence unnerved him, so that he clammed up, except with Chrissie. Was Rhona disapproving . . . ?

'Christine, if Uncle Wolf has finished his meal you can bring me the knife and fork, and the plate – carefully, mind . . .'

Her daughter complied, all sweetness that made Rhona swallow.

Returning to the table, the child met Wolf's affectionate gaze, her own no less loving. 'Shall Mummy cook for you tomorrow as well?'

'Most likely Mrs Rawson will be here tomorrow,' said Rhona hastily.

That's it, thought Wolf, make plain your dutiful visits are granted only when you feel you cannot avoid them!

Rhona rinsed away the suds, dried the last item and hung the tea towel to dry. 'Time we were making tracks, Christine.'

'Already?' Wolf protested. 'You've hardly said a word.'

She met his glance, read there his desire to keep her with him, to have her attention.

'Some of us,' she responded over her daughter's head, 'have compensated very ably.' She didn't insist on their leaving.

In the sitting room, Chrissie collected up all the scattered newspapers, folded them studiously, placed them on the table beside Wolf's chair.

'How do you do it?' Rhona laughed. 'She's the untidiest child ever.'

'That's better,' Wolf approved, smiling. 'You needed to let go.'

'You should talk!'

'I know. I do know.'

Christine had clambered up on to his lap, seemed to drowse already. Absently, Wolf caressed her gleaming hair.

His grey eyes darkened, the lines of his mouth went taut. 'I suppose I was ill-prepared for all the bloodletting of war at close quarters, for the carnage on that beach. Maybe the long wait, had taken the edge off my judgement. I should have *thought*, though, shouldn't have sent them back, unsuspecting . . .'

'But war, surely, entails calculated risks. Everyone that day was geared to getting men and tanks ashore. Your only alternative was doing nothing, watching that tank's destruction.'

'Those men were relying on me.'

'You're the last person who'd be careless.'

He snorted disbelievingly.

'I *know* you,' said Rhona earnestly.

'That's more than I do.'

'Give yourself time.'

'There's too much of that. Far too much.'

'Couldn't you return to your regiment then? Now you've rested up.'

His glance told her, and she wondered how she'd bear the truth. Blinking, she forced herself to look away, to see the mahogany sideboard, the luxurious wallpaper – the exquisite room in the heart of a beautiful home. You're killing me, she thought, destroying the man I love. *Wolf Richardson*, remember – the man who'd put fear into the folk of Vicar's Dale! And you've no intention of going back, ever. You're hiding.

'Tell me about your life these days, Rhona. What's it like?'

'Busy. Chrissie told the truth. When I'm not at the mill, I'm helping organize transport with the WVS, or round at the hospital doing what bit I can. Some of the lads can't manage to write home . . .' She shrugged, sighed. 'Phyllis is magnificent. You remember Phyl – did you know she's nursing? She married again, you know – Dan, my young brother.' She reflected for a moment. 'Things do work out, you see, love.'

'For some.'

Christine stirred, yawned, snuggled closer against Wolf.

'It is time I took her home.' Time I got her away from you, she was thinking, before I break – wanting to hold you both, for ever.

'I'll bring her out to the car for you.'

It was Christine he kissed, as he handed her into the car. Deep inside, Rhona was weeping.

'You will bring her again?'

'Why not?'

21

Despite her repeated decisions to the contrary, Rhona's visits to Farnley Carr continued. They were scarcely any easier for her, and Wolf improved hardly at all. Only with Christine was he in any way animated, recognizable. Were those brief glimpses of the original Wolf all that took her there so often?

Mrs Rawson, soon after his return, had taken Rhona aside to tell her about the unanswered telephone, unopened correspondence. From the army, she was sure. Rhona recalled seeing official-looking envelopes. Eventually, she persuaded Wolf to call in the doctor who could help him avoid a charge of desertion.

'In the last war, *my* war, they'd have called it shell-shock,' the doctor told Rhona afterwards while Wolf was dressing. 'A trauma too great for body and mind to accept. He's unfit to serve, that isn't in doubt: the army doesn't use officers who don't command themselves. What's to be done is less certain. Treatment requires a patient's acceptance.'

And accepting that he even needed medical help (or any other kind) went against the grain. Wolf had acquired the professional opinion that ensured he wouldn't be court martialled or cashiered. Whatever willpower remained seemed directed towards obstructing a cure. And as for venturing out, Rhona suspected his farthest outing was to see her and Christine to the car.

The situation had continued for nearly eleven months; she was alternately sympathetic and irritated. With Christine, he could be as appealing as the child he so patently adored. Without her, he could seem just as fractious!

Feeling guilty because she might have economized on petrol by using public transport, she was driving up the all-too-familiar road to Farnley Carr. She never used her full allocation, though, and she was exhausted today, last night she'd hardly slept.

During their previous visit to Wolf, Christine had been unwell, restless, fidgety. Now Rhona knew the cause, had half resolved to remain with her daughter, only Eve had almost pushed her out of the Gracechurch Street house.

'You get along to the WVS, I can cope with our Chris. A change of company will do you good.' If it *had* been the WVS centre she'd been attending that might have been true. She wondered how, and why, she'd kept most of her visits to Wolf a secret, and for so long?

'Where's Chrissie?' he demanded immediately, glancing anxiously towards the little Morris.

'I'm afraid it was measles,' Rhona said with a grin. 'As yet, she's not really poorly, and my mum's looking after her. I left them both as pleased as punch, they seem to adore each other.'

'Christine's an adorable child.'

She laughed. 'You'd have thought so at four o'clock this morning! She wakened up all feverish and wouldn't go back to sleep. It's times like that when I wish I wasn't on my own with her.'

This was the day when she was going to tell Wolf all about Timothy. She'd worked out that this was the way she would lead up to it. Somehow, though, she couldn't say any more, not just yet. Anything she might think of would be hopelessly inadequate. He'd wonder why the blazes she hadn't told him as soon as he came home.

'Well, come in,' Wolf invited, 'you should know better by now than to let me keep you hanging around at the door.'

The evening sun was gleaming through the stained-glass window as she followed him across the hall and into the sitting room. It was blissfully cool indoors, she imagined the thick walls of Farnley Carr would insulate against the sun.

'It's a scorcher for May!' she exclaimed, pushing up the thin sleeves of her crêpe-de-chine jacket.

'Why don't you take that off?' Wolf suggested, standing with a hand outstretched to take it from her.

Rhona hesitated. The top she wore beneath was little more than a camisole, she'd made it herself out of one of her old blouses. But without explaining her sudden embarrassment, her irrational dread of feeling half naked with him, she couldn't remain as she was. Wordlessly, she slid her arms out of the sleeves and handed the jacket across.

Wolf continued standing, though, after laying the garment on a chair. He was gazing down at her, filling the exquisite room with his presence, while she went to sit on the sofa. His grey eyes revealed that he was more, perturbed even than usual. Assuming he was annoyed because she was here alone, Rhona smiled reassuringly.

'Chrissie'll soon be better. I'm sure it isn't a bad dose of measles. And she's a resilient child, always has been.'

'I'm not thinking about her.'

'Then what is it?' Was he having another very bad day? Was he resurrecting the horrors of D-day? 'You've got to put the troubles of this war behind you, sooner or later. It can't last much longer now Hitler's killed himself.'

'I didnt know he had.'

Rhona was even more alarmed. Where was he living? Not in this world certainly.

'And you?' he demanded sharply. 'Is obliterating everything what you're trying to do? Are you trying to pretend that nothing went wrong – that Timothy's still alive, so you can prolong the charade you've been acting out for months!'

'You know,' she gasped, realizing that she sounded like somebody in a cheap novelette, not understanding how to sound otherwise.

'I had to get at the truth. Since you don't trust me sufficiently to be straightforward.'

'I wish you hadn't.'

'I wish I hadn't needed to. For God's sake, Rhona, you could have confided in me.'

'Aye.' Ridiculously, tears rushed to her eyes now. She

could see how she'd hurt him, and saw also that there had been no need.

'You could have told me without my assuming our relationship would automatically alter.'

'Am I that transparent?' She herself hadn't analysed her motivation, but recognized now her enduring mistrust of the attraction he generated.

Wolf shrugged. 'Perhaps I'm just extraordinarily receptive to your determination to keep me out of your life.'

'It wasn't like that.'

'No? He'd been dead for over a year when I came back. Yet you still let me believe he was a prisoner over there. I'd never have found out now if I hadn't made feeble attempts to get Red Cross parcels to him.'

'Oh, no! Oh, Wolf, it was only that . . .'

' . . . I am divorced, and you're determined you'll have nothing to do with me!'

'Nay, that's not fair! Haven't I come here week after week . . .'

'And withheld all warmth.'

'You didn't want any of that. You only had eyes for our Chris.'

Only because she's yours, he thought despairingly. Have you lost your sight, Rhona, all your intuition? How could anybody be so blind?

'Do you think your abhorrence of my status hasn't registered, after all these years? For Christ's sake, Rhona, I'd have given anything to have been single when we met, but facts are facts, irrefutable. Ineradicable. I've hated the knowledge that I had been married. Just as I first hated that bloody reservoir for turning you against me.'

His face was ashen with anger, as if this was draining life itself from him. Rhona couldn't be surprised: she felt as though her own blood was dribbling away through her feet.

She shivered, but didn't speak. What was there to say? She was in love with this man whom life had made an impossible partner for her, and all she could do was sit here while he drove one hatchet blow after another through the friendship that was all they permitted.

Wolf had grown silent. Waiting for her to speak? Well, he'd be disappointed, wouldn't he? How could she contradict what he was saying, when no one knew better than Rhona herself how true it was that there never could be anything between them!

'When I came back here,' he continued at last, so quietly that Rhona had to look at him to make out the words, 'it was only through you that I held on to life. There was no other way that I'd have continued to exist.' He paused, and she recognized now that he hadn't been waiting for her to say something, but to win enough control over his emotions to be able to talk.

'You – or you and Chrissie – were the only people I couldn't desert. I had to keep going, somehow, just to – be with you.' He choked and Rhona sprang to her feet.

By the time she'd crossed the few feet of blue carpet tears were running down her face. 'You daft thing!' she exclaimed, 'talking like that! A man who's done all that you've done. Planning and constructing things like that reservoir, then joining the army, becoming an officer in no time at all. Have you forgotten the recognition you've warranted – how the Prince of Wales opened that first stage of your reservoir.'

'And he's shown since that his judgement isn't all that reliable, hasn't he?'

'How do you mean? He stuck out to marry the woman he loved, against all the odds, no matter what he had to sacrifice.'

'You think that's *good*? You don't hold with divorce . . .'

'I didn't, for me, but that's a long time since. I was terrified, as well, because I'd never be as lovely, nor as sophisticated as your wife was.' Now she'd managed to get that out, it was her turn to hesitate. 'And I'm right sorry, love, that I've annoyed you by being like that.'

'Annoyed, that's hardly the word!' He pulled her to him. For a long while they stood very still, holding each other. When Wolf kissed her it was amicably, without any trace of passion. Rhona understood that the kiss misrepresented his feelings, just as surely as so much that had occurred during the past year and more had misrepresented her own.

Never, since long before she'd been married to Timothy, had she allowed Wolf near enough for her to recognize the effect she was having. Somehow, she understood that he'd always responded in this way to her.

'Wolf . . .'

He met her searching gaze unflinchingly, seemed to be smiling the first real smile she'd had from him since he returned. Why had she been resisting? *Why?* From the first moment that they had met.

'I only love young Chrissie because she's the image of you. And, as for sophistication, that conceals a multitude of shortcomings.'

Was it possible that her admission of being daunted by his previous marriage was all that had been needed? He drew her against him again, pressing her to the firm evidence of his ardour. His lips remained tender, though, trailing kisses over her closed eyelids, an ear, her throat.

Rhona slid her hands to either side of his haggard face, covered his lips with her own, probed with her tongue. He was strong and warm through the thin stuff of her skirt, she yearned to be a part of him.

Breathless with her kisses, Wolf moved away sufficiently for his serious grey eyes to verify her intention. Rhona moved her hands down over his shoulders and around his back, held him, and raised her lips for his.

He brushed the corners of her lips with his own, planted feather-light kisses on her chin and cheeks, then desire made his kisses more forceful, demanding. Ecstasy sighing in her throat, Rhona stirred against him.

Hazed by longing, she went mutely with him up the cool stone staircase, along a thickly carpeted corridor and into his room.

'Rhona, my love, my life.'

Again, she was in his arms, cherished. His lips sealing

hers once more, he slid aside her strap, baring one shoulder. His mouth followed gentle fingers, tracing the line of her breast, caresses soft as a spring breeze, awakening bliss deep within her. His touch unhurried, near-reverent, he took each garment from her. He held her close again, stilling his own passion to savour her pressure against him.

Rhona opened his shirt, explored, her fingers eager. And wept within her heart over ribs that were so angular. He shrugged his arms from the shirt, enfolded her again, making her flesh tingle with the contact of his skin.

'Time somebody looked after you,' she murmured huskily, torn between need of him and concern for his well being. 'Fed you up a bit . . .'

'Your daughter did offer, when she grows old enough. Do you think I'll survive that long?'

'I'll not let even her take over what's my job!'

'Possessive now, are you?'

'Happen it's time we both were – permitted ourselves to be so . . .'

'Happen so.'

His Yorkshirism made her laugh. He took her mouth again, hungrily, his tongue plunging between her teeth, its rhythm echoing the life surging through him.

The bed was only a pace behind her. Hypnotized by all the senses willing her entire attention to Wolf, she had noticed nothing about the room. As, imperceptibly, he eased her backwards, she felt herself surrendering. That the bed was there, its satin quilt soft to the back of her thighs and then its mattress supporting, seemed synonymous with the security she'd found in Wolf.

The eloquent grey eyes holding her gaze, Wolf followed, fitting himself to her side, tracing her lips with his own till need anchored them there. He touched the line of her waist, her ribcage, her breast, his fingers at first tentative till passion increased their pressure.

Rhona caressed his shoulder where the bones, again over-prominent, generated an ache of compassion strong as the aching urgency within her. Her hand slid around to his spine, plunged downwards, made his kisses intensify.

Light as hovering breath, his hand found the curve of her calf, traversed her knee, progressed. Awakening to his fingers, Rhona sighed, smiled, her body taut, waiting.

His eyes already making love, he held her without touching, briefly, while discarding his remaining clothes. Rhona drew him to her, the length of him instantly firing her: lean limbs, the hardness of his fleshless chest, that other hardness.

'God, but I need you, Wolf Richardson! My darling . . .'

She felt his smile as his mouth took hers again, sensed the joy in his movement across her, and sensed the restraint tempering his eagerness. He pressed without entering, alert to her slightest stirring; skin against skin, constraining himself for her needs.

He caressed her with his body, offering himself. Rhona took him to her, eagerly, savouring the amazing strength in him, the shimmer of sensations, her own massive longing, its intense, heart-beat urgency. Wolf grew more insistent, fiercely assertive, as he responded to her impulse. Yet still he heeded her every movement, governed his own to be its complement, until they were responding, each to the other, the yearning and its answer, pausing, interchanging, in increasing awareness.

I want you for ever, she thought, like this, *holding* . . . Yet then there'd be no fulfilment, no giving you completion, no final surge of *living*. I want you, I want you, every sense was screaming. Each nerve in her body alert, every pulse an echo of her yearning, the love of years was centring on this glorious means of belonging. And then she was taking from him, greedy for all he would give, yielding his ultimate satisfaction.

'I love you,' Wolf gasped, his breathing noisy against her ear, and the final tumult of his love snatched away her last atom of control. The love she'd curtailed for what felt like a lifetime was released in smiles mingled with tears.

'Did I hurt you?' All concern, Wolf touched her lashes with a finger, showed her the tear.

Choked with a multitude of emotions, Rhona shook her head. 'Was there ever more consideration, more *caring* . . . ?' She marvelled that she never had suspected what kind of man he was, never had supposed being loved might be so exquisite.

'You don't long for twelve years without learning some discipline,' he told her gravely. Gently, he kissed her mouth.

Rhona drew him close to her, wrapped her arms about him. The ferocity of her need of Wolf was so small a part of a many-faceted love. He made her feel well-cherished, she ached to show him there'd be no more striving alone, no more solitude.

'Lord, but I made life difficult, didn't I?' she exclaimed, appalled.

Wolf's response was light. 'I certainly prefer this.'

'You should be heaping me with recriminations . . .'

'And waste our being together? I don't even know if I may count on your being here through the night.'

'Mother told me to leave Chrissie undisturbed, with them.'

'You're not going back to Apsley Road alone.'

'No, I don't believe I am. What I will do, if you don't mind, is telephone later – only to check Christine's no worse.' She'd not forget how guilty she'd felt about Tim, she'd not risk anything happening to his daughter.

'You must send her my love, with get-well wishes.'

Rhona smiled. 'I'm not supposed to be with you, am I? Mother thinks I'm at the WVS centre.'

Wolf laughed heartily. Rhona gave a look of mock-reproof – and hugged him furiously. 'You shouldn't be encouraging me to be devious!'

'I wouldn't, if I didn't know that's the last thing you'll really become.'

Wakening with Wolf beside her, then going downstairs together to make breakfast, was like a fantasy. Rhona was dreadfully afraid of really wakening up, of finding last night a dream. Sitting either side of the kitchen table, they ate in near-silence, loving each other with enduring glances.

'Mind if I hear the news?' Wolf inquired. 'Just the headlines.'

Rhona agreed readily. He was much better already, concerned for the rest of the world.

They listened to the entire, extended bulletin. At six twenty-five the previous evening, Friday May 4th, on Luneburg Heath in the presence of Field Marshal Montgomery, five German plenipotentiaries had signed the surrender of the German Armies of the North,

'Oh, thank God!' Her eyes were full of joyful tears again, her voice shook.

Across the table Wolf grasped her hand. Wryly, he smiled. 'So yours wasn't the only capitulation!'

She raised an eyebrow. 'Evidently not.' And what better way to celebrate the start of the restoration of peace!

Just as quickly, though, Wolf's expression changed. The raw pain told her of the men who'd never know peace, *his* men.

'It's up to us now,' she said softly. 'To make what we can of whatever remains. Make it all – worthwhile.'

'H'm.'

He was struggling against emotion, fighting to conceal it from her. Can't you just let go, she thought, willing him to cease this unhealthy restraint.

'If I may use your telephone again to speak to Bill, I'm sure I needn't go in to work. This surely is one Saturday morning when, if anybody wants to have the mill running, they can manage without me.'

'No,' he said hastily. 'You go along – much the best idea.'

Uneasily, Rhona prepared to go out. She hated leaving him, so soon after they had at last made love, and when he was so obviously disturbed again. But perhaps, alone, he would just snap – give way to the grief suppressed for too many months.

Wolf walked her to the car, hugged her beside its door. 'Take great care of yourself, my dear.'

By the time the war with Japan ended, Wolf certainly appeared to be recovering. Almost, the three of them were like a family. When they were together. With the end of hostilities, Rhona became increasingly busy at Bridge House. Her father-in-law retired which, although no great surprise, thrust more responsibility on to her at a time when she'd have chosen less in order to concentrate on her relationship with Wolf. But, having decided that she would resist the temptation to sell out, the alternative was restoring production of coloured yarns for cloth, as well as the knitting wools that were her speciality.

'Thank goodness our Christine's starting school – that'll keep her occupied during the day,' she remarked to Eve. 'I can't expect you to look after her for ever.'

'I shall miss having her here, you know that,' Eve said, smiling. 'But are you certain you're right taking all this on? What about Wolf?'

There had been no secrets from her mother since that morning when, following news that the war in Europe had ended, Rhona had returned to Gracechurch Street and admitted where she'd been.

Eve hadn't been surprised. 'Well, there's nothing more sure to encourage our Chrissie to get over this bout of measles than having you both spend more time with her beloved Daddy Wolf.'

'You knew!'

'*You* don't know your daughter if you imagined she'd hold her tongue! Nay lass, you might think I'm not very up to date, but I'm not quite ga-ga! Did you really believe I'd encourage you to go to the WVS that often of an evening, when you were working that hard during the day?'

'Does Dad know how friendly Wolf and I have become? What does he think?'

'Same as me – we'd like to see you married. But if you

don't get round to that, we've lived through far worse things since 1939.'

Marriage, though, was Rhona's intention. Once Wolf was himself again. She supposed, knowing him, there'd be no wedding until.

She and Christine spent most weekends at Farnley Carr. She imagined the news would have percolated around Halfield, but had sufficient self-possession, these days, to disregard the opinions of people who were not involved.

She had confided in her mother-in-law. Ellen Brightstone had wept a bit, without saying one word about Timothy, but then she'd patted Rhona's arm. She'd managed a wan smile. 'Young Christine needs a father, just as much as you deserve to have a man about you, we'll never criticize what you've done. Wolf Richardson didn't have an easy war, either – and if your situation now isn't ideal, there's lots of couples have found making it legal wasn't enough to guarantee happiness.'

Auntie Norah's reaction surprised Rhona most of all. When Wolf was up to visiting people again, Auntie Norah's was the first home he agreed to go to with Rhona. Wondering what kind of a reception they would have, Rhona had left Christine with the Brightstones.

Driving was one thing Wolf had neglected so it was in her car that they drove over Moorland Road.

'Does Auntie Norah know?' Wolf asked, his anxious expression making Rhona laugh.

'Afraid she's going to tell you off for being naughty, are you? A bit late now, my lad, to think of that! Happen you should have asked if it was all right by her before you took me into your bedroom every Saturday and Sunday.'

'I think we're both mature enough to make our own decisions.'

'That's a relief! I wondered if you were going to say it was all my fault, that I'd led you off the rails, or something.'

'Which you have,' Wolf teased.

'Get away with you! I'm close on thirty-three, remember, not a young bit of stuff!'

'If that's inviting proof of what you still do to me, you'd better draw off the road and park somewhere secluded.'

'Eeh, you posh folk do talk dirty!' Rhona exclaimed, but laughter spoiled the effect of her mock reproof. 'And you'd better straighten your face before we get there, Wolf Richardson. Or Auntie'll be telling you this is nothing to grin about.'

Moments later, Rhona contained a smile, glancing sideways at Wolf who was walking decorously beside her up the path to the cottage. He couldn't have looked more like a small boy anticipating being caught scrumping apples.

'Well, come in then,' Auntie Norah welcomed them, beaming. 'I was wondering how long it'd be before the pair of you would come here together, admitting what you were up to!'

'Up to?' Rhona inquired, kissing the old lady.

'You know what I mean, both on you,' she said, and looked directly at Wolf. 'Aye, and I can see why you're not putting a ring on her finger yet. Had a bad war, haven't you, love? You'll be wanting to straighten yourself out before you take on responsibilities.'

Relieved, smiling slightly, Wolf nodded.

'Aye, well – it's a good idea to find something to take your mind off your worries. They do say as there's one sure way of letting go of all the bad things that's happened. And I've always known you two belonged with each other.'

Feeling they belonged, however, was one thing; wishing for tangible evidence of their union began to plague Rhona. Eventually, after months of living with Wolf at weekends, she decided that if he wasn't prepared to raise the subject of a wedding, one person *was*.

It was a Sunday night. Replete after lovemaking, she ought to have been feeling happy. Instead, the familiar pain generated by knowing she and Christine would be gone tomorrow was gnawing into her.

'Don't you wish we could simply stay like this, darling?' she asked, one hand locating his in the warmth of the large bed. 'Never to part, never to go separate ways.'

'Don't I do enough of remaining here – when I should be out there, working, earning to keep you and Christine?'

'I didn't mean that. And you will, in time.'

'You reckon? How many months has it been now, I've lost count, *have chosen to*, perhaps – because I can't face the truth.'

'No one's stopping you working.'

'I've no company, now, have I? That was wound up when I enlisted.'

'I didn't know that. You've never let on. But you could start up again, surely. You haven't lost your skill, nor any of that knowledge.'

'No?' He snorted. 'Don't imagine I haven't considered this, Rhona, I've thought of little else. But I can't even visualize constructing anything, much less start to put it all into practice.'

'Oh. I'm sorry. I know how much it means to you, love. But that wasn't what I was on about anyway. I meant us – I don't like not belonging with you all the time. I don't like taking Chrissie and walking out on you every week.'

'You don't have to.'

'I should sell-up, you mean? Move in here permanently, be a kept woman.'

'That's likely – you're the one that's earning!'

'And you don't like that much either . . .' Despite the million behind you.

'Not a great deal. And, yes, I'd like it less if you were legally mine, my wife.'

'So – there'll be no wedding bells, yet awhile.'

'Unless you issued an ultimatum. And I'm not certain that would generate the desired response in me, anyway.'

'You're very straightforward, if nothing else.'

'Amongst the many things I owe you, my love, that's one of the most important.'

'Wolf, I'm not trying to force your hand, I wouldn't do that to you. But you do know I want us to have a proper home life, where we can bring up our children, *yours*.'

'I've had more than a suspicion that you felt this way,

yes. There's nothing would give me greater joy. But I have to know I'd be the father they should have.'

'You ask our Chris! Don't you know what a lot she thinks about you?'

'Would that we all had her capacity for living for present happiness.'

'And are you happy, Wolf?'

'Do you need to ask? In today, while you're here. I've known no joy like this.'

'*But . . . ?*' She sighed, resigning herself. 'I never did get what I was after without a bit of a struggle. Why should everything change now?'

Trying to be philosophical, being glad that Wolf was improving mentally as well as physically, *keeping occupied*, Rhona continued on.

At the mill she was enjoying returning to producing the yarns that she loved, and was designing patterns again. Christine, growing into a bright little schoolgirl, was becoming more of a companion, and helped to keep her mind from Wolf during every week, while her soul as well as her body was aching to be with him.

It was Jack Hebden who told her she was looking tired, one Saturday when she was collecting Chrissie from them before driving over to Farnley Carr.

'Have you never thought of packing it all in, selling the mill?'

'Aye, I have and all – three or four times every week, regular!'

'But you won't contemplate it, will you?'

'Oh, Dad, how can I? Now? It's not just the way I inherited them shares, I married Tim, whether or not I should have done. I owe him keeping Bridge House going.'

'You owe him nowt! Nay lass, don't think like that. You and Tim got wed because it was what he was after. You gave him a kiddie, and that made him happy for as long as he lived. Life now, though, is for you to make the best of – for yourself, not only for our Chris. Aye – and for that man you've loved since long before the war.'

'You think I should be living with him at Farnley Carr, don't you?'

'I don't see much future for you and him, while you keep to-ing and fro-ing. I thought your mum and me might have proved that second marriages can work.'

'You always have shown that. But you two *are* married.'

'So, that's the way the land lies . . .'

'Until, or unless, Wolf sorts himself out, there doesn't seem much prospect of anything any different.'

The situation began getting her down. Wolf was just as ardent, still considerate of her need for fulfilment, and he was no less exciting. The impermanence of their living arrangements, though, removed a lot of her enjoyment, even made her feel guilty that his lovemaking continued to thrill her. *Was* she totally committed?

And yet none of this was responsible for her spending less time with Wolf. The business was escalating. Although clothing still was rationed, everyone seemed eager to spend their precious coupons, and knitting was an economical means of having something new.

Rhona had taken a week's sales trip to London, calling on magazines and retailers who had featured their wool and patterns before the war. She herself had recaptured much of her enthusiasm and had returned feeling as exhilarated as following her first visit. And she had generated so much interest in their products that, afterwards, she spent most of each Saturday working in the office at the mill. Quite often, even when she and Chrissie were at Farnley Carr, Rhona was designing patterns. There soon seemed little point in going to Wolf late on a Saturday evening, she began spending Sundays only with him.

Towards the end of September Rhona drove Christine out to Farnley Carr one Sunday morning, and Wolf was not at home. He went out so rarely, and never without telling her if it was a day when she was expected to join him, that she was immediately alarmed.

Trying to quell her panic, she turned to Christine as they walked back to the little blue Morris. 'Let's go and see Grandma and Grandpa Brightstone instead, shall we?'

Rhona left her daughter with Bill and Ellen, then drove through heavy rain over the moor towards Dale Reservoir.

She found him, as she had suspected she might: motionless, staring out over the barren drained valley, closed in on himself.

'Hallo.' Hurrying over wet tussocks of heather that scratched at her ankles, Rhona reached his side. She slid a hand through his arm. 'Bad day?'

'Are any of them any different?' He was frowning, hadn't even turned to look at her.

'You used to say, once, you were at least glad when I was with you.'

'You *were* with me then, completely, if only for two days a week.'

'I've got to build up the business again, you know I have.'

'All right. But nobody's expected to work a seven-day week.'

'Six.'

'I dispute that. How many Sunday afternoons do you sit drafting designs?'

'I'm sorry. Afraid it's a part of the way I am.'

'Sure. Okay.'

'And there's your job – there,' she told him, pointing. 'If you got on with that you'd have less time for fussing about how I was occupying my life.'

'Are you saying you want me out of it?'

'Anything but! I want you happy again, Wolf, that's all. If you were contented, I wouldn't care if you never worked again. But I know you – this construction business is as much a part of you as the mill is of me.'

'And you're sick of me the way I am.'

'You're putting words into my mouth. They're not true, love.'

He sighed. 'Well, I'm sick of everything.'

Rhona gulped. She *was* sickened now, if not greatly surprised.

'Very well. We can always call it a day.'

'No, I didn't mean . . .' Again he sighed, but as though she exasperated him.

'We're not very good for each other, are we, as things are.'

Wolf did not argue. A long silence developed, while they stood miserably side by side, enveloped in lashing rain.

'You – you'll not stop bringing Chrissie to see me?'

'I don't resort to emotional blackmail, Wolf.' Even when I'm being ripped in half.

'And I suppose I shouldn't, either . . .'

22

I'm only forty-two, Wolf thought that evening. I'm not going to die to order, nor even suffer some debilitating illness. If death or sickness had been intended, Normandy was the place. During that massive conflict had been the time.

Peace was a major irony. For him. At least, he now knew where he stood. There was nothing more to lose. He'd gone through every room of the house in the past few hours. Each had been well furnished, tastefully as well as expensively supplied with quality that had come through the war years unspoiled. And his home mattered not at all to him, now. Without their voices, their bright hair, their *radiance*, all it did was mock. He could surrender Farnley Carr tomorrow . . .

For an hour or more he'd shifted around in his brain the prospect of selling everything, getting right away. But that would be *running*. Until that moment, it really had not hit him that running was precisely what he had been doing since June 1944.

And this is where I stop: enough!

Not wishing to test the durability of his resolve, he began immediately to telephone. First, he spoke with his accountant, ensuring that his resources would be available the instant he required them. And then he spoke with Sir Reginald Newbold.

'I'm planning reconstruction of Dale Reservoir. The firm most involved in its original construction would be best fitted for the work. How are you placed?'

'Well, Wolf, I'm not exactly looking for a job. There's more than sufficient building to hand to keep me going for as long as I plan on working.'

The news seemed a fatal blow. Wolf inhaled sharply, sorely disappointed to meet problems this soon.

'On the other hand, mind,' Sir Reginald continued, thinking rapidly, 'there's nothing to prevent my expanding the company. Men are being demobbed to right and left, I daresay some might be tempted into building, who've been in other trades . . .'

'How soon can you let me have your decision?'

'How soon do you need to know?' Hearing from Wolf had been totally surprising, he'd have preferred a bit of warning to allow time for thinking this through.

'Tomorrow preferably, first thing. I've got to act on this, and act fast. Otherwise – well, I'll admit to you that I'm afraid that I won't.' Ever.

'As bad as that?'

'I've done damn-all since D-Day, Reg. You must have heard. It's growing insidiously habitual, not sure I can cope.'

'Oh, what the hell – yes, count me in. I doubt if there'll be much difficulty mustering enough men. If they're not as skilled as you might wish, don't go blaming me, just remember I had reservations.'

'A lot of the workforce will be labourers, anyway. It isn't as if we're starting the job from scratch.'

'How will you go on for supplies of necessary materials?'

Wolf smiled wryly. 'Give me time – I've only this evening decided to go ahead. What I have ascertained is that my assets will be converted into ready money by the time I need to draw on them. I suppose, if we should experience trouble over obtaining materials, I could always pull the proverbial few strings. I did all that work to government contract early on in the war.'

'There you are then – all tied up. We must get together in a day or two, finalize a few details.'

Wolf managed a taut smile. 'You make it sound deceptively easy. Glad I spoke with you!'

Sir Reginald laughed. 'Make me a packet, and the satisfaction will be mutual. I was planning on expanding the business once we got on our feet after the war. My youngsters are growing up fast, I'm doing my best to get the girls interested in the admin side, as well. The boy wouldn't dare follow any other line!'

'Er – quite.'

Wolf permitted himself a few minutes only of regretting. There seemed nothing he could do, now, about the family for which he had longed for such a large proportion of his life. Work, however, was a different matter.

Far into the night he was drafting plans, referring to details of his original construction of Dale Reservoir. As the early autumn mists drifted away from the valley at first light next morning, he began a detailed inspection of the damage sustained. On the following day he called Sir Reginald Newbold to the first site meeting.

That Monday seemed interminable to Rhona. No matter how busy she might be at Bridge House Mill, her concentration was abysmal. Increasingly, since seeing Wolf yesterday, she was realizing that this break was final.

By the time she trudged along Gracechurch Street to collect Christine from her grandmother, Rhona felt utterly weary and dejected. When she opened the door, though, Dan was there, smiling, full of himself. Recently returned from the navy, he was enjoying married life. Phyllis, now expecting a baby, had persuaded her father to have structural alterations done at Lavender Court, providing them with the whole of the upper floor as a self-contained flat.

'There's only one thing wrong with civvy street,' Dan told Rhona, 'and that's going back to weaving carpets. Can't stand being cooped up all day.'

'What do you want to do, then?' she asked him. 'Besides nothing – and somebody to help you do it!'

Her brother laughed. 'Now steady on. Who said I'd come home wanting to be idle? Specially now I'm going to be a dad. As a matter of fact, there's one or two things I might try. I wondered if you might come up with some suggestions . . .'

'Me? Nay – how would I know what you want to do? You'll have to make your own decisions, lad, you're old enough now.'

'Have I said I wasn't? I only thought – with you running your own mill, you might manage to come up with something for your favourite brother.'

'Oh – favourite now, are we? Don't kid yourself! Are you serious, though, about working at Bridge House?'

'What I was wondering was – have you got anybody lined up to go out selling? You know, trips to London – aye, and to Manchester, Birmingham, that sort of thing?'

'I've always covered London myself. The rest we do mostly by advertisements, correspondence . . .'

'You could do more by the direct approach.'

Rhona was studying him. Dan was a personable young man. He'd always been likeable. Anywhere in the North, he'd go down a treat. That might do for a start. Living with Phyllis, he was changing all the time . . .

'You'd have to know spinning inside out. They'd spot a mile off if you knew nowt about it. That'd mean six months, at the very least, going through the mill, every process – like I did for a beginning. If you're prepared to be cooped up inside for that length of time, I'm prepared to let you have a go. We'll see how you frame – if I think you'll be a good advert for Bridge House Mills, I'll give you a chance to prove you can sell.'

'When do I start?'

'As soon as you've discussed this with Phyl – I don't want her complaining to me that her husband's always traipsing off selling my stuff!'

'We've talked already.'

'Oh, you have, have you? Did she put you up to this?'

'No, I had it all worked out. It's given me something to think about, standing at them carpet looms.'

'Sounds like the first task'll be teaching you to keep your attention on the job!'

'I'll see you have no cause for complaints.'

'Just keep that in mind. Because you're going to work for family doesn't mean you'll be treated soft! Although I'm beginning to wonder if you're soft in the head – you've agreed to come, without one word being said about what I'll pay you.'

Daniel grinned. 'So long as I don't earn less than I'm getting at present, I shan't grumble. Later on, there'll be commission, an' all, won't there?'

Rhona contained her amusement. 'Aye – that'll be a good way of making sure you try as hard as you can.'

Dan was telling her what he could earn on a good week weaving carpets when Phyllis walked through the door. As soon as she realized that Rhona was agreeing to Dan's suggestion, she beamed.

'There's nobody fairer than you, Rhona. I know you'll give him a good start.'

Rhona grinned at her friend. 'I'll teach him what hard work is, that I do promise!'

Since Dan and Phyllis were staying for tea at Gracechurch Street and Christine was begging to eat there as well, Rhona agreed when her mother suggested that they should all gather round the table. She had no heart for cooking for herself and Chrissie anyway. All she wanted was this day over and done with. That house in Apsley Road was going to seem very big for the two of them, and no prospect now of them moving from it to Farnley Carr.

Phyllis was watching Rhona's expression and when she went into the kitchen for more milk Phyllis followed her and closed the door behind them.

'What's up, Rhona? Has Danny twisted your arm about setting him on at the mill? Weren't you so keen?'

'Nothing's up, I don't know what you mean. And I'm pleased about Dan. I reckon he'll most likely make out all right, though you needn't tell him that, not yet. I shan't be sorry if somebody can take charge of boosting sales. And I can't keep tripping off here and there. Mum's been a brick looking after Chrissie while the war was on, it's time I stopped relying on her such a lot. Now Dad's firm is reverting to their normal line of business he has more time at home, and I'm going to see they both enjoy it.'

'Well, there'll be me to baby-sit as well, don't forget, when I have to pack in nursing.'

'Thanks, love. It's high time I did more at the house,

as well – it were all a bit makeshift when I was getting the home together. I know that there utility furniture isn't very exciting, but some of it's not so bad and would modernize a few of the rooms. They all could do with another coat or two of distemper, as well. I'm going to make it into a real home, one where our Chris will be happy growing up, having friends to stay if she wants.'

'But . . .' Phyllis was staring and staring at her, as she leaned against the wooden draining board, totally bewildered. 'What about you and Wolf, you'll be living at . . . ?'

Her voice had evaporated beneath Rhona's dismal expression. And now the lovely red-brown head was being shaken from side to side.

'Oh, no! Heaven's above, Rhona, what's happened?'

'Sssh . . .' Rhona glanced warningly towards the door. 'I don't want them knowing, and certainly not our Chrissie. Not for as long as I can keep it to myself. It's all over, Phyl. It – just wasn't working out. I'm busy all the time, Wolf resents it . . .'

'Poor Wolf . . .'

'What about "poor Rhona" for a change? He's the one who can't accept the way things are. Never once have I tried to get *him* to change, I've bitten my tongue time after time. Look how I went and slept there, that was something I'd never have dreamt of a few years ago. Neither of us were happy as we were, and he won't do anything any different. Won't get wed, won't talk about working again, won't let me work . . .'

'Be fair, old love, he has let you.'

'Grudgingly, as if he were humouring me! Any road, he's admitted he wasn't happy either with the way things were working out. So – there we are.'

'You do know how much he's always loved you, and for how long . . .'

'Love? I wonder.'

'Rhona, listen . . . I – couldn't tell you at the time, there wasn't much point afterwards. Wolf came to me once, just after the war had started. He came to ask if I

367

knew – what you felt for him, if there was any hope you'd – end up together.'

Rhona felt the blood draining away from her face, then rushing upwards again to colour her neck and her cheeks. 'Why the blazes didn't you say? Why didn't *he*?'

'I'll never forget the way it happened. He was just beginning to – talk, when the telephone rang. It was you, Rhona, telling me you'd married Tim Brightstone.'

'Oh, God!'

'You see now why I had to keep it to myself. Wolf had started by asking me to consider our talk confidential, anyway. After your bombshell, there wasn't any good purpose to be served by not doing so.'

Appalled, Rhona shut her eyes, pressed hands that trembled to either side of her face.

'What – what did he say when you told him?' she asked eventually, when she'd controlled herself enough to speak.

'I don't think he said one word. He just turned away swiftly, walked straight out of the house.'

'Aye – he would. Lord, I've made a right pig's ear of it, haven't I, Phyl? Right from start to finish.'

Phyllis put an arm around her shoulders. 'Not just you, love. Him as well. He ought to have gone about it differently from the start, spoken to you of the way he felt, never mind sounding out your friends.'

'But he *did*, don't you understand! Time after bloody time, in all sorts of ways. Since long before he was free of his wife, and lots of occasions after that – when I was too set in my ways to even contemplate becoming his second! But that was before what the war did to us both. And as soon as I got round to seeing it were no use going on cutting off my nose to spite my face, he'd somehow lost the capacity for enjoying any of the time we spent together.'

She sighed, blew her nose fiercely, swallowed. 'Get us that drop of milk out, will you, love? We'll have to go back in there. They must be wondering what on earth we're playing at.'

'In a minute. Rhona, you can't simply let things stay

as they are, you know that, don't you? You'll have to see Wolf, patch things up.'

'No. Oh, no. You didn't see how he looked this last weekend. I *am* making things worse for him, we're destroying each other. There's no going back, Phyllis, ever.'

'But . . .'

'Phyllis, *please*! Drop the subject. I don't want to even discuss him ever again – do you hear?'

During the next two months Rhona prepared for Christmas. In every moment that she wasn't working for Bridge House Mill, she was busy on the house, or at her stove. She'd invited everybody for Christmas Dinner: her parents, Timothy's, Stanley, Phyllis and Dan, Clive, Phyllis's parents. They'd all pooled their coupons and she reckoned she could lay on a pretty good spread. And if that doesn't keep me from brooding, she thought, I'm giving up!

She was trying to make herself feel festive. The Paris shops already were displaying longer-length skirts and fragile, lace-trimmed blouses. Through a buyer in a Leeds store, Rhona had bought a dark green coat and skirt, and a white lace blouse, all pin-tucks and so feminine she wondered privately if she hadn't overdone it this time.

What she had tried not to wonder was how Wolf would have reacted to seeing her in something so lovely. Most weekends during their time together, she'd dressed for cooking in that massive Farnley Carr kitchen, and for their games with Christine.

They all arrived at once, as she was putting vegetables into pans. Fussing over Christine, who always adored attention, they surged into the living room. Even Bill and Ellen were struggling to overcome their sadness.

'You're looking very smart, Rhona lass,' Bill exclaimed. His wife said nothing. She had seen her daughter-in-law's face, almost as white as that exquisite blouse.

After kissing Rhona, Phyllis took charge of everyone's coats, while Stanley and Dan offered round drinks.

Eve and Jack Hebden converged on Rhona in her kitchen.

'It's nice to see you in something new, love,' said her mother, then was unable to ignore Rhona's staring eyes. 'Pity you're not looking better in yourself.'

'I hope preparing all this hasn't been too much, Rhona love,' her stepfather said.

'Course not. I'm better with plenty to do.'

They were watching her concernedly, just the same, as they gathered around the table. Again, while Phyl, Dan and Stanley kept conversation moving while they ate, Rhona remained aware of Ellen as well as Mum and Dad, eyes riveted on her plate, as she picked at her dinner.

Phyl tackled her afterwards, under cover of helping to bring in the pudding. 'I know that skirt has a nipped-in waist, old love, but you can't tell me you have to go starving yourself so's you can get it on. And if you were matching your face to your blouse, you forgot to do something about the dark circles beneath your eyes.'

'Thanks for nothing!' Rhona exclaimed, but had the grace to give her sister-in-law a rueful smile. 'Did they put you up to saying summat?'

'They didn't have to. I have eyes in my head, as well. I wish you'd look after yourself better, old love.'

'Happen I will, once Christmas is over.'

Feeling she was being inspected for signs of wear and tear didn't help to ease her awful weariness. And sitting down, while the others were clearing away and washing up, allowed too much time for thinking.

Within the next few days she would be seeing Norah Lowe. Poor old Auntie Norah, she was neglecting her. Not that she'd forgotten her birthday, she'd been making plans for that. But deep down in her heart she knew the reason she'd kept away. Since splitting with Wolf she'd curtailed her visits, to avoid Auntie Norah finding out.

I'll make it up to her, she resolved. I'll give her an evening she'll remember for the rest of her days! She'd been hoarding rations for weeks, with this in mind as well as Christmas.

Preparing ahead for a special meal for the old lady, as soon as Christmas was over, ought to have been satisfying, but it took a lot of doing. Rhona felt no less tired, no less unhappy. Ever since October, Christine had been pestering to see 'Daddy Wolf'. Although he wasn't mentioned quite so frequently now, every mention was just as hurtful. But she couldn't burst into tears, could she, in front of the child? Wearied to death with it all, Rhona could hardly summon enough energy or concentration to bake for Norah Lowe's surprise party.

The strange white reflection on her bedroom ceiling awakened Rhona on the old lady's birthday. The first real snow of the winter. From the windows of the house in Apsley Road, Halfield looked quite beautiful. Snow continued throughout the morning. At lunchtime she drove down to Gracechurch Street and picked up her mother and stepfather.

'Are we going for Norah Lowe now?' he inquired, getting into the car.

'No, I've got one or two things still to do. I thought maybe you'd look after our Chris while I go and pick her up.' She wanted an opportunity for a quiet word with Auntie, out of Christine's hearing. She didn't know how much her daughter understood of her reasons for not seeing Wolf. Her own family were in the picture by now, but she didn't want Auntie Norah coming out with awkward questions.

'You don't think this lot'll be worse later on?' Jack persisted. 'That sky's full of snow, if you ask me.'

'Will you help me make a snowman, Grandad?' Christine asked persuasively, bouncing around in the back of the car.

'He won't if you don't sit still, Madam,' Rhona cautioned her daughter, glancing at her in the rear-view mirror. She was thankful, though, that her plans for fetching the old lady appeared to be accepted.

It was later than she'd intended when she set out for the cottage, the snow was coming down again, and more heavily over Moorland Road. But she'd soon be there.

And if the weather worsened during the evening she could easily accommodate Auntie Norah, who might enjoy sleeping away from home for once.

There was no response when Rhona rattled the door knocker. She hammered on the door, waited, hammered again. She called, 'Auntie Norah,' although she'd sensed by now that the cottage was deserted.

Picking her way carefully through the snow drifted up against the wall, she reached the window and tried to peer in. Seeing anything was difficult because of the net curtain inside and the external scattering of flakes, but she could see no one. And where she'd expected a blaze in the grate of the black leaded range, she could discern a dying glow of embers.

Alarmed already, she was returning to the path when she noticed her footmarks weren't the only ones. Some while ago – snow was filling the indentations – somebody had left the cottage.

She can't have gone out! Rhona thought, not somebody her age, not in this! Wherever would she have gone . . . ? Whatever had possessed her to stir from her own hearth? Bewildered, apprehensive, she looked all round for clues as she walked back down the slippery path and closed the gate.

The footprints appeared to continue a little way away from the gate, but her own shoes had made a mess of the track. And, for four or five yards to either side of where her Morris was parked, the road had been swept clear of snow by the wind blowing down off the Moors.

'I'll have to try and find her,' she said aloud, getting back into the car, sitting for a minute with the engine running till the wipers cleared the windscreen. Why on earth had the old lady taken to wandering off?

Was it because it was her birthday, and she thought they'd all forgotten, that nobody cared . . . ? Guilt sickened Rhona as she recalled how she'd been avoiding Auntie Norah, afraid of what she might say about her deserting Wolf. There were reasons, she thought, and

knew at once she'd not consider her own excuses absolved
her.

I'll find her now, she resolved, *somehow*, I'll find her.
I've got to do that, and take her home for the party that
might make up for everything.

Where would she go, though . . . ? What could have
induced her to set out . . . ? Unless – had she taken it
into her head to see her old home, Branby Cottage? Had
she been so disturbed that she'd disregarded the blizzard
and set out all that way?

'Norah? Auntie Norah? Are you in there . . . ?'

Rhona flexed hands that stung from battering at the
door, and called one last time. Alarmed, she thrust all her
weight against the wood, rusted hinges fractured, and the
door crashed inwards.

Wings flailing, a big, black bird soared from the hearth
to land on an exposed rafter. Roof and windows gaping,
Branby Cottage was derelict, its stone floor deep in drifting
snow. There wasn't one footprint.

Auntie Norah couldn't be here. And *she'd* reached the
end of her tether. It was time she went home. There'd be
no party; the chief guest was missing.

Why search out here? Would anybody, whatever their
age, trudge over Moorland Road in this? Rhona dashed
for the prewar Morris Eight.

The keening wind savaged icy flakes, rushing them
at the windscreen. Beyond labouring wipers, she could
scarcely see the heather, gorse, and tussocks obliterated
by snow. Was it the hope of finding Norah Lowe, or her
own longing, that had brought her this way, towards the
silver valley?

The place had meant a lot to her for . . . how long?
Eight years, nine? Since before the war, anyway, when
she'd come out here with him. And on that harrowing
night, despite the previous forty-eight hours, she'd had
her breath taken by its strange serenity and beauty.

Only the frosted moors looked the same, though now.
With the reservoir's draining waters, the valley had died;

and there was neither purpose nor justice in this second destruction.

In the gateway near the deserted reservoir keeper's premises, Rhona turned the car carefully. The blue-grey setts bared by the gale were icy. Before driving off she waited a moment, controlling her dejection, and stared straight ahead. 'At last,' she gasped, 'at last!'

Over by the reservoir site – where, earlier, she'd avoided glancing – was an area glowing in lamp-light. Against the snow, contractors' vehicles looked black, parked with massive concrete blocks stacked beside them, and cranes waiting, ready.

The rare tears filled her eyes now, thickened her throat, and made her laugh, quietly, self-consciously. Joy and relief banished all the day's disappointment. Nothing could be as bad, not now. He would be fine again, just fine . . .

If only she didn't feel so tired, though! Despite having the car, going anywhere seemed far more difficult than when she used to do so much walking. I wasn't as tired then, thought Rhona; nor as old!

She'd never admitted before to feeling any different. Maybe the war was to blame. Or its ending. Ever since Japan surrendered last August and eased the worst of the tension, she'd been drained of the will that had driven her on. Only her responsibility had not lessened, nor her hardest fight of all – against her own emotions. But there had been no other way, right from the beginning. *Had* there . . . ?

Toughened by stark Yorkshire moors and a town gloomy with mill-smoke, she'd grown up practical, with too much sense to allow dreams much space in her head. Organization was her maxim, and it appeared to serve her well.

The engine of the little car made a strange wheezing noise, shuddered, and stopped. Braking gently so she didn't skid, Rhona drew up close to the frosted heather bank. Without much hope she tried the engine again, frantically scanning the dashboard. The petrol gauge read empty. But she never neglected filling the tank! 'Damn it all, why today?' She wouldn't readily forgive her own carelessness.

Wearily she got out of the car, secured all the doors, and braced herself to stay on her feet. She'd have to walk as far as the next bus stop, if no more than that. She hadn't seen one bus in either direction all the time she'd been driving around. This desolate route always was first to pack up in wintry weather.

Rhona turned up her collar and crammed the bottle-green beret well down over her hair. Her matching coat and skirt were of the longer length, fashionable since the war ended, but she wore thin shoes unsuitable for these ice-bound roads.

Her flare of red-brown curls and trim figure made the driver of the Daimler smile as he reached the brow of the hill and saw her. Warm though the car interior was, the sight of her straight back sent a glow surging through him. He might have known she'd be out here.

He spared a hasty glance towards his construction site. Delight supplanted his earlier concern for her, she couldn't have missed seeing that.

It wasn't the bus, Rhona could tell, and didn't bother looking over her shoulder. Keeping her feet required all her attention. But the signs of renewed activity across the valley cheered her. She had known he would have to reconstruct. They couldn't manage without Dale Reservoir. What had she always told him . . . ?

Innate straightforwardness made her smile wryly at her own selective memory. Well – for twelve years or so, anyway. Looking back, it seemed a lifetime since she'd thought differently, and had fought for what she believed right. It had been winter then, just as cold as today.

'I hope there's nothing wrong with your car?'

The driver of the Daimler wound down his window as he drew level with her. It was Wolf. Why wasn't she surprised?

Ruefully Rhona smiled. 'Not a thing. It just runs better on petrol, like most cars.'

'You haven't . . . ?' His grey eyes glinted wickedly.

'I'm glad it's making somebody's day, any road!' she retorted, torn between annoyance because of being the source of his mirth, and thankfulness to see Wolf looking so greatly improved.

He opened the door of the car. 'Come on, dear . . .'

It was no good letting the trouble between them prevent her accepting a lift, specially on a day like this. The heat inside the car enveloped her at once, if she'd felt easier with him, it would have made her relax. As she settled into the passenger seat beside him, she felt Wolf scrutinizing her expression, and sensed his humour waning.

'What's wrong, Rhona?'

'Nothing. Just – fed up.'

'About running out of petrol?'

'That was the final straw. I'd been planning it all for days, you see. I might've known it'd go wrong! I always seem to be flogging my guts out for nothing.'

'You certainly look as though you've had more than you should take.'

His grey eyes were warm with concern – more than that, with love. She'd had enough of steeling herself to carry on. What was this battle about, she wondered, this daily battle that seemed, more than anything, to be with herself?

'I had it all planned out,' she said, aware that she was repeating everything; most probably, making very little sense to him. 'I've been hoarding rations specially for today as well as for Christmas. As soon as that was done with, I baked her a cake. Last night I sat up decorating it. I made a trifle, of sorts, it's only that synthetic cream. And I can't find Auntie Norah anywhere. Her cottage is empty. I've searched most of this wretched moor. Even went to check that she hadn't wandered off to what's left of Branby Cottage.'

'Maybe you've been looking in all the wrong places.'

'I'd worked that out for myself, thank you very much!' Aghast, she checked. 'Sorry, Wolf, there's no excuse for me going on at you. I must be more tired than I believed.'

'Then why not simply let go and, this once, have somebody else take charge?'

The notion was most appealing. Thank goodness he couldn't tell how much she longed to take him up on it. There'd be no resisting then, just as there'd be no resisting the attraction that already was setting up its old familiar heart-beat tattoo deep within her. He was looking his old self again now – no, *better*, even. His brown hair was immaculately cut, and the scattering of grey above his ears seemed to soften the effect of his rugged features. His overcoat appeared new, but he'd always bought good stuff, it might simply have been kept very carefully until he was out of uniform. And over the leather smell of the luxurious upholstery she recognized the scent of the soap he'd used before the war. That more than anything weakened her – so much so that she had to will herself not to reach out to him.

'Where were you off to anyway? Am I delaying you? Were you going somewhere important?' To her own ears, she was babbling, she only hoped he couldn't guess how nearly she was slipping out of control.

'Very important, yes.'

That jolted her. Badly. *Almost*, she'd been willing to believe that when he'd spoken of letting somebody else take charge he'd meant . . . No, but things didn't happen like that. Not here. Not for her. Wasn't that why she'd had to go on and on, coping, resisting . . . And she couldn't hold out against her own feelings any longer. Not in this car, *his* car.

'Well, perhaps you'd drop me at the first garage we come to, so's I can pick up a can of petrol?'

'I'm afraid that doesn't coincide at all with my plans.'

Rhona gave him a look. Just before his awareness of her glance, a smile had curved those fine lips. Was he laughing at her predicament? Now he'd overcome all the traumas of his past, was he ready to make a joke of *her*? She shook her head, as if to be rid of the exhaustion generated by so many years of constraint. Instead, it made her dizzy, she grappled with the door handle.

'Let me out here then, I was walking, wasn't I? You'd better get on your way, if your business is so important.' And let me have a bit of space round me again, so's I can control all this *yearning*. I've controlled it before, always – except for those few months. I've always been good at not giving way to my feelings . . .

Why, though, *why*? something inside her head began persisting. Why had she resisted Wolf, for most of the time that she had known him, why now was she gathering her insubstantial strength to leave him yet again?

'Let me do the worrying about that,' he said firmly, taking her hand and removing it from the door handle, holding it secured in his fingers.

His touch completed the unstringing of her. She noticed his glance flicking sideways towards the reservoir site, and back again to her. He was containing a smile.

'Yes, I've seen what's happening over there,' she said warmly, thankful she could be entirely honest about her feelings regarding the reservoir. 'I can't tell you how relieved and delighted I am, love.'

'Thank you. You were right, you see, I have emerged, at last.'

'And look heaps better for it! I'm that glad I've seen you, Wolf!'

Just let me go now, while you carry on to meet whoever you're supposed to be meeting. Let me have my hand back, while the touch of your fingers is only imprinted deep into mine . . . nowhere else.

'I'd better be getting home. Happen I'll have an early night, now I haven't managed to find Auntie Norah. None of this would have happened if she hadn't been that stubborn about a telephone. I'll have to have another go at finding her tomorrow . . .'

'I don't think you need do anything of the kind.'

'You've grown very callous! She's *a hundred years old, Wolf* – that's what the party was for.' His grey eyes were more beautiful than ever, gazing concernedly at her. And she was so tired and disappointed, she wouldn't hold back tears much longer. If she started crying, he'd feel obliged to take her home. 'Oh, let's get moving, Wolf. We can't sit here all night, specially if you've somebody to meet.'

'I've met her, you dear idiot! I was looking for you . . .'

'Rubbish! Not out here. Normally, this is the last place I'd . . .'

'Where did you leave Christine?'

'At home, of course. Don't look at me like that, my mother's there, Dad as well. All they were waiting for was Auntie Norah . . .'

'I know where your mother is, she answered the telephone.'

'You rang?'

'To invite you and Chrissie to Farnley Carr. To celebrate, with Auntie Norah . . .'

'*She's at Farnley Carr?*'

'Just this once, I actually remembered a birthday. I picked her up early, because of the snow.'

'You – you planned a party as well?'

'A small dinner – Norah Lowe, myself and, of course, you and young Chris.'

'*Of course?*'

'You're the people I love.'

Rhona sighed.

'So, that's how you feel still?' Wolf frowned. 'My loving you is one massive problem.'

'Well – well, hasn't it been, right from that very first day?'

'Why, I wonder, are you always looking back?'

'I'm not, I – ' Thoughts as well as words ran dry on her. She wondered yet again why she needed to dwell on past reasons for *not* seeing Wolf. 'Look – can we leave this just now? Mother and Chrissie will be out of their minds with anxiety. I said I'd only be half an hour. That was *hours* ago.'

'And this all really is pretty silly, isn't it? You worry when you're not with young Chris, you expect she'll be anxious about you. And I worry about the pair of you. All the time, all my life, there's nothing else. Why the hell can't I be taking care of you both, as a family, under the one roof?'

Astounded, Rhona gazed at him.

'I do mean married,' Wolf asserted. 'I didn't find second best any more acceptable than you did. *Now* . . .' He glanced again towards the reservoir site. 'I can offer some stability.'

All she could think was that she wasn't the only person who'd be feeling this relieved. 'Chrissie's never stopped calling you Daddy Wolf.'

'So, on her behalf, you'll accept.'

'You know I've always loved you.'

'Against your better judgement.' He crushed her hand against his lips.

'Aye – that was the way of it, for a long time. But I'd have married you, you know, when you came back after D-Day.'

'I know,' he said gravely.

'Ay, I am glad!' she exclaimed. 'We'll not waste any more time now. I'll give you the children you want . . .'

'Do you think that will wait? At least till we've picked up Auntie Norah, and driven to your home?'

So long as I can look at you, she thought, and go on looking. Can see that smile that's lighting up your glorious grey eyes, can watch your hands, capable on the wheel. So long as I may sit like this, outwardly calm, inwardly seething with excitement because you're so close to me again, so close I'm hardly aware of anything but awakening to the pulses you generate. And so long as I may know, as I know at this moment, that we will endure, and no circumstances in the future can be so dreadful as when we parted . . .

'Happen I were daft,' Rhona observed presently, 'not taking more notice of how I feel about you.'

'Happen you were.'

ROWAN'S MILL

Elizabeth Walker

**bestselling author
of VOYAGE**

At sixteen she wouldn't have had the nerve. At eighteen
she would have known better. But at seventeen Rowan
Judge was prepared to tackle the toughest job in town
single-handed: saving the family woollen mill from
closure. Bradford's hard-headed business community
had seen nothing like it since the rise of James Barton,
the textile baron who had broken up Rowan's family
and blighted their lives. Determined to prove herself
more than his equal, in the space of a few years Rowan
achieves the impossible – she drags the mill from the
brink of disaster to Stock Exchange success. But at what
cost to herself and those she loves?

Saul, Rowan's husband, bears the brunt of her driving
ambition. Charming, mercurial, a supremely successful
salesman, he finds himself in constant clashes with her
over the development of the business. And when she
meets Richard, son of her arch enemy, Rowan sees in
him her perfect match in talent and temperament.
Which will she choose? Or does Rowan's mill mean
more to her than either?

A finely meshed and enthralling saga, *Rowan's Mill* is
the powerful novel of a remarkable woman whose
desire for revenge unleashes an invincible ambition.

FICTION/SAGA   0 7472 3237 7   £3.99

More Compulsive Fiction from Headline:

THE LAND IS BRIGHT

A Liverpool saga in the great tradition of Catherine Cookson

ELIZABETH MURPHY

'Better is a dinner of herbs where love is than a stalled ox and hatred therewith.' Proverbs 17

When her Mam dies in childbirth, little Sally Palin becomes a second mother to her two brothers and baby Emily, the apple of her eye. Sally is determined that her sister shall leave the mean streets of their Liverpool home and enjoy a better life, but the success of her dream is bittersweet.

To escape a fever epidemic that ravages the city, Emily is sent away to her rich, childless Aunt Hester, to grow up in the healthy country air with luxuries the Palins could never provide.

But despite these material advantages, Emily fails to find happiness, and settles for a loveless marriage to an elderly widower, while Sally enjoys love and fulfilment with her husband and children, even though they must struggle against unemployment, illness and tragic loss . . .

'. . . an evocative novel of life behind the scrubbed doorsteps at the turn of the century. Gently paced, it nonetheless conveys the grinding miseries of poverty and making ends meet in the pre-welfare days . . .'
Books

'Elizabeth Murphy draws on her knowledge of her home town Liverpool to conjure up a cast of colourful characters . . . in a family saga that you just won't be able to put down.' *Prima*

FICTION/SAGA   0 7472 3192 3   £3.99

GRACE THOMPSON

A Welcome in the Valley

**A heartwarming story of Welsh
village life in the tradition of
Christine Marion Fraser's RHANNA**

The little Welsh village of Hen Carw Parc – the
old deer park – seems to be an island of rural
tranquillity. But the inhabitants are a lively and
varied community – and none more so than
Nelly Luke, the cheerful Cockney widow
whose eccentric lifestyle is the despair of her
social-climbing daughter Evie.

Yet Nelly's amiable warmth brings her many
friends – Fay, the young newly-wed whose
marriage is haunted by the all-too-substantial
ghost of her lost love; Amy, the village
postmistress, whose private life is colourful
indeed; the dignified Mrs French, whose family
cupboard contains several unlooked-for
skeletons.

Against the mounting excitement of the
Coronation summer, Nelly steers her friends
and family through storm and sunshine alike . . .

FICTION/GENERAL   0 7472 3361 6   £2.99

A selection of bestsellers from Headline

FICTION

TALENT	Nigel Rees	£3.99 ☐
A BLOODY FIELD BY SHREWSBURY	Edith Pargeter	£3.99 ☐
GUESTS OF THE EMPEROR	Janice Young Brooks	£3.99 ☐
THE LAND IS BRIGHT	Elizabeth Murphy	£3.99 ☐
THE FACE OF FEAR	Dean R Koontz	£3.50 ☐

NON-FICTION

CHILD STAR	Shirley Temple Black	£4.99 ☐
BLIND IN ONE EAR	Patrick Macnee and Marie Cameron	£3.99 ☐
TWICE LUCKY	John Francome	£4.99 ☐
HEARTS AND SHOWERS	Su Pollard	£2.99 ☐

SCIENCE FICTION AND FANTASY

WITH FATE CONSPIRE The Destiny Makers 1	Mike Shupp	£3.99 ☐
A DISAGREEMENT WITH DEATH	Craig Shaw Gardner	£2.99 ☐
SWORD & SORCERESS 4	Marion Zimmer Bradley	£3.50 ☐

All Headline books are available at your local bookshop or newsagent, or can be ordered direct from the publisher. Just tick the titles you want and fill in the form below. Prices and availability subject to change without notice.

Headline Book Publishing PLC, Cash Sales Department, PO Box 11, Falmouth, Cornwall TR10 9EN, England.

Please enclose a cheque or postal order to the value of the cover price and allow the following for postage and packing:
UK: 60p for the first book, 25p for the second book and 15p for each additional book ordered up to a maximum charge of £1.90
BFPO: 60p for the first book, 25p for the second book and 15p per copy for the next seven books, thereafter 9p per book
OVERSEAS & EIRE: £1.25 for the first book, 75p for the second book and 28p for each subsequent book.

Name ....

Address ....

....

....